TAKE HEIGHT, RUTTERKIN

Millie Thom

Copyright © 2021 by Millie Thom

The moral right of Millie Thom to be identified as the author of this work has been asserted in accordance with the Copyright, Designs and Patents Act 1988.

All rights reserved. No part of this publication may be reproduced, stored in a retrieval system, or transmitted, in any form or by any means, electronic, mechanical, photocopying, recording or otherwise without prior consent of the publisher.

Contents

Cast of Characters	5
A note about the pronunciation of two names	8
Map of Central Bottesford, showing some of the places in the book	9
Plan of Lincoln Castle as it would have looked in the 17th century	10
Sketch of Cobb Hall from outside the castle	11
Sketch of Cobb Hall from inside the castle	12
Prologue	13
One	14
Two	34
Three	53
Four	81
Five	99
Six	126
Seven	155
Eight	170
Nine	194
Ten	206
Eleven	220
Twelve	244
Thirteen	257
Fourteen	272
Fifteen	290
Sixteen	311

Seventeen	324
Eighteen	344
Nineteen	363
A thank you from the author	378
Acknowledgements	379
About the Book	380
About Millie Thom and her Books	385
Links to the Author	387

Characters

Joan Flower: Goodwife (formerly Mistress Flower) of Bottesford

Margaret and Phillipa: her daughters (Phillipa the eldest)

John Flower: Joan's husband

Rutterkin: Joan Flower's cat

Samuel Fleming: Reverend at the Bottesford Anglican Church of Saint Mary the Virgin and Rector for Bottesford Parish

Sir Roger Manners, fifth Earl of Rutland: elder brother of Francis

Lady Elizabeth (countess): Sir Roger's wife

Sir Francis Manners, sixth Earl of Rutland: younger brother of Roger

Lady Cecilia Manners (countess): Sir Francis's second wife

Henry, Lord Roos, and Lord Francis: Sir Francis and Lady Cecilia's two young sons

Lady Katherine: Sir Francis's daughter to his first wife, Frances, who died 1608.

Sir George Manners: younger brother of Sir Roger and Sir Francis

King James I of England, Ireland and Wales (and VI of Scotland)

Prince Henry: elder son of James 1

Sir George Villiers: favourite of James 1 and neighbour/friend of Sir Francis Manners

Mistress Abbott: housekeeper at Belvoir Castle

Anne Baker of Bottesford, Joane Willimot of Goadby, and Ellen Greene of Stathern: cunning women known to Joan Flower

Alice Nicholls: Samuel's housekeeper

Gilbert Nicholls: Alice's husband and Samuel's gardener

Esther Davenport: Samuel's sister

Thomas Davenport: her husband

Peter Jenkins: innkeeper at the Belvoir Inn in Bottesford

Thomas Simpson: Phillipa's lover

Hugh Allingham: farmer from Normanton

Goodwife (Goody) Jessie Simpson: Thomas's shrewish mother

Goodwife (Goody) Agnes Peate: wife of Joan Flower's former lover

Goodwife (Goody) Mary Hewson: another villager

Kitty Beddows: another villager

Lord Willoughby, Sir William Pelham, Henry Hastings, Matthew Butler: interrogators at Lincoln Gaol (along with Sir Francis, his brother Sir George, and Rector Samuel Fleming.)

Harry Beddows: Gaoler at Lincoln Gaol

Mary Ingram: Lincoln Midwife and 'examiner' of witches

Sir Edward Bromley and Sir Henry Hobart: Judges at Lincoln Assizes

A note on pronunciation of two names used in the book:

Belvoir – as in the Vale of Belvoir and Belvoir Castle – is pronounced as Beaver, like the animal and not as it is in French. However, it still means 'Beautiful View'.

The River Devon – which flows through the village of Bottesford – is pronounced as though it has two letter e's (Deevon) and not one, as in the English county in S.W. England.

Map of Bottesford

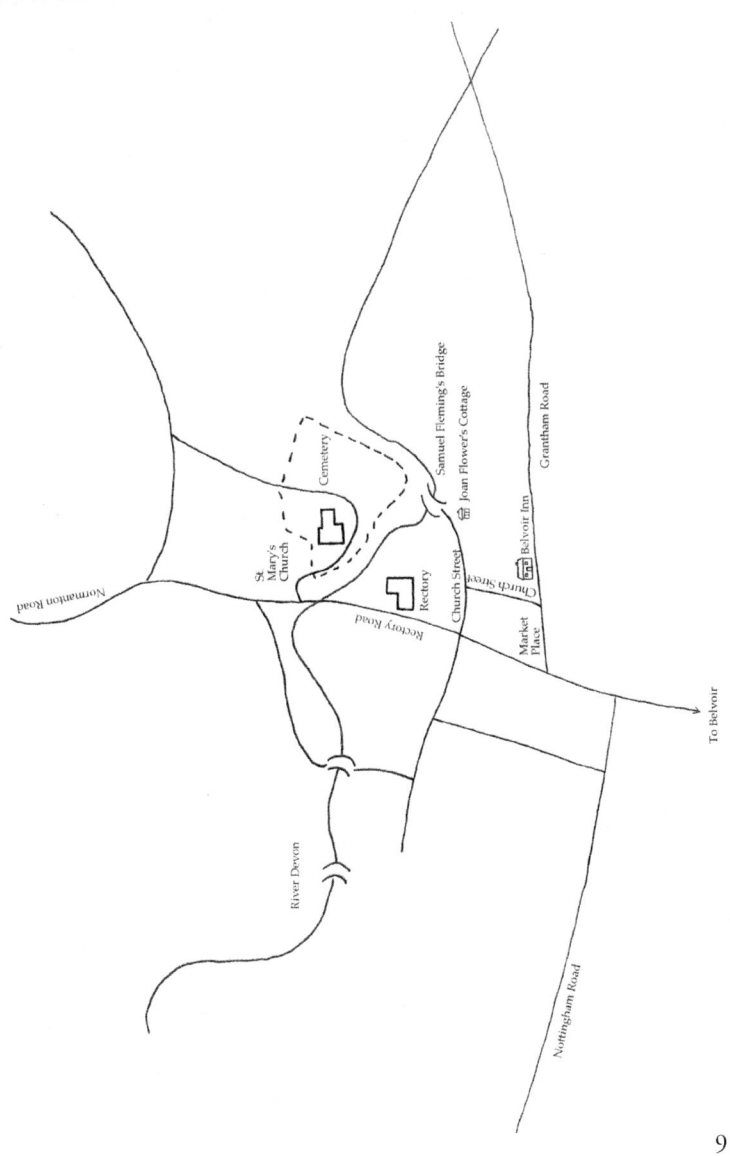

Map of Lincoln Castle in the 17th Century

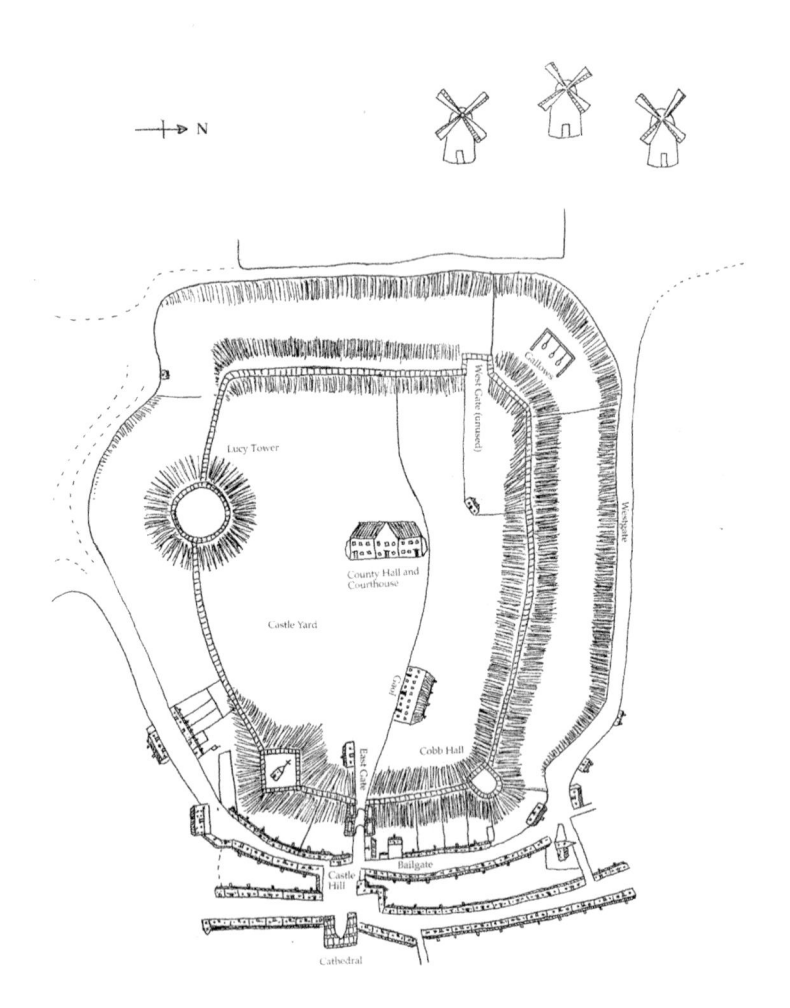

View of Cobb Hall from inside Lincoln Castle

11

View of Cobb Hall from outside Lincoln Castle

Prologue

Rats! Dozens of them scurried across her wasted body as she lay on the foetid straw, frozen in terror at the touch of their tiny, claw-like feet on her skin.

'Get them off me!' she screamed to the stone walls of the cell as one of the creatures sank needle-like teeth in her neck. 'Help me…!'

But no one came to her aid as more rats joined the masses, drawn as a magnet to iron by the scent of blood and the chance to feed on tender flesh. Knowing she would die in this malodorous place, she closed her eyes and hoped death would take her soon…

'On yer feet,' the gruff voice ordered, as the toe of a boot connected with her side. 'They've got something interesting for you today, so best not keep them waiting, eh? You can play with the rats once the interrogators are done with you. I'm not sure yer'll be in a state to do that, though.'

Shaking with fear and dreading facing her inquisitors again, she heaved herself up. Another day of such pain and she'd be begging for the hangman's noose.

Chapter One

In which a happy weekend turns sour

Bottesford Village, Leicestershire: mid-September 1611

Margaret Flower pushed her way through the crowds milling around the closely spaced stalls, struggling to keep sight of her mother as she darted hither and thither a short way ahead. As usual on a Friday, folk from neighbouring villages vied for the freshest foods and most useful household wares. Ma had bought so much already that Margaret's arms ached. It would serve her mother right if she dropped the baskets here and now and everything in them got trampled underfoot.

Margaret frowned as she considered the injustice of her role while her mother haggled over the price of yet another cut of meat. Why was *she* always the one to carry everything they bought while Ma strutted around the market with her nose in the air like she was some kind of queen? Margaret could well understand why so many village women whispered unkind words behind Joan Flower's back. Only today Margaret had heard one of them mutter, 'Who does she think she is, anyway, the stuck-up hussy? Just 'cos her family found favour at the castle. She's no better than the rest of us!'

'Place this carefully in one of your baskets.' Joan's commanding tones cut through Margaret's thoughts. 'And mind you don't drop it. I'd never face the countess again if it got broken after she'd paid for it.'

Chapter One

Margaret eyed the pretty glass bowl before doing as she was told. 'If you're so worried about it, why can't you carry it? My baskets are full to bursting but one of yours is almost empty.'

'Don't you speak to me like that, my girl!' Joan snapped as she headed past the Butter Cross that stood pre-eminent in the market place, leaving Margaret hoping they were going home. 'I need my hands free to inspect the items we buy. I'll not be fobbed off with inferior goods by conniving villagers. Most of these low-born goodwives would be pleased to pull the wool over my eyes. They're all jealous of the generosity shown to our family by the Earl and Countess of Rutland – and the fact that *my* title is *Mistress* Flower and not *Goodwife* Flower. At least I'm mistress of my own house.'

Margaret knew that was true. Her father's position as personal manservant to Sir Charles Manners, a relative of the earl's, ensured their favoured status with the whole Manners' family. Even her mother's family had been long-time employees at Belvoir Castle. Unfortunately, Sir Charles's estate was in Hucknall, over twenty-five miles away, which meant that Margaret and her elder sister seldom saw their father. But his monthly visits were a delight, especially as he always came home laden with gifts for the three of them.

'Why can't Phillipa come to market with you sometimes instead of me?' she persisted, unwilling to be side-tracked from her grumbling for long. I can stay at home and tend the herb garden for a change.'

'Don't make me laugh, girl – and you can take that look off your face right now. You aren't even fourteen till December, whereas your sister will be sixteen next month. Phillipa's already a woman, a*nd* she knows her herbs. *You* don't know the difference between a buttercup and a dandelion, let alone chamomile and feverfew.'

Ma's scornful words made Margaret scowl. 'But I can learn. All you have to do is teach me.'

'I'll think about it when I get time. Now, we've got everything we came for, so we need to get home before this bowl gets broken. And it's time to get the pastry made to bake some meat coffins for tonight's meal. I've bought a nice piece of veal, a peppercorn and a pot of nutmeg, and we should already have enough cloves and mace in the house. I also bought a flagon of white wine. What we don't use in the sauce we can always drink.'

'Veal pies… and wine! Does that mean Pa's coming home?'

Joan nodded. 'I left your sister with orders to get some bread baked while we were out and I won't be pleased if she's forgotten. I had a sack of best wheat flour delivered from Easthorpe Mill yesterday especially for them. Just think, if you'd changed places with Phillipa today, it would have been you baking the bread.'

Too happy thinking of Pa's imminent arrival to worry about anything else right now, Margaret just shrugged.

*

The evening was a pleasant one as the Flower family enjoyed a meal together in their cottage beside the River Devon for the first time in over a month. A bright fire crackled in the stone hearth, sending sweet-smelling wood smoke up the chimney, occasional wafts drifting round the room. Oil lamps and can-

Chapter One

dles cast their flickering glow into otherwise dark and gloomy corners. The sturdy cast-iron oven stood empty in the hearth alongside the fire, at rest after almost a day of continuous use.

The two girls were delighted with the bolts of finely woven wool their father had brought to provide them with a new dress apiece and remained in happy mood, chatting together as their parents caught up with each other's news. But Phillipa's ears picked up at what her father said next, a dark cloud momentarily spoiling her evening.

'The earl asked Sir Charles if he could manage without me this weekend, and seeing as it's my weekend off, I wouldn't have been in Hucknall anyway.' John Flower looked thoughtfully at his wife. 'Sir Roger's holding a ball for his niece's birthday tomorrow night. It's hard to believe Lady Katherine will be eight this year. It seems like only yesterday that she was a tiny babe and her mother was still alive.'

Pa was quiet for a moment as he took another bite of his veal pie, seeming to Phillipa to be pondering on past times when the Earl of Rutland's brother, Sir Francis, lost his first wife, Lady Frances, to smallpox six years ago. Pa had often told them how badly Sir Francis had taken it until he'd met and married his second wife, Lady Cecilia. 'Anyway,' Pa continued at length, taking his wife's hand, 'they need an extra footman because one of his regular men has been taken ill. Don't worry, I'll get my weekend off next week instead, so I'll be back here late Friday afternoon.'

'When do you have to go up to the castle, Pa? It's not tonight, is it?'

Pa shook his head, his collar-length hair pale beside his

wife's dark tresses. 'No, Phillipa, it isn't. At least I've got tonight to be with you all, but I'll be off to Belvoir first thing in the morning, just as soon as I've collected the horse and cart from the stables at the inn. Peter's a good landlord and never charges much for stabling and feed, and always makes sure the horse and cart are hitched when it's time for me to get back to Hucknall. Guests will be arriving at the castle in time for a banquet with the Manners family before the ball later on and I need to be up there earlier to make sure I know what's expected of me. Once they've all left on Sunday afternoon, I'll be heading straight back to Hucknall.'

'Then that's that, I suppose.' Ma stood to top up the wine mugs from the flagon, causing Margaret to grin from ear to ear when even she got a refill. 'And before you two start bleating, you heard what your pa just said. He'll be back next weekend, so we'll have had him home for an extra night.'

'Not only that,' Pa added, grinning round at them. 'Sir Roger promised to pay me for the two days' work – with a substantial tip for my trouble, I might add – when Sir Charles has already paid me my usual wage. So, seeing as I'll collect a second wage on Sunday, I'll be bringing some extra coin when I see you next week. It should help out with household expenses.'

Ma nodded. 'Extra cash always comes in useful. The cost of food alone seems to be constantly going up these days and there's the upkeep of the house to think of. We're fortunate my grandmother persuaded the last earl to sell her this cottage. Having no rent to pay is a great help, though I know Roger Manners lets out the cottages in his villages for a minimal rent. He's kind like that.'

Chapter One

Pa pulled a face, one that always made the girls giggle, and feigned an indignant tone, 'Aye, well, he can afford to be kind, can't he? They say the Earl of Rutland's one of the wealthiest men in England, and the many villages and rich farmlands in the Vale of Belvoir must bring him in a tidy sum. And don't forget, he also has a large estate at Haddon in Derbyshire, with its big, fine hall. He even has estates in Warwickshire and Yorkshire. Folk like us simply can't imagine such wealth. But you're right, Joan, it's good of him to keep the rents so low. Other rich lords still charge their tenants ridiculous sums and don't care a whit that some can't even afford to feed themselves. But let's not get downcast tonight. I'm about to let that tasty-looking custard slide down my throat before I pour another mug of wine.'

John Flower squeezed his wife's shoulder. 'It's a fine meal I've come home to, wife, and I thank you for it. We're having our own banquet tonight and memories of it will keep me going while I show all the rich folk into the castle to enjoy theirs tomorrow.'

Ma smiled at the praise. 'The three of us enjoyed baking this afternoon, didn't we, girls?'

'It was fun making those veal pies,' Phillipa agreed, her dark eyes shining in the lamplight. 'I always enjoy baking.'

'And now I know why people call them coffins,' Margaret put in. 'We make the pastry stiff enough for the pies to stand on their own without being held in a dish. They do look like tiny coffins once the lids go on. I also liked learning about some of the spices and herbs we put into them. They smell really nice, too.'

'Well, let's finish our banquet before we get ourselves off

to bed; we'll be up at the crack of dawn. Oh, and husband, seeing as you're not delivering cages full of pigeons to the earl on this visit, if you'd take the new glass bowl for the countess with you, I'd appreciate it. It will save me the job of trekking up that hill with it tomorrow. Lady Elizabeth may well want the bowl to put some delicacy or other into at the banquet. Or, thinking about it, the bowl might even be a gift for her niece. Lady Katherine might not be of marriageable age yet, but it's never too early to start a collection of household things for when she is. Even daughters of rich folk like to have their own set of lovely things when they wed.'

*

Margaret followed her dark-headed elder sister around the large garden behind their cottage, waiting for the opportunity to ask her question. They wound their way past the hen coop with its long run behind a wattle fence and netted roof to a patch full of colourful herbs. A tall, weeping willow, still clinging to its summer foliage, stood sentinel on the garden's far boundary, flanked by a prickly holly tree and a study oak. Although it was late afternoon, the September sun was still warm on her face and Margaret was glad to be outdoors. It seemed to lessen the nagging pains she'd been feeling all day.

'Phillipa, will you teach me the names of the different herbs and what they're used for?'

'I will if you really want to learn. You've never wanted to know anything about the garden before, so I thought you weren't interested.'

Chapter One

Margaret averted her eyes from the probing dark stare. 'Well, I wasn't when I was younger, but now that I'm a woman, I am. When I have my own husband and a house to run, I'll have to grow some and –'

Phillipa's laugh put an end to Margaret's ramblings. 'What's so funny?' she demanded, pouting. 'I don't intend to stay here with Ma and Pa all my life, you know. I'll be on the lookout for a nice handsome husband very soon.'

'Oh, Margaret, you've got a few years before you need to think of such things. Even I'm not thinking about needing a husband just yet and Ma and Pa haven't mentioned they're looking for one for me. Just enjoy being a girl while you can. Being a woman brings responsibilities, and there's time enough for them later on. I'm only just entering womanhood, and you're still a child.'

'No, I'm not! My courses started over a year ago, as well you know, and today, I'm cursed with this monthly torment again. This is the first time I've felt so ill and I want to know if one of your herbs can make these awful pains go away.'

Margaret had not intended to divulge that so abruptly, but there it was, out in the open. Desperate for pain relief, she needed her sister's help.

Phillipa gave an understanding smile and put her arm around her younger sister's shoulders. 'I see… Do I take it you haven't asked Ma for one of her potions?'

'How could I when she's been out for most of the day? You know she always meets with those cunning women at Anne Baker's house on Saturdays when Pa isn't here. They seem like strange friends to me.'

'Ma enjoys their company, and we can't begrudge her a little time out on her own, can we? She also learns a lot about herbs and potions for curing folk's ailments from them. Besides, she was expecting to have Pa here until tomorrow, and I know she was disappointed when he said he was leaving this morning.'

Margaret nodded, knowing how disappointed she'd been herself. None of them could be miserable when Pa was at home.

'Well then, let's have a look for a suitable herb, shall we?' Phillipa took Margaret's hand and led her round the patches of herbs, their skirts sweeping the winding paths as they walked. 'Some of these can be used to treat a number of ailments as well as relieving pain; some are used to make colourful dyes and others to flavour different foods – but we'll look at all those another day. For now, we'll just pick one that is always useful for women's pains.

'Perhaps motherwort,' she said, bending down and using her clippers to cut a small bunch of the purple-pink flowers. 'Now we'll go indoors and boil some water to make a potion you can drink. Then you can curl up in your bed with a pillow warmed by a bed pan held against your tummy. Your pains will soon ease.'

'Thank you, Phillipa. If I'd known being a woman was this painful when I was younger, I would never have wanted to become one.'

*

Reverend Samuel Fleming, rector of the Anglican church of Saint Mary the Virgin's in the parish of Bottesford, rose

Chapter One

from his bed soon after dawn, careful not to jar his aching back or strain his creaking knees. He hobbled over to pull back the window drapes, allowing the morning sunlight to stream into his bedchamber on the first floor of the rectory. A wave of sadness engulfed him as he stood there, taking in the view of the lovingly tended garden with its abundance of late blooming flowers and the many trees with their gold-tipped leaves or bright evergreen sheen. It was on the eighteenth day of September, five years ago to this day, that Samuel's younger brother, Abraham, died in this very house after travelling up from Cambridge to spend a few happy days with Samuel, their sister Esther, and Esther's husband, Thomas. Yet after two short days, that happiness was abruptly curtailed.

That a seemingly healthy man should simply die in the chair in which he sat had seemed unreal to Samuel. Yet his brother's Cambridgeshire physician assured him that Abraham's heart had been weak for some years, attested by his constant shortness of breath and the debilitating pains in his left arm and chest. So, perhaps, their brother's death hadn't been too unexpected after all. But knowing that fact hadn't made Abraham's loss any easier to bear for Samuel, or for Esther. The three of them had always been close. Samuel found comfort in his firm belief that his devout brother was now with God. He was glad that Esther had a loving husband whose shoulder she could cry on.

Before her marriage twenty-six years ago, Esther had been Samuel's housekeeper, which was how she had met the friendly and jovial visiting clergyman. Thomas Davenport was minister at the church in the village of Harston, seven miles from Bottesford, and after her marriage, Esther moved to live there, obliging Samuel to appoint a housekeeper from the village.

Alice was a kindly soul, punctual and hardworking and entirely trustworthy. She came in to cook and generally keep house on a daily basis and her husband, Gilbert, was the competent gardener who kept the grounds in such impeccable condition. Fortunately, their Bottesford cottage was a mere five-minute walk away from the rectory, so Alice often arrived at the crack of dawn. She had her own key so she just let herself in and got on with her work.

Alice and Gilbert Nicholls kept Samuel's loneliness at bay during the day, and he thanked God for bringing such good people to help him. But he greatly missed the company of his sister in the long, quiet evenings. He and Esther would talk for hours about a multitude of things and on many an occasion she had helped him to write a difficult sermon. Esther had fussed over him like a mother hen, ensuring his home was as neat, tidy and comfortable as it could be. And how she could cook! All Samuel could do now was look forward to Esther and Thomas's next visit.

He headed over to the dresser, close to the door along the wall opposite his four-poster bed, thoughts of his siblings still playing in his head. Lifting the heavy ewer, he tipped the cold water into a large pot bowl and splashed his face before patting it with a drying cloth. Never a man to demand luxuries, Samuel had become used to washing morning and night in the chilly liquid – even during winter's iciest months – before garbing himself in the vestments required for the day's work ahead. Already in his sixty-third year, he thanked God daily for giving him such a long life, and enabling him to spend forty of those years in service to the Church. Even as a child, Samuel had known he was destined to become a Man of God and could not wait to begin his training.

It was Sunday again, Samuel's favourite day of the week. Today, his flock, the good people of Bottesford, would come to worship in the beautiful church, known to most people hereabouts as simply Saint Mary's or often as the 'Lady of the Vale'. The church's lofty steeple of two hundred and ten feet could be seen for miles across the Vale of Belvoir and looked magnificent when viewed from the castle up on the hill. He smiled to himself, thinking how truly awe-inspiring Belvoir Castle looked when viewed from Bottesford.

The quiet knock on his door told him that Alice had arrived.

'Will you be ready for your breakfast soon, Rector?' she called through the door. 'I know you like to break your fast early on a Sunday so you have time to go over your sermon before Morning Service.'

'I'll be down as soon as I finish dressing and have brushed what's left of my hair. Dare I hope you have some of those delicious pork sausages for me again?'

'I daresay you'll know whether I have or I haven't as soon as you open your door,' Alice teased. 'The smell of sausages being cooked has a way of drifting into every room in the house – though perhaps not as much so as bacon.'

'Then I'll finish dressing quickly, in anticipation of being greeted by that errantly drifting aroma when I open my door.'

'Breakfast will be ready for you as soon as you come down,' she called, her echoing voice gradually diminishing as she descended the stairs. This rambling old rectory had a disconcerting way of bouncing sounds from wall to wall.

Samuel perched on the edge of his bed, bending to buff his shoe buckles as he thought about his service for this morning. Unfortunately, the earl and his family would not be attending today; it was Lady Katherine's birthday and Belvoir Castle would be full of guests. Sir Roger had given his apologies last Sunday and assured Samuel that things would be back to normal the following week.

Although Samuel understood the reason for the absence of the Manners family today, he could not help feeling disappointed. It was particularly unfortunate on this occasion, since not only Sir Roger and Lady Elizabeth would be absent, but also the earl's younger brother, Sir Francis, and his wife, Lady Cecilia. Services never seemed as uplifting to his congregation without the presence of at least some of the earl's family. Nor was the large church as full. If people knew in advance of the earl's intended absence, some of Samuel's flock evidently saw no need to leave their folds. Not that all of them came every week, anyway. The Flower family, in particular, never came more than once a month, generally on weekends when John Flower came home from Hucknall. John was an upright man and had been a churchgoer all his life. Samuel recalled him as a lad with his fair-headed parents, such a cheerful and happy couple, who loved the Church and had doted on their only son.

John Flower had inherited his parents' religious zeal and happy attitude to life and he loved his wife and daughters dearly. Samuel sighed. He just wished that Joan Flower shared the same zeal, if only for their daughters' sake. After all, Samuel

Chapter One

himself had christened both Phillipa and Margaret in Saint Mary's.

He left his room, shutting the door behind him, and followed that tantalizing odour of sausages – or was it bacon? – down the creaking stairs.

*

On Sunday evening after a busy afternoon making potions from some of the herbs in their garden, Joan Flower sat with her daughters in their little cottage. It had amused her that Margaret had watched carefully how things were done, which Joan decided was no bad thing. Her younger daughter was old enough now to assist Phillipa in the task, and it would allow Joan time to catch up with other chores. Joan found sewing particularly relaxing, especially after hours spent over the cooking pot or wash tub, or physical exertions around the garden. Pottering round the quiet herb garden was one thing, but keeping on top of all the cooking and cleaning was a different matter. Fortunately, both of her daughters were old enough to help with such work.

'Ma, what did Anne Baker want this afternoon? You were only at her house yesterday.' Phillipa's voice cut through Joan's thoughts. 'It's unusual to see her out on a Sunday. Did she need one of our potions? We've sold a few jars this week for one thing or another.'

Joan laughed. 'That'll be the day. Anne knows more about herblore than I'll ever know. You should see inside her cottage. The number of pots full of potions and ointments she has on her shelves makes our few dozen look like child's play. She must have remedies for every complaint going.'

Joan was silent for a moment, wondering whether she should answer the question honestly while Margaret was still up. Phillipa would understand, but for all her boasting about being a woman, in many ways Margaret still had the mind of a child. 'No, Anne didn't want any potions,' she went on. 'She was just passing and called in to say that Joanne Willimott from Goadby wouldn't be coming to our gathering next Saturday. She has a funeral to attend in her village.'

That was not a lie, of course, but it was not the main reason for Anne Baker's visit. Anne was one of the cunning folk, after all, and dealt with requests for remedies for many kinds of ailments. She was also teaching Joan additional skills in the art in order that she eventually pass some of the trade that was presently overwhelming her to Joan and her daughters.

'Pull up the stool and sit beside me, Phillipa,' she urged, once her younger daughter was sleeping upstairs. 'We need to speak, woman to woman.'

But the reaction her subsequent words engendered was more impassioned than Joan had anticipated.

'You're telling me that a woman visited Anne Baker for a potion that would kill her unborn child. Surely, that's an evil thing to do. How could any woman murder her own child?'

Phillipa looked appalled and Joan reached out to take her hands. 'The answer to that is not a simple one. There are a number of reasons why a woman may not wish to bear a child, whether it be her first or one of many.'

'I can understand that a woman from a poor family could

Chapter One

feel anxious over the cost of another mouth to feed, but I can't accept that killing it is the answer. Surely she and her husband would find a way of making ends meet so that the child could be born and reared?'

'I'm sure many a husband and wife have done that, Phillipa, but if they can barely feed themselves and the children they already have, another one in the household could mean the whole family suffers. Little ones may even starve. But there are other reasons why a woman would ask for such potions, which you won't like to hear. But hear them you must.

'Imagine what would happen if an unwed woman got herself with child by a man who refused to marry her. Or, as in the case of the woman who came to see Anne Baker, a wife found herself with child by a man who was not her husband.'

Phillipa gasped. 'How could any wife betray her husband like that? We are taught that marriage vows are sacred. I can see that if the husband found out the babe wasn't his, he would probably never trust his wife again and the marriage would be tainted for ever. I doubt that few husbands could forgive such betrayal.'

'That's exactly my point. The goodwife who needs Anne's help is already four months into her term and it won't be long before her shape gives her away. She managed to hide the sickness in earlier weeks and is now frantic to be rid of the babe.'

'I understand what you're saying, Ma, but it still doesn't make it right in the eyes of God.'

'Pah! What do I care about God? He never stopped my pa from dying so young. Going to church is for folk who think God will help them in life – but I know different. If there *is* a

God, he has a funny way of showing how much he loves his people. I was only three when Ma and me were left on our own. It was a good thing Sir Roger's mother took pity on us and made sure my ma always had work at the castle, even if it was only scrubbing floors.'

Phillipa's face told of the shock of hearing her mother speak this way and Joan instantly regretted allowing herself to vent long-suppressed anger. She took a deep breath before continuing. 'What this woman wants to do may well not be right in the eyes of the Church, but she has four other children to consider. It would be a sad home for them to grow up in with a ma and pa who barely spoke to each other – or with no ma at all. Some husbands have been known to kick unfaithful wives out the door.

'Now, I think it's time we headed up to bed. It's Monday again tomorrow and we only have five days before your pa's home again. That's something good to look forward to.'

*

Daylight was just seeping through the shutters of the upstairs bedchambers when pounding on the cottage door had Joan and her daughters leaping from their beds and charging downstairs in a panic. No one had ever called at such an early hour, or banged so hard to be heard.

Joan unbolted and pulled back the door and stared at the two men on her doorstep as a feeling of dread crept over her. Something was very wrong.

'Mistress Flower?' A big burly man with a kindly face fingered his hat with obvious disquiet as she nodded. 'And these are your daughters, Phillipa and Margaret?'

'They are, but who wants to know, especially at this early hour?'

'I'm Robert Sudbury and this is my lad, William. Reverend Fleming's housekeeper sent us here. She was on her way to the rectory as we pulled into the lane and told us where you lived. If we might step inside for a moment, what we have to say might be easier for you to hear if you were sitting down.

'My son here and me, we're farmers, from over at Whatton-in-the-Vale, three miles this side of Bingham,' Mr Sudbury said once they were seated. 'You know it?'

Joan's fear at what she might hear intensified. 'I only know those places as being on the way to Nottingham… and that they're along the route my husband takes to and from Hucknall.'

'Aye, we know that, Mistress,' young William put in with an appreciative sidelong glance at Phillipa. 'We've chatted to John a time or two when he's stopped by our farm for a mug of milk. It's only a hundred yards from the Nottingham Road, you see. Always had a smile on his face and a friendly word to add. Told us he had a wife and daughters in Bottesford and how much he missed you all when he went back to work in Hucknall.'

'Then perhaps you'll know that he's only just gone back there after spending the weekend here, mostly working up at the castle? He said he was leaving Belvoir on Sunday afternoon.'

'That fits with what we'd already guessed.' Robert Sudbury's face was grim and Joan knew he was about to tell them something they didn't want to hear.

'Whatever it is you have to tell us, say it quickly and get it over with,' she said with forced composure. 'It's obvious that something has happened to my husband, so we need to know exactly what that is. Is he hurt in some way?'

Robert Sudbury took a breath. 'Mistress Flower, there was a nasty accident not far from Whatton and the horse and cart your husband was driving went off the road and ended up thirty yards down the hill to his left. I'm sorry to have to tell you that he didn't survive.'

'Pa can't be dead!' Margaret shrieked, jumping up from her stool. 'He was used to driving that cart and he told us the horse was a steady old plodder.'

'That may well be,' William said, 'but from what we saw of the scene, we can only think that something startled the horse, it bolted and the cart hit a rut in the road. It's not the smoothest of roads, considering it's the main one into Nottingham from here. As to what scared the horse, it could've been a deer running across in front of him, or something as small as a rabbit or stoat.'

Robert held out upturned palms. 'It could even have been a carriage of one of them fancy lords that caused the accident, hurtling past too close and expecting all other traffic to pull over. We see them doing that often enough. I don't suppose we'll ever know what caused it, but you have to accept the truth that John Flower is dead and we're all deeply sorry about that. The horse was as good as dead, too, so we put him out of his misery. We've brought your husband's body back in his own cart and put his few belongings in a sack.'

He reached into his coat pocket to retrieve a leather pouch

Chapter One

which Joan instantly recognised as John's. 'Mr Flower had this fastened to his belt and there are a good many coins in it. Looks like he might have just been paid for whatever work he'd been doing at the castle over the weekend. I imagine it'll come in useful for paying for the funeral and such like.'

Too stunned to speak as her two daughters sobbed, Joan just nodded.

'Me and William will carry him in for you before we get off, Mistress, and unhitch our horse from your cart.' The two of them stood, ready to leave. 'Reckon you'll have to lay John out and prepare him for burial until the reverend gets here.'

Joan thanked them both for their kindness and passed a half crown from the pouch to each of them. She tried to push all thoughts of money to the back of her mind, but they refused to do as bidden. How she and the girls would survive without John's regular wage loomed before her like the threat of their inevitable grave. She wanted to hide herself away and weep until the pain of it all left her body.

Chapter Two

In which heads need to be kept above water and a cat joins the Flower family

Bottesford: early October 1611

Joan Flower disliked being the object of pity, but few people in Bottesford offered their sympathy regarding her newfound lowly status in life, though several expressed their condolences on the death of her husband. She had known how popular and well-liked the handsome John Flower was long before they were married seventeen years ago; many girls in the village had hoped to win him as their own. But John had chosen Joan. 'My beguiling dark one,' he'd called her. 'I could not have stopped myself falling in love with you if I'd tried.'

Joan knew he'd meant every word and trusted he would never stray; she'd been told how beautiful she was on many occasions in her younger days. But to Joan, John was simply a man whose family had long been in the employ of the Manners family, and could maintain a good lifestyle and a certain, elevated status in the village as a consequence. To Joan's way of thinking, marriage to John Flower would ensure that she and their children would also enjoy such standards, just as her own grandmother had once done.

If Joan's mother hadn't gone her own way when it came to marriage instead of marrying a man deemed more suitable by the family, she, too, might also have become a well-placed

Chapter Two

lady-in-waiting at Belvoir Castle. Joan's father had never been liked around here. 'Too dark and foreign-looking for these parts... Wouldn't want t' turn me back on 'im,' the men had said. Admiring glances from the women told a different story. A Spaniard by birth, Joan's father had passed his dark good looks on to his only child – which in turn, she had passed on to Phillipa.

Thankfully, the new earl and countess had overlooked Joan's parentage, seeing her as a good, steady worker around the castle and intelligent and trustworthy enough to do a little shopping now and then for Countess Elizabeth. Similar tasks still fell to Joan after she'd needed to stop working at the castle when her children were young and had continued until John's death. But that had changed everything. Joan had heard nothing from the countess since – not even acknowledgement in receipt of the pretty glass bowl.

Such thoughts filled Joan's head as she stared down at John's grave in Saint Mary's churchyard, no more than a hundred yards from her cottage. She could not afford to spend what little money she had left on a headstone and the grave was marked only by a simple wooden cross. Some days her anger at his death overrode all else; the loss of his income was a severe blow. Love was not something Joan had ever felt for John. She liked him well enough, but the love of her life had wed another eighteen years ago, and still, after all this time, seeing him around the village caused umpteen emotions to run amok. If Jonathan Peate came to her now as a lover, she knew she would not say no – his wife be damned.

It was barely two weeks since her husband was buried and

Joan was desperate to find alternative sources of income before winter set in and they had no money left to buy food. It was something she planned to talk over with her daughters tonight.

*

'No, Margaret, I don't want to sell the hens – not unless we really have to. We need the eggs, as well as the meat now and then. I wouldn't mind getting rid of that noisy cockerel, but we'll get no more chicks if we do.'

'Well then, why can't we grow more herbs?' Margaret suggested next, undaunted. 'You already know how to make a lot of potions and ointments, Ma, so if we grow more herbs, we'll have more jars to sell. You told us that Anne Baker's already asked you to take some of the trade she hasn't got time for.'

'That's one of the things I'd thought of, too,' Phillipa added, her attention swinging from Margaret to her mother, 'and it's something all three of us could be involved in. But I also think we need to be growing a few more vegetables for our own use instead of having to buy them at the market. We've enough unused space in the garden for a good-sized vegetable patch as well as extending the herb garden. If we grow enough, we could even set up a stall in the market place and sell them, just like other folk do.'

Joan Flower stared vacantly at the colourful rag rug on the cottage floor, deep in thought. 'It's too late in the year to be sowing herbs, but we can do that early next spring. We could get a vegetable patch prepared this month, though, and get the seeds and tubers in the ground before winter. I'll see if Hugh

Chapter Two

Allingham along Normanton Lane has any spare. He grows lots of crops on his land and will probably sell me a few quite cheaply if I talk nicely to him at the market next Friday.'

'We could probably do with onions and garlic, and a few roots like turnips, carrots and beet. As for different greens, we should have as many as he grows,' Phillipa added, evidently pleased that her idea hadn't been brushed aside. 'Margaret and I can do the sowing and planting, Ma.'

Joan smiled at the daughters. 'I like the idea of growing our own food. It would save us a lot of coin and by next year we'll even have our own seed. What clever daughters I have to think of all that. But what we need to think about now, is how to find some immediate sources of money.'

Joan swung out her arm to indicate a few items in the room. 'There are some good, solid pieces of furniture in this room that your pa bought over the years. They might look nice but we don't need all of them and the cottage is full to bursting anyway. We could sell some pieces to bring us a few coins. We only need to keep enough chairs and stools for us to sit on, one dresser and chest for storage, and a table where we can prepare our potions and suchlike.' She heaved a sigh. 'I just need to swallow my pride for long enough to stand in the market place to do this. Those gloating goodwives will have a heyday knowing how low we've fallen.'

'Phillipa and me will do the selling, Ma. You've no need to be there. None of the women have cause to give us the evil eye.'

Joan pulled her two daughters to her and kissed each brow in turn. 'I must have done something good in my early life to be blessed with daughters like you.'

'You do believe in God, then,' Phillipa quipped. 'The reverend would be pleased to know that.'

'Who says I have to be blessed by the Christian God?' Joan said, laughing. 'I have the old gods to bless me…' She let that thought hang as they headed up to sleep, she in the large bed she'd shared with John Flower for seventeen years, and the two girls on their pallets on the other side of the wooden divide.

By mid-morning the following day, Joan was readying herself to walk round to Anne Baker's house when there was a knock on the door.

'I've a letter and a crate for you from Lady Elizabeth, Mistress,' the messenger said, handing the letter to Joan. 'Sorry if I got your title wrong,' he added, lifting the heavy crate into the cottage before turning to head down the path to where he'd tethered his horse and cart in the lane.

'What did he mean by that? What title was he talking about?'

Margaret's voice from behind startled Joan, and she spun round, thrusting the unopened letter into the girl's hands. 'Take a look for yourself and tell me what you make of it. I can see very well what the esteemed countess is saying.'

'It's addressed to "Goodwife Flower". Oh Ma, the countess knows very well that you are *Mistress* Flower.'

'But I'm not… not any more. Your pa's death has left me a widow, and no unmarried woman can claim to be "mistress" of any household – despite the fact that this cottage belongs to *me*.' Joan made no attempt to conceal the contempt in her voice and Margaret stared at her. 'Having no husband to keep

Chapter Two

me in my place and provide me with an income lowers my status to goodwife.'

'Then it was cruel of the countess to rub that in, after all the work you've done for her over the years,' Phillipa added, coming in from the garden to join them. 'I suppose many folk will be thinking you should be considering marrying again.'

'Well, that will never happen. The three of us will manage on our own, at least until you two are wed. Until then, we'll think of some useful ways of earning enough to keep us going.'

'Aren't you going to open the letter to see what Lady Elizabeth has to say?'

'Yes, I am, Margaret, as soon as I'm calm. It will only be further condolences and suchlike.' Joan broke the envelope's waxy red seal and retrieved the folded paper. 'Oh, my goodness, it seems the countess has sent us some money, a tidy little sum, too. Listen to what she says:

Goodwife Flower

As you see, I have sent you six gold crowns, two for each of you, perhaps to purchase clothing and shoes or whatever items you may need before winter comes. You also have a goodly number of shillings to spend however you see fit. I can only hope it helps until you find gainful employment. I am sure the foodstuffs will also help in this respect. The cheeses, meats and sausages are from our own farms, as are the onions, plums, apples and pears. The fish is from our ponds and the bag of flour was purchased from Easthorpe Mill.

I will organise more provisions to be sent to you in the near future. Until then, it would probably be wise for you and your elder daughter to seek out employment. You will not survive without some form of income for ever.

My thoughts have been with you since hearing of your sad loss.
Elizabeth Manners

Joan nodded, happy to know that the countess had not forgotten them. 'Perhaps we'd better open the crate and have a look.'

Margaret reached in and lifted a sackcloth pouch sitting atop several wooden and metal containers inside the crate. She loosened the drawstring and tipped the coins onto the table, delighted to count out not only the six crowns but thirty silver shillings as well.

'Oh Ma, Lady Elizabeth has been so generous. We won't have to worry about starving for some time.'

'Perhaps we won't but that doesn't mean we should get too comfortable about it all. As the countess has pointed out, her money won't last forever, so we make sure we only buy things we really need.' Joan's raised finger halted Margaret's inevitable reminder. 'Yes, I know you're both in need of a thick winter coat, and your two crowns will buy you one and still leave you coin for your purse.'

'What about you, Ma? I seem to remember you saying you could do with a new winter shawl.'

'That's true enough, Phillipa, but I can weave one for myself for half the cost. I'll just spend some of my two crowns on some raw fleece, and do all the spinning, dyeing and weaving here in the cottage. We've some pretty dyes made from our herbs earlier this year. You know how I enjoy making things and it will give me something to do on cold winter days.

Chapter Two

*

Late November, 1611

Late on a Friday afternoon, little over a week before the start of Advent, Phillipa returned to the cottage to find a small white cat curled up on the rug at her mother's feet as she sat in her chair by the fire, sewing.

'Well, there's a sight I never thought I'd see in this house,' she said, closing the door to the darkness outside. 'Are you looking after that animal for someone, Ma? It seems to have made itself nice and comfortable by your feet. You always told us you detested cats.'

Joan put the woollen stocking of Margaret's she'd been darning aside and focused on her elder daughter. 'Yes, I did say that, didn't I? And I meant it at the time. It's just that this poor thing wouldn't go away from our doorstep and it's so cold out there. He's only a kitten – not more than a few months old by the looks of him – and would probably have died if I hadn't brought him in and fed him. All right,' she added, smiling at Phillipa's raised eyebrows, 'I've probably grown soft as I've aged. Besides, every time I chased him off, he came back.'

'So it's a tom, is it? You've already checked that little detail?'

'I've checked. It's a tom all right.'

Phillipa bent down to stroke him. 'Ouch!' she squealed, clutching her hand. 'The little monster scratched me!'

'Get your hand into a basin of cold water and the bleeding will soon stop,' Joan ordered, lifting the cat onto her lap to a chorus of loud purrs. 'Perhaps he thought you were about to

Take Height, Rutterkin

put him outside. He's just got to learn to trust the three of us if he's to live here.'

'You're planning to keep him, then? Well, you have surprised me, though I can see he really likes you. And, with any luck, he'll help to keep the number of mice down in the house and hen coop. I can't wait to see Margaret's face when she gets home. We'd best warn her that he's likely to scratch, though.'

Joan nodded as she absently stroked the pretty white cat. 'Margaret should be back soon. She went out to meet some of her friends at the market this morning and promised to pick me up some spices I need while she was there. I wouldn't be surprised to find out they'd planned to meet up with some of the village lads, either. She was a bit secretive about the names of the friends she was meeting.'

'I didn't notice her in the market-place on my way home and there were very few people still there.'

'She would probably have headed up to Anne Baker's by then. Anne has recipes for the ointments we hope to make from the new herbs we'll be growing and she promised to have them copied out for me by today. I asked Margaret to pick them up before she came home. I hope she remembers and isn't still gallivanting around with her friends. I'd like to read them to make sure we'll be able to make them in the cottage.

'Oh, I almost forgot... How did you get on at the castle? Any luck, or was Lady Elizabeth overwhelmed by applicants?'

Phillipa beamed. 'There were six of us there, hoping to fill just three positions. And I'm happy to say that me and two others – Jennifer from Redmile, and Rosy from Sedgebrook – were the lucky ones. The countess told us that nine young

Chapter Two

women had already been taken on from Muston, Barkestone and Stathern, and we were the last. We start on Monday and we'll be there until a few days after Twelfth Night.'

Joan couldn't hide her relief in hearing that. The cash was sorely needed. 'I don't know the exact jobs we'll be doing yet,' Phillipa went on, 'but the countess said we could be placed anywhere in the castle, depending on what the housekeeper wants doing. We could be in different places each day, like the kitchens one day, the laundry the next and cleaning bed-chambers the next. Or we could be in several different areas in a single day.' She shrugged. 'I don't mind what I do, so I'll go where I'm sent. It will be almost seven whole weeks' paid work, Ma, as well as my board and lodgings at the castle, so you won't need to spend as much on food for just the two of you. I'll also be provided with a uniform, so everyone who sees me will know I work at the castle. I'll have a day off every week, though I don't know which it will be at the moment. But whichever it is, I'll come home and hand you my wages.'

'I'd rather you kept your coin in a safe place over the weeks you're there and brought it home altogether once you've finished. It will be a tidy sum by then and it will help see us through to the spring. It will also save you the needless trek back here every week, when you could be resting up at Belvoir.'

Joan heaved a sigh. 'I can't deny I'll miss having you here over the Christmas, and so will Margaret. It's bad enough knowing your pa won't be here. It will be very quiet with just the two of us.'

'But you'll also have this little cat to keep you company—that is, if no one comes to claim him. Have you decided what to call him, yet, Ma? How about James, after the king, or possibly Jaimie? Or even Roger after the earl, or better still, Rogue? From what I've heard, that's exactly what the earl is. Lots of Bottesford folk call him Rogue Roger.'

They both laughed at that. 'Well, I can't see the cat as a Jamie, and I doubt if the earl would be pleased to know we thought of him as a rogue, despite what the gossips say. This cat will be called Rutterkin. I don't know why, but the name popped into my head the moment I saw him on our doorstep.'

'Oh Ma, you're a strange one at times. But it will be nice to have a cat about the place, although I hope he keeps his claws to himself in future.'

*

Belvoir Castle, Lincolnshire: late November 1611 – early January 1612

Phillipa had never worked so hard in her life. Throughout the last week of November, the dozen new temporary servants at the castle scrubbed and cleaned every room, hallway and staircase from top to bottom in readiness for putting up the wonderful Christmas decorations that the Manners family were known for. The housekeeper, Mistress Abbott, a middle-aged lady whose rigid stance and sharp tongue kept the staff on their toes, was never far away. Any lapse in endeavour was severely reprimanded. By the end of the week, Phillipa's hands were rough and red, every fingernail broken and ragged. But the receipt of her first wages made her realise how worthwhile all that hard work was.

Chapter Two

She duly stashed the coin away amongst her few belongings in a small set of drawers allocated to her in a room she shared with several other young women, including Jenny and Rosy. Both were cheerful and chatty and Phillipa thought herself fortunate to be placed with people she liked. Not all the other servants were amenable, particularly some of the older women from Bottesford who were regular employees at Belvoir. She even overheard snippets of gossip amongst a group of them in which they used blatantly callous words to describe Joan Flower. Observing Phillipa passing by, they rapidly dispersed.

'They said my ma was a no-good whore!' Phillipa confided to her friends once they'd finished work and were back in their room for the night. 'I know Ma refuses to go the church on Sundays, but those women had no cause to say she needs to confess her sins to the reverend – especially when my pa has only been dead a few months. And they said that Ma flaunts the fact that Lady Elizabeth favours her.'

'Folk can be cruel at times,' Jenny consoled, folding her grey, workaday dress ready for morning and sitting down to begin the nightly ritual of brushing her long auburn hair. 'They can also be very thoughtless. I don't know why they should call your ma a whore, but those accusations might simply come from someone who is jealous of her standing with the countess. Jealousy is a strange thing and makes people say things they don't always mean. Don't take their idle gossip to heart.'

Plump and rosy-cheeked Ruby nodded in agreement as she clambered into her bed. 'Try to pretend you heard nothing the next time you see them, Phillipa. Smile sweetly and say good day. If you start shooting hostile glances their way, you may end up being the victim of their vicious tongues.'

Over the next few weeks, Phillipa took her friends' advice, smiling at everyone she passed and throwing herself into her work, determined to give no one cause to call her 'lazy' or 'just like her mother'. She feared they might think she got this job because of her mother's long-standing connections with the castle, and had the uneasy feeling that it might be true. But she heard nothing further and the weeks of the Advent flew by.

With Christmas only a week away, the gruelling work of scrubbing, cleaning and polishing, washing bed linen and making up guest beds drew to a close. Cooks declared that all the Christmas puddings and cakes were made and that meats and mince pies and various sweets and desserts would be ready in time for the arrival of the many guests. Barrels of ales and scores of the newly produced glass bottles filled with colourful wines stood waiting in the cellars below, and Mistress Abbott informed the staff that players, mummers and minstrels would be descending on them over the next few days – and to keep well out of their way.

Every surface, table-top and window pane gleamed, ready to accept the festive mantle that would adorn them until after Twelfth Night. Estate groundsmen and gardeners carried in mounds of greenery to accompany the few Advent ornaments. Prickly holly with blood-red berries, bay, rosemary, ivy, branches of fir trees and even a few sprigs of mistletoe were draped with sparkling tinsel and tied with red ribbon to deck walls, mantle pieces, tables and window ledges. Glittering stars, moons and snowflakes hung from high ceilings, doorframes, windows and silver chandeliers.

Chapter Two

Phillipa had never seen anything so splendid and vowed she'd remember such sights till her dying day. How could she not feel a tinge of envy that people like the earl and countess could afford such luxury whenever they chose, while many poor folk across the land would be lucky to have bread and cheese to eat this Christmastide?

*

Bottesford: January 1612

January began with a spell of mild weather, for which Joan was thankful and could only hope it lasted. A few cold months would mean buying more logs for the fire and spending longer outdoors collecting kindling, neither of which were prospects she relished.

Phillipa came home on the afternoon of the thirteenth day of the month, a week after Twelfth Night. She had spent over seven weeks at the castle and been paid for eight. On top of which, all twelve of the temporary staff were given an extra crown as a Christmas gift from Countess Elizabeth.

Despite having spent the last week helping to restore the castle to a state of clean and tidy normality, Phillipa was full of exuberance. Tales of Christmas at Belvoir Castle with the dozens of rich guests in their fancy clothes, elaborate plays and magnificent feasts and balls, poured from her lips as they sat round the fire in the cottage that night.

'A few of the earl's brothers and sisters were there with their families, and of course Sir Francis and Lady Cecilia, who live at the castle most of the time anyway. Even their younger brother, Sir George, was there for a few days, but he needed to go back to his hall at Fulbeck before getting back to work in January. Did you know he's the Member of Parliament for Grantham, Ma?'

Joan nodded. 'I did, and I can recall seeing him around when he was a lad. He married a Lady Frances, we were told, but as far as I know, they have not yet had children.'

'Anyway,' Phillipa pushed on, 'no expense was spared on decorating not only the main rooms, but also along the stairs and bannisters. I've never seen so much greenery, not to mention glittering stars, tinsel and red ribbon. As for the food…'

Joan only half listened, having witnessed a few Christmases at Belvoir in past years, but she could see that her younger daughter was rapt.

'Well, that's how the rich people live,' she explained when Margaret gasped at Phillipa's description of the ladies' silk gowns and sparkling jewellery. 'And there's no point in the likes of us feeling jealous. Believe me, it isn't only at Christmas when the Manners family indulge in elaborate entertainments and dress up in their finery. The birthday feast for Lady Katherine at which your pa assisted as an extra footman would have been just as grand, but without the Christmas greenery and tinsel.

'No, Margaret, such things are not for us to enjoy. Be thankful your pa's family and mine have worked for the Manners family for years and we are held in high regard by the earl and countess. There are many folk in this village who are envious of *us*.'

Joan's words jolted Phillipa's recollections of the harsh criticisms she'd overheard, but she kept them to herself, intending to broach the subject with her mother once Margaret was out of the room.

'I know, but I can dream, can't I, Ma?' Margaret replied. 'Perhaps next year I might be chosen to spend Christmas at the castle like Phillipa. I'll be almost fifteen by then. All that food sounds unreal.'

Joan sighed. 'It *is* unreal for people like us. Don't forget, Margaret, the servants aren't invited to the feasts and balls. Phillipa will tell you that, once she's finished marvelling about everything. Extra servants are only hired to make sure the castle is made spotlessly clean, ready for the rich folk to enjoy themselves.'

Phillipa held out her rough, red hands for Margaret to see. 'Ma's right. We had a few weeks of really hard work cleaning the castle, before and after Christmas. And we weren't allowed anywhere near while the guests feasted and danced. The earl and countess have their own special servants to serve food and wines at table – not mere cleaners like us. But I caught glimpses of the food while tables were being laid and the music from the balls and plays could be heard in most parts of the castle. I admit, I felt very jealous and wished I could be part of it all.'

Joan took Phillipa's hands. 'The redness will soon go if you keep your hands away from harsh lye soap and hot water for a few days, and your nails will recover. I can't tell you how much the money you've brought back means to the three of us.' She glanced at the sackcloth bag of coins sitting on the table before refocusing on Phillipa. 'When you look at your broken nails, just remember that the coin all your scrubbing helped you to earn will mean we won't need to worry about food or fuel for the fire until the spring. I can't thank you enough, and perhaps next year, Margaret might find employment at Belvoir, too.'

*

'Ma, what you said about some of the village goodwives envying us…' Phillipa started, once Margaret had gone to bed. 'I overheard some of them at the castle saying nasty things about you.'

'That bothers me not one fig!' Joan retorted. 'I know full well what they think of me and I won't be losing any sleep over it.'

Phillipa nodded and opened her mouth to continue, but thought better of it and clamped it shut again.

'Come on, Phillipa, out with it. If there's something on your mind, let's hear it. Nothing you say connected to those miserable servants up at the castle is going to upset me.'

Phillipa stared at her mother's resolute face and decided she was probably right. 'They said you were a whore, and they have no cause to say such things! Why must some people always be so spiteful?'

Joan Flower was silent for a moment, as though trying to think of a suitable answer. But what she said left Phillipa reeling. 'It's true, I have become a whore – but only since the middle of November, and I've only given myself to one man. No, I don't feel good about it,' she said at Phillipa's outraged expression, 'despite the fact that he's a widower. And I'd like to know how any of those gossiping goodwives found out about it.'

Chapter Two

Phillipa just stared at her mother, not knowing what to say, so Joan pushed on, 'You have to understand that by early November, I had no idea that you would find work at the castle, nor did I know if the countess would keep her word and send us more food. As a mother, I had you and Margaret to think about, and no mother wants to see her children go hungry. As it turned out, Lady Elizabeth sent us more provisions a week before Christmas but no money came with them this time.'

'But *whoring*, Ma? Could you find no other way to earn money? What about selling your potions, and perhaps a few eggs? We always have eggs to spare.'

'Phillipa, until we make a lot more potions and ointments, we don't earn enough from sales of them to keep Rutterkin fed, let alone the three of us. And I can't sell precious foods for a meagre groat or two. Giving myself to this man twice a week enables me to buy the weekly bread, milk and cheese, as well as a few vegetables. I still have a little of the coin the countess sent us, but that won't last for much longer.'

Phillipa didn't know what to say, and although she hated the thought of what her mother was doing, she could understand the reason for it. 'I don't want to know who this man is that you sleep with or where the two of you meet, and I know that whatever I say won't stop you going to him. I also know that you're doing it for Margaret and me. I just wish we could find some better way of earning coin than that. Are you still willing to sell the furniture you were intending to take to market before the first coins and provisions came from Lady Elizabeth?'

'It's always a possibility, but for now, we have your earnings to keep us going for a while as well as the little we make from our potions. Spring isn't too far away, when we'll be able to get the new herbs sown and, hopefully, see some signs of the vegetable seeds we sowed in October.'

'I was happy to earn this money for us, Ma, and only wish my work at the castle could have lasted a lot longer. I'll keep looking for other jobs I could do, and Margaret isn't too young to find employment. A couple of the girls taken on at Belvoir this Christmas were not yet fifteen.'

There was little more to say and they headed up to bed, Philippa with a heavy heart at thoughts of what her once proud mother had been reduced to.

Chapter Three

In which the king visits the earl

Bottesford: late June 1612

Belvoir Castle was in mourning. Sir Roger Manners, Fifth Earl of Rutland, was dead. News was carried to villages across the Vale by the castle's heralds, who duly nailed proclamations onto the doors of churches and market halls, or onto tree trunks in tiny hamlets, after first reading it aloud to the groups that readily gathered round.

Although no cause of death had yet been cited, the earl's failing health had been general knowledge for some time. Villagers had even speculated at to its cause after he'd been spotted hobbling into church, relying heavily on the support of his younger brother and their coachman. But not a word of explanation passed down from the castle. Even servants shook their heads, claiming ignorance as to the nature of their lord's ailment. Yet it was already known that Sir Roger's wife, Countess Elizabeth, had grown frail and sickly-looking over the past year in particular, and the gossips took no time in airing their views. Only one thing could be the cause of the early death of one partner in a childless marriage and increasing ill health in the other.

'It could only have been syphilis,' Anne Baker declared, her steady green gaze moving between her three companions as they sat in her Bottesford cottage two days later discussing some new potions she'd created. Anne was an intelligent woman, a year or two older than Joan, who loved to take centre stage, and generally succeeding in keeping her audience rapt. Joan Flower listened intently from her seat between the other two cunning women, the older and shrewish little Joanne Willimott and the rounded and comely Ellen Greene.

'I've seen the symptoms often enough and I've been told that Sir Roger rubbed his head and arms a great deal, which suggested to me they were aching. I was also informed that he constantly yawned and sneezed – *and* he shivered and sweated a lot as well, all at the same time as he sat in church. Being constantly tired, aching all over and feeling feverish, are the first signs of syphilis I look for when a person is fully dressed. I also caught a glimpse of a bright red rash on one of the earl's hands not long since, and I guessed then he'd probably have warts and lesions in places he kept well covered, like his nether regions.'

'When did *you* manage to get close enough to him to notice this rash, might I ask?' Ellen's voice held more than a little scepticism and Joan smiled to herself, watching Anne's scowl soften as she decided not to reply in kind.

'It was when he and Lady Elizabeth stopped alongside the Belvoir Inn and one of the coachmen was sent to buy a couple of mugs of ale. I just happened to be walking past, you see. The day was hot and muggy, and the earl and countess were out in an open coach. I'd have thought no more about his need of a drink if he hadn't raised his arm to swipe the back of his hand across his sweating brow, exposing his palm. Needless to say, bright red rashes on the palms of hands and the soles of feet

Chapter Three

are another sign that the disease is rampant in a body.'

Joan listened with interest to her friend. She had never liked the raucous and sometimes vulgar Sir Roger, who was known to absent himself from the castle for months at a time, gambling his fortune away and pursuing liaisons with women of ill repute. But thoughts of the gentle Lady Elizabeth being stricken with the same disease filled Joan with sadness and she could only hope that the earl and countess had not shared a bed for many years.

*

The village of Normanton: last week of July 1612

'We won't be able to meet like this after next week, Hugh – for a while, that is.'

Joan ran her long fingernails down the length of her lover's back before shoving his weighty body from her own and pulling herself up to gaze down at him. The late July day was hot and sweat glistened on his suntanned skin. Hugh Allingham was a handsome man, tall and dark-haired, muscular, too; just as Joan liked a man to be. But the petulant pout her words had engendered made her cross. He was not her husband and had no call to demand her time, even if he did pay her for it. Still, she needed his coin and didn't want to upset him. Though not exactly a wealthy man like the rich folk in the castle, Hugh was a yeoman farmer and he and his only son worked hard on their strips of land and made a good living. Unlike many, Hugh could afford to hire a labourer during busy periods in the farming year. He also owned his own cottage and barn as well as a pair of oxen, three sturdy ponies and a covered wagon.

'Oh, don't look so vexed, Hugh. As I said, it will only be for a while, no more than two or three weeks.'

She stroked his cheek and moved herself close to deliver a passionate kiss on the lips, pulling quickly away before he became aroused again. 'And before you ask, I cannot refuse the new countess. She's offered all three of us work at the castle during the king's visit in August and, as you well know, we need the coin. This will be the first real work any of us has had since Phillipa was up at Belvoir over the Christmas season.'

Hugh pulled a face and removed a strand of straw from Joan's dark hair. His barn was comfortable and private enough for their meetings, especially when his son and labourer had begun harvesting the oats on their strips in a field closer to Bottesford, almost a mile from the cottage and barn. But straw in a person's hair was as good as announcing the fact that they'd been enjoying a sexual romp. 'Are you saying I don't pay you enough? I thought what I gave you each week would be enough for foods you need.'

'You pay me well enough, and I'm not complaining about that. But we have other expenses besides food. I have fuel for the fire to think of, even in summer. We'd have nowhere to cook if I didn't light it each day. We collect small branches and as much kindling as we can from the woods but I like to keep a store of stout logs, which we have to buy. The three of us also need new clothes every now and then. Shoes don't last forever, you know, and nor do dresses. Once they wear thin and start to fray, they soon fall into holes. I darn and mend

Chapter Three

garments until there's little left to darn, and only then do I purchase cloth to make new ones.'

'Aye, well, go if you must, but just tell me this: who's going to feed that cat of yours, and the chickens, when you're gone?'

'Anne Baker agreed to do that every day, which was kind of her. I've told her to take as many eggs as she wants in payment.'

'I'll be an unhappy man without your visits to look forward to. You know how much I care for you, don't you, Joan? And I'll be forever wondering whether some man or other up at the castle has tempted you to his bed. The earl has a lot of fit-looking servants.'

Joan stayed his hands from roaming around her still curvaceous body, knowing how besotted this man was with her. If it were up to him, he'd be having her every day of the week instead of a mere two. As a widower with only one grown-up son and making a comfortable living as a yeoman farmer, Hugh would be a good catch in marriage for most women. But not for Joan; she valued her independence too much.

'Sweet Hugh,' she said in a tone she hoped would appease as she pulled her shift and grey woollen dress over her head and stood to tie a black cord around her waist. 'The three of us will be sharing a sleeping chamber with a number of other women and none of us will feel like doing anything other than sleeping after a day of scrubbing floors, washing bed linen or pots and pans, or running errands for any household member that asks. We'll be dogsbodies for all and sundry up there. No more than lowly scrubbers and charwomen. If you think we'll feel like rutting with anyone all night as well, you can think again. Besides, I'll be saving myself for when I come back to you.'

Hugh nodded, evidently having nothing to say to counter her reasoning, and Joan moved away from their love nest in the straw, ready to leave. 'I know you don't like me working away from the village, Hugh, but I think you understand that I have to take whatever work comes along. I have my daughters to think of.'

'Aye, I understand that.' He stood and moved to pull Joan to him for a final kiss. 'But I wish you were coming back to your own cottage each night so I wouldn't have to worry about other men jumping into your bed – or dragging you into theirs. You're still a beautiful woman, and I know there'll be other men desiring you.'

Joan felt an overwhelming compulsion to laugh. Although only just nearing her fortieth year, she had felt so old since John's death. The worry of coping without a husband's income was wearing her down, and having what seemed like the weight of the world on her shoulders made her feel like an old hag. She knew herself that she wasn't the wrinkle-free, dark-headed beauty she'd been not so long ago; more than a few grey hairs snuggled betwixt the black. No, a fresh-faced young beauty she was not. It was Phillipa and Margaret who now turned heads.

She reached the barn door, thoughts of her daughters filling her head. Chalk and cheese, those two, just like she and John had been. Pretty, blue-eyed and fair, Margaret had always favoured her father, while Phillipa had Joan's dark, sultry looks. Joan was proud of both of them, though she constantly worried about their futures and their prospects of finding husbands willing to take a wife from such a poor background.

Chapter Three

'I wonder what kind of earl Sir Francis will make.' Hugh's voice cut through Joan's thoughts. 'Although, we all know he was as wild as Sir Roger in his younger days – and so was their younger brother, George. Taking part in Essex's rebellion against Queen Elizabeth two years before she passed did none of them much good, but at least Sir Francis and Sir George settled down after their youthful misdemeanours. Sir Francis has been running the various family estates since his marriage to Lady Cecilia four years ago. Let's face it, Sir Roger cared naught for any of them, other than they provided him with coin for his decadent pursuits.'

Joan turned to face him as he sat on a bale of straw. 'Sir Francis has always spoken civilly to people in the village, more often than not with a smile on his face,' she replied. 'He seems as pleasant as his wife, and Phillipa said he was always kind to the staff during the Christmas festivities. 'It can't have been easy for him and Lady Cecilia living up there, especially when Sir Francis was busy managing the different estates while his brother was off somewhere, squandering as much coin as the estates took in each year. But from what I've seen and heard, Lady Elizabeth and Lady Cecilia are good friends. It was Lady Elizabeth's idea to hold the ball for Lady Katherine's birthday; she is a caring aunt. It's unfortunate she wasn't blessed with at least one child of her own.

'Best be off now,' she shouted back as she left the barn. 'Thanks for the coin, it will be put to good use. See you next Tuesday.'

*

Take Height, Rutterkin

Belvoir Castle, Lincolnshire: August 1612

Lady Cecilia Manners heaved a sigh of relief. After a couple of hectic hours, their royal guests were now seated around the banqueting table in the castle's spacious great hall and the meal was underway. The king's party had not arrived until early evening so everything had been such a rush, and time for the welcoming drinks, niceties and chats had been limited. While the visitors enjoyed the light refreshments, servants carried in the weighty travel chests from the coaches and delivered them to the respective rooms. The esteemed guests were then able to bathe and change into their evening wear.

Yet the delay had had its advantages. It had given Cecilia time to check that the banqueting table had been draped in the household's most decorative linen cloths and laid with its finest glass, silverware and earthenware. She had also managed to visit the kitchens to check that the guests would be treated to an array of rich meats and pastries and some of the finest wines offered anywhere in the country.

In honour of his revered status, the king was seated at the centre of one side of the long, rectangular table. Garbed in a striking, long-sleeved doublet of patterned gold brocade, with the lace collar and cuffs of a fine linen shirt proudly on display, he looked the epitome of wealth and power. The waves of his thick dark hair cascaded down his shoulders to complete the look.

Immediately to James's left was Sir Francis, and Cecilia was seated next to him. Other guests included a number of local dignitaries, many accompanied by their wives. Amongst them

Chapter Three

were the earl's younger brother, Sir George Manners, with his wife, Lady Frances. All had donned their most splendid apparel for the occasion.

Sir Francis stood to deliver a short, but warm, welcoming speech, expressing his hopes that his majesty would find his visit to Belvoir both enjoyable and memorable. Francis's final quip – that the king would undoubtedly be relieved to get home to rest at Whitehall after the vigorous lifestyle of the Vale – engendered chuckles around the table.

The king replied in kind, thanking Francis for his hospitality and declaring that no one had ever yet managed to tire him out. But he'd be delighted if Francis succeeded in doing so – and since he was famished, could they now get on with the meal?

Cecilia watched as the dark gaze of King James the First of England and Ireland, and the Sixth of Scotland, swept those gathered around the table as they laughed at his little witticism until his focus eventually settled on her husband.

'Do you recall the last time I was here, Francis?' he asked, sitting back to allow a servant to place a generous helping of roast beef on his plate, his nose twitching at the tantalising aroma. Cecilia smiled, knowing how hungry their royal guests must be after travelling for most of the day. 'It seems like only yesterday,' James continued, 'yet it was over nine years ago, and under vastly different circumstances. So much has occurred since then, has it not? The fact that I am still alive is a miracle in itself.'

Cecilia listened to the Protestant king, hoping he would say nothing offensive regarding the Catholic faith. Though she and Francis hid the fact that they were of the Catholic persuasion from the general public – and attended services at the Anglican Church of Saint Mary's in Bottesford for appearances' sake – King James was well aware of the family's Catholicism. Due to the friendship they had shared over the years, his majesty generally chose to overlook the fact, but he *would* keep dropping derogatory remarks about the 'damnable Catholics'.

'I remember it well, Your Majesty,' Francis replied as the king chewed a mouthful of beef. 'It was in the April of 1603 when you were on your way to London to claim your throne following the death of Queen Elizabeth.' King James merely nodded as he swallowed. 'The long journey from Edinburgh was arduous and you and your entourage were sorely in need of an overnight rest. Of course, my elder brother, Roger, was earl here at the time.'

'I hope you will accept our deepest condolences on the death of your brother, Francis. Sir Roger was dear to us all, and as your good self, he paid numerous visits to our court over the years. I'm told his wife, Lady Elizabeth, retired to Nottingham to stay with some of her family after the funeral. Do you think she will ever come back to Belvoir?'

Cecilia knew what her husband would reply. Thoughts of her absent friend always caused a stab of sadness in her breast.

Francis shook his head. 'Probably not to live here permanently, though my wife will sorely miss her. They were very close; like real sisters in many ways. But Elizabeth has promised to visit us before September, if she is fit enough to travel. She hasn't been at all well for some time and I'm afraid we all fear

Chapter Three

the worst will happen before long. But let's not dwell on that tonight. You were saying, my lord?'

'Er… oh yes. Since my initial visit all those years ago, I have never done you the courtesy of visiting your home, for which I most heartily apologise. I confess, the treacherous Catholic plot to blow up Parliament two years into my kingship quite put me off travelling for some years, so I limited my summer progresses to our southerly route. This year, however, I decided that the midland route would suit us better. The people to the north of our capital need to see their king, after all. Though to my shame, I have not yet returned to Scotland, nor have I visited Ireland since my accession to the English and Irish thrones. I hope to rectify that with visits to both in the near future, although, whether that will ever be possible remains to be seen.'

James heaved a sigh. 'It is by no means easy being the monarch of three nations, Francis, and I had little choice other than to keep London as the seat of my government.'

'I understand, Your Majesty, and you have no need to explain to me. I can only admire your skills of rulership and administration. It is a feat beyond the ability of any ordinary man.'

'I value your loyalty, Francis, and know that several of the areas to the north of our capital are safely under your control. But that does not mean you need to stay away from London. I would be grieved if you missed too many of our courtly celebrations.'

'On this occasion, it is we who are honoured to be entertaining you at Belvoir, my lord, and can only hope you find our castle to be comfortable. We will endeavour to make your stay pleasurable and interesting. There is fine hunting in our woods and across the open lands of the Vale, and I know hunting is a particular passion of yours. We have several groups of musicians, including the one playing quietly for us now, and on some evenings my wife and I have arranged for plays and masques to be staged for your amusement. In fact, on two evenings, plays of my good friend Will Shakespeare will be performed. I selected two that feature witches and their craft, a subject I know to be close to your heart. I hope *Macbeth* and *Julius Caesar* will give us something else to discuss over the days of your visit. And naturally, my wife will ensure that only the finest foods and wines are served to Your Majesty.'

Francis gestured to Cecilia at his side and she smiled at King James.

'It is a pleasure to see you again, Lady Cecilia,' the king said, returning her smile, displaying a set of perfect white teeth. 'We have seen little of you at Court, although I know you visit your London house on occasion. Bedford House, is it not?'

'It is, Your Majesty, although I have not had the pleasure of staying there since our two sons were born. Henry is presently but three years and his brother, Francis, a mere fifteen months.' She smiled in acknowledgement of the king's understanding nod. 'I would hope to visit Bedford House, and of course your splendid court, when our sons are both a little older and travelling becomes easier. My step-daughter, Katherine, is almost nine and travelling is no burden to her. Henry has also proven to bear up well on short journeys. But Francis is a sickly babe and I fear that travelling by coach would do him little good.'

Chapter Three

'Nor anyone in the coach with him, I should think.' The king's shoulders moved up and down as he laughed with the guests at his own jest. 'But I shall eagerly await your visit, as will my dear wife. Queen Anne will understand the need to attend to young children, having had three of our own. Thankfully, our youngest, Prince Charles, is twelve now and causes few problems in that respect.'

Cecilia smiled again at a man she had always seen as foppish and unmanly. Compared to her husband, James fared rather badly. He was not as handsome as Francis for one thing, and despite being as equally tall and broad-shouldered as her husband, James's spindly legs could not be missed when he stood. Yet she could not deny that he was charming, witty and affable enough in company – if one overlooked the strange, muffled timbre of his Scottish voice, which, she had heard, was a result of his tongue being too big for his mouth.

Cecilia was not prone to listening to gossip, but rumours of King James's sexual predilections were hard to miss when she and Francis were in London. His insistence on surrounding himself with handsome young men at court was constantly whispered about. Gossips even went as far as suggesting the royal marriage was a charade and the three royal children were sired by different fathers of James's choosing. Cecilia knew there was rarely smoke without fire but she kept an open mind on the issue and had never discussed it with anyone but Francis, who suggested they disregard it as nonsense.

'How is Prince Henry, my lord?' Francis asked, glancing at the empty seat to the king's right that should have been filled by the heir to the throne. 'He is evidently another who does not travel well. He looked quite ashen on arrival, as though his stomach had rebelled at the need for a journey. Some of our roads are badly potholed and do not allow for a pleasant ride. I hope he will be recovered enough to join us in the morning.'

'Indeed, Henry has never travelled well, and I should not have jested at your present predicament with young Francis, Lady Cecilia.' James flashed her another of his white-toothed smiles. 'In actual fact, I do sympathise with you. The queen and I had hoped Henry would grow out of his travel sickness as he aged, but at eighteen, journeying anywhere still makes him nauseous and weary. He will be better after a night's sleep; his cheerfulness and good looks will return and I expect he will join us for whatever entertainment you have planned for tomorrow. He's quite a charmer of the ladies, you know, although I say so myself.' King James beamed at the thought. 'They say he is handsome and dashing, and who am I to argue with that? He is also intelligent and a born leader, and will make an excellent king one day. Naturally, I hope to be here for some years yet, which will give Henry time to prepare for the crown. Now, I'd like to sample some of the excellent-looking syllabub, if I may.'

Little was said while the various desserts were savoured but eventually, Cecilia excused herself and the ladies and directed them to their withdrawing room, where they could chat about everyday life and family problems whilst enjoying another glass of wine or a cup of cocoa. The men would move to more comfortable chairs in this large hall, ostensibly to discuss important events occurring in the country and on the continent, and generally to catch up with each other's news.

Chapter Three

*

Ever the genial host, Francis ordered port and brandy and waited until servants had poured for the guests and left the hall before enquiring after the latest news at court. But King James had one overriding interest, besides which most other issues paled into insignificance, and soon steered the conversation that way.

'I hope you're continuing to encourage the people of the Vale of Belvoir to be vigilant in their quest to seek out signs of devilish practices,' he started, addressing his host, seated in an armchair close to his and taking a sip of port before resuming. 'I know you share my feelings of revulsion for those who dabble in such diabolical works. They are instruments of Satan's evil and we must rid our land of them before we are all controlled by their heinous spells.'

Francis did not interrupt, knowing that James was only just warming to a topic he could speak about all night. He smiled to himself as most of the guests suddenly became engrossed in topics of a lighter nature. Not that it mattered; the king had not even noticed, since Francis was the focus of his attention.

'Since the publication of my treatise, *Daemonologie*, fifteen years ago, witchcraft has been increasing across Europe and Britain alike – which I'm sure you're aware of having toured Europe yourself. After witnessing how witches and sorcerers were dealt with there, I assume you follow news of such events as it arrives in England?' Francis merely nodded. 'The stench of witches burning at the stake is not something to be easily forgotten. In Scotland, witches are hanged but their bodies are then burned, whereas in England we continue to hang them and bury them wherever their gaolers see fit. That could be in consecrated ground, or not, depending on the gaoler's own convictions. Sometimes, of course, a family might request to take the body for burial and in general, I don't think they are refused.'

Francis had no desire to see the barbaric punishment of burning at the stake become customary in England. 'Hanging kills a witch just the same,' he remarked, 'and doesn't take as much time and effort on behalf of the gaolers. Nor do we have to suffer the stink of roasting flesh.'

'Ah, but Francis, hanging allows a witch's vile spells and curses to continue working their evil, whereas flames purify the body, permitting the soul to return to our loving maker, ending their evil forever. But, since witchcraft is seen as a felony in England, the punishment for which is hanging, we will continue to hang those convicted.'

'I believe you know my younger brother, George,' Francis said quickly in an effort to change the topic of conversation, and gestured at a sturdily built, brown-headed man sharing some jest with a family cousin close by.

'Yes, I've met both George and his wife, Frances, on a few occasions at court. I noticed them during the meal but we shared no more than an affable nod. I wondered if they lived here in the castle or were simply visiting on this occasion.'

'They have a suite of rooms here, just as my wife and I had when Roger was alive. But, like myself and Cecilia, George and Frances have a house in London, and George purchased Fulbeck Hall when he became Member of Parliament for

Chapter Three

Grantham eight years ago. The hall is a little further from Grantham than Belvoir but, as an MP, George has constant streams of visitors and holds regular meetings, and did not wish our privacy at the castle to be invaded.'

'They have no children, as yet?'

'Unfortunately, no. After seven years of marriage, George seems resigned to the fact that he and Frances are not to be blessed with offspring of their own.'

King James evidently chose not to pursue such a personal matter, reverting instead to a more general topic. 'I believe George wasn't with you on your Grand Tour of European countries, but he did join with you and Roger in the Earl of Essex's rebellion eleven years ago. How the three of you escaped the executioner's block we'll never know.'

The grin on the king's face made Francis laugh. 'We certainly had a lot of explaining to do, Your Majesty, but it wasn't we three who persuaded Queen Elizabeth to be lenient with us. It was the Earl of Essex himself we have to thank for that. As you will know, he was found guilty of treason and beheaded.'

'So, you had the overly ambitious Robert Devereux to thank for your continuing existence.' King James chuckled at the thought. 'It must have cost Elizabeth dear to execute one of her favourites, though perhaps if she had not, many more of her subjects would have lost faith in her. There were already those who doubted her ability to rule in her old age, and if she had pardoned Essex, there would probably have been riots. There was never any doubt of his guilt, after all. But, that's all in the past.'

The king finished his port and stared vacantly ahead, seeming lost to his thoughts as his forefinger circled the rim of his glass in a regular motion. Francis waited, debating with himself whether he should say something to break the silence, when the sudden, high-pitched note created by the motion of James's finger caused chuckles around the room.

'The three of you were reckless in your younger days, Francis,' James declared, with a smile that said he was not admonishing. 'I'm glad to see that you and George appear to have settled and are a little more staid nowadays. Unfortunately, from what I saw and heard of Roger's gambling, I don't believe he ever reached that stage.'

Francis knew that anything he said to counter what the king had said about Roger would be an outright lie, so he simply nodded.

'It must be over a year since George graced our London Court, so I'll have a chat with him later. But for now, I am content to converse with my good host.'

Francis inwardly groaned, knowing too well what the conversation would return to.

'As I was saying, witchcraft has become a disease that we must stamp out, and that can only be done if God-fearing people everywhere watch their neighbours carefully. They must denounce anyone – man, woman or child – they believe to be practising the dark arts, or of attending the heinous gatherings with the Devil they call Sabbaths. They say that the naked dancing and cavorting and overall debauchery at these Sabbaths is more offensive to good citizens than anything we could imagine. Some witches have described these events during their trials, and judges have almost choked in revulsion. The mere thought of what these evil creatures can do in our

Chapter Three

country fills me with terror and we must never cease striving to wipe them out'.

'I agree we need to be constantly watching for signs of devil worship, Your Majesty, but, as yet, we have had no accusations made against anyone on the Belvoir Estate. No one has died in suspicious circumstances and, although we have a selection of cunning folk, from what I gather, they do no more than offer herbal remedies for fevers and various other aches and pains. Villagers trust those people, and since they cannot afford the fees of trained physicians, we cannot begrudge them paying a few coins for such remedies. I confess to having an interest in herbs myself and have brewed a few remedies for fevers and headaches from plants in our own gardens.'

'Devil worshippers come in all forms, Francis, so be on constant guard. Many are old hags, it is true, but others may have a pretty face or a beguiling manner that draws you in before you realise it. Make sure your villagers know this, and urge them to be aware that many witches house creatures they call their familiars. These loathsome beings can be seen in several forms, the most usual being a cat, of course. But there have been incidences of witches confessing to their own familiar being a dog, a rat, toad, insect, or even a grotesque mix of several creatures. That these abominations feed by suckling on a witch's blood through a teat put there by Satan is beyond repugnant.'

Francis nodded, having heard all this on every visit he'd made to court over the past nine years. He'd been alert to any signs of evil doings since his European tour when he was twenty, but King James was obsessed with the subject and rarely spoke of anything else.

'I imagine you've heard of the witch trials taking place in Lancashire this very month?'

'I have, Your Majesty. It is appalling to think that such a large number of witches could have been working their evil, and not have been apprehended for it, for as long as they did. Most of them are from the same family, and all from Pendle, I believe.'

'Mmm, that is true. I am told they were initially tried at York Assizes in mid-July, where one of the eleven charged was found to be not guilty. The remaining ten are currently being held in Lancaster for a further trial at the Assizes there. As far as I'm concerned, Francis, all ten must be guilty, but we'll see what the judges decide in two or three weeks.'

'We have organised our first hunt for tomorrow,' Francis said, once again aiming to divert the king's thoughts elsewhere. 'Fox hunting has becoming popular in many places over the past fifty or sixty years, particularly so in Norfolk and more recently, in the Vale. Of course, when pursued by the pack, the fox invariably heads for the woods, which is not a problem for our beagles. They are keen hunting dogs and we train them specifically to sniff out foxes.'

'This is a new sport to me, Francis, and I will need instruction in what to do.'

'All you need to do, Your Majesty, is to follow where the dogs lead and enjoy the ride. There will be more than a score of us riding tomorrow, so you won't be getting lost. I know you and Prince Henry are skilled horsemen and used to riding across open country, jumping low hedges and riding through streams, so you should have no problems at all. I assure you,

Chapter Three

you will both come back feeling exhilarated, particularly if our pack doesn't lose the scent and the fox is caught. The wretched animals cause havoc with our chicken farmers and they even take lambs in the spring. If they'd keep to rabbits, their usual food, we'd have no need to hunt them.'

King James laughed. 'I'll look forward to that and will explain to Henry what is planned. I just hope he feels well enough to join us. If not, he can stay behind and recover.'

'If another day to recover is what the prince needs, there will be a host of trusted servants around to ensure he has meals and drinks while we ride out. There will be plenty more days to venture out before you return to London, my lord. In a day or two we could go hawking, if you wish.'

'I'll leave our entertainment in your capable hands, Francis. You know I rarely refuse a day's hunting, or hawking, or even fishing. A day spent simply riding out to some of your quaint little villages would also suit me perfectly.'

*

Prince Henry rose from his four-poster bed in the large, sumptuously furnished room in Belvoir Castle, wondering how to persuade his father he still wasn't well enough to accompany him on this hunt. In truth, after a good night's sleep, the nausea created by the coach journey had gone and Henry was refreshed and in need of food. He would feel guilty lying to his father, yet he knew that the king would never accept his aversion to hunting. No prince of the realm had ever disliked the sport.

As much as he loved to ride, Henry took no pleasure in

the killing of helpless creatures, especially when their meat wasn't needed for food. Fox hunting was not something he'd tried before and it sounded quite barbarous. To Henry's way of thinking, seeing a terrified animal cornered and torn apart by a pack of hounds brimming with blood-lust should not be classed as sport.

Any moment now, his manservant, Henshaw, would arrive to assist him to dress in fine apparel that would display Henry's elevated status yet be suitably practical for a day in the saddle. He needed to be quick, so he grabbed a faded green tunic and brown breeches from his travel chest, the well-worn garments intended to convey the impression of him being too ill to dress with care. He stood in the middle of the room, repeating his excuses several times inside his head in order to make them sound real and convincing. After all, he had no intention of sounding like a lying little weasel. His face must also be fixed in a way that spoke of continuing sickness and that he was downcast at the need to miss a good day out hunting.

Henry ran his fingers through his tousled red-brown hair and picked up the finger ring from the mantelpiece above the hearth, the only piece of jewellery he wore every day without fail. The thick gold ring with the initials *HS* engraved on it was a gift from his mother on his eighteenth birthday and he held it on his palm, staring down at it, reminded of her kind face and wondering what she would be doing back in London. Queen Anne never accompanied her husband on his progresses, but Henry was not surprised at that. It was common knowledge that love between his parents had long since died.

His servant's knock on the door made Henry jump and the

Chapter Three

ring fell from his palm and bounced off the hearth's grating into the ashes beneath.

'Damnation,' he mumbled, knowing that retrieving it would involve rummaging through great piles of ash. To retain his dignity, he needed to get rid of his servant.

'I don't need your help today, thank you,' he called, knowing that although Henshaw would wonder why that was so, he would not question it. That done, Prince Henry, heir to the throne of England, Wales, Scotland and Ireland, got down on his knees, picked up the poker and tentatively rooted through the burnt-out remains of last night's fire.

'Why are you in here and what are you trying to do down there? This room is on my route for today, so it can't be on yours as well.'

At the sharp tones of the unfamiliar voice, Henry leapt to his feet, spinning round to see a fair-headed young woman – well, more of a girl really – dressed in a brown woollen dress topped by the white pinafore, and a mop cap on her head. She was obviously a servant, and he couldn't help smiling at her audacity. But then again, garbed in his oldest tunic and breeches, this girl wouldn't have a clue who he was.

'I need to clean out the ashes,' she went on, 'so you'd best go and ask which rooms you're supposed to be cleaning because it isn't this one. And I need to get on because I've got a few more rooms to deal with after this. Thankfully, this is the only one with a hearth to clean out.'

'Yes, I suppose I should go, but I need to find my ring first. I dropped it in the ashes down there. I was just about to look for it when you came in.'

'I'll look for it as I clean the ashes out then,' the girl said, making shooing motions with her hand as she came to the fireplace. In the other she carried a sack, seemingly to put the ashes into. 'Just get out of the way and let me do my job. Stand or sit as you please, but give me space to work.'

Henry backed up a few steps and the girl pulled on a pair of old gloves she retrieved from her apron pocket and knelt down to commence her work. She riddled the cinders through the grate with the poker so that more of the ash fell through to the hearth below. 'I'm surprised whoever slept in here last night needed a fire,' she remarked. 'It's August for goodness' sake. Whoever heard of a having a fire in a bedchamber at this time of year?'

'I believe the gentleman was quite ill yesterday. You know the sort of thing, feverish and sweating, yet shivering, all at the same time – brought on by the nausea caused by travelling so far.'

'Oh, I suppose that makes sense, though I've never travelled further than the three miles up to the castle from our village, and that in a horse and cart with plenty of fresh air around me. I can't imagine what it would be like to be shut inside one of those fancy coaches outside. But if this man travelled in one of them, he must be some kind of important lord.

'Yes, I think he must,' Henry said, grinning as the girl continued to shovel out the ash. A few moments later, she halted and turned to stare up at him, a scowl on her face. 'Tell me, what were *you* doing with this ring I'm looking for? I doubt if it's yours, so how come you had it in your greedy paws? You weren't thinking of stealing it, were you? The gentleman who has this

Chapter Three

chamber won't be happy if you run off with his ring. Oh, don't tell me you were about to steal from one of the king's men?'

Henry couldn't help a chuckle. 'I'm not sure which question you'd like me to answer first, but believe me, I'm no thief. The ring is mine and was a gift from my mother, so I do cherish it. Now, you answer my question: how do you know this isn't a woman's room?'

'You don't know much about this job, do you? I know because the bed covering isn't all flowery and pink or some other pretty shade. Bed coverings in the male rooms are generally a darker colour with a bold pattern instead of flowers. In double rooms the bedding tends to favour the women's style.'

'Oh, I see,' Henry replied as the girl carefully shovelled out the ash, checking each load for a ring. 'Here it is,' she said at last, picking it out and wiping it on her pinafore before standing to hand it to him. It's a handsome ring, I'll say that.'

'I don't know how to thank you… What is your name, by the way?'

'It's Margaret. Now, be off with you and let me clean up this hearth.'

'Don't you want to know what my name is?'

'No, why should I? Look, I don't want to be rude but you need to go and find out which rooms you should be cleaning.'

'We need to get you dressed in finer clothing than those for the day, my lord,' Henshaw declared, striding across the room from the doorway, eyeing Henry from head to toe. His gaze swung to Margaret, squatting with her sack of ash by the fireplace. 'How *dare* you enter to clean while my lord is still in his chamber!'

Margaret gasped and stared at Henry, and he realised she'd be wondering which 'lord' he was and why he was dressed in such shabby clothes.

'That's enough, Henshaw,' he said. 'The girl was retrieving my ring, which I carelessly dropped in the ashes; I won't have her kindness repaid by harsh words. I was about to head down to the hall to break my fast and explain that I am still not fully recovered from yesterday. I will not be joining the hunt, and these clothes were, quite frankly, the first that came to hand and I lack the energy to look further.'

'Very well, Prince Henry. Your father is hoping you are fit to ride with them, but you alone know the state of your stomach. I'm glad this girl found your ring for you. Queen Anne would be saddened to know of its loss. I'll leave you to send her on her way.'

Henshaw left and Henry grinned at Margaret as she stared, agog, at him. 'I apologise if the revelation of my name was a shock to you. But now at least you believe that the room is mine, the ring belongs to me, and I am not some thief with… now, how did you phrase it…? Oh yes with "greedy paws".'

Henry laughed out loud and Margaret smiled back. 'I'm sorry I was rude to you, my lord…I mean, Your Highness. I didn't know who you were, and in those clothes, you looked like a servant.'

'It is I who must apologise, Margaret. I should have told you who I was when you came in, and not kept it from you for so long. As it was, I was enjoying listening to you chastising me. It was quite charming, and I can say that I wish everyone was as honest as you. Theft is obviously something you would not

Chapter Three

condone.' He pulled open a dressing table drawer to retrieve a small item and held out his closed fist, indicating she should hold out her hand.

'You have no need to give me anything, Prince Henry.' Margaret suddenly curtsied, and he grinned at the confusion on her pretty face. 'I can't believe I'm standing here, talking to the heir to the throne. My mother and sister will never believe me.'

'Take it, please. A gold crown is little enough for the favour you did for me, and the entertainment you provided. I carry little coin on my travels as I have no need of it, and would happily have given you more. I realise it's not every day that village girls meet royalty, and it was good for me to have someone putting me in my place instead of grovelling before me simply because my father is the king,'

Margaret curtsied. 'When you become king, Prince Henry, I will know that our country is ruled by a very wise and kind man. I thank you for the coin. It will be put to good use once we return home.'

*

'Don't you go bragging about your meeting with the prince,' Joan warned Margaret as they returned to the servants' sleeping quarters for the night. 'The vicious tongues of those goodwives from the village will never stop wagging if you do. We've got another three weeks up here and we can do without their low opinions of us reaching the countess. They already think of me as a whore, so we can't afford to give them anything else to tattle about.'

'I'll try to keep it to myself, Ma. After all, I don't see much of any of them while I'm working, and they haven't time to stand and gossip, either. It's only when we go to the kitchens to eat that we're all together, and no one's likely to start slinging insults in front of Mistress Abbott or any of the earl's stuck-up servants. Anyway,' Margaret added, her face taking on an expression of insult. 'Nothing happened in the prince's room that I should be ashamed of. It's not as though he dragged me into his bed or anything, and those women can't make up stories about things like that while the king's party is still in the castle.'

'Well, if you do happen to pass groups of them tittle-tattling, just do what I was advised to do at Christmas. Hold your head high, smile sweetly and say "Good Morning" or "Good Afternoon", as it suits.'

'Yes, Phillipa,' Joan said with a grin. 'That's something the three of us need to remember, even if we feel like giving their smug faces a good old punch.'

Chapter Four

In which there are hard times ahead

Bottesford Village: last Week of August 1612 – mid-April 1613

To Hugh's chagrin, Joan was happy to accept Countess Cecilia's offer of a further three weeks' employment at Belvoir Castle following King James's return to London at the end of August. For Joan and Phillipa, the offer was extended as day servants only, starting on the first day of September, whereas Margaret was offered the chance to continue living and working at the castle with the possibility of the employment becoming permanent.

'We don't need to think too hard as to why Margaret's been favoured over us, do we, Ma?' Phillipa pulled her chair across the cottage floor to sit beside her mother whilst they chatted, something they'd found little time to do since their return to Bottesford yesterday. Joan had had errands to run and both she and Phillipa had clothes to wash and cooking to do. Having meals cooked for them at the castle had been a real treat.

Phillipa looked quite peeved, and Joan knew how she felt. For a younger daughter to be favoured over the elder rarely went down well, especially so in Phillipa's case. After all, it was she who had impressed Lady Elizabeth with her hard work over the previous Christmas.

'Prince Henry must have dropped a good word in the

countess's ear,' she said, stroking the purring Rutterkin curled up on her lap. 'Margaret said he was impressed by her honesty. His vouching for her will have meant much to Lady Cecilia.'

'So, you and I have to walk up there and back every day. After a hard day's work, we'll be fit for nothing.'

Joan shrugged. 'That's what most of the cleaning women who work at the castle do, Phillipa; they have no other choice. The higher-ranking servants who live in the village will have their own horse and cart, or even a small carriage. As a rule, only cleaners and washerwomen employed from villages much further away are offered live-in positions. So, yes, Margaret is privileged.'

'I imagine I'll get used to walking over six miles every day, but I'm worried about you, Ma. You're not as young as you were.'

Joan laughed. 'I should clip you round the ear for that remark, my girl. I'm not in my dotage yet. But we won't be walking, anyway. Don't forget, we already have your pa's cart, which is fine now that Peter Jenkins has mended the damaged parts for us. And I asked Hugh if we could use one of his ponies for the three weeks. He kindly agreed and he knows we'll take care of the animal. It'll be unhitched and put into one of the castle paddocks while we work, and stabled at Peter's inn overnight, just as your pa used to do with his old horse when he was home. The stable-boy, Joseph, will see he's well fed, and will hitch and unhitch him to the cart for us morning and night. Peter's agreed to a small fee of a sixpence a week – three of it for the lad. So, we're all happy with that.

'By the way,' Joan continued, lifting an indignant Rutter-

Chapter Four

kin to the floor and standing, ready to resume work, 'Peter mentioned that Lady Elizabeth died at her family home in Nottingham. Seems he heard about it from one of the castle's footmen who lives in the village. As far as anyone knows, Lady Elizabeth will be taken down to London for burial, in Saint Paul's Cathedral, I think he said. Her husband's family at Belvoir will have an effigy made of her to lie beside her husband on his tomb here in Saint Mary's.'

'I'm sorry to hear of the lady's death, Ma, and I know you were fond of her. It's only a couple of months since Sir Roger died. You always said that neither of them had looked well for some time, so perhaps they'd both had some kind of illness.'

'Possibly,' Joan said, not wishing to explain what Anne Baker had said about syphilis. 'If they did, at least they'll be at rest now, if you believe what Reverend Fleming spews out in his sermons every week. Oh, I forgot to mention, Anne's agreed to carry on feeding Rutterkin and the hens, and she'll collect the eggs for us every day, so we don't need to worry about that before we rush off every morning.

'Now, let's get outside and do a bit of tidying-up around the garden. I also want to cut a few herbs for making some new potions and ointments tomorrow. Winter will be upon us before we know it and folk will be needing more cures for chills and aches and pains. Our earnings from the castle will see us through most of the cold weather, but extra cash from selling our herbal remedies won't go amiss. And of course, once our own wages have run out, we'll have regular money from Margaret for our food. So, Phillipa, be glad that your sister is in the countess's good books.'

Take Height, Rutterkin

*

The late November day was drawing to a close as Samuel Fleming hastened back indoors, harbouring a heavy heart. A bitter iciness hung on the air, seeming to penetrate even the thickest of coats to find its way through to a person's very bones. No snow had yet fallen, but on first glance, the sheen of white swathing the rectory roof, as well as the trees and lawns of the garden, could have been taken as such.

The day had started well. Samuel had spent most of it calling at villagers' homes, hearing of their grievances and various ailments, or sharing their happy news of an upcoming marriage or the birth of another child. It was the part of being a clergyman that Samuel most cherished. He deemed it a privilege to be allowed into their lives, offering what help or advice he could, or generally just brightening their day with a chat. It was earlier this afternoon, on encountering Peter Jenkins, the seemingly tireless landlord of the Belvoir Inn and font of knowledge regarding news from around the country, that Samuel's contented day came to an abrupt end.

'Typhoid fever, no less,' Peter said, sounding half-choked himself. 'Prince Henry was such a popular and handsome young man, clever and learned, too… not a complete fop like some of those other young lords who pass through Bottesford at times. He made a big impression on the women who worked up at the castle this summer. I'm told he died in the Palace of Whitehall during preparations for his sister, Elizabeth's wedding. By now the whole country will be in mourning. His poor mother, Queen Anne, must be distraught. There's never been such a well-liked heir to the throne, and his concern for the welfare of everyday people was known to all. To have been taken away from life so soon can't be right…

'Well, Reverend, I know you would preach a sermon to me on that one, but Prince Henry will be sincerely missed.'

'So, James Stuart's heir is now his younger son, Charles,' Samuel had absently replied, his thoughts still on the cheerful face of Prince Henry. Having been invited to dine at the castle on a few occasions during the king's visit, Samuel had taken an instant liking to the prince, whose cheerful and caring manner had seemed at variance with the intense and often dour conduct of his father, whose conversation invariably revolved around the need to annihilate every witch in the country. 'As you say, Peter, we must hope Prince Charles turns out to be as pleasant and level-headed as his elder brother.'

The rectory seemed unnaturally quiet as Samuel entered, the single oil lamp, lit by Alice before she left a short while ago, casting flickering shadows around the hallway. Not for the first time he recalled the days when Esther was living here. Her cheerful voice, undoubted intelligence and sharp wit were ever a balm to his troubled thoughts. Alice had left a fine beef stew keeping warm for him beside the stove, but thoughts of Prince Henry's death had taken away any appetite he'd had earlier today. He sank into his comfortable chair by the hearth in his study, watching the logs shifting positions as they burned. Perhaps he would tackle the stew later.

*

Take Height, Rutterkin

Joan and Phillipa spent Christmas that year together in their cottage. It felt lonely without Margaret, although Joan admitted that things had been little different last year when it was Phillipa up at the castle. On a few evenings, Joan even found herself with just Rutterkin to keep her company, and could only imagine that Phillipa had found herself a man. Yet if she was meeting him in secret, it said much for his intentions regarding their relationship. Such meetings were likely based on lust rather than any sense of lasting affection or long-term plans. Still, Joan hoped they found somewhere warm and dry to meet.

Margaret continued to come home on her day off every week, bringing a large proportion of her wages, keeping an odd sixpence for any small item she might wish to buy for herself. Joan was grateful for the coin. It kept Phillipa and herself fed, though little was left for anything else they might need, such as strong winter boots, logs for the fire, or even chickenfeed. For those, she still relied on the coin that Hugh generously gave her after their own clandestine meetings, and on whatever she made from selling her potions and charms to anyone in need of them.

The cold, snow-covered days of the early new year brought more villagers to Joan's door. Remedies for a multitude of ailments were in high demand, including dried willow bark, which people could brew as a tea or simply chew to combat a number of aches and pains. Folk suffering the pain of injury from various accidents vied for places in the queue with those with rheumatics and lumbago, runny noses, coughs and sore throats, toothache, earache or rashes on the skin. Two women

Chapter Four

required Joan's service as a midwife, bringing new life into the world and one young girl needed her skills in ejecting an unborn babe from her womb. Although not a task Joan relished, to have turned the girl away would have resulted in her being banned from her family home as soon as her rounded belly became evident. With nowhere to live and no way of feeding herself, the girl would have likely ended up a corpse in a ditch somewhere.

Still other folk wanted charms or sigils to make someone they loved reciprocate the feeling, or to stop bad things happening in their lives. Reasons for requesting charms and sigils were as diverse as Joan had expected as she listened and supplied what was asked without judgement. She had learned her lessons from the other cunning women well, and had begun to love the work, which made her feel needed in the community. Not that is stopped many of the goodwives from gossiping about her and the many lovers she supposedly enjoyed. Hugh was enough for her to cope with at present. As for Phillipa, she seemed to be content enough with whoever she was meeting three times a week.

On one of her weekly days off at the beginning of March, Margaret arrived home a little later than usual. In addition to her wages, she handed Joan something wrapped in a piece of linen, looking exceedingly pleased with herself. 'It was the best I could do this time, but who knows, I might manage to get more for you in future.'

Curious, Joan took the package, unwrapping it with Phillipa beside her, eagerly waiting to see what it was. 'Dear God, I hope this didn't come from where I think it did.' Joan's appalled reaction evidently threw Margaret, and her glance shifted to Phillipa whose expression reflected their mother's.

'Margaret, tell us exactly where you got this from.' Joan's voice was stern as she put the large ham on the table, staring at it as though it might jump up and bite them.

'Well…' Margaret started, her blue gaze darting between her mother and sister. 'It was quiet around the castle this morning because Sir Francis and Lady Cecilia have taken their children to visit Sir George at Fulbeck and won't be back for almost a week. We heard it was a last-minute decision, but the head cook threw a strop because no one had told him they were going. He'd already baked enough bread and pies and roasted enough meat for their luncheon today and he left it all on the kitchen table and told us to help ourselves, so we did. I was near the front and grabbed the roasted ham before it disappeared. There was nothing left on the table by the time everyone got something, so we all left.'

'You didn't steal it, then? That's the honest truth?'

'It is, Ma. I took the ham because I was thinking how hungry you both must be with so little coin to live on, and would rarely be able to buy meat.'

Joan nodded and forced a smile. 'We appreciate that you're worried about us, Margaret, but very relieved that the food was offered to you. Stealing is something people resort to when they are really starving and have no other way of getting food.' She tilted her head toward Phillipa. 'We aren't in that position yet, as long as you keep your work and we sell plenty of our herbal remedies. We should also have some spring greens to sell at market in a few weeks so if nothing changes, we should

Chapter Four

manage quite well until we find more work, either at the castle or in the village.'

Phillipa put her arm round her sister's shoulders. 'The ham looks and smells wonderful, and I think we should all enjoy some of it tonight while you're here. Knowing it was given to you is a relief. As Ma said, we aren't starving yet, and still have money coming into the house from various sources.'

Joan shot a look at Phillipa, urging her to silence. Margaret didn't know that her mother had a lover, and what she didn't know couldn't hurt her.

'Come and sit down,' Margaret,' she said, shooing Rutterkin from her own comfortable chair and urging Margaret to sit there. 'You must be tired after your walk and you need to rest before rising at dawn tomorrow to get back in time for another day's work. Let's hope the cook's temper has cooled a little by then.'

*

Spring seemed bent on evading them that year, and by mid-April, cloudy skies and frequent rain had become the everyday norm. Although Joan longed for the sun to appear, this depressingly cool, wet weather brought her and Phillipa one advantage. Requests for herbal cures for chesty coughs and head colds continued. Although their income from sales of her potions and ointments had fallen overall, Joan was not unduly worried.

'We still have the coin Hugh gives me and Margaret's wages coming in every week,' she said to Phillipa one evening when they were sitting in the cottage discussing their money situation. After a busy day spent weaving cloth, they were ready for their beds. 'There'll also still be some folk calling at the cottage in need of herbal cures in the summer, and charms can be requested at any time of year. So I don't think we need to worry too much just yet.'

Phillipa nodded. 'Let's hope we make a little profit from our sales at the market tomorrow, too. It's a good thing the winter wasn't too wet while our spring vegetables were growing. Most were doing really well before the weather became so miserably wet. At least we have a good crop of spring cabbage, if not much else. The soil out there is nothing but mud this week.'

'You're right, and I'm hoping we won't have lost the early root vegetables.'

Having booked a space in the market place, the following morning, Joan and Phillipa set up a small trestle table to display their wares. In addition to their first crop of spring greens, they set out a dozen newly laid eggs and several pieces of woollen cloth, most big enough for children's dresses and three of them long enough for women's. By early afternoon, their table was bare.

'I'd say we've done really well, considering it's our first time as market traders,' Phillipa gushed, packing away their belongings and dismantling the trestle table. 'I was amazed how quickly it all went. Perhaps next week we could bring a few pieces of the furniture you said you didn't need a while ago. If we load all we have onto the cart, we should manage to pull it between us. If not, we can ask Peter if he could spare one of his own horses for a few –'

Chapter Four

Phillipa's words were cut short as vendors and shoppers rushed to the edge of the market place to see what the commotion was. A covered wagon was hurtling along Rectory Road, heading towards them, and folk were scattering out of its way. Jostled along amidst the others, Joan and Phillipa watched as the wagon swerved left onto Church Street. People were soon speculating as to whom the wagon belonged and where it could be going.

'Looks like one of Hugh Allingham's wagons,' a man's voice called. 'I've seen him bringing his produce to market in it. Though why he's driving at that speed is anyone's guess.'

'It's not Hugh driving it today,' another man said. 'It looked like Jack Willows…'

'There's only the church and rectory along that road, so perhaps Jack's in a rush to see the reverend and beg forgiveness for his sins,' another man jested. 'There must be half-a-dozen youngsters in Bottesford the spitting image of Jack.'

They all tittered, knowing that Jack had a job keeping his breeches on whenever a pretty woman caught his eye.

'Let's not forget, the Flower women's cottage is also up there,' a skinny young woman with bright ginger hair yelled. 'Perhaps Jack can't wait for a night-time romp with the three of them. Good value for money is that: three whores for the price of one.'

The woman spat venom, not light-hearted jest, and Phillipa grabbed Joan's arm lest she hurled herself at the malicious bitch and tore her hair out. Joan was strong and short-tempered and the feeble-looking red-head would stand little chance if it came to a one-to-one fight.

Take Height, Rutterkin

The woman's cronies crowded round and holding her head high, Phillipa pulled Joan away. But, emboldened by their retreat and her ring of bodyguards, the woman called out again, her caustic words aimed at Joan.

'Go on, you evil witch, get back to your cauldron. We know what you're up to every night in that cottage of yours, with all those potions. Casting spells on our menfolk to make them come to you, that's what you're up to. Poor Tom Simpson can't keep away, even though he promised himself to me… Why don't you tell us why you never come to church on a Sunday, *Goodwife* Flower?'

Fuming with rage and wounded pride, Joan wrestled to keep self-control, like a wakening volcano with its innards gurgling after sleeping a thousand years. She'd never been liked in this village, and had generally been unmoved by it, but to be accused of being both whore and witch in front of so many others was hard to bear.

They turned away and headed home before Joan did or said something she'd later regret.

'If that red-head had said one more thing I'd have given her a thrashing. She's got no right to make such allegations.'

'Kitty Beddows isn't worth getting yourself worked up about, Ma. She's a bit simple, if you ask me, and always says the first thing that comes into her head.'

Joan heaved a sigh of resignation. 'You're probably right, but I get so angry when people say such things. We say nothing of this to Margaret when she comes home in a couple of days. Is that clear?' Phillipa nodded. 'If she's to keep her place at the castle, she needs to be cheerful about her work, so the longer she

Chapter Four

knows nothing about these ridiculous accusations the better.'

Nothing more was said until they drew near to their cottage to see Hugh's wagon close by, with Reverend Fleming, Jack Willows and another young man whom Joan recognised as Hugh's son, Michael, in conversation beside it. Although surprised and more than a little eager to know what was going on, Joan was reluctant to become involved in their discussion.

'Whatever they're saying has nothing to do with us,' she said to Phillipa, 'so just keep walking as though you haven't seen them.'

But it seemed that Samuel Fleming had other ideas. 'Goodwife Flower,' he called, beckoning Joan over as Jack and Michael stood to one side. 'We are in need of assistance, if you could spare a moment.'

Joan sent Phillipa on to the cottage and walked over to join the three men. 'I hope there's nothing wrong, Reverend. Everyone at the market saw Jack heading up this way and wondered why he was driving so fast.'

The reverend sighed and shook his head. 'I'm afraid something has happened to Hugh.'

Joan strove to keep her voice calm, even though alarm bells were ringing in her head. 'An accident, you mean? Is he all right?'

'I'm afraid not, but thanks to the speed in which Jack and Michael got here, Hugh lived long enough for me to give him his last rites. He died very soon after.'

By now, Joan knew that the panic would show on her face, and she breathed deeply while Reverend Fleming explained, his voice filled with sorrow. 'From what both of these men tell me, Hugh was working inside the loft of the hay barn, replacing what he believed to be only two sections of rotten floor planking. It seems that several other planks beneath the hay were also completely rotten and must have given way as Hugh stepped on them.'

'He fell through…?'

Samuel nodded and Joan fought back the tears as immense sorrow overtook her. She may not have felt love for Hugh, but she had been very fond of him. A kinder and more generous man would be hard to find. 'Oh, the poor man. He must have fallen hard to do so much damage as to bring about his death.'

Michael's eyes brimmed with tears as he explained what had happened. 'We'd just moved the ploughshare in there yesterday and Pa landed on it. One of the blades cut deep into his thigh. There was so much blood.' The young man thrust his fingers through his hair, attempting to conceal his anguish behind his arm as his face crumpled. 'Me and Jack were out in the fields. None of us knew the floor in that loft was as rotten as it was.'

Samuel Fleming placed his hand on the young man's shoulder. 'There's no blame to be laid at your feet, Michael, or at yours, Jack. It was an accident, and remember, it could easily have been any one of you up there, replacing those planks.'

There were a few moments' silence as Michael composed himself, and the reverend addressed Joan. 'I wondered if you might help me to prepare Hugh's body for burial? Michael and Jack will carry him into the rectory, and we'd be grateful if you would wash him and help to lay him out, much as you did for your husband. My housekeeper, Alice, has done this

Chapter Four

for us in the past, if no relatives were able, but she is away visiting her mother in Grantham for a few days, so I am afraid I'm on my own.'

Although a little surprised that the reverend should ask her, Joan agreed. It would give her the opportunity to say her own goodbye to Hugh.

'After washing Hugh, we will wrap him in a linen shroud and tomorrow Michael will bring him a clean set of clothes, which he will be dressed in once his body has relaxed after its initial stiffening. So, would you be able to return to the rectory tomorrow afternoon as well, Joan?'

'Yes, I have no other plans.'

'Thank you, Mistress,' Michael said. 'Only last week, my father told me what a kind-hearted woman you were. I didn't even know you knew each other.'

Joan shot a panicked glance at the reverend before replying but his face was impassive. 'When you live in an area for as long as your pa and I have, Michael, there are few people you don't know. Hugh and I were childhood friends, and I always thought well of him. He was popular with everyone in the village, including my husband. He will be missed, and I know you'll take care of the farm now it's yours.'

'I will, Mistress, and Jack will still come over daily to help out. I'll need to find another labourer to help, though. There's too much work for two of us.'

'I must go home and tell Phillipa what I'm doing before I come over to the rectory, Reverend. She'll wonder where I am if I don't, and it will give Michael and Jack time to carry Hugh inside.'

Phillipa was saddened to hear of Hugh Allingham's death, knowing him only as a friendly farmer she saw occasionally at the market. But she gasped when Joan revealed that it was Hugh who had been her lover, and paid her so generously. Joan knew she'd be wondering how on earth they would they cope now, with only Margaret's small wage coming in. She tried to put all thoughts of money behind her, which wasn't hard as she grieved for Hugh himself, berating herself for not loving him more when he was alive. She and Phillipa would find some way of earning coin, even if it meant Joan walking up to the castle and begging Lady Cecilia for work. But for now, she would pay her respects to Hugh.

The wagon was leaving the lane as Joan hurried over to the rectory. The front door was open and Samuel Fleming stood there, ready to lead her through to a room off the hallway. It was small and barely furnished save for the long oak table upon which Hugh lay, a wooden chair and a stout oak dresser. The reverend had already removed Hugh's farm clothes, soiled from hours of work on the land and now ripped by the vicious blades of the ploughshare and soaked in blood. Reverend Fleming had covered the body with a thin woollen blanket. A bowl of warm water and two cloths sat atop the dresser, a small one for washing Hugh down and a larger one for drying him. A linen sheet was draped over the back of the chair.

'I'll leave you to wash Hugh down, Joan, and I imagine you'd like to say goodbye to him in private.'

Joan stared at him, not knowing how to answer that. Why the reverend should think she'd wish to speak to Hugh, she could only guess.

Chapter Four

'I only realised that you and Hugh were lovers when Jack handed me this earlier,' Samuel said, holding out his hand to reveal an ivory comb, of a type often used by women to keep their long hair in place or simply as decoration. 'He found it amongst the hay in the barn where Hugh fell to his death. This particular comb is distinctive in that it has a scarlet butterfly painted on its outer rim and I'd noticed you wearing it a time or two. Naturally, I drew my own conclusions. It had obviously fallen from your hair as you lay with Hugh.'

'I won't deny it and make myself a liar. Hugh and I *have* known each other since childhood, as I told Michael, but we have only lain together these past eighteen months. I was never unfaithful to John Flower, despite him rarely being home.'

Samuel nodded. 'I believe you, and will not pry further.' Joan almost laughed at the reverend's rare smirk when he added, 'I imagine Jack only handed the comb to me after it had fallen from his pocket when he pulled out a handkerchief and he saw me staring at it. With the number of women Jack visits around Bottesford, he could have given it to any one of them.'

'Thank you for returning it to me, Reverend. I knew I'd lost it, though I had no idea where. It was a gift from John when we were first wed, and it has proven to be useful, especially when the wind blows wild.'

Once Samuel Fleming had left the room, Joan set to with her ministrations. Tears rolled as she swabbed Hugh down, relieved to see that the reverend had already washed and bandaged the deep gash in his thigh. She whispered her farewells and her gratitude to Hugh for his generosity, knowing that some of the teardrops were induced by her own self-pity. Her lover's death meant that she and Phillipa desperately needed to find ways of earning coin. And after the confrontation at the market today, she was not inclined to try selling anything again.

After a while, the reverend returned and together they wrapped Hugh in the shroud. Samuel Fleming said little, except to convey his thanks to Joan, for which she was grateful. At that moment she would probably have broken down in floods of tears again.

'I'll come back tomorrow afternoon to help you to dress him,' she said as she walked through the rectory door into the pouring rain.

Chapter Five

In which life becomes a downhill slide

Belvoir Castle, Lincolnshire: early May 1613

Watery sunshine filtered through the clouds that had obscured the blue since the end of March. Joan trudged up the hill to the castle, hoping the rain would hold off until she got home. Few days had been rain-free for well over a month and spring sunshine seemed to be deliberately keeping out of sight. Views across the Vale dressed in its fresh spring foliage were stunning, nonetheless, although the normally profuse white May blossom on trees alongside the road was scant in places. Songs of nesting birds carried to her ear and she tried to pick out the different chirrups and trills, as she had done since she was a child. Yet neither the beauty of the Vale nor the sweet birdsong could lift Joan's spirits. Her head was filled with thoughts of how she could beg the countess for work for Phillipa and herself without sounding as though she was grovelling. To be seen by Lady Cecilia as a beggar was the last thing she wanted. But without work, beggars could be what she and Phillipa would become.

The countess was bidding farewell to guests as Joan arrived, intending to knock on the servants' entrance at the rear of the castle. But as the coach pulled away, Lady Cecilia caught sight of her.

'Goodwife Flower,' she called, walking towards her after assuring the vigilant sentries patrolling the grounds that Joan was known to her. 'Is something amiss, or are you hoping to speak to someone inside – your daughter, perhaps? No doubt she will be working, but a few moments of her time would not be a problem. Like your elder daughter, Phillipa, Margaret is a good worker, and both myself and Mistress Abbott are pleased with her. She has recently been given responsibility for the wash house as well as looking after the poultry. Both are positions reserved for people we can trust and a small increase in her pay will reflect that.'

'That is good to hear, my lady, and I will be sure to tell Margaret how proud I am of her when I see her next.' Joan shuffled, suddenly feeling stupid, standing here in her drab, grey dress beside an elegant countess in her fine blue velvet gown, her rich auburn hair adorned with jewelled combs, while the words Joan needed to use in a simple question continued to evade her. 'But it isn't Margaret I came to see. I was hoping to speak to you.'

'We have had too many cloudy days, have we not, Joan?' Lady Cecilia said, not waiting for an answer and continuing her prompting. 'The weather really is quite depressing and, like most people, I long for the sun to shine. Fortunately, the views of the Vale are still lovely from up here, sunshine or not… although I am sure you have not walked three miles uphill just to survey the views. Are you and Phillipa well and coping since poor John passed away?'

'We are not ill, thank you, my lady, but we are worried. Phillipa and I have been unable to find employment in Bottesford and we are in need of coin to pay for logs for the fire and food for our hens.'

Chapter Five

'Are you seeking employment here, with us? Is that why you have come?'

The countess's green eyes seemed to bore into Joan's and she looked away, shamed by the need to admit her poverty. 'It is, Lady Cecilia. You have been kind to our family, as was Lady Elizabeth, and I despise myself for having to ask you this favour. You have employed the three of us at times, which enabled us to pay for things we needed to live from day to day. But now, with only Margaret working, we are even struggling to buy food.'

'Come, Joan, walk with me in my garden while we speak.' The countess strolled towards the decorative iron gates into her personal garden, leaving Joan no option but to walk beside her. 'The roses and lilacs are not yet showing signs of budding thanks to this unseasonal coolness, but there are daffodils in abundance and a few hyacinths and irises still in flower in places. I am pleased to have found a gardener who keeps my garden so colourful for most of the year…'

The countess halted her steps and turned to face Joan. 'But you haven't come to hear my praises of our gardener, either. Regarding employment for yourself and Phillipa, I can persuade Mistress Abbott to find work for both of you for a few weeks, if that will help your situation.' She smiled and continued strolling along the winding path between the flower beds. 'However, we are not in need of extra staff for long-term employment at this time, and the servants' quarters are full, so your employment would be as day servants as before. Perhaps you could travel in the cart as you did when you worked here last year?'

'Thank you, my lady. I can never repay your kindness.' Joan blinked back the welling tears as gratitude and relief washed over her. 'And, as you rightly say, if I can hire a pony for the time we are here, travelling by cart would make things much easier.'

*

Michael Allingham willingly loaned the same pony to Joan and Phillipa that his father, Hugh, had loaned them the previous year. He was a gentle-natured animal, compliant to the mere touch of the rein or softly spoken words. As before, Peter Jenkins agreed to stable and feed him each night for the same rates as before, and during the day he would graze in a grassy paddock at the castle. When all was finally arranged, Joan released a further sigh of relief.

They started work in the second week of the month and although tired after the usual scrubbing and cleaning or stripping and making beds, by the time they got home, all weariness paled into insignificance at the thought that they were earning coin. They saw little of Margaret other than during the midday meal, since most of her work was focused in the outdoor wash house or hen house.

Things continued this way for the rest of May and until the Friday of the first week of June, when Mistress Abbott called them both to her room.

'Lady Cecilia has asked me to thank you both for working so well over the past four weeks,' the housekeeper started once they were seated before her desk. 'She also asked me to say how sad she is that the work cannot be extended for longer.'

Chapter Five

That single statement was enough to dash Joan's hopes. A few more weeks would have given them enough coin to last throughout the winter.

'However, there is also a little good news to pass on to you,' Mistress Abbot continued, treating them to one of her rare smiles. 'The countess believes we can employ one of you, at least until after the busy Christmas season when the house will be full of guests. Whichever of you accepts this position will be required to live in at the castle, as you did over Christmas the year before last, Phillipa.'

The housekeeper's attention swung between the two of them. 'Would you like a few moments to think about the countess's offer?'

'No, thank you, Mistress Abbott,' Joan replied. 'Phillipa will accept the position. It will give me chance to catch up with tasks in the cottage that have been neglected while we've been busy here.'

Phillipa nodded enthusiastically. 'I would be happy to continue my employment here, Mistress Abbott, and you won't be disappointed in my work.'

'Then I shall pass that good news on to Lady Cecilia. You will start work this coming Monday, so I suggest you come up here on Sunday evening in order to get yourself settled into the servants' sleeping quarters first.'

Nothing more was said about that and they received their last week's wages and turned to leave, intending to collect the pony and cart and return home. Mistress Abbott suddenly remarked, 'Oh, Joan, might I have a quick word in your ear before you leave?'

Joan nodded and sent Phillipa on to the paddock.

'I must confess to being relieved it will be Phillipa continuing to work for us,' the housekeeper started once the door was reclosed.

Joan stared at the woman, wondering if that was intended as insult or the woman had simply phrased it badly. 'I mean no offence to you,' the housekeeper continued, as though reading her thoughts, 'but it has come to my knowledge that the women of Bottesford employed here have been most unpleasant to you since you started work in May. Their spiteful comments and whisperings are groundless, I'm sure, but it does not make for a happy working atmosphere when such accusations, or speculations, are being bandied about. For your sake, I hope most of the things they say are false, but either way, you must be hurt by them. The words "whore" and "witch" come to my ears every day, and I don't want this kind of thing reaching Lady Cecilia. So, you see, although I gave you the choice regarding which of the two of you would continue at Belvoir, I trusted you would make the right decision. As yet, I have heard nothing directed at either of your daughters, and hope I never will. Both are good workers and we are pleased with them.'

'I admit that the women's comments have been getting worse these past months, Mistress Abbott. As far as I can see, their spite is because I'm a widow, and I'm not the first widow who has not remarried to become the object of such vicious talk. Some of them heard the earl asking me about the use of various herbs a few days ago, and even that set their malicious tongues wagging again. Yet I could not have refused to speak to Sir Francis.'

Chapter Five

'Of course you couldn't, but as I said, your leaving is probably the wisest thing to do. I'll make sure they all know you have not been dismissed but left after completing the four weeks' work initially agreed upon.'

'You're right, Mistress Abbott, it is best that Phillipa be the one to stay. She knows how to ignore their gossip or simply pretend not to hear. And Margaret is well placed outdoors, away from them for most of the time. I thank you for my earnings and I'll be on my way. Phillipa will be here Sunday evening, as arranged.'

*

Joan and Phillipa had each earned four weeks' wages and by the time they had paid Peter for stabling the pony and Anne Baker for feeding Rutterkin and the hens, what remained of their joint wages would have been enough to see them through the rest of the summer. But now that Phillipa's work was to be extended, they would have enough coin to see them through the following winter for food and fuel.

Not rushing out every morning at the crack of dawn seemed strange to Joan at first, but she soon settled back into the routine of tending the cottage garden and making her potions. Margaret and Phillipa came home on their days off every week with their wages, although their free days rarely coincided. Margaret had also fallen into the habit of bringing home food from the castle kitchens, which she said was freely given to her simply because the cook, Master Simon, had an eye for a pretty woman.

Take Height, Rutterkin

'Are you saying you're the only pretty servant working at the castle, Margaret?' Joan looked quizzically at her daughter, wanting to believe what she was saying but finding it hard to do so. 'Master Simon gives you these pies and cakes because he likes the look of you?'

'Well, I don't know of any other servant who is so favoured,' Margaret chirped. 'Phillipa doesn't have food given to her, does she? But if that greasy fool thinks he's getting into my bed or romping in a haystack with me because of his gifts, he can think again. I've got a couple of others in mind for that.'

'You be careful, my girl,' Joan said as alarm bells rang yet again. 'You play a man along like that, then drop him flat, he might just turn nasty. So no more hovering around this cook in the hope he'll give you special treats. We can do without those and I won't sleep at night thinking he might come after you. The same applies for those "others" you have in mind, whoever they are. Do you hear me, Margaret?'

'So it's all right for Phillipa to be out with a man, but not me? Don't you think I'd like a man's body next to mine at times, Ma? I'll be sixteen in December, and many girls I know are married by then. After slaving all day in that steamy laundry or traipsing through the filthy hen house, my evenings are mine to do as I please – what's left of them by the time we've all eaten and cleaned up in the kitchens.'

Joan knew all too well that the castle rules banned relationships between servants, but she also knew that whatever she said to Margaret would likely go in one ear and out of the other. She could only hope that her daughter had wit enough to know what was right or wrong.

Chapter Five

But as July came in, as cool and dreary as June had been, Joan learned that her trust in Margaret had been sadly misplaced.

*

After spending a hot and sweaty morning in the laundry, Margaret sauntered across the courtyard, heading for the castle kitchens where the servants' midday meal would be served. She was in no rush to be indoors again, loving the sensation of the cool, outdoor air on her skin. The constantly cloudy weather might be something others complained about, but after being in the laundry for hours it was sheer bliss. She was nearing the castle door when one of the housemaids approached her.

'Mistress Abbott wants to see you, Margaret. She's waiting in her room.'

'What... now, Sally? It's almost time for the meal so can't it wait until later?'

The girl shrugged. 'She said "this very minute" and I'm not going back in there to tell her she'll have to wait.'

Margaret nodded, knowing the fusty housekeeper's temper only too well, although so far it had always been directed at other people. She followed Sally into the castle, hoping the housekeeper only wanted to ask about egg production over the past week or some particular item of clothing she was about to send to the laundry that needed particular attention.

'Enter,' Mistress Abbott responded to Margaret's hesitant knock, the coldness of her tone telling her that this interview would not be a pleasant one. As she stepped inside, she knew immediately that her employment at the castle was in question.

It was not Mistress Abbot sitting behind the desk but Countess Cecilia, her normally smiling face uncharacteristically severe.

Lady Cecilia signalled for her to sit on a wooden chair in front of the desk, while the housekeeper stood, grim-faced, by the fireplace.

'I'll come straight to the point, Margaret,' the countess started, 'and inform you that our cook has complained of food going missing from his kitchen. And we have reason to believe that you are the one taking it.'

Margaret's heart seemed to skip a beat before pounding wildly in her chest. Guilt washed over her as she thought of the many loaves, cakes and pies she'd helped herself to over the past few months. Not that she'd admit to any of it to the countess. She knew of at least three others who pilfered things from various rooms, like bits of jewellery from the bed chambers, or a pretty, small ornament now and then from the ladies' withdrawing room. None of them had ever been caught. All she took was food, and that was because Ma was poor and needed it to live and run the house. That oily cook, Simon, was getting his own back because she refused to lie with him.

Thoughts of what her mother would say made her stomach lurch, especially if she was dismissed. Ma was counting on her wages for the foreseeable future.

'Several members of staff can testify to having seen you loitering around the kitchens late at night, each confirming Master Simon's suspicions regarding the culprit. Have you anything to say in your defence, Margaret?'

'Yes,' she said, nodding as the tears welled, all intentions of denying the charge, gone. They would know she was lying,

Chapter Five

and that would make her look even worse in their eyes. 'I have taken a few pies and cakes, and even a few loaves. But they were for my mother, not for me.'

'I see, but stealing things to give to someone else does not make you any less guilty of theft. Does your mother know the food you take to her is stolen?'

Margaret shook her head. 'Ma thinks the cook gives it to me, because that's what I told her. She'll be so angry when she knows he didn't. I know stealing is wrong, your ladyship, and I promise never to do it again if you just let me stay. Ma will be struggling even more if I lose my position here.'

Lady Cecilia waved away her excuses. 'A number of your family have worked at this castle over the years, and this is the first time we have ever had cause to chastise any of them. We cannot overlook theft, or it will lead to others thinking they, too, can do so without reprimand. In addition, we have your other misdemeanour to consider – or perhaps we should refer to it as your indiscretion.'

Margaret stared at the countess, knowing exactly what she was talking about, but trying to look puzzled by this further accusation.

'It appears that when the earl and I were visiting our hall at Haddon last week, you and a male member of staff had the sheer audacity to use the bedroom shared by the earl and myself for your own sexual gratification. The housemaid who entered to clean the room claims to have found the two of you in our bed! How embarrassing for all three of you – but an absolute disgrace on behalf of you and your lover. The maid didn't know his name, but she certainly recognised you.'

'I can't deny what's been reported, my lady. We entered on impulse because there was no one around to see us. That it was your room fills me with shame, though at the time we simply did not think.'

Having kept silent until now, Mistress Abbott evidently could not allow such a feeble excuse to pass. 'It was quite scandalous of you to even consider entering the earl and countess's room, let alone use their bed to satisfy your carnal desires. A shocking affair, all round, and I, for one, have strongly urged Lady Cecilia to terminate your service at Belvoir, as from this moment. How disappointed Prince Henry would have been to know that someone he believed to be so honest was in fact, quite the opposite.'

The countess nodded. 'Terminating your employment with us is the only thing I can do in the circumstances. I have always held your mother in high esteem, and I hope she will understand that I have no other choice in this. Your sister will keep her post, unless we are given cause to dismiss her, too. Naturally, I would not send you home without some form of remuneration. Mistress Abbott will ensure you receive ten shillings, which is what you would normally earn in three months, so you will not be destitute whilst you seek employment elsewhere. You will also take with you the wool mattress and bolster from my bed. Neither the earl nor I would use them again after they have been defiled by others. I'll send one of my drivers down with them in a cart. If you want a lift home with him, you need to wait at the stables. He will be there in thirty minutes, which will give you time to collect your belongings from the servants' quarters.'

Chapter Five

Countess Manners stood and said a few words to the housekeeper before turning again to Margaret. 'Good day, Miss Flower. These incidents mean that I could never employ you at the castle again.'

*

Bottesford Village: early July 1613

Joan was furious with Margaret. It was the first day off that Phillipa had had since her younger sister had been sent home in disgrace four days ago, and Joan was venting her anger. Phillipa understood how she felt. Barely two months ago, her once-haughty mother had swallowed her pride, admitted their desperate poverty to the countess and begged for work.

Margaret had rarely been in the cottage since being excluded from the castle, too scared of facing her mother's continuing rage. 'How many times did we both tell her we weren't desperate for food just yet? By getting herself dismissed, Margaret's put us dangerously close to being just that. I sometimes wonder if she's completely witless.'

Sensing her mother hadn't finished, Phillipa said nothing, while Joan continued to stroke the purring Rutterkin on her lap in an effort to calm herself.

'As for her sullying the earl and countess's bed, what on earth was she thinking? She's a stupid and thoughtless girl, and Lady Cecilia had every cause to dismiss her. But what I want to know is why the housemaid who found Margaret in bed with her lover didn't know the man's name. Margaret told me that this Mr Vavasour holds a responsible position in the castle and is well known to all of them. Yet he got off scot-free! Where's the justice in that?'

Joan closed her eyes and rubbed her brow, as though the worry of it all was too much to bear. 'How we'll manage without Margaret's wage, I don't know, and I doubt she'll find work elsewhere.'

'Thankfully, I still have employment, Ma,' Phillipa reminded her, 'at least until January. But if that isn't enough coin for you, you know what you and Margaret must do. You said yourself that your potions don't bring in enough money, so I'm sure you realise that we have only one way of earning coin left open to us. Unfortunately, I won't be able to join you until January.'

'Yes, Phillipa, I realise only too well where things are heading.' Joan rose from her chair to open the door to let Rutterkin out, allowing scents of herbs from their garden to pervade the room. 'The goodwives in this village already believe we run a bawdyhouse here, enticing their men to us with our potions. What difference will it make if we actually do just that? I don't have Hugh paying me every week now, and as far as I know, the man you've been meeting on your days off doesn't pay a groat for your services.'

She shot an enquiring look at her daughter. 'Tom Simpson, isn't it? I recall that name being mentioned by that redhead at the market.'

'Not much gets past you, does it?' Phillipa said. 'No, Tom hasn't paid in the past but when I see him later, I'll tell him that things will be different from now on.'

Chapter Five

Joan harrumphed. 'You think he'll pay for what he's already been getting for nothing? He's more likely to look elsewhere for a free ride in the woods.'

'Tom will do whatever I say, especially when he knows he can come to the cottage now, even though it's only once a week while I'm working at the castle. Meeting in the woods isn't much fun when it's pouring down. But I only have to look at Tom and he follows me like a little lost sheep, despite the efforts of his shrew of a mother. Goody Simpson wants to keep him tied to her apron strings, and that's a fact. But we need more than a couple of men round here if we're to make enough money to live on. And seeing as Margaret has caused all this, she can become as much of a whore as you and me, Ma. As far as I can see, it's an easy way to earn some coin.'

Joan nodded, already resigned to the idea. 'Well, you've changed your tune about whoring since last year. It's strange how desperation forces people into doing things they once thought contemptible. I'll leave it to you and Margaret to pass word of our intentions round to likely customers, Phillipa. Perhaps when you mention it to Tom, he'll get word round for us. We may only get a couple here to start with, but men brag of their exploits, and I'll wager that before too long we'll be entertaining most nights of the week.'

Margaret returned at that moment, red-eyed and looking sorry for herself. 'Phillipa wants a word with you,' Joan said curtly as she stood and headed for the door. As it's Saturday, I'm off to visit the cunning women.

'Remember to let Rutterkin back in when he mewls at the door.'

*

The following three weeks passed slowly for Phillipa and she looked forward to her days off, especially to being brought up to date regarding how many visitors Ma and Margaret had entertained recently. Word had soon got round and business was booming. Margaret took delight in telling her sister how much more fun it was tending the sexual appetites of their 'guests' than rubbing her hands raw washing clothes in the castle laundry. In truth, Phillipa found her work at the castle to be dull and repetitive. Cleaning all day was not for her and she would have much preferred to have been at home while her mother and sister were setting up the workings of a bawdy-house. Still, she supposed, it wasn't long until January, and this extra coin she was earning would come in useful for Ma.

By the last week of July, word of the debauched goings on at the Flower women's cottage had spread through the village, and servants at Belvoir Castle wasted no time in hurling spiteful and vicious comments at Phillipa whenever their paths crossed. On a few occasions Mistress Abbott appeared just as groups of these bitter women were closing in on Phillipa.

As expected, it wasn't long before she was summoned to the housekeeper's office. Nor was Phillipa surprised to see the countess sitting behind Mistress Abbott's desk.

'I imagine you know what I'm about to say, don't you?' Lady Cecilia started, and continued before Phillipa could draw breath to reply. 'These past two weeks, the atmosphere around our corridors has become most unpleasant. Mistress Abbott tells me she has needed to be on constant watch lest the women

Chapter Five

physically attack you. What your mother and sister are doing in their home has been on everyone's lips, as are allegations of witchcraft, and they are venting their anger and disgust – yes, I did say disgust – on you, although you are not even at home at present. That their grievances are brought to the castle, and their working day and that of Mistress Abbott is disrupted because of it, tell me it is time to act.'

Cecilia Manners fixed her cool blue gaze on Phillipa. 'In a nutshell, I have no other choice than to dismiss you from service here. On consideration that the fault is your family's and not yours, I am prepared to give you a week's notice.'

Phillipa inwardly sighed in relief that the countess had no knowledge of her regular meetings with Tom Simpson. 'Since today is Thursday,' Lady Cecilia continued, 'I suggest you go home now. You will be paid for the rest of this week and you will return on Monday morning to work your notice. I intend to speak to the rest of our staff regarding the way they will behave towards you next week, but I am not prepared to risk the potential violence of this situation continuing further. Your leaving is the only way I can be sure of that.

'I wish you well, Phillipa, but the best thing you could do would be to persuade your mother and sister to change their lewd ways and the three of you to become God-fearing members of the Bottesford community.'

*

'She actually said that did she?' Joan couldn't believe what Phillipa had just related. 'Countess or not, Lady "high and mighty" Cecilia has no right whatsoever to preach God-fearing ways to us. She has no idea what life is like for the poor of this world. Trying to exist from one day to the next is no easy matter, and I doubt the "lady" would survive for two minutes if circumstances such as ours were suddenly thrust upon her.'

'I'm sorry, Ma. I shouldn't have told you, but you did ask. I was angry with Lady Cecilia, too, and suppose I just needed to get it off my chest. I'd done nothing wrong.'

'You have every right to be angry, Phillipa, Joan soothed, embracing her daughter as they strolled round the herb garden that evening. 'Unlike Margaret's, your dismissal was unfair. You've always worked hard at the castle, and been praised by the countess and Mistress Abbott, and this is how you're rewarded. Lady Cecilia should not have taken her so-called "disgust" at what Margaret and me are doing out on you. And I can't deny that the loss of your wage leaves us no other choice than to keep the bawdyhouse running.'

'At least Lady Cecilia has given me a week's notice, so I have a little more coin to come before I can join you in entertaining the men. I can't see anyone in this village offering me work. The women here all really despise us now.'

'Lady Cecilia is no friend to this family!' Joan suddenly ranted. 'And she's a miserable liar for telling Margaret she holds me in high esteem. I'll get my own back on her and her family for their heartless treatment of us if it's the last thing I do. Exactly how, I haven't quite decided. But, one way or another, I'll make them pay.'

*

Chapter Five

The three women stared at Joan as though she were mad. 'What makes you so sure that we dabble in witchcraft?' Joanne Willimott glanced at Anne Baker and Ellen Greene, trying to keep her pinched, shrewish face from smiling. 'We are all cunning women here, nothing more.'

'But I know different, don't I?' Joan grinned back. 'Everyone in Bottesford believes you to be a witch, Anne Baker, and you two are tagged as "witch" by many in your own villages. So I'm asking you to show me how to make a spell that would make a person ill, perhaps eventually kill them. I've a score to settle and I know exactly how I want to take my revenge. I just need the right spell to do it.'

Ellen Greene's brow creased as she thought. 'There are several spells that could cause harm to a person. But they say the most reliable one, if you want a decline in health rather than immediate death, involves using an item of clothing that belongs to him or her, or even a strand of hair or a few nail clippings. None of us has tried this spell, since we have never craved revenge as you do, Joan. Are you sure you want to know how to cast it?'

'I... yes, I am,' Joan said, the gravity of what she was contemplating suddenly overwhelming. But thoughts of the treatment of her daughters by the Manners family were enough to strengthen her resolve.

'Then listen carefully and I'll explain what you must do.'

*

Phillipa returned to the castle to work her one week's notice the following Monday, with orders from her mother to find some small items of clothing belonging to the earl and countess's two sons, five-year-old Henry, Lord Roos, and two-year-old Lord Francis. She was to bring them home after her last day at the castle.

This was quite an easy task for Phillipa, since most of her work for the week involved cleaning the living rooms and bedchambers used by the Manners family. While they breakfasted in the great hall, housemaids set to with their cleaning, and today, breakfast would be a little longer than usual as the family had a visitor for a few days. The servants knew only that he was a Leicestershire man called Sir George Villiers, one of the earl's many friends.

Phillipa slipped into Henry's room. At first, she could see nothing small enough to take, until she opened an oak chest into which old or faded items were thrown ready for disposal. In there was an odd glove, one of a pair which had seemingly lost its other half. She stuffed it quickly into her pocket and continued to make the bed and tidy and dust the room. Next, she cleaned and tidied in little Francis's room. He was a sweet-natured child who Phillipa could have been very fond of in different circumstances. But she rummaged through old clothing in a chest in the child's room and eventually found a pair of tiny, frayed linen gloves which she tucked in her pocket with the one of Henry's.

How her mother planned to use these gloves in exacting revenge on the Manners family, Phillipa had no idea.

*

Chapter Five

During the three weeks after Phillipa had brought home the gloves, Joan's determination to take revenge on the Manners family constantly wavered. At times, targeting the earl and countess's two sons loomed before her as a measure too drastic to take; the little boys were innocents, unaware of decisions made by their parents. Then Joan would dwell on what she saw as Margaret and Phillipa's callous dismissal and her resolve to retaliate would be sparked anew. Harming two of the Manners' children for harming two of her own, would be fitting retribution.

Phillipa's bitterness at Lady Cecilia's actions still stung and she constantly harassed her mother to take action. 'I got you the gloves, so why don't you get on with the spells you said you wanted them for?' she goaded on Thursday morning as they tidied the cottage after last night's entertainments. 'It looks like you've lost your nerve to me.'

Already fraught from her own internal struggle, Joan launched herself at the girl, her right arm raised ready to knock her flying for her insolence. Only Margaret's quiet voice halted the strike. 'If you give Phillipa a black eye or a broken nose, she won't be very presentable for our customers for a week or two.'

Joan's arm hovered in mid-air as Margaret's words hit home, then she crumpled, laughing hysterically before the tears emerged. Deep inside, uncertainty and helplessness mingled with the many emotions she'd held in check since John Flower's death. Deflated pride and resentment at her loss of status ignited her interminable envy of the rich folk up at Belvoir. The Manners family wanted for nothing on this earth and had money enough to burn. Yet they would cast someone out because of the cruel tongues of others, or for stealing a few loaves of bread, merely to keep her family fed. Joan and her daughters were reduced to prostituting themselves to keep from starving. They had become common harlots, despised and spurned by the community in which they lived.

Phillipa and Margaret knelt beside her, their arms around her as she sobbed. At length, Phillipa led Joan up to her bed for a few hours' sleep before their guests arrived later on.

The following morning, once Phillipa and Margaret had returned from the market, Joan turned to her elder daughter. 'Fetch me Lord Henry's glove, Phillipa. We've got work to do.'

The small cauldron of water bubbled as it sat on the iron grid swung out over the fire. Joan took her thickest drying cloth and carried the pot over to the table where she stood it on a smooth, square piece of oak that acted as a stand. On the table, Joan had already placed a sharp, pointed knife that she used for skinning rabbits beside the small, brown kid glove.

'Now,' Joan said, her gaze moving between her two daughters. 'My friends have never tried this spell, so they could give me no advice on how to cast it. But they trust those who have had success with it. The spell requires no words; the actions alone bring about the desired outcome. But I will say a short piece of my own, so not a sound from either of you.'

Joan mopped the beads of sweat from her brow, suddenly feeling overwhelmingly hot, standing in front of the glowing fire and over a pot of steaming water. She picked up the glove, tiny in her long, graceful hand, and placed it in the hot water, prodding and pricking it several times with the knife point. As she stabbed, she chanted:

Chapter Five

In the name of the Devil
this glove I destroy
Deep in the earth
will I bury it
May it turn putrid and rot
As the family who cast us aside
will gradually wither and die.

Wide-eyed, Phillipa and Margaret watched as Joan used the knife to lift the steaming glove from the water, placing it on the drying cloth on the table to cool. Then she lifted it with her fingertips and rubbed it along Rutterkin's back, instructing the cat to do as she bid:

Take height
and to the castle goSeek out
young Henry Manners
and do some hurt unto

An indignant Rutterkin bolted through the open door. 'We'll bury the glove beneath the roots of the willow tree,' Joan declared.

'Why there?'

'Because the tree weeps, Margaret, no other reason. Beneath the weeping willow just seems the right place for it.'

'Ma, you prayed to Satan… the Devil!' Phillipa sounded horrified. 'You're no devil worshipper, even though you don't go to church. Be careful you don't bandy such words about in this village or you'll be arrested as a witch. What made you say such a thing? And what was that all about with Rutterkin?'

'The words just came into my head. I worship neither God nor the Devil as you both well know. I'm answerable only to the old gods, and taking revenge for wrongs done is acceptable to them. And everyone knows that witches are supposed to have familiars. You know, animals that can take different shapes and sizes and do their mistress's bidding. They can even fly, and carry the witches to gatherings of the coven, and their Sabbaths, where they meet to feast and dance, and have orgies with the Devil. Besides, you obviously weren't listening properly. If either of you had been alert, you would have realised what I actually said.'

Joan picked up the glove and headed for the door. 'Tell me, do either of you know of any bodies buried in the earth that don't gradually turn putrid and rot – or of any person alive today who will not eventually wither and die in old age?' She smiled for what felt like the first time in weeks. 'At least I feel as though I've done something useful now. And tomorrow, we'll cast a similar spell on Lady Katherine. I have a pretty lace handkerchief of hers from when I last worked at the castle. It was on her bedroom floor, so I helped myself to it. I'll do the spell without the chant this time and throw the handkerchief on the fire, and we'll see what happens.

'Nothing will come of either spell, you'll see.'

*

Joan's rage continued to fester as she left the rectory late the following Wednesday afternoon. What right had Reverend Fleming to send for her in order to chastise her as though she were a child! The way she and her daughters chose to earn a living was no concern of his, and he didn't even ask why they had resorted to whoring to earn enough money. He was no better than his fancy friends up at the castle. That rectory was like a palace inside, as far as Joan could see.

Realising she needed to calm down before going home, Joan decided to take a longer route from the rectory, which meant heading to the front of Saint Mary's Church. From there she could walk back into the village along Rectory Lane, on past the Market Place and Butter Cross before turning left off Grantham Road towards her cottage.

It had rained on and off all day; footpaths and roads were muddied and puddled, and Joan quickened her pace, hoping to get home before the rain started again. As she neared the Belvoir Inn and made to turn towards her cottage and the back of the church, a group of nigh on a dozen goodwives appeared, heading straight for her, laden with stones they'd collected. Joan stopped in her tracks. That they intended her harm was plain to see.

'The whore's left her bawdyhouse. Aren't we in luck today, ladies?'

'As mouthy as ever, Jess Simpson,' Joan sneered. 'No Tom tied to your apron strings today? He's probably off somewhere, having a good old romp with Phillipa.'

'That's where you're wrong, witch. My lad's at home, helping his pa with his carpentry.'

'You call me whore and witch, and I'll admit to the first. But what do you know of witchcraft to throw accusations about with such ease?'

Take Height, Rutterkin

The women jeered. 'We've always known you were up to no good, Joan Flower,' Agnes Peate glowered at the woman who had always lusted after her husband. You have the look of a witch, always scruffy with that wild hair and indecent gypsy clothing you wear when the fancy takes you.'

'There's evil in those dark eyes of hers, too,' Jane Thompson agreed. 'And she's always been hostile, spewing her venom and thinking she's better than all of us because the earl and countess thought the sun shone out of her backside.'

'That mouth of yours needs washing out with lye soap, Joan Flower!' Agnes Peate yelled, evidently enjoying belittling a woman she saw as her rival. 'Especially now that the earl and countess have dismissed your whole family from their service. And while we're at it, all good folk go to church on a Sunday, but you don't. We don't need to think too hard as to why, do we? You're a devil worshiper, and you've passed your evil ways on to your daughters. John Flower would turn in his grave if he knew.'

'So yes, we are right to label you whore and witch,' Jessie Simpson yelled, picking up the thread again. 'Let's show Joan Flower what we think of witches in Bottesford!'

Stones large and small were hurled straight at Joan, most of them finding their target. Joan clutched her brow and blood covered her fingers, while a second round of missiles hit her body and arms. Uncontrollable rage welled and she thrust out her hands, chanting a curse that seemed to just sound in her head:

In the name of the Devil, I curse you all!
May your crops perish and rot

and flesh fall from your bones
Of starvation you will die
Strumpets lewd will take your men
leaving your children
alone and unloved

A sudden flash of lightning followed by a loud thunderclap added to the women's terror. As one, they fled.

Chapter Six

In which the harvest fails and a child becomes ill

Bottesford Village: Late August - September 1613

By the third week of August, a cheerful face was hard to find amongst the goodwives of Bottesford. Not only had the weather remained cool and wet for most of the summer, it was common knowledge that those Flower women were drawing their menfolk to them every night of the week. It was also obvious that their cottage had become a regular meeting place for witches.

Several women attested to spotting ugly, gnarled witches on their broomsticks flying to and from the cottage, some of them naked beneath their black cloaks. Others recalled seeing witches flying across the sky on the backs of monstrous animals, from snarling cats and dogs to croaking toads and buzzing insects. Still other women professed to have seen truly grotesque creatures, a mix of several types. Goody Hewson particularly remembered seeing a terrifying creature with the body of a giant spider, the head of a lion and the tail of a dragon.

That these women believed what they had seen puzzled Samuel Fleming. Oh, he believed the tales of the Flower women's lewd behaviour well enough, having returned to the rectory on a few evenings to witness the comings and goings of village men, while raucous laughter or drunken singing issued from the cottage. But the tales of fearsome beasts were a different matter. Samuel already had enough on his plate without

Chapter Six

attempting to discover who was putting these goodwives up to describing such creatures. He sighed, knowing he wouldn't rest until he had answers as to exactly what was going on in this once quiet and pleasant village.

It had been a long and tiring day and Samuel wanted nothing more than a hearty meal and his bed. He'd spent all day at the castle, where the earl and countess were at their wits' end. Their firstborn son, five-year-old Henry, heir to the earldom of Rutland, was seriously ill, and by all accounts, becoming worse with each passing day. A number of known physicians had already been called but nothing they'd prescribed had improved the child's condition. Samuel's heart ached for his old friend, Francis, and he'd spent several hours with him and Cecilia, praying for little Henry's recovery. Lady Cecilia vowed she would not rest until she found a physician who knew how to deal with this illness.

After a good night's sleep, Samuel hoped he would feel refreshed enough to start asking questions about the sightings of flying witches and their creatures. Tomorrow was Wednesday, the day he'd planned to start preparing his sermon for the harvest festival next week. Yet even that had become another area of worry. Several villagers had reported poor harvests in many summer vegetables this year. Carrots, turnips and summer greens were rotting in their gardens. There would be little to be proud of in the harvest display in church. Naturally, fingers were pointing at Joan Flower. After all, Joan Flower had cursed their crops.

The following morning Samuel left the rectory as soon as he'd donned his cassock and broken his fast. Leaving Alice to her chores he threw on his hat and cloak and headed about his business. He had no definite plan for the day and decided to follow wherever his questioning took him. The August morning was cool, although the sun occasionally peeked through the clouds that had darkened the skies for much of the summer. Today, the air held that freshness that Samuel loved, and it caused him to linger a while longer than usual in the rectory grounds before heading down to watch the ducks on the River Devon.

He stood on the pretty stone bridge over what for centuries had been a ford, often used by people coming to church. It was such a delightful little river, meandering through the village with alders and drooping willows adorning its banks. But charming as it looked during the summer months, in winter and early spring, the Devon would be full, often flooding its banks, and crossing the ford became a perilous feat. Samuel's thoughts returned to that near-fateful day in late March eight years ago when he had almost been swept away and drowned while riding across that ford. He had determined there and then to have a bridge built to keep his people safe, and felt immensely proud that it had become known as Fleming's Bridge.

The glossy foliage of trees in the dense woods behind Joan's cottage was beautiful, though he knew that for many an amorous couple those woods were favoured for a different reason, despite the rain.

Samuel loved this village and it filled him with such sadness to think of the turmoil encompassing its people now. He was not naïve enough to believe that people were always perfect, but he knew he would never stop trying to save a single soul

Chapter Six

seen to be sliding into the paths of sin, or into the clutches of the Devil…

People like Joan Flower and her daughters.

He decided his first stop would be the Belvoir Inn, just around the corner on Grantham Road. The innkeeper was someone whom folk talked to, so little happened in Bottesford that Peter Jenkins didn't know about.

'Well, Reverend,' Peter said, grinning as he wiped down the long oak table on which his kegs of ale stood, 'I can't say I've seen any flying witches and grotesque beasts myself, but my wife has heard the gossip spewing from the mouths of those goodwives. She says they really believe it. It sounds like madness to me, and like you, I don't know what to make of it. But they all think Joan and her daughters have given themselves to the Devil. Where's their proof of that, I ask? The three of them have always been pleasant with me, and paid for use of the stable a time or two when they were working at the castle. My guess is that a couple of local women have made up all this nonsense and convinced the rest it's true. You know as well as I do, Reverend, stories often become more fanciful with each telling.'

Samuel sat on a bench at one of the customer tables, ready for a lengthy chat. 'Perhaps you're right,' he replied, hoping that was true. 'I'll try to speak with some of the women later, but no doubt they'll stick to their tales, and their complaints about the Flower women. I suppose we can't blame the women for feeling angry with those three for tempting their men away, but as far as I can see, the men have shown great weakness in giving in to such temptation.'

Take Height, Rutterkin

'I imagine you've heard about the cereal harvest, Reverend,' Peter said, suddenly keen to change the subject.

'I have, and that's another thing worrying me. I was over at Easthorpe Mill the other day and I've never seen Matthew so downhearted. He tells me that both the rye and the wheat harvests have been disastrous this year. Many of the grains are black and hard, and not fit for grinding into flour. You know, Peter, I've heard of this happening elsewhere.'

'Aye, most of the farmers who come in here know of it, and dread it happening to their crops. It's a well-known disease in cereals, and can affect most grasses. Seems to be caused when we have a cool, wet spring, just at the time when the crop's in flower and needs the sunshine. Some kind of fungus gets hold of the plants, and if the weather stays the same till the harvest, this fungus really takes hold. A lot of what should be good, golden grains are these black or purple fungus seeds. Unfortunately, Reverend, we've seen few dry days and little sunshine this summer.'

'That tallies with what Matthew told me. Since harvesting began a couple of weeks ago, farmers have been frantically removing the black seeds from wheat and rye grains before sending them to the mill. It seems there are still enough good wheat grains left to grind into flour but far fewer of the rye because rye is affected even more than wheat by this fungus. Farmers and millers will both suffer losses in profit this year, thanks to this wet weather. Many folk will go hungry, too, especially the poor who rely on rye bread to fill their bellies, along with the few vegetables from their gardens.'

Samuel didn't mention who the villagers held responsible

Chapter Six

for their rotting vegetables this year. Peter's chatting could spread those rumours even more.

Peter put down his cleaning cloths and came over to sit opposite Samuel. 'I've heard some strange tales about flour made from grains with these black seeds among them. If people eat bread or pies made from that flour, they seem to do weird things.'

'What kind of weird things?'

'They usually get sick and vomit a lot to start with, which is bad enough, but then they can go a bit funny in the head,' Peter added, making circles in the air by his head. 'They often start seeing things that aren't there, or they feel itchy, as though insects are crawling over their skin.'

Samuel was suddenly alert. 'They start seeing things that aren't there…?' Peter nodded. 'Then I need to find out where these goodwives have been buying their flour from in recent weeks. It isn't from Easthorpe Mill because Matthew hasn't milled any of this year's grains yet.

'Thank you, Peter,' Samuel said, heading for the door, 'you've given me a good place to start.'

Samuel Fleming's next stop was at the home of Goody Hewson, since she claimed to have seen one of these monstrous flying beasts. The friendly little woman welcomed him into her modest but beautifully clean cottage, and once they were seated and had exchanged a few words about the awful weather, he asked after the family's health.

'None of us have been too good of late, I'm afraid, Reverend,' Mary Hewson replied, getting up to place another log on the fire. 'I've kept our three young 'uns in their beds because

Take Height, Rutterkin

they're still feeling sickly. There seems to be a lot of it about in the village at the moment, and I've even been feeling ill myself. My husband's the only one of us feeling well, although even he felt a bit out of sorts on Saturday morning.'

'I'm sorry to hear that,' Samuel said sincerely, always concerned about illness in his flock. 'Is there anything you've all eaten that might account for the sickness – perhaps some meat from the market that wasn't as fresh as it should be?'

The little woman re-seated herself, her wrinkled brow telling Samuel she was thinking about his question. 'Not unless the rest of the village has eaten the same cut of beef as we have these last few days, which is unlikely. Many of them rarely buy meat at all. The cost, you see… No, Reverend, it can't be the meat, or the fish, for the same reason.'

'What about bread, or pies? Do you buy them ready baked from the market, or bake your own from purchased flour?'

Mary shook her head. 'We haven't needed to buy flour for some time. Robert usually takes the cart over to Easthorpe and buys a few sacks at a time, some wheat and some rye. It's enough to last us for several months. But now you mention it, I usually bake my own bread, but there was a stall on the market last Friday selling ready baked loaves. It was rye bread and a lot of us in the village bought some, to save us time over the weekend, you see. It tasted all right to me, though Robert said it had a strange tang about it and ate no more than a mouthful. He said it wasn't anywhere near as good as my bread. But he would say that, wouldn't he? He always said I make the best bread in the village and –'

'Do you know who ran this stall, or where it came from?'

Chapter Six

Samuel was well used to Mary's long-winded replies and felt rude for cutting her off, but he needed to push on.

'I'm afraid I don't. Two men I've never seen before were serving – could've been father and son. They smiled a lot but didn't say a great deal, so I doubt they'd have chatted to anyone, especially as folk were queuing to buy their bread. There was no sign up with their names on, either, come to think of it.'

'On another matter, Mary, I was told you had seen a fearsome-looking creature flying around recently. Is that true?'

'Oh, it is, Reverend, but the ugly beast wasn't alone.' Mary's eyes opened wide at the memory. 'There was a half-naked witch riding it and lots of other terrifying creatures with witches on their backs flying over Joan Flower's house as well. My eyes were specially drawn to one monstrosity because it had the tail of a dragon, all zig-zagged it was. I won't be leaving this house at night again for a while, I can tell you.'

'Which day would that be?'

'Two nights ago, so that must have been Monday.'

'Were there other people around who also saw these terrible creatures?'

'Yes, there were quite a few of us. We'd been watching Joan Flower's cottage, hoping to see which of the village men went there. Most of us were feeling sick in the stomach and one or two complained of headaches and that their eyesight had gone blurred. I felt that way myself and started to wonder if I was going blind. Then everything went quiet for a moment, before someone shouted, "Look, witches on broomsticks up in the sky with their monstrous familiars. Just look at the head on that dog! Looks like a toad's to me…"

Take Height, Rutterkin

Everyone started yelling about this beast or that, and we stared for a few moments. Then we ran.'

'Did you recognise anyone riding these beasts?'

Goody Hewson shook her head. 'They were too small to make out, and some were hidden by the creatures' wings.'

'Do you remember who the first person was to spot these creatures – the person who shouted out?'

'It was Jessie Simpson. Is that important?'

'I don't know yet. It's what to make of you all seeing these creatures that I'm puzzling over. Did you all just go home after that?'

'As I said, we all ran and the only people we saw were four men heading our way. Let me think who they were… Oh yes, there was Peter, the innkeeper, Jessie Simpson's lad, Tom, and that young man who helps on Michael Allingham's land. I believe his name is Jack Willows. I only know that from what my eldest daughter says about him. Sounds quite a rummun, if you ask me. Now I can't be certain of the name of the fourth man, but he looked like someone who works up at the castle. I've a feeling he could be called Jonathan something or other.'

Samuel thought for a moment. He could recall the names of two or three Bottesford men who worked at the castle, but one in particular had been sweet on Joan many years ago. 'If it's who I think it is, Mary, his full name, is Jonathan Peate.'

'Aye, of course it is… Agnes' husband. Thank you, Reverend. They must have come out from the inn to see what we were all screaming about. Not that they bothered to ask us. They carried on walking, probably to see the flying beasts for themselves.'

Chapter Six

'Yes, I imagine they would have wanted to look,' Samuel said, unsurprised to learn that Jonathan Peate frequented the Flowers' house, but very surprised that even Peter had succumbed to temptation.

*

Nothing came of the visions of flying witches and strange creatures over the Flowers' house. Over the following few weeks, tales of the sightings were rarely spoken of, recalled only when one or other of the Bottesford women felt she was losing her husband or sweetheart to the whores at the bawdyhouse.

Having since discovered that the visions were caused by a fungus called ergot, which thrives in wet and sunless years, Samuel Fleming was relieved that the gossiping had eased. But he continued to pray daily on behalf of the Flower women, asking God to help them to forego their licentious night-time activities with all their drinking and rowdy singing. More particularly, Joan Flower must cease cursing everyone who crossed words with her, invoking the name of the Devil to do it.

By the second week of September, it was apparent that the vegetables sown in the spring by the villagers had gradually rotted in the sodden earth. Samuel could see that the months of constant rain, with little sunshine to dry out the mired earth, was the cause of it. But to the superstitious goodwives of Bottesford, the cause was Joan Flower's curse.

'She put that curse on our crops. We all heard her.' Agnes Peate waited for Samuel to respond, but he was taking note of the names of the nine women protesting here. If Esther had still been living at the rectory, she would never have let them in. But Alice was not as forceful or stern-faced as his sister could be when the need arose.

'Yes, I believe we've heard that before, Agnes.' Samuel's patience was wearing thin. 'I've already explained to you all why your garden crops have rotted over the summer: the same reason why the wheat and rye have become diseased. We cannot control the weather therefore we must accept what God has ordained for us and pray He looks more favourably upon us next year. Many people will go hungry this winter, but I am certain that Joan Flower's curses are not the cause of too much rain, or ergot in our flour.'

'She caused lightning and thunder to come as soon as she'd spoken her curse, Reverend, so it looks to us like she can control some of the weather. We all saw and heard *that*, too.' The red-headed young woman cast her green gaze around her companions, nodding in response to their agreement.

'We must agree to differ on that, Kitty, and I shall need much more proof than a sudden flash of lightning and a thunderclap to believe that any of the Flower women are witches. Now,' Samuel added, rising to his feet behind his big oak desk, 'if none of you has anything further to say, I have work to attend to.' He picked up a small hand-bell and shook it, and within moments, Alice was there.

'Show these good people out, would you, Alice?' Suddenly relenting displaying his impatience, Samuel said, 'If and when you find further proof, ladies, I will be happy to hear of it. Until then, I bid you all good day.'

Chapter Six

Alice rushed back into the room once the women had gone. 'You haven't forgotten your sister and her husband will be arriving in two days, have you, Reverend? You told me they said Saturday.'

'Saturday it is, Alice, sometime in the afternoon, I believe. Which is why I need to finish writing my sermon today. If I hear another thing about those Flower women from anyone else in this village before Esther and Thomas leave here next Tuesday, I will not be overly pleased.'

'Then I'll spread your wishes around once I leave the rectory today,' Alice responded cheerfully. 'Now, I'll fetch you a nice mug of cocoa. That never fails to cheer you up.'

Samuel smiled at Alice's retreating back, thinking how much his being cheered up was to do with her cheerfulness. But as he started writing his sermon, so many of the year's events darkened his thoughts and worry set in again. If it wasn't Joan Flower and her daughters he was concerned about, it was the bad harvests and thoughts of a winter of little food. But at this moment, it was events at the castle that dominated his mind.

Tomorrow would be Samuel's last chance to visit the castle before Esther and Thomas arrived. He knew it would not be a pleasant visit. The earl and countess would need his advice, and his prayers. The health of their five-year-old son, Henry, had declined rapidly over the past two weeks and Sir Francis had sent for Samuel in the belief that the child would soon be with God. He and his wife needed the comforting presence and prayers of their chaplain.

Samuel would pray for the child tonight, and hope that his many prayers would not be in vain.

*

On approaching the castle the following morning, Samuel was surprised to see a splendid coach and four black horses waiting outside the imposing arched doorway. His own small coach drew up behind and Samuel alighted, just as the heavy wooden doors swung back and the earl emerged. Accompanying him was a young man whom Samuel recognised as one of Sir Francis's many associates.

'Good to see you, Samuel,' the earl said. 'My wife will be relieved to know you're here. You are acquainted with George, I believe.'

'Indeed, I am, Sir Francis,' Samuel said, offering his hand to the earl's friend. 'It's a pleasure to see you, again, Sir George. I believe we met during the Christmas festivities last year.' George Villiers nodded, smiling. 'Sir Francis tells me your travels in Europe have kept you away from home a great deal this year.'

'That is true, Reverend. I was in France for the first six months, until the end of June, though I can't say I find that country unpleasant. I spoke a little French before I went, but can happily say that my knowledge of the language is infinitely better now. And thanks to the many tutors my mother insisted I had after my father died, I am passably good at dancing and fencing.'

Sir Francis laughed. 'You are too modest by far, George. You are the best dancer I have ever seen. Your grace and fluidity of movement make the rest of us seem like carthorses on the dance floor.'

Chapter Six

'And you, dear Francis, are very kind, though you know full well that flattery makes me blush. But, to continue what I started to explain to Reverend Fleming, I have found that a life of travelling suits me. However, I have decided it's time to stay home at Brooksby for a while. As you probably know, our hall is barely twelve miles from here and it's good to be able to visit close friends again.'

Samuel smiled. 'Then perhaps we will meet again before too long.'

'Cecilia's in the nursery with Henry, if you'd care to go in, Samuel. I'll be there as soon as I've said my farewells to George.'

Samuel left the two men at the doorway and hastened to the nursery, where he found a distraught Lady Cecilia kneeling at her young son's bedside, silently praying. The child's nursemaid tactfully picked up a pile of soiled bedsheets and disappeared, presumably to the laundry.

Samuel came to stand beside Cecilia who acknowledged his arrival with a wan smile.

'Thank you for coming, Reverend,' she said, rising to her feet. 'I can think of nothing else to do other than constantly pray. Henry is so weak today. He vomited and soiled his bed sheets so many times during the night, he is completely drained. Never have I seen his face so white or his lips so parched.' She reached down to stroke the sleeping child's cheek. 'Every day he seems worse than he was the day before, and I fear he won't be with us for much longer.'

Cecilia's tears welled anew and Samuel put a comforting arm around her shoulders until she composed herself.

'We have tried remedies from our most eminent physicians,

Samuel, but nothing brings improvement to Henry's condition. I thank God that the convulsions are rare. It is so hard to watch our child turning blue in the face while he loses control of his body. The writhing and jerking seem to go on for so long and sometimes we think he will not survive the attack.'

'But he has survived them so far, Cecilia,' Francis said as he entered the room. 'We must focus on the positive as well as continuing our prayers and doing our utmost to help him recover. George will be adding his prayers to ours when he is in London. It distressed him to see Henry looking so ill when he came in to see him yesterday evening. It seems Henry was refusing to take his soup until George took the spoon from his nurse. She tells me that George managed to get four whole spoonfuls into him – the most Henry's eaten at one time for weeks.'

'It's unfortunate that he vomited so much during the night that the soup would have done him little good.' Cecilia's eyes brimmed with tears yet again. 'My prayers all seem to be in vain, and I have just been informed that Katherine isn't feeling at all well this morning. She has also vomited during the night and her nurse insisted she stayed in bed.'

'Then we must hope that whatever ails Katherine is not the same affliction that has brought our son so low. I will sit with her later, but at this moment our prayers must be with Henry.' Francis turned to Samuel. 'Might we prevail upon you to pray with us once again? You have been my dearest friend since you came to Belvoir when I was a boy, and have been with me through so many ups and downs in life. Henry is not only our heir but a delightful child and our hearts will be broken if he should… he should…'

Chapter Six

Samuel laid his hand on his friend's arm. 'I know, Francis, and my heart weeps to see little Henry in such distress. I will gladly pray with you.'

'I would be grateful if you could say The Lord's Prayer. It always sounds so much more meaningful when you say it.'

'Then we shall kneel beside the child's bed and say it together.'

*

On Saturday evening, Samuel rested in the spacious sitting room in the rectory with his sister and brother-in-law after enjoying a delicious stew cooked for them by Alice. Having arrived in the late afternoon and eaten little since early morning, Esther and Thomas were quite ravenous and very much appreciated Alice's efforts on their behalf. Although most vegetables were already hard to come by, Alice had managed to buy a few carrots, onions and a turnip, as well as enough mutton to create a delicious meal.

'Dearest Samuel, you really must take more rest,' Esther declared. 'You look so tired I fear to stop speaking for a moment in case you fall asleep where you sit. I can't say you look undernourished – quite the opposite in fact – and I know that Alice feeds you like a king.' Esther glanced at her husband, nodding in agreement with her. 'So, brother, pray tell us what is upsetting you so deeply that you are losing hours of precious sleep over it.'

Samuel smiled at his beloved sister, in her sixtieth year and six years younger than he was, Esther was a woman who thrived on keeping busy. She was particularly good at organising things, and people, which was just as well, since Thomas Davenport was happy to share his life with someone who could bring order into his otherwise chaotic existence. Yet Thomas was a gentle and genial man, and he and Esther had shared twenty-seven years of happy marriage, despite it being a childless one.

'You know me too well, Esther, and as always, you are right. I have a great deal on my mind at present, little of which is pleasant. Much as I would love to share my worries with someone, it would be selfish of me to burden you with them. We so rarely see each other these days and your visits are so short. No, I do not lay the blame for that at the feet of either of you,' he added, raising his hand to halt Esther's intended remark. 'Both Thomas and I are men of the Church, and have little time for much else in our lives. Visiting friends and relatives is a rare treat for all of us and I don't wish to spoil your visit here. We have little more than two full days together as it is.'

'I can understand your reasoning, Samuel,' Thomas said,' but I implore you to tell us or Esther will keep me awake all night grumbling about you being selfish and unreasonable.'

Samuel roared at Thomas's words, seeing the funny side of them as well as the probability that he was right. Esther had always been like a dog with a bone when she knew someone was hiding things from her.

'Well,' he started, 'I will tell you of the three main things that plague my mind, Esther, if you promise not to keep speaking of them after tonight.' He grinned at her feigned expression of affront. 'Do we have an agreement on that?'

Chapter Six

'I suppose we do, Samuel, although we can't help you with anything if we cannot speak of them.'

'I doubt if anyone in this land could help change some of the things occurring in our beautiful Vale at this moment. Which problem to speak of first, I don't know. Two of them directly involve people in Bottesford and Belvoir whom I know well. The other thing is something you will know about yourselves and is of concern to all of us. If I mention this year's harvest you will understand.'

Thomas nodded. 'The ergot in our grain crops. None of us in this region, or perhaps even the entire country, has escaped that – or the rotting vegetable crops. It will be a hard winter for many, particularly the poorest amongst us who rely mostly on rye bread,'

They spoke a little longer about the diseased harvest before Samuel explained about the Flower women, including their dismissal from service at the castle and the accusations of fellow villagers. The topic of witchcraft was one that raised its ugly head all too often. Esther was forced to admit to not knowing how to deal with the situation and stressed her concern at the king's insistence that all his subjects should be ready to condemn and report anyone they suspected of being a witch.

'It can only lead to mayhem, injustice and tragedy,' she declared. 'Many innocent people will find themselves arrested on the grounds that they are simply old and haggard and look like witches. Widows and any women who have chosen to live alone will be particularly targeted, especially if they happen to keep a cat or sell herbal cures for various ailments. Cunning men and women from all walks of life who sell such cures and charms will be under constant suspicion of dealing with the Devil, especially if one of their cures fails to work and a patient taking it still dies.

'If such things are happening in Bottesford, I can understand your deep concern.'

'Indeed, Esther, I fear that very soon, things may come to mayhem in this village and I dread that day.'

'You mentioned a third thing, Samuel…?'

'It is the one causing me the most worry at this moment, Thomas. The Earl of Rutland's son is desperately ill and worsening by the day. I feel so inadequate to help. My own constant prayers and those with the family seem to have been in vain, and my heart goes out to the earl and countess.'

Esther came to kneel by Samuel's chair and take his hand. 'Naturally we had heard that the child was unwell, brother, as most people in the Vale will have done. But we had no notion of how ill he really is. And you must never label yourself as inadequate. By praying with the family as well as for them, you are doing the most needful thing of all. If you say even skilled physicians have failed to cure the boy, then prayer is the only thing left. God will take the child if that is what was ordained for him in this life.'

*

Belvoir Castle: Late September 1613

In the early hours of the twenty-second day of September, five-year-old Henry Manners, Lord Roos, heir to the earldom of

Chapter Six

Rutland, died in his bed at Belvoir Castle. He had been very ill for the past few weeks and not one physician had been able to save him – or to identify the particular illness that caused both convulsions and great sickness. A pall of immense sadness hung over the castle and notifications of the boy's death were sent out to the many villages of the Vale.

Samuel spent the day with the family, offering condolences and prayers in the castle's small chapel. As grief-stricken as he was, he could only imagine how Francis and Cecilia were feeling. Although Henry's death had been expected at any time over the previous week, the actual event hit them like a thunderbolt.

Lady Cecilia was too distraught to speak and spent most of her day at prayer. Francis sought solace in Henry's room for a time, sitting beside the bed upon which the child had been laid out ready for burial in Saint Mary the Virgin's Church in Bottesford. It was here that Samuel found him in the late afternoon and they sat together for some time. To start with, Francis said nothing about Henry, his life or the illness that had deprived him of it. Instead, he steered the conversation to his and Samuel's old university days in Cambridge and the pranks that the students were wont to get up to. Though their periods of study were years apart, students' sense of fun hadn't changed, even amongst those destined to become men of the cloth, like Samuel.

'It's hard to think that we were once so young and mischievous, isn't it, Samuel? Me and a few others could have been tossed out of university for any one of the tricks we got up to. Perhaps putting that grass snake in the principal's bed was going a bit too far – but then, there was that huge spider we dropped into Master Hubbard's ale when he wasn't looking. He almost swallowed the thing.'

They laughed at their memories, though their laughter was hollow. Suddenly Francis said, 'Katherine wasn't seriously ill when you were last here, you know. It appears she'd been feeling unwell the previous day and had vomited a couple of times in the night. But she pretended she still felt sick in the morning in the hope that I would sit with her. I did so for an hour or two after you left and she eventually confessed to her crime. But how could I scold her when she has seen so little of me since Henry became sick?'

'She did not ask for Cecilia?'

'In truth, Samuel, Katherine has found it hard to accept Cecilia into her life. The death of her real mother was a massive blow to her, even though Frances died when Katherine was quite young. Yet Cecilia has tried so hard to win her affections and I had thought things were improving between them. But it seems that Katherine resents all the hours Cecilia spends with our sons and feels somewhat pushed out.

'It will be only one son from now on, of course,' Francis added, his voice breaking as his sorrow welled. 'Cecilia and I must hope for more children while we're both still young enough. We now only have one heir and as we have seen with Henry, anyone's life can be cut short at any time.'

'I foresee a number of deaths from starvation amongst the poor this winter,' Samuel admitted. 'Food will be hard to come by after the disastrous harvests in both grains and vegetables. I'm just hoping the sickness that took dear Henry isn't some-

Chapter Six

thing that has been seen in the villages. If it has, it will probably spread like the plague and our communities will be decimated.'

Samuel rose and patted his friend's arm. 'I must go home before it gets dark. I will continue to pray for you all and will come back to see you the day after tomorrow to finalise arrangements for the funeral.'

*

Bottesford: September 26, 1613

'It's a good thing our cottage is at the back of the church, Ma,' Margaret declared, coming through the door at midday to find her mother sitting in her chair by the fire with Rutterkin on her lap. It had become a familiar sight for the past month. Joan seemed resigned to just sit there and issue orders to her daughters to get on with this or that. 'There would have been even more people in their dreary dark mourning clothes swarming past our house than there already are if we were at the front. There are four coaches waiting along our lane, so goodness knows how many there will be on Rectory Road.'

'It's only one day, Margaret, so hold your patience. Lord Henry was an important young man and there will be lords and ladies from miles around come to pay their respects. But I, for one, say good riddance to another member of the haughty nobility.'

Margaret dragged a stool across the room and sat beside her mother. 'Do you really think the boy died because of that spell you did with the glove? Couldn't he have died from some illness he picked up from one of the dozens of visitors they get at the castle? You said yourself at the time that nothing would come of it.'

'You really don't want to be held responsible, do you, girl.'

'I can't help it Ma. I thought the spell you did was just pretend, to make us feel as though we were getting our own back on those miserly Manners. But if it really worked, then we are murderers. We could all be hanged.'

'Too late to turn back now. The spell was cast and today's funeral may or may not be the result. At least I know now that the spell *might* have worked. You can pretend you had nothing to do with it, Margaret, but the three of us know you did. After all, it was you getting yourself dismissed that made me do the spell. Phillipa was only dismissed because of you.'

'That's not all true!' Margaret shrieked, jumping to her feet and prompting a hiss from Rutterkin. 'Phillipa was dismissed because all the gossip about *you* being a witch was causing her trouble at the castle. The other women didn't want her there, so the countess told her to leave.'

Joan nodded. 'Yes, there was that, too, so I suppose you're not entirely to blame. Those goodwives want to see me hanged as a witch and I know I'm playing into their hands with all my cursing, which only spurts through my lips when I'm angry. If I were a churchgoer, it would be different, but as I'm what they call an atheist, that fits their idea of a witch.

'And I don't intend to disappoint them. Once Phillipa gets home, I'm going to cast the same spell again; the earl and countess have two sons, after all. You can be with me on this or not, it makes little difference. My loathing for the Manners

Chapter Six

family is something I cannot simply brush aside. If this spell works it will leave the saintly earl and countess without a single son and heir. If it doesn't work, we can safely say that we played no part in the demise of Henry Manners.'

*

It was late afternoon by the time Phillipa got home and Joan didn't need to think too hard as to where her elder daughter had been, or who she'd been with.

'I hope Tom Simpson's paying you for all these afternoons he's with you,' she said as Phillipa hung her coat on a hook behind the half-open door. The late September day was warm and the aromas from the cooking pot needed to escape.

'Course he is, Ma. I wouldn't be allowing him near me if he didn't. I'm only meeting him in daylight this week because he can't get here at night while his sister is visiting with her family. Tom has to look after the children while the rest head off to the Belvoir Inn.'

'I hope you've been careful to go somewhere you can't be seen. You know what the gossips are like in this village.'

'I thought we had, but today a couple of goodwives were collecting kindling in the woods and almost fell over us. I won't repeat what they said, and by now what they saw will be all round Bottesford. I've told Tom our afternoon meetings are over and if he wants me, he comes to the cottage like the rest of our customers. He sulked, but he knew why I'd said that, so he didn't argue. Anyway, I'll put what he's given me for these four days in the box.'

Joan let the subject drop. Phillipa knew what she was doing, and a few extra payments from Tom Simpson would come in useful.

'I'm casting the same spell again tonight and as I told Margaret, you can be with me or not. It's up to you.'

'I'm with you, Ma. What about you, Margaret?' she called out to her sister who was busy stirring the pot for tonight's meal.

'I'll be there. The two of you would only moan at me if I didn't watch.'

After they'd eaten their chicken broth, Joan set out the items needed for the spell on the table. This time it was one of the tiny linen gloves belonging to Francis Manners, who was still little more than a babe. Not that Joan let that thought worry her. The entire Manners family were her enemies now, no matter what their ages. Once again, Joan pricked the glove with a sharp knife tip while a pot of water came to the boil over the fire. Then she carried the pot to the table and dropped in the little glove, prodding and pricking it a number of times before lifting it from the water with the knife and laying it on a drying cloth.

'As I told you both the first time I performed this spell, it needs no words; the actions alone are enough. So, this time I'll do as I did with the second spell I cast – the one on Lady Katherine – and say nothing.'

'But the spell on the earl's daughter didn't work, Ma, so why do this one the same way?'

Joan frowned as she thought about Margaret's question. 'I believe the spell failed on that occasion because Rutterkin

Chapter Six

refused to carry it to the castle. Why that was, I don't know. I had hoped the spell was strong enough to fly up the chimney and to the castle on its own. Since it did not, I'm hoping our little cat will play his part this time. If he does, and young Francis becomes sick, we'll know that Rutterkin's role in that spell is necessary for it to succeed.'

Joan glanced at the sleeping cat purring loudly on her chair by the hearth. 'We are fortunate in having a cat to assist with these spells, although if Rutterkin does know how to fly, it would be good of him to allow us to watch him doing so one day.'

Joan grinned at her daughters and lifted the tiny glove, turning to rub it along Rutterkin's back before tossing it into the fire. Once again, Joan requested the cat's assistance:

> *Take height*
> *and to the castle go*
> *Seek out*
> *young Francis Manners*
> *and do some hurt unto*

As with the spell on Henry, Lord Roos, the cat shot through the door and Joan sat down in the vacated chair. 'Now we keep our ears open for gossip from the castle. As far as I'm concerned, nothing of our doing tonight could cause harm to any child. But performing the spell helps me to vent my anger and hatred of the Manners family for turning their backs on us.

'And tomorrow, I'll perform my fourth and final spell. If it works, my revenge will be complete.'

The late September day dawned grey and dismal, the sky obscured by menacing black clouds that threatened imminent release of their load. The bleakness of the day matched Joan Flower's mood as she prepared the room in her cottage for another spell. She had slept little during the night as thoughts of today's activities churned in her head. If the spell she'd cast yesterday and the one she was about to cast both worked, the occupation of Belvoir Castle by the Manners' family could end once Sir Francis reached his deathbed. Joan knew no better way of wreaking vengeance on the family who had turned their backs on her.

And yet, memories of happier times when that same family had shown Joan great kindness constantly caused her cravings for vengeance to waver. Lady Elizabeth, wife of Sir Roger Manners, would not have tossed Joan and her daughters aside. But Lady Cecilia was not Lady Elizabeth. In her bitter state of poverty and hopelessness, Joan could only see Countess Cecilia as a haughty woman who flaunted her wealth in the magnificent clothes and jewellery she wore and who lacked the gentle kindness and compassion of Countess Elizabeth.

'Fetch me that pair of Lady Cecilia's gloves your Mr Vavasour gave you, Margaret,' Joan ordered as she prepared the table for this final spell. 'And a clipping of wool from inside the mattress the countess gave you. I'll get the other things ready while you do that.'

Joan checked that Rutterkin was still curled up by the

hearth then placed on the table a wide strip of linen cloth, a bowl of warm water, a drying cloth and the same small, sharp knife she had used in the other three spells. She glanced at Phillipa as she came to stand by the table, studying the items in silence, eyebrows squeezed together in puzzlement. Margaret returned with the gloves and mattress wool and she, too, considered each of the items in turn but questioned nothing.

'You're both about to find out what this spell is for,' Joan said, rolling up the sleeve of her dress to the elbow and picking up the knife. She held her bared left arm over the bowl of water and drew the blade across her skin to make a small gash. Several drops of scarlet blood fell into the water before she bound the wound with the strip of cloth.

Joan's dark gaze moved between Phillipa and Margaret as she picked up the gloves and scrap of fleecy wool and placed them in the water, swirling them round in the bowl with her knife. 'Both of you, get over to Rutterkin and stay next to him. I don't want him running off before I'm finished.'

Joan lifted the gloves and wool from the bowl and dabbed off the excess water with the drying cloth before carrying them across to the still sleeping Rutterkin. 'Roll him over so I can reach his belly,' she said, kneeling beside her daughters as they eased the cat onto his back. Joan rubbed the gloves and wool over Rutterkin's white belly, then tossed them into the fire as she chanted:

> *Barren womb until the tomb*
> *Infertile seed won't do the deed*
> *Manners of yore will be no more*

Rutterkin did not run off as he had done on two previous occasions, though his yellow eyes ranged warily between the three of them before he rolled onto his side to continue his nap. 'He evidently knows that this spell needs no assistance from him,' Joan said, stroking the furry head. 'It's a long-acting spell, and we should see the results of it in future years – if it works, that is. If it doesn't, Lady Cecilia is still young enough to bear more children.'

'Ma, we don't yet know if the boy, Francis, will die. He could grow up to become the next earl.'

'He could, Phillipa, so we'll just have to wait and see what happens. After all, the spell was only cast yesterday. Besides, we don't even know if these spells work at all, do we?'

Chapter Seven

In which the countess seeks answers

Belvoir Castle: August 1615

Sir Francis enjoyed a leisurely ride back to the castle alongside King James amidst two dozen of his armed retainers. The August day was warm, with only the hint of a breeze, and the rich green landscape stretched out before them, a balm to mind and body. It was the first full day of the king's two-week stay at Belvoir Castle as part of his summer progress and they had chosen to ride out to some of the Vale's villages. As always, James spent much of the time airing his thoughts on topics close to his heart, seeming to have forgotten that he'd brought many of them up during last night's meal.

'Life can deal the harshest of blows, yet those of us in positions of authority are expected to dry our tears and continue as though nothing has happened,' James declared, twisting in his saddle to face Francis. 'To lose your elder son at so young an age was indeed a tragedy, but to know that your younger son is afflicted with the same malady must be causing you great concern. He's been ill for two years, you say?'

Francis nodded, caressing his black's long neck in an effort to keep his emotions in check. 'Little Francis suffered the first signs of this illness within days of Henry's death and it has continued to plague him since. At times the sickness seems to abate and we believe him to be recovering, only to see him writhing in pain the following day. It is such a strange affliction, my lord, and not a single physician has suitable medication to cure it.'

'Two years does seem a long time for an illness to fester. Has the child been bedridden all that time?'

'Not all of it, Your Majesty, though at times he has seemed too weak to stand and Cecilia has insisted he be taken back to his bed. It has greatly hindered his ability to enjoy the life of a normal young boy. I admit it is causing us great concern, especially as he is now our sole heir.'

'I will add my prayers to yours and Cecilia's. It is a most worrying time for you.'

'Thank you, Your Majesty. I admit it has been a difficult two years, though I am sure that anyone in the land would feel the same at the loss of a child, particularly a firstborn son and heir, as was Prince Henry. Such was the manner and personality of the prince that the entire country mourned his loss.'

James turned away, momentarily silent, and Francis knew his wound was still raw. He had doted on his firstborn. 'Henry's death was almost my undoing,' James admitted at length, 'and I don't know how I would have coped without the support of my many friends. I always look forward to seeing your smiling face at court, and of course, George Villiers rarely leaves my side nowadays. He'd be with us now except that his mother is ill and we thought it prudent for him to spend some time with her in Brooksby.'

Francis nodded, already having been informed that Lady Mary was unwell.

'I've thanked God on many an occasion for enabling me to

Chapter Seven

meet George a year ago at the Apethorpe hunt,' James continued. 'Once I'm back in Westminster, I intend to knight him as Master of the Bedchamber, and have a few more promotions in mind for the coming years.'

'George is, indeed, a personable young man. My daughter, Katherine is immensely fond of him. We've known him for years, of course, since his family home is but twelve miles from Belvoir.'

'Yes, George has mentioned his attachment to your family and your wonderful home. We both agree it is a most beautiful place to visit and your hospitality does you and Cecilia great credit. As for George, he certainly turns heads wherever he goes,' James added with a fond smile. 'He also fares well in conversation with any of my courtiers – although, I sense a degree of envy of his perfect good looks amongst them. Nevertheless, George has helped me cope with so much.

'But as I was saying, Prince Henry had been reared to know he would rule this land one day, whereas Charles has had that prospect thrust upon him. He is far less cheerful and easy going than Henry was, and can be stubborn and conceited. As much as I love Charles, he is a lesser man than Henry, in height as well as magnanimity, and will not readily gain the love of the people. But we are working on his training and, hopefully, he has a few more years ahead of him before he becomes king.'

'With your guidance, Your Majesty, I am sure Prince Charles will be well prepared for the throne when the time comes.'

The party rode on, climbing up the hill towards the castle. Francis dwelt on his thoughts, hoping that his four-year-old son was having another good day. It would be the third in a row if that happened and it would give him and Cecilia a small glimmer of hope.

They were nearing the outer castle gates when the king remarked, 'Have you considered that these strange maladies might be attributed to maleficium, Francis? The evils of witchcraft surround us and can infiltrate the most sturdy and well-guarded of homes. Witches come in all forms, and can deceive even the most perceptive amongst us. I urge you to be on your guard. You could, perhaps, start by making a few enquiries as to whether there are any known witches in your lovely Vale, especially any who might hold a grudge against you.'

'I have already considered that possibility, Your Majesty, but I can't believe that any of our staff, or villagers across the Vale, would wish our family such harm. We have always endeavoured to be fair and just landlords and employers. Besides, my wife and I, as well as my daughter, Katherine, have suffered bouts of the same sickness. Yet they've lasted but a day or two before we were well again. Only our two small sons have suffered the affliction to such a degree that it cannot be cured. In Francis's case, we're at a loss as to where we could obtain further aid.'

'Yes, yes, you mentioned all that last night,' James said, wafting his hand as though swatting a fly, 'but you are skirting around my point. There could be a witch out there – or even a coven of the foul creatures – who believes you have done her wrong, and knows that the deaths of your two sons will cause you enormous grief. That would be far more satisfying vengeance to this witch than killing your entire family. Your *suffering* is what she wants to see.

Chapter Seven

'I'll leave you to discuss that possibility with the countess, Francis. Perhaps she will know of someone who might have reason to bear a grudge against you.'

'Thank you, Your Majesty, I will do that. Although the last time the possibility was suggested, Cecilia would have none of it. She cannot accept that one of our acquaintances or someone we employ could hate us so much. We know of no one who is practising witchcraft in our villages and, as yet, we are both still hopeful that Francis will eventually recover. He has survived these past two years, and God willing, he will soon be hale and hearty again. We can only assume that poor Henry was of a less robust constitution than Francis to have succumbed to this affliction so quickly.'

James dismounted and handed the reins of his white gelding to the waiting groom. 'Just remember that witches are skilled in the art of deception, Francis. Trust no one, even acquaintances and servants you have known for some time. Be constantly on your guard for anything unusual that could be attributed to maleficium, then seek out and destroy the perpetrator. I will not rest until witchcraft is erased from our lands. Does not the Book of Exodus say, "Thou shalt not suffer a witch to live"?'

*

Belvoir Castle: Early December 1615

Cecilia Manners stared at her reflection in the dressing table mirror in her bedchamber and dabbed the tracks of her tears from her pale cheeks. Her lovely skin and glossy auburn hair were losing their glow and she admitted to herself how much she had aged in a mere few years. The continuous worry over their young son, and repeated disappointments at her inability to conceive another child, were not things conducive to a happy household.

Her monthly flow had come again, dashing their hopes for another four weeks. After two years of trying, it was becoming apparent that the earl and countess were unlikely to be blessed with another child. Francis was becoming desperate, especially as their four-year-old son suffered continuous ill health. If young Francis should die, there would be no son and heir to inherit the Rutland and other estates owned by the Manners family. When asked if the boy would ever recover, acclaimed physicians shrugged and offered yet another remedy to try. But nothing worked and the fits and vomiting continued. At times, the boy cried out, as though trapped in the depths of a terrifying nightmare.

Not for the first time, Cecilia wondered whether King James was right. Could maleficium be at the root of her family's woes? Perhaps she would look into the possibility in the new year, though she sincerely hoped the king was wrong.

Cecilia felt truly drained, so much so that thoughts of entertaining at the castle made her weep. She already relied more than she ought on the housekeeper to organise things. Mistress Abbott was highly efficient and capable and Cecilia had ensured the woman received regular bonuses in her pay. But Christmas was not simply about decorating the castle or cooking seasonal fare. Cecilia was happy to leave that largely

Chapter Seven

to her trusted staff, with an appearance from her in the corridors and kitchens a couple of times a day. Yet Christmas entertainments would require her presence. She would need to look cheerful, confident and carefree, none of which she could contemplate at present. But for her husband's sake, she had no other option than to try. The future of his family name and home were at stake.

*

By Easter the following year, Mistress Abbott had been successful in collecting statements from a number of people who worked in the castle regarding the likelihood of witchcraft being practised in their respective villages. The names of a number of cunning women were mentioned, including Anne Baker of Bottesford, Joanne Willimott of Goadby and Ellen Greene of Stathern. But the names that featured largely in these statements were those of Joan Flower and her daughters.

Cecilia rose from her comfortable chair in the housekeeper's office and paced the floor, her hands gesticulating this way and that to stress her points. 'No, I won't accept that,' she said, raising her left arm and thrusting out her vertical palm. 'I've known Joan Flower for a long time, some years before I became countess here, and I cannot accept that she's a witch – or her daughters for that matter. They were well respected members of the community in the village before John Flower died, though I realise they have struggled to earn a living since then. Joan would not have begged for work if not, nor would Margaret have felt the need to steal from our kitchens. If the girl had not despoiled my bed, I would have dealt leniently with her and allowed her to stay. Then there's this awful business of the family resorting to whoring.' She rubbed her hand across her aching head. 'Oh, Mistress Abbott, I do believe I should have helped them more. I dismissed poor Phillipa because of her mother's deeds, and now you say all three are harlots?'

'That's true enough, my lady, but I'm afraid there's worse.' Mistress Abbott shook her head at the thought. 'There are several in Bottesford who testify to evil deeds done by those three, especially those named here.' She lifted a piece of paper from her desk and handed it to Cecilia. 'All six claim to have seen witches and their familiars flying close to the Flower women's cottage *and* several people have mentioned that Joan does have a white cat, which they believe to be her familiar. Then there are those who profess to have been cursed by Joan on various occasions.'

Cecilia stared at her housekeeper and took the proffered paper. 'I refuse to believe that someone can change from being a respected woman to a witch once she reaches middle age. These are probably malicious lies simply because Joan Flower was once the respected mistress of her own house and looked down on them. I'm more inclined to believe that Joan's rapid decline in status meant they could get a little of their own back by maligning her. Naturally, the whoring would give those women something to protest about, too. I can well imagine many of their husbands heading Joan's way of a night-time.'

'Joan Flower always thought herself above the rest, my lady, but she also had a look about her that could cause a person to clam up and retreat. I think it was those deep, dark eyes passed on from her Spanish father. She has his temper and foul language, too, when she's annoyed. Then there's the fact that she refuses to go to church. Most of the villagers suspect that's because she's a devil worshipper.'

Lady Cecilia's brow creased in thought. 'They can't believe Joan to be practising witchcraft simply because she has dark eyes and a temper, and doesn't go to church.'

Mistress Abbot nodded. 'Along with all the other things, Lady Cecilia, they do. Let's not forget the curses Joan's put on a number of people, or the sightings of witches and monstrous creatures flying over her cottage. Then there's –'

Cecilia's raised hand halted the housekeeper's list. 'Have these people any evidence that Joan's curses have actually caused harm to anyone?'

'They say she cursed their crops two years ago so they rotted in the ground. It was the year the cereal crops were diseased and many villagers went hungry.'

'Well, that's poppycock. This whole region had so much rain that year, very little grew at all in the sodden earth. Surely, no one in their right mind could think that Joan can control the weather!'

'Unfortunately, many do, my lady. They say it was Satan's doing. Oh, and another thing, Joan Flower is often in the company of women who have been suspected of witchcraft for some years – though there is little proof of that about any of them.'

'I'll write to Samuel Fleming and arrange to see him as soon as he's free,' Cecilia said. 'All this talk of devil worship is worrying. He's known most of the villagers for years and will be able to make more sense of all of this than I can.

'And Mistress Abbott,' she added as she reached the door, 'I want no word of your findings, or of my visit to see Reverend Fleming, to reach my husband's ears.'

'My lips are sealed, my lady.'

Celia smiled. 'Thank you. I'll explain everything to him once I've heard Samuel's version of events. I want no accusations or arrests until we have believable evidence in our hands.

'Not that I believe those women to be witches for one moment.'

*

'Show the countess into the sitting room, would you, please, Alice?' Samuel Fleming called from his study on hearing the rap of the door knocker. 'I'll be there directly.' He closed the book in which he was making notes for Sunday's sermon and headed to meet his guest.

'I thank you for your letter, Lady Cecilia,' he said taking her outstretched hand. 'It's an honour to welcome you to the rectory. I understand you wish to know of recent events in our village, so I shall endeavour to help you in any way I can.'

'You are one of the most astute men I have ever known, Reverend,' Cecilia replied, sitting in the proffered chair in the large, square room with its floor to ceiling windows and double glass doors along an outer wall. 'Little happens in Bottesford without your knowledge of it and I'm here to prise out and share a little of that awareness, if I may.'

Samuel took a seat opposite to her. 'Prise away as much as

Chapter Seven

you like, Countess. This village and its occupants are dear to me and you are correct, I do make a point of knowing what is happening here. I have my spies, you see. They are my eyes and ears in places where I cannot be. In other words, they are simply villagers who like to gossip.' He winked at her, making her smile.

'Then your spies would doubtless have informed you that accusations of witchcraft have been made by some of your villagers; accusations aimed at certain women who dwell here. Is there any truth behind these allegations?'

Samuel regarded the countess, knowing her to be an upright and compassionate woman who would never act on any misdeed without absolute proof. He knew full well where her questions were leading. But he also knew how much it would grieve her to suggest that someone known to her could be deemed a witch, responsible for the sickness that had killed one of her sons and threatened the life of the other. The word *witchcraft* went hand in hand with Satanic deeds: evil doings at their worst.

Cecilia shuffled a little under his scrutiny and focused her gaze on the rectory garden through the window, where the blossoming colours of April contrasted with the dark green of the yews against the blue of the sky.

'You have evidently heard that these accusations of sorcery and devil worship are hurled at the Flower women, my lady.'

'I have known about them for some time, and admit to finding them hard to believe... or, perhaps, I just don't want to believe them.' Cecilia gave a heartfelt sigh. 'It was the beginnings of such rumours, together with the fact that Joan and Margaret had become whores, that obliged me to dismiss Phillipa Flower from my service two years ago. Some of the Bottesford women in my service were not only bombarding the girl with accusations of her mother's witchcraft, they were also threatening her bodily harm. Our corridors became unpleasant places to be.'

'Unfortunately, the women's allegations against Joan and her daughters still continue.'

The countess nodded. 'I also note your reference to those allegations as being made by the women and not the men. But you have no need to explain why. The men don't fear the Flower women, or at least they don't admit to fearing them. I have heard all about the bawdyhouse and am told it is Joan and her daughters' main source of income now.'

Samuel gazed absently down at his fingers as he thought. He sensed that the countess had not come here with accusations of her own, rather to seek his views on whether maleficium was at work in Joan Flower's house. Not wanting to put possibilities into her head regarding the strange sickness that plagued her family, he decided not to say anything about it unless she asked directly. 'The men flock to this "bawdyhouse" like sheep on most nights of the week, including the Sabbath, and few of them spread accusations of witchcraft. I sense that several of them have an underlying fear of what the women could do to them if they did.'

Samuel thought of Tom Simpson, whose eyes had the look of a scared rabbit whenever he was asked about his relationship with Phillipa. Then he thought of Peter's outright ridicule of anyone who could think those women were witches. But he

Chapter Seven

had no intention of revealing names to the countess.

'What do you make of the sightings of witches flying on broomsticks or on their grotesque familiars, Reverend?'

'To my knowledge, there has been only one sighting of such things and that was two years ago, at a time when many of the villagers had eaten rye bread purchased from some unknown trader at the market.'

Cecilia's tilted head and creased brow urged him to explain. 'Like the rest of us, you will no doubt remember that two years ago it rained almost constantly, causing widespread rotting of crops?'

'I recall it well, and was speaking about it with Mistress Abbott only yesterday.'

'Then you will also know that the grain crops became diseased, leaving little for the millers to grind into flour?' Cecilia nodded and Samuel continued to explain about ergot and its effects on people who had eaten bread made from infected flour.

'So you see, my lady, those rye loaves were sold by some unscrupulous and heartless farmer to make profit from his diseased crop. Our villagers bought the loaves in good faith and many became very sick as a result. Others saw things that were not really there, often things they feared – including flying witches and their enlarged familiars.'

'I had no idea of any of this, Samuel, but it certainly clarifies a few things for me. I so want to believe that Joan and her daughters are not dealing in witchcraft. What of the curses that Joan has been putting on people – and has she also been accused of casting spells?'

Samuel smiled. 'I have known Joan for many years, and know she is as hot-tempered as her father was. She can use the choicest of swear words when she is angry and can often say things she doesn't mean. It is her way of retaliating to ugly taunts from others and I believe that is why she has started uttering these curses. It certainly keeps them quiet for a while.

'As for casting spells...?' He held out his hands and shook his head, uncertain of the answer. 'She would need to know the exact procedure in order to do so, and be acquainted with people who could teach it to her.'

Cecilia averted her eyes and Samuel guessed she would be deliberating whether or not to share her fears regarding her elder son's death and little Francis's lingering torment. He also knew of Sir Francis's great concern over their inability to conceive another child.

'I won't take up more of your time, Reverend,' the countess said, standing ready to leave, 'although I do have one more question to ask, if I may?' Samuel nodded. 'Did you know that Joan Flower has been seen consorting with women who have long been suspected of practising witchcraft?'

'Ah, you mean Anne Baker and two others from neighbouring villages. I have heard that Joan has learned much from those three about the art of making herbal remedies needful to a cunning woman. And as far as I know, they all continue to help people with a variety of ailments.'

'But could those same women also be responsible for teaching Joan Flower the art of casting a spell?'

'That I couldn't say, my lady. It isn't a question I have ever had cause to ask since I have never considered any of them

Chapter Seven

to be witches. I see little of the Flower women nowadays and I know I would not be welcome in their cottage if I should call. But I fervently pray that Joan Flower has more sense than to dabble in sorcery. It could be the death of her if it became known that she did. There are many in this village who would be happy to see her hanged as a witch.'

'Then I will also pray that the allegations are false, Reverend. I have no desire to see an innocent woman wrongly charged and executed. However, should Joan prove to be guilty, I might change my mind.'

Chapter Eight

In which dreams cause distress and there are visitors at Belvoir Castle

Bottesford Village: June 1617

Searing pains shot through her. A sharp needle was plunged into the nipple of her bared breast, a second time into her navel. Her agonised scream was cut short by a flaming torch thrust within inches of her nose, causing her skin to blister and her eyes to feel they would melt. Her eyelashes and stray wisps of her hair momentarily caught light – until her naked body was dowsed by the ice-cold contents of a water pail…

'Ma, Ma, wake up! You're having that nightmare again.'

Joan's body trembled. A deep, guttural sound emerged through her lips, then she whimpered like a distressed dog, still trapped in the machinations of the cruel dream.

'Margaret!' Phillipa called. 'Fetch a mug of water.'

Phillipa wrapped her arms around her mother in an attempt to stop her from trembling. The nightmare had returned too many times in recent weeks and Phillipa knew she was letting the constant accusations and threats of the goodwives get to her.

'You'll feel better once you're properly awake,' she said, lifting Joan into a sitting position in her bed and leaning her against the cottage wall. 'Either just close your ears to those pathetic women, or give them a mouthful back, like you used

Chapter Eight

to do. They've wanted to bring you down for years but they've always been scared of you.'

Joan's dark eyes slowly opened, heavy lidded and bloodshot from too much ale and lack of sleep, and Phillipa smoothed back her wild, tangled hair. 'That was in the days when I was Mistress Flower and in favour with the Manners family, Phillipa. Now we are nothing and those lowborn goodwives are out to pay me back. Besides, I know that if I yell back at them my yells will become curses, which makes them call me "witch" even more. I know I shouldn't curse, but I can't help it when I get angry nowadays. And it chases them away.' She glanced at the dim light squeezing through the shutters. 'Is it morning?'

Margaret came to sit at the other side of the bed and held the mug of water to her mother's lips. 'The sky is lightening, though it's not yet sunrise. Few folks will be about at this hour on a Sunday and all but one of our guests left soon after midnight. Jack Willows is snoring on the hearth rug. I'll send him on his way when I go down.'

Joan nodded and drained the mug greedily. 'It's funny how water tastes so much better than ale, or even wine, of a morning,' she murmured, licking the last drops from her parched lips. 'But ale stops me worrying so much at night when we're entertaining our guests.'

'But can't you see, Ma? Those worries are coming back to haunt you in your dreams.' Phillipa took Joan's hands and waited until she had her full attention. 'Your screams are those of a woman suffering terrible pain, yet you tell us you can't remember what they were about once you waken. Is that the truth?'

'It's all the truth you're going to get. Perhaps if the night terrors continue much longer, I'll tell you. But for now, I don't want to talk about them. Now, once we've got rid of Master Willows, we have a cottage to tidy, chickens to feed and a stew to prepare for later.'

'Preparing meals is all well and good, Ma, and a good mutton stew is delicious, but don't you think it's time that you ate a little more of it? When I lifted you up just now, you felt like a bag of bones. No,' Phillipa said, shaking her head to halt Joan's indignant words,' you are half starving yourself. We have enough coin to buy good meat once a week, and wheat flour for our bread, but whatever we put on the table you barely touch. You're not the strong, robust woman you used to be, Joan Flower, and we are worried that very soon you'll just waste away. Either that, or you'll look so weak, those goodwives will have no difficulty in overpowering you.

'Think about that, Ma. Neither Margaret nor I want to lose you, or to be left on our own.'

*

Belvoir Castle: Early August 1617

Lady Cecilia gaped at her husband, then at the letter in his hand and put down her cup of cocoa. 'He's coming here next week? That's unusually short notice. Why were we not informed earlier? You know how long it takes to prepare for a lengthy visit, especially for so many people. I must see Mistress Abbott and our cooks as soon as we have breakfasted.'

Chapter Eight

Sir Francis shrugged and picked up his napkin to wipe the bacon fat from his lips, then motioned to one of the servants to remove his plate. Katherine had returned to her room and the earl and countess were at liberty to speak openly without interruption. 'I know little more than I've told you. It seems the king had intended to go straight to Burghley House in Stamford, but changed his mind last minute and decided to come here first.'

'I imagine they wouldn't be too pleased at Burghley after making preparations for the king to visit next week.'

'No, I don't suppose they would be, but who are we to question the whims of a king? Perhaps we should be proud that King James *has* chosen to come here. It seems he's made it known that Belvoir Castle is his favourite place to stay when he's on his northern progress. Shall I tell you why he enjoys coming here so much?'

'I imagine it's because you allow him to talk constantly about himself – and, of course, about his second favourite subject, the eradication of witches from his kingdom. To be honest, Francis, King James utterly bores me for most of the time, and if he makes any more disparaging remarks about our Catholic faith, I might just scream.'

'Something tells me you aren't too fond of our king,' Francis said, making her smile. 'But he has made it known that our hospitality is second to none. Which is all well and good, but you know what bothers me most about King James's visits, don't you?'

'I have a good idea.'

'They cost the earth, and if he continues to favour us so

often with his presence, we might just find ourselves penniless.'

Francis patted her hand as she gasped. 'Not really, I was making a small jest, although the king's visits do cost us a fortune. But I'm afraid we just have to grin and bear them.'

Cecilia stood to leave, a worried look on her face. 'If you'll excuse me, Francis, I really do need to see our housekeeper and cook. No doubt the king will be accompanied by a large entourage as usual, so all our bedchambers must be made ready, as well as all the rooms we normally entertain in. And our cook will need to prepare menus for all meals for the two weeks and ensure sufficient foods are purchased, or obtained from the castle farms. And once I've spoken with those two, I need to organise some forms of evening entertainment in addition to our usual musicians. Perhaps a band of players,' she mused, 'and we should probably bring out the board games and packs of cards.

'While you, Francis, will need to think about daytime entertainments. Thankfully, it's summer, and you should be able to ride across the Vale, or go hunting or hawking, or even fishing. But please, do take them out *somewhere* during the daytime so at least we'll have time to prepare for the evenings. I also need time each day to sit quietly with our son. His nurse tells me that Francis has seemed a little better these past few days. The vomiting has lessened considerably, and the convulsions are becoming quite rare. I shall pray that this continues.'

There was little more to be said, and the earl and countess set about organising the castle and its staff in preparation for yet another visit by the king.

Chapter Eight

*

King James's arrival the following week brought a further surprise to Sir Francis. Amongst the king's party was Sir George Villiers.

'I should have guessed you'd be accompanying the king on his progress,' Sir Francis said to his friend, finding a moment to themselves once they were seated in the morning room. King James was deep in conversation with Cecilia while castle staff carried in refreshments and the king's servants unloaded chests of clothes and finery from the coaches to carry to the bedchambers. 'Rumour tells me you're most definitely the king's favourite nowadays. I hear you're not only Gentleman of the Bedchamber, Master of the Horse and the Earl of Buckingham, you are now also the Marquess of Buckingham – and you've been admitted to the king's Privy Council. You have my sincere congratulations on each of these titles, George. I've no doubt you'll be a duke before too long – and what's that pet name King James has for you…? Oh yes, "Baby Steenie". Why is that?'

George chuckled. 'It is a reference to Saint Stephen, who is said to have had the face of an angel. The king embarrasses me by telling everyone that I am "one of the handsomest men in the world" and how I have a perfect complexion. He also has several other nicknames for me, and has favoured me above all other courtiers during the past few years. So much so that I hardly ever have time to go home to Brooksby. I have heard that envy is rife amongst some of the courtiers, so I try not to hog the king too much for myself.'

'I don't think you'll manage to hog him too often whilst you're here, George. We have a full schedule of events ready to entertain the king and his companions, so he'll be in the public eye for most of the time.'

'As he has been at every hall and castle we've visited during the progress, which is, of course, only to be expected. By the way, how is your son? I can imagine how it grieves you to watch him suffer month after month.'

'As a matter of fact, Francis has seemed a little improved of late, so we're hoping he's turned a corner and will not be looking back. It is our dearest wish that he fully recovers. I have never seen a child of six look so tiny and frail; a sharp gust of wind could almost blow him away. He's our only heir after all, and Cecilia and I have been unable to produce another child.'

'Oh, I'm sorry to hear that. Have you consulted physicians on that issue?'

'We have, but all they can say is that neither of us appears to have anything bodily wrong – which means little, I know, since they cannot see our innermost workings.' Francis shuffled, suddenly feeling embarrassed speaking of such personal issues. 'But enough of this dismal talk. You are here to enjoy our hospitality and entertainments, not to be burdened by our worries.'

'Then how is your delightful daughter keeping? I sincerely hope she has avoided this sickness.'

'Katherine is well, thank you, George. No one could say she has grown into the prettiest young lady in our county, which may cause concern when the time comes to find her a husband. But she is dedicated to her role as the daughter of an earl and is skilled in many domestic arts, such as needlecraft

Chapter Eight

and embroidery. She enjoys painting, too, but it must be said that music is her first love. Katherine sings like a nightingale and is an accomplished harpsichord player. My wife tells me she is now learning to play the harp.'

'Such talents would be valued in any wife, Francis. After all, entertaining is part of everyday life for people such as ourselves. But what of her ability to run a household? Which is something, I may say, that Lady Cecilia does magnificently.'

Francis nodded. 'I am always grateful for Cecilia's skills in that respect, and am happy to say that, together with our housekeeper's time and efforts, Katherine is becoming extremely proficient in the skills required to manage a large household such as this. What she lacks in looks and wit she makes up for in dedication to her duty and sound common sense. I believe she will make someone a perfect wife, one day.'

'I have always found Katherine delightful company, Francis, and believe there will be many gentlemen of noble birth who would be glad of a wife like her. The pretty ones are too often frivolous and care only for stylish gowns or costly jewellery. But you are surely not seeking a husband for your daughter yet. She is not yet of age, is she?'

'She is only in her fourteenth year, but as we all know, the next two years will probably fly by and sixteen is a perfect age for a young woman to be wed.'

'I shall be pleased to chat with her after the evening meal, Francis. There are many strangers here and she may feel a little abashed, being so young.'

'My daughter can hold her own in conversation with anyone, but knowing you from previous visits, I'm sure she'll be delighted to have your company for a while. If you wish, I can ask Cecilia to arrange for you to be seated next to her at the meal.'

'Thank you, my friend, I'll look forward to it. I'm also looking forward to seeing young Francis again, especially as you say he's feeling quite well at present. I know he likes me. I was happy to sit and feed him his soup last time I was here. His poor nurse was unable to persuade him to open his mouth at all.'

Francis laughed. 'Somehow, George, I am unable to see you as a permanent nursemaid. But if you like, I'll also ask Cecilia to arrange for you to visit the nursery at Francis's mealtime a few times whilst you're here. You may well be able to assist the nurse again.'

'I feel it my duty to see both of your children whilst I'm here. Perhaps once we're settled into our daily routine, we can decide which days would be best for me to visit the nursery.'

'As you wish, George. Now, I can see that the king has finished speaking with Cecilia and is heading this way.'

Francis and George stood and bowed, and King James grinned at them both. 'It is hard to believe it's two years since I was last at Belvoir and, I admit, I am delighted to be here again. You and your lovely wife are perfect hosts, Francis, and it will lift my spirits to ride across your beautiful Vale again.'

'You do my wife and me great honour in saying that, Your Majesty, and we will have a number of opportunities to view the Vale of Belvoir over the next two weeks. But before we discuss anything further, I insist you take refreshment after your journey. We have a number of wines to choose from or, if you prefer, there is cocoa. And as you see, we have a variety of cakes and pastries to stop your stomachs complaining. Then, you might wish to retire to your rooms to rest before the evening meal.'

'That sounds an excellent plan, Francis. Refreshments then nap. What more could a king ask for?'

*

Bottesford: October 1618

At the beginning of October, Samuel's sister lost her beloved husband to a virulent lung disease that had taken him to his bed since early May. Esther had nursed Thomas herself and kept him company during his more lucid moments, although towards the end, they were few and far between. Samuel attended the service at Thomas's own church of All Saints in Harston, and after a further two weeks to allow her time to grieve, Esther returned to Bottesford.

It was thirty-two years since Esther lived in the rectory, and although Samuel was happy to have his sister back to lessen Alice's workload, he felt her lingering sadness and loss deeply. There could not have been a more devoted couple than Esther and Thomas. Yet, having his sister to talk to of an evening was a great comfort to Samuel. And the situation with the Flower women was generally foremost on his mind.

Little had changed to improve the status of Joan and her daughters in the village for the past year and Samuel's concern for them caused him many a sleepless night. Wherever the three tried to find employment, doors were slammed shut, although many of the men openly turning them away were not averse to spending a few hours of covert sexual activity of a night-time in the little cottage by the Devon.

Inevitably, hostility, fear and mistrust continued to simmer amongst the women. So much so that there came a point at which blame for everything that went wrong in the community was laid at the feet of the Flower women. If a sick child died, the crops failed, cattle or sheep died, milk curdled or the ale turned sour, all fingers pointed at Joan and her daughters. Even a boy misbehaving in school, or a young girl becoming idle at her work, were attributed to curses and spells uttered by the Flower women.

Samuel prayed that God would help them see that their drunken and immoral lifestyle was offensive to good Christians, and that they would cease all practices that could be attributed to witchcraft. The rector had preached about tolerance and understanding for people less fortunate than themselves in last Sunday's sermon, only to be assailed by loud protests from the congregation and further shouts of flushing out and destroying witches in their village.

Samuel now truly feared for the lives of Joan, Phillipa and Margaret Flower.

*

Belvoir Castle: November 1618

The mood in the castle was decidedly woeful; illness hung over it like a shroud. Even servants kept well away as the earl and countess sat in the withdrawing room on a miserably wet November morning to discuss a missive that Cecilia was not at all happy about.

'Do you really have to go, Francis? Under the circumstances, surely the king will understand if you decline.'

Francis Manners heaved a sigh and took his wife's hand. 'I sincerely wish I could decline. I hate the thought of leaving you to deal with all the Christmas festivities, let alone our son. I will be distraught if Francis passes whilst I am at Court. How he's held on for over five years, I'll never know.'

'Is that not sufficient reason for you to refuse to go?' Cecilia's brow creased in a frown. 'Perhaps the king would be sympathetic to our plight if you explained how close to death Francis actually is.'

'Even if... and I did say *if*... James excused my presence at the Newmarket hunt, he is unlikely to do so for Christmas at Westminster.' Francis huffed. 'Which means I'll be expected to stay in London until at least a few days after Twelfth Night, or possibly until after Candlemas in early February.'

Francis threw out his hands. 'James is not the most sympathetic or understanding of men, as you know, Cecilia, which is undoubtedly why he's never been a popular king. He's done nothing during the fifteen years of his reign to make people like or admire him, and the older he gets, the more disgruntled he becomes. He locks himself away with his favourite courtiers more than ever nowadays – George Villiers in particular. Naturally, George will be accompanying James to Newmarket.'

'My main concern is that you will be away for so long. How selfish of the king to demand you spend most of November and all of December and January away from your home and family! Although, I admit, if little Francis wasn't so ill, he would have expected us all to celebrate Christmas at Bedford House and spend much of our time at Court. But James knows full well how ill our son is and still demands your presence.

'And Francis, as you know, things are astir in Bottesford. Mistress Abbott tells me that the mood in the village is ugly. The Flower women are being blamed for everything that goes wrong and have become the targets of hate. If anything should occur whilst you are away, I shall be at a loss to know how to deal with it.'

'Then, Cecilia, we must pray that nothing does happen while I'm away. But if it does, I suggest the first person you need to summon is Samuel Fleming. I have no doubt that he will know what to do.'

*

Bottesford: Christmas 1618

As December neared and the weather turned cold, Jane Simpson, younger sister of Phillipa's lover, Tom, gave birth to her first child, a boy, whom they named Daniel. Since Jane and her husband had come to stay with Tom's parents for the Christmas, Tom was unable to frequent the Flower house as often as usual. But whenever he did, it was obvious he was not a happy man.

'I wish they'd just go home,' he grumbled as he and Phillipa lay sated and sweaty in her bed after an hour of fervent

Chapter Eight

activity. 'They've been here more than two weeks already and it isn't Christmas for another two. It's bad enough that I've had to give up my bed and sleep on the downstairs floor, without the babe screaming all night. There must be something wrong with him because it sounds like he's in pain. My sister's forever whinging that he brings back as much milk as he swallows. He looks a sickly little thing to me, and he's as bald as an egg. I wouldn't be surprised if he died before long. I'm hoping he will, then I might get some peace and quiet.'

'Don't say such things!' Phillipa replied, aghast. 'If that comes true, Thomas Simpson, you'll blame yourself for wishing it.'

'Well, I think Ma's expecting him to die. I've watched her shaking her head and seen the worried look on her face when Jane isn't looking. I heard her say to Pa that the babe should be bigger that that at five weeks. I don't suppose he'll grow much if he's always being sick, will he?'

'Lots of babies and young children die. I suppose the ones who are fed well and don't catch some illness will grow healthy and strong. From what you say, it doesn't sound as though your sister's little son is going to be one of them. There must be something wrong if he can't keep milk inside him.'

'Aye, well, we'll just have to wait and see.' Tom pulled himself up on his elbows. 'I'd best be off now or Ma will be banging on your door. She gets really angry if she knows I'm coming here, especially now Jane and her family are staying with us.'

'No doubt she thinks we'll put some kind of spell on them,' Phillipa sneered, pulling herself up to sit beside him. 'Your ma despises us and would probably be the first one to cheer if we were hanged as witches.'

'That's true enough. And it isn't just Ma who says you should hang. All the other goodwives Ma knows say the same.'

'What about you? Do *you* think we're witches?'

'I... I don't know.' Tom scratched his greasy brown head as he thought. 'Margaret doesn't look like a witch, but your ma does with all that wild hair and the scowling black glares she gives people. And sometimes you scare me when you have that same look in your eye. It's as though you're about to curse me. My ma's convinced Joan Flower's casting spells and cursing everyone she hates in this village and that you're doing the same,'

Phillipa fought down her rising temper. 'If you suspect us of being witches, Tom Simpson, why do you keep coming here? Perhaps you think I'll put a spell on you if you don't... or perhaps you believe I've already put a spell on you to make you keep coming.'

She glowered at Tom's guilty face but he turned his head, unable to meet her probing dark gaze. 'That's it, isn't it? Well, I'll tell you what, I hereby release you from your compulsion to come to our cottage. In future, if you get the urge to come here but would rather not, you'll just have to do battle with your lustful thoughts, knowing they were not put there by me!

'I also know that my ma has never put a spell on yours. She wouldn't know how to cast a spell if she wanted to,' she lied. 'And nor would I. All the cursing my mother does is her way of defending herself against people who hurt or anger her. A curse is only words, Tom, and words can't inflict harm on anything.'

'They can if they're said by a witch. What about all the

Chapter Eight

crops Joan Flower's ruined and all the sheep and cows that have died for no reason at all, unless they'd been cursed. Then there was Goody Talbot's babe who died in his sleep. And he wasn't even ill. For all I know, you might have made some of those curses.'

Phillipa leapt from the bed, picked up Tom's clothes from the floor and threw them at him. 'If you believe all that nonsense, don't bother coming back here again… ever!' She held out her hand, palm upwards. 'Pay me what you owe me, then scamper back home like the scared rabbit you are. And if you aren't quick about it, I'll shout for Ma to come and put a spell on you.'

Wide-eyed and trembling, Tom reached for his breeches and drew out several coins from a pocket. Phillipa took them and picked up her shift and dress, throwing them over her head as she left the room. From her seat downstairs, she watched Tom scurry out of the cottage and silently close the door.

*

Two days after Tom Simpson's flight from Phillipa's bed, the babe named Daniel died, and it did not take long for Jessie Simpson to start hurling accusations against Joan and her daughters. Within the next few days most of the villagers were doing the same. Even the men joined in, and the once raucous bawdyhouse became eerily silent of a night-time. It got to the stage when Joan and her daughters dared not step from the cottage alone. Even wandering around their garden, prying eyes could spot them and hurl a few sticks and stones to accompany their malicious condemnations. Yet when the three visited the market together, none in the village dare utter a word.

'Why is it that when we're out together those people turn and walk away?' Margaret asked Joan one afternoon, when she'd been chased down Church Street by a group of goodwives as they emerged from the Belvoir Inn.

'Probably because when we keep together and face groups of them, they're too sacred of whatever powers they believe we possess to say a word. The three of us chanting curses on them would frighten them to death. Don't forget, they believe that you and Phillipa are as much witches as I am.'

'That's not fair, Ma,' Phillipa declared as she came downstairs. 'Margaret and I have never cursed anyone. All this is *your* fault because you couldn't hold your temper. You open your mouth and chant about all the things that could go wrong in the village, then you're surprised that the women blame you when they do actually happen! And those spells you performed were not our doing. You insisted we should watch, so we did.'

Joan knew that what Phillipa said was true. It was her own desire for revenge on the Manners family, together with the whoring, that had led to all the gossip and name-calling in the village. 'You're right about the spells and curses, Phillipa, but you can't deny that you were both as keen as I was to turn the cottage into a bawdyhouse.'

'People aren't accused of being witches just for whoring, Ma,' Margaret added. 'Phillipa's right, you're the one they decided was a witch, and because we're your daughters, they think we must be, too.'

'The villagers are banding together against us,' Joan said,

Chapter Eight

'and the men deserting us frightens me. I fear they'll be coming for us, so leaving the cottage will be impossible for a while. We could well be overcome and taken if we so much as step outside. I'm hoping people will eventually forget about this child's death and stop blaming us for it.'

'They wouldn't believe you if you told them you had nothing to do with the boy's death, Ma.' Margaret looked on the verge of tears. 'The only way we'll all escape being arrested and charged with witchcraft is by running away from here.'

'And where do you think we could go, and how would we feed ourselves? Not to mention that it's mid-winter and freezing cold.' Joan shook her head. 'We need to be here, with a roof over our heads. And here we have the hens, and vegetables from the garden, if we can manage to get out to collect them.

'I admit, life will be a struggle now we have no cash coming in from the men, but we'll just have to bide our time and see what happens.'

*

Just after dawn on a bitingly cold morning on the first day of January, Phillipa and Margaret stepped warily from their cottage into the silence of their garden, intent on collecting eggs and whatever vegetables still grew in the near-frozen earth before the village roused. Joan remained indoors, lighting a fire in the hearth with the last of their kindling and a single log. Unless they got to the woods today, she knew that by tomorrow the cottage would be little warmer than the hen coop outside. Hot food would become no more than a memory.

It was then they came. Over two dozen fired-up men pounced on the two young women, their rabid shrieks breaking the early morning silence. Joan hurtled outside, horrified by the sight that met her eyes. Armed with stout sticks and broom handles the village men, amongst them several who had recently enjoyed the pleasures of the bawdyhouse, were beating the screaming and kicking Phillipa and Margaret into submission.

Joan plunged into their midst, intent on stopping the blows to her daughters, only to be leapt upon and beaten about the head and body until she was on her knees, pleading with them to stop. Women suddenly infiltrated the mob, their shrill voices ringing out over the thuds of beating and pleas of the three captives. Someone yanked up Joan's head by her long, dark hair and before she could curse them all, a filthy piece of rag was thrust into her mouth and a gag tied tightly around it. She was hauled to her feet, blood streaming from her forehead and upper arms, and her daughters were dragged over to her, similarly bloodied and gagged.

Then Jessie Simpson, Agnes Peate and Kitty Beddows were standing in front of her.

'Not so powerful now, are you, Joan Flower?' Jessie sneered, whilst behind her, her son, Tom, attempted to hide the stick he carried behind his back. 'You've caused enough damage in Bottesford with your evil curses and spells, and we've had enough!'

The mob yelled agreement and Jessie held up her hand for silence. 'We could all list the things you and your evil offspring have done. We won't tolerate witches living amongst us under

Chapter Eight

the pretext of being cunning women, offering healing remedies and balms. But the death of the earl's son and other babes in this village cannot go unpunished. For those deeds alone you deserve to hang.'

'Swim 'em!' a man's voice called out.

Joan and her daughters were dragged along the path towards the Devon where grasping hands yanked Joan's woollen dress over her head. She shivered violently as the piercing wind cut through her thin linen shift, panicking as a thick rope was tied around her waist. The two loose ends were each long enough to span the river's breadth and on the opposite bank, two men waited to receive one of the rope's tossed ends.

Forced to sit, a length of twine was fastened around Joan's right thumb and attached to her left big toe, and her left thumb was likewise tied to her right big toe. In this ignoble position, gagged, trussed and swaying on the edge of the riverbank, they prepared to lift her and throw her into the water.

Dreading the touch of the Devon's icy flow Joan prayed to her gods to help her.

'If you sink, Joan Flower, we'll know you are innocent.' Agnes Peate's mocking voice was suddenly close to her ear, disrupting her fervent prayers. 'Only those guilty of witchcraft will float. They say the Devil saves his own, and you are one of his spawn if ever there was one. You bewitched my Jonathan into lusting after you, just as Phillipa did to poor Tom Simpson. I hope you float, then we can enjoy watching you hang.'

'Stop this barbarity!' Samuel Fleming's commanding voice rang out as he ran across the bridge to confront the gathering. But as the brutal hands withdrew their grip on her, Joan lost her balance and toppled down the shallow bank to stop, teetering at the water's edge where the slope levelled out.

'Help her back up the bank and untie her. And get rid of these gags. Now!'

The rector's orders were not to be disobeyed and Joan was hauled away from the freezing water, shivering convulsively as the rope and strings were untied.

'Who has this woman's dress?' Samuel demanded. Jessie Simpson stepped sheepishly forward. 'Get her clothed.'

Jessie did as she was told, not disguising the look of loathing on her face as she did, and Samuel wrapped his own cloak around Joan's trembling body. 'On whose authority have you done this?'

'Rector, we've been instructed by Lady Cecilia to take the three witches captive,' Agnes Peate whined, stepping towards him. 'My husband brought the order with him after finishing work at the castle. Her ladyship asked us to let her know when the three are held captive so she can send a cart to take them to the gaol at Lincoln Castle.'

The reply took Samuel aback. 'I know naught of this. To whom was this message sent, might I ask?'

Peter Jenkins stepped through the crowd. 'To me, Reverend. Jonathan Peate brought the letter to me late yesterday afternoon, and I called the villagers to a meeting last night. Between them, they devised the plan to capture the women at daybreak. The order was definitely real and it bore Lady Cecilia's signature. You know I could not have disobeyed an order from the countess. She is in charge of local affairs while the earl is at Whitehall with the king.'

Chapter Eight

Peter's face was ashen as he looked from Samuel to Joan. 'Believe me, if I could have put a stop to it, I would have done. And the letter said nothing about swimming the women.'

'I should think it did not!' Samuel fumed. 'These women would have died of cold had they been taken to Lincoln in an open cart after such an ordeal. If they had not already drowned in the freezing water!'

His arm swept out to encompass the angry mob. 'Get back to your homes. You should be ashamed of yourselves – even you, Peter. You should have come to me with Lady Cecelia's order before taking it upon yourself to gather the villagers together.'

Peter hung his head. 'I see that now, but I believed the women would simply be taken and brought back to the inn to wait for the cart to arrive. I swear I didn't know that Joan and her daughters would be so maltreated, and I got here to see them being dragged to the river.'

Samuel breathed deeply to control his rising rage with these people. Already angry that the countess had not sent the command to him, he was grieved at the way the Flower women had been treated. 'These women are innocent until proven guilty in a court of law, and not by a malicious rabble such as you have turned yourselves into. Go home and reflect on your own sins!

'Peter, help me to get these three to the rectory where Joan can get dry and they can wash the blood from themselves. Alice and Esther will be able to find them warm food and drink. Oh, and Peter, I'll take the message of the women's capture to the countess myself.'

*

'You are kind, Reverend,' Joan said as they sat in the rectory's kitchen in front of a roaring fire to eat the bowls of meaty broth with freshly baked bread and drink the mugs of warm ale. 'Your rectory is warm and the food is good.'

Samuel glanced at Esther and could see his own compassion mirrored in her eyes. The women had washed away the blood to reveal cuts and bruises, and Margaret's left eye was so black and swollen it remained closed. 'You realise, Joan, that this will probably be the last meal you have before you reach Lincoln. Although, I imagine you will spend the night at Ancaster. The journey to Lincoln with a cart is too long to accomplish in a mere few hours.'

Joan nodded and hung her head. 'The gaol at Lincoln is a filthy and stinking place, fit only for rats that constantly bite the prisoners chained in there. Why can't the gaolers keep it clean for people who have not yet been proven guilty?'

The two young women stared at their mother and Samuel realised that Joan must not have shared her thoughts with them. He shook his head, the sadness he felt at the necessity of sending these women to almost certain death evident. 'I admit, I have never been inside Lincoln gaol, but I sincerely hope you are wrong.'

'Those accused of witchcraft are given food unfit for pigs,' Joan continued, her voice little more than a whisper, 'and are tortured to make them confess to things they did not do.'

'From whom did you hear such things?' Esther asked, incredulous. 'Surely, laws have been passed banning torture in prisons…' She paused, a thoughtful look on her face. 'Except in certain cases.'

Joan's throaty chuckle held no hint of humour. 'You might as well say it, Esther. I already know that those accused of witchcraft can still be tortured.'

Esther could not hold Joan's probing stare and averted her eyes as she replied. 'Perhaps it's best you don't frighten yourselves even more by believing such tales to be true of Lincoln.'

'I don't know what others prisons are like, but my dreams are rarely wrong. I know what goes on in that dungeon at Lincoln Castle. But I've heard there's an ordeal that anyone accused of witchcraft can demand. It involves eating a piece of bread. I'll insist on this ordeal before we reach Lincoln if I can.'

'The countess has asked to be notified as soon as the women are captured so she can send a cart to carry them to Lincoln,' Samuel said to Esther. 'I've told Peter I'll take the message myself, so if you'd ask Gilbert to get my carriage ready, I'll be on my way. Peter's stable boy will be my coachman so that Gilbert can stay in the rectory with you and Alice.'

Esther left the room to find Gilbert, and Samuel turned to the Flower women. 'You will be taken to the reception room until I return and, unfortunately, I will need to lock the door. Gilbert will be in the rectory with Alice and Esther and I'll ask Peter to join them. Under no circumstance will they open the door until the cart arrives.

'It is a sad day when I have need to hold three of my parishioners under lock and key.'

Chapter Nine

In which Samuel speaks with the countess and a journey to Lincoln proves traumatic

The castle was unnaturally quiet as Samuel Fleming was admitted by a footman and led towards the morning room by one of the housemaids. The absence of Sir Francis seemed to hang over the majestic building, repressing all attempts at jollity.

'Lady Cecilia,' Samuel said, bowing as the maid closed the door behind him. 'I hope you and Lady Katherine are well and that young Francis's condition is stable.'

The countess gestured to a plush, blue velvet armchair opposite to her own by the fireside and Samuel sat, waiting for her to reply.

'I am sad to say that our son has taken a turn for the worse in recent days, Reverend. The convulsions and vomiting are taking their toll and he is too weak to even sit up most of the time. I am praying they will lessen soon, as they usually do. The poor child has had few happy moments in his eight years of life and it is tearing me apart to see it.'

'I shall pray for him tonight, my lady.'

'I would greatly appreciate that. As for Katherine and I, we are as well as can be expected under the circumstances. Events in Bottesford have been an added burden during the earl's absence, and if I am not mistaken, those events are the reason for your visit today. I imagine you are here to ask me why I authorised the arrest of the Flower women?'

Chapter Nine

Samuel nodded. 'Naturally I would like to hear your reasons for that, my lady, but I am here to inform you that Joan and her daughters have been arrested and are being held in the rectory. Peter tells me you intend to send a cart to transport them to Lincoln.'

'Yes, I'll send the cart as soon as we have finished our conversation. You probably think I acted in haste and should have waited until my husband was home. But you need to know that Francis granted me full authority to have anyone suspected of witchcraft arrested during his absence, particularly anyone who could be responsible for causing the death of Henry and this prolonged agony of little Francis.'

Samuel's sympathy for Lady Cecilia's suffering momentarily hardened his heart to the plight of the Flower women, but he would need substantial evidence against them if he were to believe the three women capable of murder by witchcraft.

'I have come to accept that Joan Flower bears our family a grudge because I dismissed her daughters from my employ,' the countess continued. 'You know, of course, that several of our servants from Bottesford have informed us that Joan has thrown numerous curses at her fellow villagers which have come true. She has also cast spells to cause the deaths of more than one of the village children. It took me a long time to come to terms with that, but I am now convinced that Joan Flower has already k… killed one of our sons and is slowly killing the other. There is no other explanation for our misfortunes, or for the fact that the illness cannot be cured by any treatment recommended by physicians.'

Samuel shuffled in his seat, aware that the countess was

on the verge of tears. 'My lady, your distress is clearly understandable but if these women are to be tried in court, we need more proof of their guilt than the mere suspicions of villagers. You said as much yourself not so long ago. Joan's daughters have never been liked in Bottesford either, doubtless because of who their mother is, and we must be certain that lies have not been fabricated in order to cause deliberate harm to the women.'

'I know all that, Reverend, and I never wanted to think ill of Joan, or her daughters. But it was almost two and a half years ago when I explained that to you, and things have changed since then. We now have proof of the Flower women performing a spell against Henry, Lord Roos, and it is likely there have been others that we don't know about.'

Samuel gaped. This was news to him, and if Peter had known of this spell, he would surely have reported it to him. 'Do you know by whom this information was provided?'

'I do and I am certain that those concerned will need to be questioned in court.'

'They will, indeed, my lady.'

'No doubt you will recall that when I visited you with my concerns two years ago, we discussed Joan Flower's close association with other cunning women in the area, three of them in particular?' Samuel nodded. 'I particularly remember you saying that their only influence on Joan was in their roles as cunning folk.'

'And wasn't it?'

'I can't say with certainty that any of them deals in witchcraft, Samuel, but it seems that two of them were taken into

Chapter Nine

Joan's confidence regarding one of the spells she performed. It is thought that the method of implementing it was given to Joan by them in the first place.'

'I see. Then those women will undoubtedly be called to court in due course. Their evidence could be damning, for themselves as well as the Flower women.'

'Witchcraft is a shameful practice and I regret scorning King James's obsession with wiping out witches in our country for so long. I now see that he was right. Witches cause unimaginable pain to many, as we have seen in Bottesford… and here at the castle. I believe I have done the right thing in arresting the women. I've heard it said that once a witch has been put to death, any spells she has inflicted on people will end, and sufferers will soon recover.'

Samuel was highly doubtful of that but decided it prudent to say nothing on the subject. 'Joan Flower is adamant she has not participated in witchcraft,' he said, instead, 'and is determined to prove her innocence by demanding an ordeal in which consecrated bread is eaten. She is terrified at the thought of being incarcerated in Lincoln gaol, so I imagine she will do this as soon as they reach the city, or before if they make an overnight stop.'

'They'll be spending the night in the cells at Ancaster. But this ordeal will do her no good. I'm convinced she is guilty, as are her daughters, and I doubt that any ordeal she undergoes will prove differently. Joan is an evil and vengeful witch and we are determined to ensure she pays for her crimes. One of the cunning women was adamant that a spell Joan cast was aimed directly at the earl and me.'

Cecilia took a small lace-edged handkerchief from her pocket and dabbed the tears threatening to spill down her cheeks. 'For several years I have been unable to conceive, and now I know why. Joan Flower and her daughters cast a spell to ensure that Francis and I would never have more children.'

The countess stood and offered her hand to Samuel indicating that the interview was over. 'I thank you for coming and for your kindness over the years. Who would have thought we'd be facing a crisis such as this when you came to the castle as chaplain all those years ago? It was long before Francis and I had even met, of course, but he tells me it was thirty-seven.'

'It was indeed. I recall it being soon after I became the rector at Saint Mary's.'

'I confess, speaking with you of recent events has helped me to clear my thoughts, Samuel, as it always does.'

Samuel smiled. 'Then my visit has not been a wasted one. But now I will take my leave. Thank you for allowing me to share my thoughts with you, Lady Cecilia. And you have given me much to contemplate, especially regarding the evidence of the three cunning women. As rector of the parish of Bottesford, I am required to attend the Lincoln court in order to interrogate those charged, and any witnesses to their alleged crimes. I will ensure the cunning women are called to testify. The next Court of Assize is not until early March, but I imagine Sir Francis will be back before then?'

'He will. I wrote to inform him of my intention to arrest the Flower women over a week ago and his reply arrived yesterday. King James was expecting my husband to remain in Westminster until after Candlemas at the beginning of Feb-

Chapter Nine

ruary, but Francis is hopeful that James will see the gravity of this situation, and permit him to leave earlier. As Lieutenant of Lincolnshire and a Justice of the Peace, it is Francis's duty to be involved in the interrogation of the women.'

'If the king did prove stubborn in this, my lady, Francis would have less time to organise and carry out the interrogation of the women. In many cases of witchcraft, several weeks of questioning and persuasion are needed to make those charged confess to their sins. But knowing how keen King James is to eradicate witches, I am inclined to think he will permit Francis to forego the Candlemas festivities and leave soon after Twelfth Night.'

Cecilia sighed. 'I sincerely hope you're right. Whenever Francis gets here, he will not be staying longer than it takes to gather fresh clothing. He intends to take his fastest coach and his three usual footmen and carry straight on to Fulbeck to collect his brother, Sir George.

'Tell me, Samuel, when do you intend to leave for Lincoln?'

'Within the next week, I hope, as soon as the young cleric who will take my place at Saint Mary's during my absence arrives. I shall have little time to speak with him so I intend to leave written instructions regarding my sermons and general duties in the parish. I'm sure that Esther and Alice will be of great help to him.

'Thank you again, Lady Cecilia. Your comment about witchcraft being "a shameful business" sums this situation up well, although I'm inclined to add a couple of words to it:

'Witchcraft is a shameful, wicked and sordid business… and an extremely sad one.'

Take Height, Rutterkin

*

From Bottesford to Lincoln: January 1619

It was a journey of almost forty miles from Bottesford to Lincoln along the route taken by the countess's drivers across the low-lying lands of Lincolnshire. For most of the first fifteen of those miles the country road was little more than an unsurfaced and unkept path, pitted and muddied, and highly unsafe to both wheeled vehicles and horses. The drivers ensured they moved slowly in an effort to avoid the deeper potholes, many of which were invisible beneath the mud. The cart bounced along regardless, giving the three women a very uncomfortable ride. To make matters worse, stinging, icy sleet drove into them as they huddled with their wrists tied and fastened to the iron rings on the sides of the uncovered cart. Garbed as they were in only their woollen dresses, the single blankets given to each provided their only protection from the bitter weather of early January, and were soon soaked through. In contrast, the guard sitting in the back with them had the benefit of a thick woollen coat, a wide-brimmed hat and thigh-length leather boots.

After sixteen miles they reached the village of Ancaster, sitting astride the old Roman road of Ermine Street. The short January day was fading and the women had been exposed to the biting wind and freezing sleet for almost five hours. They were drenched to the skin and had long-since become stiff and numb and almost insensible. Joan had become delirious and mumbled constantly of the tortures awaiting them in Lincoln

Chapter Nine

gaol. Here they stopped to spend the night before resuming the journey in the morning.

Joan and her daughters were taken into the reception area of what appeared to be the local gaol, with Joan still muttering incomprehensibly about what she had seen in her dreams. She caught sight of the cells with their heavy wooden doors and their iron grilles and whimpered like a terrified child.

Their wrists were untied, and the two younger women were shoved into one of the cells and Joan into the other. Joan screamed and hammered on the grille with her fists until the gaoler opened the door and forcefully thrust her back, rendering her whining on the straw-strewn stone floor like a whipped dog.

A couple of hours after daybreak the three women were hustled back to the reception room to be given a mug of weak ale and a dollop of gruel before they continued their journey to Lincoln. Their hair had dried off overnight, though their clothing was still cold and damp. Joan refused to eat or drink, and constantly demanded to see a clergyman. One of the gaolers seemed to take pity on her and sped off across the square to the village church and vicarage.

'I am innocent of the crime of witchcraft, and of giving myself to the Devil, Vicar,' Joan said, throwing herself at the clergyman's feet the moment he entered the room. 'I demand an ordeal that will prove the truth of that.'

'Stand up, woman!' The scrawny little vicar in his long black cassock had a pinched and overall cruel-looking face, and Joan was dismayed that he lacked the air of kindness that Samuel Fleming had. This man was not her friend and seemed to have already convinced himself of her guilt. 'Explain which ordeal you refer to.'

'It is one I know to have been practised for many years. They say even Earl Godwine, father of King Harold who was killed at Hastings, was put to the test in this way. But he died during the ordeal, so was not found to be innocent of his crimes.'

The vicar nodded. 'You wish us to test you with a piece of bread and butter. Are you suggesting that a wicked hag like you should be permitted the same privilege as a high-ranking member of the nobility such as Earl Godwine? Woman, you are in no position to demand anything!'

One of the gaolers seemed intrigued by the idea. 'Why shouldn't we let her try, Reverend? She said the earl in question died during this ordeal, so it would seem she is willing to take the risk of that.'

'There will be no risk,' Joan put in, 'because I am innocent.'

'I say we let her try,' the same gaoler said, as the two others nodded in agreement. 'Unfortunately, we have no bread and butter here, so if you could spare a small morsel of it from your kitchen, Vicar, we'd be grateful. It will be of interest to see the outcome.'

The unsmiling vicar heaved a sigh. 'I have work that needs my attention, but if you insist on doing this, we need to make it quick. I'll do as you ask and bring the buttered bread from my vicarage, but it needs to be consecrated before the woman eats it, which I must do in front of you all.'

Ten minutes later he was back, carrying a wooden platter with a small but thick piece of buttered bread on it. Standing before them all he said a few words over the bread, blessing it

Chapter Nine

in the name of the Father, the Son and the Holy Ghost while the women and gaolers heeded the words with clasped hands. Then he offered the bread to Joan, who put it into her mouth and chewed.

Suddenly, she clutched at her throat, unable to speak or even breathe, as her face turned crimson. She held out her hands to the vicar, stepping forward, desperate for help. Phillipa and Margaret cried out and made to move to help her, but were restrained by the gaolers, while Joan dropped, stone-dead to the floor, her unseeing eyes staring at the ceiling.

'No!' Margaret cried out, breaking away from her captor to fall on her knees beside her mother's prostrate body. 'Ma, you can't be dead! We won't cope in prison without you.'

'Your mother was a fool to have undertaken this ordeal,' the noxious vicar sneered. 'It was obvious to us all that she was a witch and would choke on food blessed by God. She had given herself to the Devil – as, I am sure, have her daughters – and would never be permitted into Heaven.'

He tore his gaze away from Joan to address the gaolers. 'I suggest you get these women onto the cart waiting outside. When they're safely on their way, you will gather together a few local men to get this body to the nearby crossroads and bury it in an unmarked grave. No witch should contaminate any churchyard hereabouts.'

*

By late morning, Phillipa and Margaret were back on the cart, tied as they had been the previous day and on the twenty-five-mile journey to Lincoln. Sobbing for most of the journey at the loss of their mother, and after hearing her mutterings about tortures and vermin-infested cells, dreading what would happen to them once they got there. They paid little heed to their driver's orders to be silent, which earned them a few sharp raps with a stick from their guard.

Despite being further than the journey of the previous day, the road from Ancaster to Lincoln was a good one. It followed the course of the old Roman Ermine Street, atop the higher land of the Lincoln Ridge, so mud was almost absent and even potholes were few and far between. In addition, the drenching sleety-rain had stopped, enabling the journey to be finished by the time the January daylight had faded.

They entered the city between the old, crumbling turrets of the Roman East Gate, close to the towering medieval cathedral. Phillipa felt physically sick as her mother's words rang in her ears, and she trembled as the great buildings around her seemed to close her in, taking her captive before she even reached the gaol. Beside her, Margaret had retreated inside herself. She stared ahead, seeming not to notice they had reached their destination.

'Be brave, sister,' Phillipa whispered. 'No matter what, we know we are innocent of practising witchcraft. The judges will surely see that.'

The sharp pain as the stick connected with her shoulder put an end to further words.

The cart trundled along the old cobbled streets and eventually entered the castle through its commanding eastern gate and into the castle yard. The two young women were hauled

Chapter Nine

from the cart with their wrists still bound, gazing up with foreboding at the surrounding walls at the top of the grassy slopes that shut them off from the city beyond. Around them people were moving to and fro among the scattering of buildings, in pursuit of their daily business. Few gave the hapless prisoners more than a passing glance. Phillipa opened her mouth to offer words of hope to her younger sister, but once again, she was struck across her back with a stick.

'Say one more word and I'll knock your teeth out and drag you along the ground up to Cobb Hall.' The guard pointed his stick at the squat, flat-fronted tower at the north-east corner of the castle wall. 'The dungeon rats will probably wake you up nibbling at your feet.'

Phillipa's last thought before they were shoved through Cobb Hall's door was that the whole place looked nothing like Belvoir Castle, the only other castle she had seen in her entire twenty-three years of life.

Chapter Ten

In which the interrogators arrive in Lincoln and discuss how to proceed

Lincoln Castle: Mid-January 1619

Ten days after Phillipa and Margaret had been thrust into the castle's dungeon, an elegant coach pulled by four well-groomed horses came to a halt in the castle yard. With his younger brother, Sir George Manners, Sir Francis, Earl of Rutland, alighted and glanced about, shivering as the bitter north-easterly gusted through the castle grounds. As always when he attended a court case at this city castle, Francis thought how blessed he was to call Belvoir his home. But on this occasion, his own close connection to the case weighed heavily upon him, and thoughts of home and family came with a stab of anger and pain. By all that was holy, Francis swore, he'd make those witches pay for the grievous harm they had done to his family.

Francis waited beside his brother while his coachmen retrieved their travel trunks from the carriage roof. 'We'll take our baggage ourselves, Robert,' he said, addressing the eldest of the three men. 'The inn we'll be staying at is just across the way on Bailgate. You have my thanks for getting us here so quickly,' he added, retrieving four gold crowns from his leather purse and handing one to each of the men and keeping one in his hand. 'I'd say you deserve at least a mug of ale and a meal

Chapter Ten

at The Ram in Newark. This fourth crown will pay for food and lodgings for yourselves, stabling and feed for the horses and, of course, housing for the coach.' Francis handed the extra crown to Robert. 'You should make it back to Belvoir before dark tomorrow, as long as you leave early enough. I'll get a message to you when our duty here is done, which could be up to several weeks.'

'Very well, my lord,' Robert said with a grin on his ruddy face at the coins, 'and you have our sincere thanks for your generosity.' The other two voiced their thanks and Robert added, 'We'll reach Newark easily before nightfall. The Fosse Way is a reasonable road, as you know, Sir Francis.'

'Then we'll wish you a safe journey and hope you find The Ram comfortable.'

Francis and his brother watched the coach turn around and head through the East Gate. 'I'm missing our glorious Vale already,' Francis declared, 'and I'm eager to get this trial over with so I can see these witches hanged.'

George nodded. 'My sincerest hope is that their deaths will break those cursed spells on you and your son. I shall enjoy interrogating them, as I am sure you will yourself, Francis.'

'Only time will tell whether the witches' spells can be broken by their deaths. King James maintains that only the cleansing flames of burning can do that. Of course, I'm praying he's wrong and that hanging serves just as well. And yes, I will indeed enjoy wresting the truth from their lying lips.'

Francis heaved a sigh. 'But now we need to let the clerk in the Shire Court over there know of our arrival, then we'll head to the White Hart to get out of this wind and have a meal before we settle into our rooms. We'll start discussions when the other five interrogators arrive, hopefully within the next few days. My old friend Samuel Fleming will be one of them.'

*

As the second week of January ended, Samuel Fleming left Bottesford to make his way to the city with its exalted cathedral and castle that presided over the surrounding lands from atop the Lincoln Ridge. Having travelled to the city on a number of occasions by taking the same route as that of the cart carrying Joan Flower and her daughters, he saw no reason to do otherwise on this occasion. Knowing the route was too long to cover in a single day in his small carriage, especially with the neglected state of the roads, he had already booked two rooms at the Fox and Goose in Ancaster, one for himself, the other for his coachman, Peter Jenkin's stable boy, Joseph. He had also written to the landlord at the White Hart in Lincoln and managed to secure himself the last available room, for which he was inordinately thankful. Walking too far put a strain on his creaking knees and lower back nowadays.

The meal was a hearty one, the duck roasted to perfection. Samuel licked his lips to retrieve any last drops of the deliciously thick gravy and leaned back in his chair to relax in front of the inn's roaring fire with his mug of ale. The food and warmth made him feel drowsy and the voice of the innkeeper's wife as she collected his platter startled him.

'You look ready for your bed, Reverend. Have you travelled far?'

Chapter Ten

'Only sixteen miles, Mistress, but I was up before dawn to make sure everything was ready for my journey and to place my sermon notes where the young vicar taking my place can easily find them. So it's been a long day, especially for a white-headed old man like me. And tomorrow I have almost another twenty-five miles to suffer in the little box I call a carriage.'

She laughed, the creases around her eyes indicating she was not a young woman, though still an attractive one. 'Well, it's good to know that not all members of the clergy are as miserable as the vicar we have to put up with here.' She lowered her voice and leaned a little closer to Samuel's ear. 'Between you and me, I don't know why he joined the Church in the first place. He's not interested in the villagers, or their problems. I'm glad he wasn't vicar here when Sidney and me were wed. The previous vicar was a happy soul, but he passed away and this sour-faced weasel seems to be here to stay.'

Samuel could not help smiling at the look on the woman's face as she spoke. 'I'm sorry to hear that. Joining the Church is a calling for most of us, and taking care of our parishioners is something we should take to heart. The wellbeing of my flock is important to me.'

'Are you heading to Lincoln on Church business, Reverend… if you don't mind me asking?'

'I am, in that it involves three of my parishioners who are to stand trial at the Assizes. As rector I am called to assist in their interrogations, and those of any witnesses to their crimes.'

'They wouldn't be three women, would they – a mother and her two daughters?'

Samuel nodded. 'No doubt you recall them passing through

a short while ago. They would have been held in the village gaol.'

'I remember the incident well, Rector. The three of them were witches, we've been told.'

'The incident…?'

'The mother asked for some kind of ordeal in which she would eat consecrated bread and butter.' The woman hesitated, seeming to expect some kind of reaction from him.

'Please go on,' Samuel urged. 'I knew Joan Flower was intending to ask for this test, but I've heard nothing further. I would appreciate you enlightening me regarding the outcome.'

'It seems the woman ate the bread provided and blessed by our vicar – the snivelling little man I've just been talking about – and she choked on it.'

'You mean she's dead?'

The woman nodded. 'Reverend Simons ordered the gaolers to ensure she was buried at the Ancaster crossroads, where all condemned witches from around here are buried.'

A wave of immense sadness washed over Samuel as his mind filled with images of Joan Flower as a happy, vivacious young woman with her two young daughters. The death of John Flower had changed their lives forever.

'The daughters were taken on to Lincoln?'

'They'll have been in the castle gaol for almost two weeks now, Rector,' she said with a frown. 'Witches or not, I hope they've got strong stomachs. From what we've heard, that dungeon they throw criminals into is a filthy, stinking place, riddled with vermin and freezing in the winter.'

As he sat in his room that night, leaving Joseph finishing

Chapter Ten

his meal in the room below, Samuel contemplated the gravity of the task ahead. It was not one he looked forward to. He had believed Joan Flower to be exaggerating the appalling conditions in the gaol, but it seems they were generally known the closer one got to Lincoln. Phillipa and Margaret would be in need of spiritual guidance as they faced the incriminating charges against them. The interrogations and examinations would be gruelling and likely to involve pain, if Joan Flower's words were to be believed. He knew the interrogators would be relentless in their determination to elicit confessions from the women. Then there would be the trial when the sisters would face the learned and solemn judges in their long dark robes and hoods. The prospect of the terrible fate ahead of them if they were found guilty would loom over them like some huge, preying beast.

Until he had heard all the evidence and what the women themselves had to say in their defence, Samuel resolved to keep an open mind.

*

Over the next few days all five of the other interrogators arrived in Lincoln. Sir Francis welcomed each before they settled into their respective rooms at inns within walking distance of the castle. He realised what a strong and celebrated team he had. Amongst them were two renowned members of the Lincolnshire aristocracy, both close friends of his and regular visitors at Belvoir Castle. Lord Willoughby of Eresby was also Francis's Deputy Lieutenant of Lincolnshire. He was a tall, stout man of middle age with a short, dark moustache and beard, and the reputation of not suffering fools lightly. By way of contrast, Sir William Pelham was shorter, fair-headed and slightly built, the most noticeable feature on his face being his prominent green eyes. These he used to good effect. A piercing glare from the High Sheriff of Lincolnshire would make most men quiver and wonder what they'd done wrong, especially since Sir William was known to be greatly experienced in matters of the law.

Another two eminent members of Francis's group were Henry Hastings and Matthew Butler. Henry was the ageing Sheriff of Leicester and a member of the Earl of Huntingdon's family. He was a strong Protestant with a deep interest in cases of witchcraft. Mr Butler, like Francs himself, was a renowned Justice of the Peace; a middle-aged, self-possessed man, well accustomed to prising the truth from those accused.

Then there was Sir George Manners. Francis's thoughts focused on his younger brother, whose political achievements he could only admire. Five years ago, George had risen from being the Member of Parliament for the town of Grantham to that of the Member of Parliament for the whole of Lincolnshire. George had already made his intention of ensuring these women hanged clear to Francis.

As colleagues and acquaintances of the earl, dignitaries in their own right and conversant with the law and courtly procedure, Francis thanked God that this small group of men were determined to see the heavy hand of justice strike down the Flower women. The witches had brought death and immense pain and suffering to a member of the nobility – for which they would pay dearly.

Chapter Ten

By way of contrast, Francis's old friend and his family's chaplain, Reverend Samuel Fleming was not born into the nobility, and his profession in the Church set him apart from the earl and other examiners. Yet Francis held Samuel in high esteem. Now in his seventy-first year, the Rector of Bottesford was an extremely intelligent and well-educated man, renowned as a writer and academic. Francis knew that, unlike the other interrogators, Samuel would show the sisters kindness and if they were proven guilty of witchcraft, he would help them to repent and ask God for forgiveness. Samuel would want more than anything to save the women's souls from everlasting damnation.

All that would be acceptable to Francis… as long as Samuel did not attempt to prevent the witches' death. Nothing must stand in the way of ending those spells on his family, even if it meant an end to his and Samuel's close and lengthy friendship.

*

On Saturday the twentieth day of January, Francis called all interrogators to a meeting in his spacious room at the White Hart in order to discuss how the examinations of the women should be conducted. Once they were seated around the large, circular table and the wine had been delivered and poured by the cheery innkeeper, Francis opened the meeting.

'Four of you in this room came to Lincoln with the expectation of examining three women, a mother by the name of Joan Flower and her two daughters: Phillipa, aged twenty-three, and Margaret who is twenty-one. Other than Sir George, Reverend

Fleming and myself, you will probably not have heard that Joan Flower died during the journey to the city.

It seems she demanded the ordeal of eating consecrated bread in the hope of proving she was innocent of witchcraft or of giving herself to the Devil. The outcome was that she choked on that bread, provided and blessed by the vicar of the church of Saint Martin's at Ancaster, and simply dropped dead.'

The room fell silent while the men digested that news and Francis noticed Samuel staring down at the table top. 'I would like to stress two things here,' Francis continued. 'The first is obvious, in that we now only have two women to examine instead of three. This gives us more time to wear each down with our questioning. But the second thing is even more to our advantage. The ordeal the mother demanded did the very opposite of what she had hoped. It proved, without doubt, that she was a witch.'

Francis glanced round at the nodding heads and threw out his hands. 'If the mother was a witch, casting spells and cursing man, beast and every crop that grows, it stands to reason the daughters are, too.'

Sir William Pelham raised his hand requesting to speak, and Francis nodded. 'That point may well be one of the first things we should work on. Get these women to confess that they were involved in casting spells with their mother. After that, we want confessions regarding them making pacts with the Devil. A single confession to the latter will be enough for us to see them both hanged. Confessions of casting spells alone would be insufficient.'

'Indeed, Sir William,' Francis replied, 'and I'm sure the

two women will be more than aware that now their mother has been proven to be a witch, they will have little chance of proving they are not.'

Samuel Fleming raised his hand and Sir Francis nodded.

'In all the trials I attend here at the Lincoln Assizes, my main concern is for the spiritual well-being of those convicted. That does not mean I overlook the evidence for or against their alleged crime, or object to the prescribed punishment should they be found guilty. If we have valid proof of these two young women practising witchcraft – or more importantly, of them having given themselves to the Devil – then they will hang.'

Francis wondered where Samuel was leading; so far, he had said little that had not just been said by Sir William.

'Other than the women's own confessions, proof presented by others having witnessed their crimes is generally enough for us to convict them,' Samuel stressed. 'I have been given the names of two cunning women in the Vale of Belvoir who claim that Joan Flower told them of the spell she cast on your elder son, Sir Francis. And since these women, plus one other, are believed to have supplied Joan with the spell in the first place, it is likely that they are witches themselves. I suggest these three be brought to Lincoln to testify regarding that spell. They can be tried in respect of their own dealings in witchcraft at a later date.'

'Our primary task is to ensure the witches hang,' Lord Willoughby declared, his dark gaze sweeping those gathered. 'Since that cannot take place until the women have confessed to giving themselves to the Devil – *or* witnesses can verify that they have – questioning those cunning women could prove invaluable. If, for example, those women can verify that the

Flower sisters have been involved in those heinous Sabbaths, where witches gather to celebrate their wicked deeds with Satan, confessions from them would not be necessary. The law clearly states that those charged with witchcraft can still be convicted on the evidence of others.'

'So, it seems we are agreed about our ultimate goal,' Francis said, acknowledging the nodding heads. 'Then I put a few points to you regarding the organisation of our interrogations and areas I feel we should focus on. Anyone who disagrees, or has anything to add or suggest, can simply raise his hand in order to speak.

'First and foremost, we examine the sisters separately. That will give them no chance of agreeing with each other when answering questions. However, we *do* need to use the same line of questioning with each so that answers can be compared – which will require us to make a careful note of any inconsistencies in their responses. It follows that if one of them confesses to anything incriminating which the other denies, we repeat that same question to the other sister over and over until we wring the same confession from her.

'But before we delve into more searching questions relating to witchcraft and devil worship, I suggest we first ascertain the characters and lifestyles of the women. It would be useful to the judges to whom we present the findings from our interrogations. This can generally be done quickly by asking a few pertinent questions as well as by our own observations whilst they speak. I know I have no need to itemise what type of things to note to any of you, and since I already know what is said about Phillipa and Margaret Flower, I don't wish to put

Chapter Ten

ideas into your heads. Naturally, any negative points regarding their characters can be used during your later questioning.'

Matthew Butler raised his hand. 'I will add to Sir Francis's point about the repetition of questions in order to extract the required answers. We must allow neither of the accused respite from our questioning, and if we are still unsuccessful after a few days, there are methods of persuasion available to us at the castle.'

'I hope such methods will be used only as a last resort,' Samuel put in, forgetting any protocol of raised hands.

'In my experience, Rector, most criminals will admit to their sins at the mere threat of torture, or the sight of instruments used for it.' Matthew acknowledged the murmurs of agreement. 'I imagine our interrogations of the women will include the usual physical examination by a local midwife, Sir Francis?'

Francis nodded. 'The court clerk informed me that one would be available as soon as she was needed.'

Henry Hasting raised a hand. 'If teats or devil's marks are found on the women's bodies there will be no possibility of them denying they were put there by the Devil. The teats are needed in order for the woman's familiars to feed on her blood and, as we all know, familiars are the links between the witches and Satan. Physical examination is generally a painless process for the women – although there are ways of discovering for certain whether teats or other strange marks were put there by the Devil that are not so painless. It is sometimes needful to resort to those measures.'

'Being stripped naked and having a stranger conduct a search of every inch of the body is surely humiliating enough without causing great pain,' Samuel said, again forgetting to raise his hand.

Henry threw Samuel a placatory smile. 'In Lincoln, at least there is a woman to do these examinations, Rector. At some courts they are carried out by men, sometimes the interrogators themselves. As for resorting to painful measures during physical examination, we must hope we have no need for that. But if no teats or devil's marks are found on the women, we pursue our interrogations relentlessly in the hope that at least one of them will utter something incriminating that we can work on. If those methods still fail to elicit a confession, the threat of thumbscrews or even the rack, is often enough to do so.'

'I suggest we simply take things as they come,' Francis put in, 'and make our decisions regarding how to proceed accordingly. I think we're all agreed that we allow these women no respite. Our onslaught of questioning must be relentless, so that in the end the accused will be so tired they would rather confess the truth of their crimes than let the questioning continue.'

Once again, Samuel requested to speak. 'I fear that if the women are so totally exhausted, they might confess to any charge, true or false, simply to make the questioning stop.'

George Manners held out his upturned hands. 'I doubt if any sane person would confess to practising witchcraft or dealing with the Devil if they were truly innocent. Surely they would know that to do so would mean certain death?'

Samuel shook his head. 'No, my lord. Innocent or guilty, most people would confess to any crime they were charged with rather than be tortured, day after day. Death would appear as a relief from it all.'

Chapter Ten

'I agree, Matthew Butler said, 'but most witches are stubborn creatures and will not confess readily to their sins. They generally need some form of persuasion. And let's not forget, King James recommends that torture is used.'

Francis had no intention of allowing the meeting to become an argument regarding the use of torture. 'We have one final point of organisation to resolve before we all part. As interrogators we will examine the women in pairs, but since there are seven of us, I suggest that William and Matthew be the first to do so, followed by Lord Willoughby and Henry, and George, Samuel and I will be last.'

No one had objections to that, so Francis continued, 'Interrogations will begin on Monday, the twenty-second of January, so William and Matthew, you may wish to meet tomorrow in order to plan what you will focus on. I suggest you question Margaret first, the younger of the two sisters. And Samuel, I believe you wish to assess the women's state of mind before any questioning starts, so perhaps you could do that tomorrow, after you have been to church?'

'Thank you, Sir Francis, it would be most useful to me to speak with them first.'

Francis nodded. 'All interrogations will take place in the upper chamber of Cobb Hall There are no prisoners held there at present, which is fortunate.

'My friends, trials such as this are never pleasant, nor are the crimes committed easy to understand. But we must do our duty and, as our king constantly reminds us, we must try to eradicate the practising of witchcraft from our country.'

Chapter Eleven

In which the interrogation of the Flower sisters begins

Lincoln Gaol: Late January 1619

The manacle around Phillipa's left wrist had rubbed her skin almost raw but to say anything to the grubby, repulsive gaolers would only result in another slap around the head, or a kick in the belly. She struggled to stand, desperately needing to relieve herself and moved as far as the five-foot-long chain would allow to squat down to the filthy, stinking straw. During the three weeks that she and Margaret had been imprisoned in this reeking dungeon, not once had the straw been changed, nor had the mounds of human excrement beneath it been shovelled out. But Phillipa had passed the point of retching at the stench and, somehow, had become able to ignore it.

The dungeon was a putrid hole at the base of Cobb Hall, a tower that had defended the north-east corner of the castle in earlier times. The dungeon had been created by digging down, into the sloping hillside of the Lincoln Ridge. The floor above was shut off from the dungeon by a trapdoor, and descent into the cold, dark, place was by climbing down a wooden ladder. The icy, January wind whistled through the arrow slits in the narrow, end walls of a number of tapering recesses, whilst allowing little light to stream in. Phillipa glanced at her sister curled on the flea-ridden straw, three feet away from her. Margaret had long-since shrunk inside herself rather than

Chapter Eleven

acknowledge the reality of her surroundings, or the situation they found themselves in.

Several other prisoners were manacled to the walls, five men and three women. Phillipa had ceased to be embarrassed at squatting to relieve herself in view of the men within a day or two of being imprisoned, and kept her ears closed to the sexual slurs and outright assertions as to what they would do to her if they were not chained to the wall.

The sudden creaking of the opening trapdoor sent a wave of fear through her. It was not yet evening, the usual time for the gaolers to bring the watery sludge they called stew, and she wondered if she and Margaret were about to be interrogated.

One of the four, usual gaolers descended the ladder. He was a burly man with a gruff voice, who made no effort to disguise his contempt for prisoners. The fact that he was alone was enough to induce further trembling in Phillipa. There were always two of them when the scraps they called a meal were being dished out, one staying at the top to pass food to the other who balanced on the ladder.

'There's someone to see you,' he barked, stepping from the bottom rung and coming to glower at Phillipa. 'And he's insisting on coming down here, even though I told him it'd be easier for you to get up there. But he's very persistent… What's wrong with your sister?' He moved over to Margaret and shook her until she roused, mumbling under her breath.

'Can't you see what's wrong with her?' Phillipa shot at him. 'She's sick, obviously from eating the slimy rat fodder you call food!'

Phillipa's brave words came without thought and the burly

man stepped towards her, fist raised, aiming to punch her in the head – then evidently thought better of it with the trapdoor open and the person waiting to talk to her and Margaret up there.

'Get her on her feet and talking sense while I get back up, ready to help your visitor down here.'

The gaoler headed up the ladder and Phillipa explained to Margaret what he'd said. 'Why would anyone want to come down here to all this filth?' the younger woman asked, staring up at the trapdoor. 'If he wants to question us, why didn't he have us taken up there?'

Phillipa followed her sister's gaze to see the same ugly gaoler backing down the ladder, followed by another pair of legs encased in a dark cloak of some kind. She gasped as the rest of the cassock-clad visitor came into view and a small ray of hope embraced her. He turned as he stepped onto the straw from the bottom rung and Phillipa was unsurprised to see his hand move to cover his flaring nostrils as the stench assailed him.

But hope and relief at seeing a friendly face were marred by the knowledge that Samuel Fleming would not have the power to order their release, even if he wanted to.

'Has the reverend come to say prayers with us before we are hanged?'

'No, Margaret,' Phillipa replied, adamant. 'We must face interrogators and a trial to prove we are guilty before that can happen. We are not to die yet and Reverend Fleming is probably here to see how we're coping in this stinking place.'

'You can leave us,' Samuel snapped as the gaoler stood his

Chapter Eleven

ground. 'I wish only to speak with these women and nothing we say will be of interest to you. They can hardly escape with those manacles still attached to them and you on the other side of the trapdoor.'

The disgruntled gaoler slunk off and back up the ladder.

'I'll be making a formal complaint about the conditions in this dungeon,' Samuel said, taking everything in from floor to ceiling before focusing on the sisters. Phillipa could not miss the sympathy emanating from him and knew he'd be recording every detail. 'I cannot deny how shocked I am at the way you both look,' he remarked. 'They must surely feed you, and yet you are both so painfully thin. And have either of you been able to wash since you came here?'

Phillipa gave a mocking laugh. 'We haven't washed our bodies or our clothes since we left Bottesford three weeks ago, Reverend, and the only food we've been given has been mouldy or turning rotten.' She shook her head, trying to hold back her tears, but failing miserably. 'As you see, we are filthy and starving, and probably stink, too – which is difficult to tell when everything in this dark hole reeks. We sleep on this foul straw, which has mounds of human dung beneath it and rats come out at night to gnaw at any bit of flesh they can find. Is it any wonder that so many people die in here, even the innocent who are flung down here to await trial? There were three others down here until two days ago, but they were carried out with their own liquid dung covering them. Gaol fever, they call it.'

Samuel didn't answer and Phillipa could see that his anger equalled his pity. Eventually he said, 'Shall we pray together?'

'Why?' Margaret asked. 'Our mother didn't want us to go to church, or pray to the Christian God. He wouldn't be able to stop them hanging us, would he?'

'My sister's right, Reverend. No one can help us now, not even God. They will find us guilty no matter what we say.'

Samuel sighed, and Phillipa knew that, deep inside, Reverend Fleming would know that was true. 'Remember this,' he said, his sad gaze moving between the two of them, 'if you are innocent of the crimes with which you are charged, you must pray to God to give you strength to endure imprisonment in this reeking dungeon and the rigours of the coming interrogations and trial. If you are found guilty and condemned to die, you must pray sincerely to Him for forgiveness. If you truly repent your sins, the Heavenly Father will forgive you and take you into Heaven. I shall pray daily on your behalf. No one should be incarcerated in such a rank and unwholesome place as this.'

Samuel rapped on the bottom of the ladder and the gruff gaoler made his descent. 'You go up first, Reverend, then if you lose your footing, I'll be behind to steady you.'

'I'll see you again during your interrogations,' Samuel assured Phillipa and Margaret. 'I cannot yet say whether I believe you to be guilty of practising witchcraft, but I truly hope you are not. And yet, innocent children have suffered at someone's hand, and if you are guilty of such evil you will need to be sincere in your repentance if your immortal souls are to be saved.'

*

Chapter Eleven

Cobb Hall, Lincoln: January 22 – February 25 1619

Margaret realised it was morning when the blackness beyond the window slits gradually lightened to a pale shade of grey. It had been a particularly cold night and she had sat with her back against the rough stone wall for most of it, fending off the rats that had persistently tried to bite her bare legs. Margaret had been particularly angry with the creatures last night because she'd been trying to remember everything that had happened to her and Phillipa to result in their imprisonment in this stinking place. She wondered if Hell could be any worse, and whether the Devil welcomed rats into his domain.

She choked down a sob, remembering Ma's strange death, and thinking that if Pa had still been alive, he would have been ashamed to call her and Phillipa his daughters. She gasped, realising she couldn't even remember Pa's face.

The trapdoor creaking open brought all the prisoners awake and their eyes fixed on two gaolers as they climbed down the ladder. One of them came to stand before her with the usual contemptuous smirk on his face.

'Margaret Flower, on your feet. You've a treat in store for you: two nice gentlemen have come for a little chat.'

'What about me?' Phillipa said, pushing herself to her feet. 'Can't we be questioned together?'

'Your sister's got a tongue in her mouth, hasn't she?' the gaoler sneered, grabbing Margaret and forcing her mouth open. 'Looks like there's one in there to me. And you'll be expected to use it up there 'cos if you don't, those gents have plenty of clever ways of making you talk.'

Take Height, Rutterkin

He unlocked the manacle around Margaret's wrist and shoved her towards the ladder, which she obediently climbed behind one of the men whilst the one who had grabbed her took up the rear. She emerged in the upper chamber, which she had seen little of on the day they were brought here, the warmth from a few torches around the walls seeming to wrap around her stone-cold body like a blanket.

In the centre of the room, two men were sitting behind a wide table, on which were stacks of papers, a couple of inkpots and two quills in their stands. The stern demeanour and dark attire of these men, along with the small, low stool in front of their table – which she guessed was for her to sit on – left Margaret with little doubt that these were her interrogators and she focused on her surroundings to stop herself from trembling.

The chamber was similar in shape to the dungeon, although it had a stout wooden door leading out to the grassy slope down to the castle yard, and the stone-flagged floor was devoid of straw. There was also a door at either side of the room which, Margaret guessed, would lead out to the battlements at the top of the castle wall. Some of the deeper window recesses were closed off from the room by wooden doors, seemingly to create small chambers, perhaps even cells, behind. The two gaolers disappeared into one of them.

'Sit down,' one of the seated men said, pointing at the stool. Margaret obeyed, unnerved by the penetrating glare from his bulging green eyes, 'You will speak only when requested to do so. Is that understood?'

'Yes,' she replied, in barely a whisper.

'You'll have to do better than that, woman! I ask you again,

Chapter Eleven

is that understood?'

'Yes, my lord. I will speak only when told to.'

'Very well,' he went on. 'First, I will introduce my colleague and myself to you. Beside me is Mr Matthew Butler, who is a Justice of the Peace for Lincolnshire, and I am Sir William Pelham, High Sheriff of this county. You will address my colleague as Mr Butler and me as Sir William. Alternatively, you can refer to either of us as my lord. Is that clear?'

Margaret nodded, quickly adding, 'It is, Sir William,' when he scowled at her.

'State your name, age and place of abode.'

'I am Margaret Flower. I am twenty and one years and I live in Bottesford.'

She watched as they wrote those details down.

'Now Margaret,' Sir William continued, 'tell us which crimes you are charged with.'

'They say I am a witch, and that I was involved in putting a spell on Sir Francis and Lady Cecilia's young son, Henry, Lord Roos, and causing him to die. But I –'

Sir William held up the palm of his hand. 'You were not asked to express innocence or guilt regarding your crimes at this point. What other crime are you charged with?'

Margaret stared at him, uncomfortable at having to constantly look up and confused as to which crime he referred to. 'It must be that of causing the earl's youngest son, Francis, to become sick, too.'

'Are there any other crimes you have been accused of committing?' Mr Butler asked as Sir William again wrote on his paper with his quill.

Take Height, Rutterkin

'No, my lord, at least, I don't think there are.'

Mr Butler continued to stare at her and she shuffled, wanting to look away but not daring to.

'You mean you don't know of any, or you don't want to say?'

'I really don't know of any, Mr Butler,' she said, further unnerved by his strange smile and the glance he shared with Sir William.

Mr Butler leaned forward, resting his elbows on the table and steepling his fingers beneath his chin. 'Do you enjoy living in Bottesford?'

Margaret thought that a strange question. 'I like it well enough, my lord, 'but I don't know what it's like anywhere else because I've lived in Bottesford all my life.'

'And did you have plenty of friends when you were growing up?'

'I did, Mr Butler. We had a lot of fun chasing through the woods and paddling in the fords in the Devon.'

Sir William looked up from his writing. 'Do you still have a lot of friends now?'

Margaret momentarily stared down at her hands, as though examining her fingernails, then looked back at her questioner. 'Yes, I still have all my childhood friends. Few people have left the village, so sometimes we meet just to chat, or visit the market on a Friday.'

Sir William returned to his writing and Mr Butler resumed his questioning.

'How do you earn a living, Margaret?'

Again, Margaret stared down at her hands, now clasped tightly together. 'I have sometimes found work at Belvoir

Castle, cleaning and such-like, my lord. I have also helped my mother to make her cures for various ailments from the herbs in our garden.'

'Are you saying you have no regular form of employment?'

'I am, Mr Butler. Finding work in our village has not been easy.'

'Why is that?'

'I… I don't know. Perhaps there isn't enough work to go round. I did find employment in the castle laundry for a few months once, but that came to an end, too.'

Again, Sir William looked up from his papers. 'What was the reason for it ending?'

Margaret's answer did not come readily and Sir William snapped, 'Stop wasting our time, woman! It's a simple enough question and you must know why you left.'

'Because being in the heat and steam of the laundry made me ill.'

The two men shared a glance. 'Are you sure you were not dismissed?'

'I was not dismissed, Sir William, why should I be? I was good at my work but the steamy, hot air in the laundry wasn't good for my health.'

'Were your mother and sister in gainful employment at that time?'

'My sister had been given work at the castle for a few weeks and was living in the servants' quarters, and my mother was earning a little from selling the potions and herbal remedies she made. We had vegetables in our garden and hens for our eggs and sometimes meat, so Ma wouldn't have starved.'

Take Height, Rutterkin

'So, your mother wasn't angry that you just left your place of work, considering that yours was the only permanent wage coming into the house at that time?'

'She wasn't happy about it, but she said we'd manage, at least as long as Phillipa was still employed.'

'We'll come back to that point again,' Sir William said. Margaret was relieved he hadn't pursued it now and hoped he'd forget about it later.

'We are told that your mother is no longer alive and of course, your sister Phillipa is in the dungeon below, held on the same charge as you. Tell us how Joan Flower died.' Mr Butler tilted his head as he waited for her to answer.

Margaret swallowed hard. Her mother's death was too recent and too strange to talk about. 'Our mother died on the way to Lincoln.'

'Oh, and what, pray, did she die of?'

'She choked while she was eating some bread and butter.'

'How unfortunate,' Mr Butler remarked. 'Why would she be eating bread and butter when she was under arrest and on the way to Lincoln Gaol?'

'Ma swore she was innocent of practising witchcraft and making a pact with the Devil and when we reached Ancaster, she demanded a test… an ordeal… to prove it. The ordeal involved eating a small piece of bread that had been blessed by a priest.'

'Go on,' Sir William ordered. 'Tell us the rest.'

'If she had eaten the bread and lived, my lord, it would have proved she was not a witch. But she choked on it and died.'

'And what do you think that proved, Margaret?'

Chapter Eleven

'I don't know.'

Sir William's fist came down hard on the tabletop. 'Of course you know! Say it, woman!'

'It proved that she was a witch… but she wasn't.'

'Tell us which crimes your mother was charged with,' Mr Butler urged as Sir William again wrote on his papers.

'They said she cast a spell to hurt and cause the death of Henry, Lord Roos.'

'And did she?'

'No, my mother would not have done that, and nor would Phillipa and I.'

'Do you tell lies, Margaret?'

'No, my lord.'

'Isn't that answer a lie in itself?'

Margaret shook her head vehemently but Mr Butler was not placated. 'I put it to you, Margaret Flower, that you often tell lies.'

'I don't know why you should say that, when you don't know me.'

Mr Butler gave a contemptuous huff. 'Sir William and I know a lot of people who do know you, though.'

'Well, I don't know who they are, my lord, or why they should have cause to tell lies about me.'

'Tell us again why you left your employment at Belvoir Castle,' Sir William said, the contemptuous look on his face filling Margaret with unease.

'It was as I told you before, my lord… the heat and steam were not good for my health.'

Neither of the men commented, but she watched as both

wrote things down on their papers.

Sir William put down his quill. 'Explain to us how your mother, sister and you have been earning a living for the past few years.'

'We entertain people in our cottage, and they are kind enough to pay us for the drinks and food we provide.'

Sir William threw out his hands. 'Are you saying you make enough to live on by doing that? Surely, you would have to buy the food and drinks you sold, so there cannot have been much profit.'

'We made enough to get us by, my lord.'

'These guests that you "entertained", were they both men and women?'

Margaret could not hold that green gaze and stared at the floor. 'They were mostly men, if I recall.'

Sir William's scornful laugh frightened her. 'Do you deny that you ran a bawdyhouse?'

'I… I didn't run it, my mother did.'

'But you participated in the various "activities", did you not?'

'Yes.'

'Then stop lying and tell us, did all of your income come from the bawdyhouse?'

'Mostly, Sir William, although, as I said, at first, Phillipa still worked at the castle and my mother made a little from her herbal remedies, especially in the winter with so much illness about.'

'Now that's better,' Mr Butler declared. 'Why lie in the first place?'

Chapter Eleven

'I don't know, my lord. I suppose I was ashamed to admit it.'
'What else have you lied about?'
'Nothing.'
'Are you a thief, Margaret?'
'No, I am not, Mr Butler.'
'You have never stolen anything in your life?'
'No.'
'Not even from Belvoir Castle?'

Margaret shot a panicked look at Sir William, who was glaring at her again, and she realised they knew.

'Tell us again why you left your employment in the laundry at Belvoir Castle,' Mr Butler said.

'I had taken food from the castle kitchens because my mother had little money coming in at that time and I thought she'd be starving. Mistress Abbott, the housekeeper, found out and told the countess, who dismissed me.'

'Was that the only reason for your dismissal?'
'Yes, my lord,'

Sir William snapped. 'Stop playing games or I'll have you flogged for wasting our time!'

Margaret fought back the tears that threatened to flow. 'A maid found me in the earl and countess's bed with one of the other servants, a man I'd been seeing for some time. When the countess was told about it, as well as the stealing, she was very angry and told me to leave the castle, and that she would never employ me again.'

'So, we have seen that you are a liar, a thief and a strumpet, earning a living in the most disreputable of ways, and brazen enough to defile the bed of the Earl and Countess of Rutland!'

Take Height, Rutterkin

Sir William shook his head and threw out his hands. 'I put it to you, Margaret Flower, that you also lied about having friends in Bottesford. In truth, your family was abhorred, especially by the women whose husbands frequented your bawdyhouse. I believe that most people in Bottesford have suspected the three of you of practising witchcraft for some years.'

Margaret knew that to deny what Sir William said would be pointless so she said nothing.

'So,' Mr Butler said, leaving Sir William writing his notes, 'having established the fact that you are dishonest in a number of ways, how do you expect us to believe a single word you say? You have lied while answering almost every question so far.' He shook his head, and stared at her, as though deciding what to ask next. 'Do you practise witchcraft, Margaret, and have you made a pact with the Devil?'

'No! I have done neither of those things.'

'Have you indulged in sexual activity with a familiar?'

'No, I've never seen a familiar.'

'But we know that you're a born liar, so how can we believe that?' Sir William asked, looking up from his writing and glaring at her again. 'Answer Mr Butler's questions *honestly*.'

'I lied about those other things because I am frightened. I've never been questioned before. But I am not lying when I say that I am not a witch or a follower of Satan. And I don't have any familiars.'

'Then we will leave you for a short time so you can reconsider your answers. Then we will return and start all over again.

'Gaolers!' Sir William yelled. 'Take this woman back to the dungeon and bring up her sister.'

Chapter Eleven

*

The first thing that hit Phillipa as she stepped from the ladder was the warmth in the room compared to the permanently freezing cold of the dungeon. She could see no hearth, and realised that the heat must come from the torches along the walls. The second thing she noticed was that no one was sitting behind the table ahead of her and, apart from herself and the two gaolers, the room was empty. Then she noticed the filthy state of her dress, stained by the stinking, unchanged straw. At least the dimness of the dungeon had kept the full extent of her foul appearance from her.

'Sit on that stool over there,' one of the gaolers said, giving her a shove. 'The gentlemen'll be back soon, and they'll expect you to talk nicely to them.'

Phillipa did as she was told, staring up at the fine vaulted ceiling, her anger at her mother for bringing them to this mingling with her fear at what these interrogators could do to her and Margaret if they didn't get the answers they wanted. Margaret had simply dropped to the straw when they'd brought her back to the dungeon, though she didn't look to be physically hurt. She hoped they'd get a chance to talk once she was taken back to the dungeon.

Two well-dressed, haughty-looking men came though the outer door, their stern expressions matching the darkness of their clothes. They seated themselves behind the table and glowered at her, seeming unimpressed by what they saw. Phillipa glared back, refusing to be intimidated before they started.

The two men introduced themselves, and once she had stated her name, age and place of abode, Sir William picked up his quill and focused his sharp green eyes on her. 'It seems that neither you nor your sister has been able to secure permanent employment in your village. Why do you think that is?'

Phillipa wondered what her sister had said, realising that these men were aiming to compare her answers to Margaret's in order to catch them out. But the only thing she could do was give her own opinions.

'I believe it's because my mother was not liked in our village, particularly by the goodwives. Both of our parents came from families that had been in favour with the earls and countesses at Belvoir Castle for many years. Because our mother was mistress of her own house – in fact, the house was her own through inheritance – her title after her marriage was Mistress Flower, compared to the lowlier term of Goodwife Flower.'

Phillipa paused, realising she was saying a lot, but Sir William told her to continue.

'When our father died, the women took advantage of our mother's lowered status to ridicule and snub her to get their own back for the many years she had snubbed them. If Joan Flower had not still been in favour with Countess Elizabeth and Countess Cecilia after her, they may well have turned to violence some years ago. As Joan's daughters, we became targets for their envy and dislike too, and few people in the village were prepared to employ us.'

'Tell us about your experiences of working at Belvoir Castle,' Mr Butler said.

'I worked there twice, my lord. The first time I was em-

Chapter Eleven

ployed by Countess Elizabeth as an extra servant over the Christmas period.'

'When would that have been?'

'It was the Christmas after my father died in the September, so that's almost eight years ago now.'

'And the second time…?' Mr Butler persisted.

'That was a year and a half later, over the summer. Margaret was already working there, in the castle hen house and laundry, and our mother and I were taken on for a few weeks by Countess Cecilia. We would both have liked to have stayed longer, but it was not to be.'

'Why?' Sir William asked, his manner curt and to the point.

'We were called to the housekeeper's office to be told that there would only be a place for one of us from then onwards. Mistress Abbott was very pleasant about it, and said we could decide which of us would do it. It was Ma who said that I should stay on for a little longer and Mistress Abbott was relieved about that.'

'Why relieved?'

Phillipa averted her eyes and Sir William snapped. 'Well, out with it. What did Mistress Abbott dislike about your mother?'

'Oh, she liked Ma well enough, Sir William, but many of the servants at the castle did not. A lot of them came from Bottesford and they had started calling my mother a whore, and saying that she was making potions to lure the village men to her cottage. They had taken to calling her names, even in the castle, and Mistress Abbott was finding it hard to keep the peace.'

'But Margaret left her work at the castle a little before you,' Sir William persisted, his attempt at a smile more unsettling to Phillipa than his glower. 'Why would she do that, if she was enjoying the work?'

'I… I don't really know.'

'Nonsense!' Sir William exclaimed. 'You know full well why she left.'

'And I am sure she must have told you, so why are you asking me?' Phillipa instantly regretted her forthright words, but she was tired of being asked all the same kind of questions.

Sir William's fist slammed the tabletop. 'I remind you, woman, that you are here to answer every question you are asked, not pick and choose those you like best. If you speak that way again, I'll have you chained outside for the night – which will leave you desperate to get back to the dungeon – if you survive the freezing cold, that is.'

The questioning switched to Mr Butler, while Sir William continued to glare at her. 'You stopped working at the castle a short while after that, too, Phillipa. Was it your own choice to do so?'

'No, I was also dismissed. The women started picking on me and shouting at me in the corridors. Some of them even closed in on me a few times and I would have had a few beatings if Mistress Abbott hadn't come to stop them. The countess thought it best that I leave.'

'Tell us,' Mr Butler said, 'changing the subject, 'which crimes you are charged with.'

'Witchcraft… which I deny! I'm no more a witch than either of you.'

Chapter Eleven

The two interrogators stared at her, then glanced at each other, and Phillipa could see they were searching for words with which to admonish her for her audacity. But when Mr Butler resumed his questioning, he chose to overlook her reply altogether.

'Have you made a pact with the Devil?'

'No, my lord, I have not.'

'Have you ever indulged in sexual activity with a familiar?'

'Never, Mr Butler.'

'Tell us how your mother, Joan Flower, died.'

'She died in Ancaster Gaol, where we stopped for the night on the way to Lincoln. She asked to be allowed an ordeal that she believed would prove her innocent of the charge of witchcraft. She was given some consecrated bread to eat, but she choked on it, and died.'

'And what did that prove?'

'They said it proved she was a witch and had made a pact with Satan. Devil worshippers can't swallow bread that has been blessed by a priest. But my mother wasn't a –'

'Did Joan Flower have any familiars?'

'No, Mr Butler, she did not.'

'All three of you were arrested on charges of witchcraft, were you not, Phillipa?' Sir William remarked, taking his turn at the questioning.

'Yes.'

'So, what do you think your mother dying in that way tells us about you and Margaret?'

'It obviously makes you think we are also witches. But we are not!'

'Explain, then, what you have done to bring such a charge upon yourself, and precisely which deeds you are charged with.'

'I have done nothing, Sir William, but they have charged me with causing little Henry, the earl's son, to become sick and die.'

'Any other charges?'

'Francis, the younger son of Sir Francis and Lady Cecilia is also now ill, Sir William, and they believe that my mother, sister and I put a spell on him, too.'

'Are you charged with anything else?'

'No.'

'It seems you're as big a liar as your sister. But I'm sure that by the time we've finished interrogating you, we'll have the truth from you both.' Sir William continued to glare at her, and shouted, 'Gaoler, fetch in the pilniewinks.'

Phillipa knew that whatever the pilniewinks was, it would be used to cause her great pain unless she told them what they wanted to hear. She felt suddenly sick and regretted giving her brash and cocky answers.

'Fetch the instrument over here for the accused to inspect,' Sir William ordered, as one of the gaolers appeared and placed a small metal implement on the table.

'See if you can guess what our pilniewinks can do, Phillipa.'

Phillipa stared at the fairly small object, which had two horizontal metal bars with three short metal bars protruding upwards from it, the middle one having threads for a screw on it. It looked like some kind of vice, and she dared not think how these men would use it on her.

Chapter Eleven

'Look carefully, Phillipa,' Sir William urged. 'See how the top bar moves up and down, so that if anything is placed in here,' he added, pointing at the space between the two horizontal bars, 'we could turn this screw to move the top bar down, crushing whatever had been placed in there very badly indeed.'

Phillipa knew they were wanting to see her reaction. But she just stared at the device and said nothing, though her heart pounded so fast and loud, she feared they might hear it.

'If I tell you another name for our pilniewinks, you'll know exactly what we use it for.' Mr Butler waited until she looked at him. 'We call it the thumbscrew, and it is exceedingly good at crushing either thumbs or toes so they will never be of use again. And, I forgot to add, our little pilniewinks is also very clever at making people scream.'

'Now, Phillipa,' Sir William said with that sickening smirk again, 'you seem to be a much more intelligent and sensible young woman than your sister, and we know you can give us the answers we want. We have no need to introduce you properly to the pilniewinks today, but before you return to your comfortable straw, we have just a few more questions to put to you.'

Mr Butler looked up from his papers. 'Are you a thief, like your sister?'

'I am not, Mr Butler,' she said, making sure her manner was a little more civil than it had been earlier. 'I have never stolen anything in my life.'

Mr Butler nodded and went on, 'Are you a liar?'

'I don't often lie. If I don't give you the answer you want, it doesn't necessarily mean I'm lying.' She shrugged. 'But no doubt you'll make your own minds up whether I am or not.'

'Do you admit to being a lewd strumpet and having indulged in a life of wantonness and sin?'

'I imagine you know about our bawdyhouse, so I can hardly deny that I have become a strumpet, yet only as a means of earning money to keep us alive. But I have never knowingly committed a sin against, or hurt, another person.'

Neither man commented on her answers and Mr Butler continued, 'Have you put a spell on Thomas Simpson in order to keep him coming back to you for sexual pleasure?'

'He thinks I have, but I wouldn't know how –'

'Do you confess to practising witchcraft and having made a pact with the Devil?'

'I deny both of those allegations. They were made up by Bottesford villagers because they hate our family.'

'And yet, the charges of causing the illness and subsequent death of Henry Manners and the ongoing illness of young Francis Manners, were not made by villagers, were they?' Sir William's voice was sharp and hostile compared to Mr Butler's and Phillipa could not help smiling, just to annoy him even more.

'No, they were not, Sir William.'

'So, are you calling the Earl and Countess of Rutland liars, too?'

'They are not liars, but they have been led to believe we are responsible for those things by the malicious gossip of the village women who work at the castle. It is Bottesford folk who put those ideas in their heads. It is they who are –'

Chapter Eleven

Sir William's raised hand halted the rest of her reply. 'Believe me, Phillipa Flower, your answers are not convincing and next time we see you we'll expect you to be more truthful.

'Gaoler,' he called, 'take this woman back to the dungeon and ensure that she and her sister are chained in recesses some distance apart.' He focused on Phillipa. 'That way, you can, individually, consider the questions you have been asked today and how you will respond to them the next time we meet.'

Chapter Twelve

In which interrogations continue

Lincoln: Lincolnshire: Late January 1619

After enjoying a meal together in the inn room below, Sir Francis Manners glanced at the men seated around the table sipping their port in his room at the White Hart. It was time to get down to business. 'As you all know,' he said, 'I've called us together to enable William and Matthew to share their initial thoughts on the Flower sisters. Hopefully, their doing so will give us a better idea of how to proceed and the best way in which we could elicit confessions from both women.'

'Sir William and I agree that we are dealing with two very different characters here,' Matthew Butler started. 'The younger sister, Margaret, is the weaker of the two, and will be the easier to crush. She does not stand up well to questioning and would be quickly reduced to tears. She also seems to be a compulsive liar, which is something we should continue to work on.'

Sir William nodded. 'Margaret doesn't have sufficient fortitude to withstand constant interrogation. I suggest that after several hours of questioning again tomorrow, if she still hasn't confessed, we should inflict a night of sleep deprivation on her before we resume interrogations. Margaret's lies may catch her out when she's exhausted, so we must be alert for any differences in her answers, no matter how slight.'

Chapter Twelve

'And Phillipa?' Francis asked. 'In what ways is she different to Margaret?'

'She is bold and brazen, and not easily cowed by sharp words or even threats,' Matthew continued. 'She has a better command of words than her sister and some of her replies are insolent in the extreme. Phillipa has a degree of self-confidence I have rarely seen in women of her class, especially one charged with witchcraft and facing likely death. Would you agree, William?'

'I would, and I will add that Phillipa Flower has a way of staring into a person's eyes with a certain look – almost as though she is trying to bend them to her will. It can be quite disconcerting.'

Francis grunted. 'I know someone else known for doing the same.'

'I admit, I have cultivated my own stare over the years, Francis, and it has generally had the desired effect on criminals I interview. But with Phillipa, it was useless. She simply stared back at me, defiance radiating from her. She even had the temerity to smile at me on one occasion. I have to admit, it is Phillipa I will take the greater pleasure in breaking.'

Samuel Fleming raised his hand, requesting to speak. 'Mr Butler, you mentioned that Phillipa was not easily cowed, even by threats. Might I ask, in which way you threatened her?'

'It was I who threatened her, Reverend. I said we'd use the pilniewinks on her if she continued to be stubborn.' Sir William paused, glancing round at the interested faces. 'I asked one of the gaolers to bring one into the room so she could inspect it but she just stared at it impassively as Matthew and I explained how it worked.'

'And do you intend to use this instrument soon?'

'No, Francis. We want to wear the women down with interrogation first, and we have other methods of persuasion to try before we get to instruments of torture. I admit, I allowed the woman's arrogance to annoy me, and saw the pilniewinks as a way of bringing her down a peg or two.'

Francis nodded. 'What I suggest is that we deal with Margaret first, and leave Phillipa in the dungeon until we get something useful – preferably a confession of witchcraft – from Margaret. That way, we'll have a head start on Phillipa and she'll find it hard to deny the charges once her sister has admitted them.'

He noted the murmurs of agreement and continued, 'Tomorrow, I'd like Sir William and Matthew to interrogate Margaret again. Start in the morning and continue throughout the day, with just a short break to enable the two of you to find refreshment. Margaret will be given nothing to eat but she must be permitted water. Then, arrange with two of the gaolers to ensure she is subjected to a night of sleep deprivation. Offer the men extra coin for this, as they will be losing sleep, too – although they will probably swap rotas with fellow gaolers in order to catch up on sleep the next day.

'I'm sure the gaolers need no explanation of how to carry this out, but you could remind them that the prisoner must be walked around the room at the merest sign of falling asleep. I want Margaret to be exhausted and hungry when she is questioned the following day. As William suggested, over-tiredness dims the mind, especially when combined with hunger, and I'm hoping she will say something she has so far concealed.'

Chapter Twelve

'Do we still pursue the night-time plans if she admits to casting spells or anything else connected to witchcraft during tomorrow's interrogation?'

'I see no reason not to, Matthew. Once something has been confessed, even if it's to making a pact with the Devil – which will be enough for us to hang her – further questioning may result in confessions of Phillipa's involvement in witchcraft, or even those three cunning women.'

Francis fixed his steady brown gaze on Samuel. 'I forgot to mention that men have been sent to bring those three women here. It will take some days, since they will need to ride out to Stathern and Goadby as well as Bottesford. But we need to question the women about the information they gave relating to Joan Flower casting spells. Hopefully, they'll also tell us of Margaret and Phillipa's participation in them, and of the sisters being Devil worshippers.'

'They will also be required to give evidence at the trial, won't they?'

'Probably, Samuel, but that will depend on the judges. And once the sisters have been hanged, the three women will, doubtless, be interrogated regarding their own dealings in witchcraft. They're likely to be sent to the gaol at Leicester for that, of course, since Bottesford and the surrounding villages are in Leicestershire, whereas Belvoir Castle is in Lincolnshire…

'So, tomorrow night, perhaps we could dine together at the White Hart again?'

Everyone agreed they'd be pleased to do that. 'We'll only need to meet in this room to talk if William and Matthew feel there have been any developments,' Francis added. 'I'm inclined to think we'll have more to discuss after Margaret's sleepless night and another day of questioning, although the woman might turn out to be stronger than we've given her credit for. I'm hoping we'll only need to use more painful forms of torture as a threat to the women. But it will be necessary to do so if they resist gentler forms of persuasion for too long.

'Lord Willoughby and Henry, you will be interrogating the day after tomorrow. I trust that is still agreeable to you?'

Both men affirmed that it was and Francis ended the meeting. All except Samuel Fleming left to return to their respective lodgings. Francis smiled at his old friend. 'You look worried, Samuel. Have I said something you don't agree with?' He pointed to two fireside chairs. 'Sit with me awhile so we can talk.'

'It isn't anything you have said,' Samuel assured him, once they were comfortably seated and Francis had poured them each another glass of port. 'I simply wanted to stress how disgraceful conditions are in that dungeon. It is truly filthy, and not fit for humans to be confined in, especially considering that some of them have not yet been proven guilty. There are multitudes of rats down there, and Phillipa and Margaret are both wretchedly grimy. Prisoners must relieve themselves on the same straw on which they sleep and the stench of it turns the stomach. I doubt if any of them get much sleep with the rats and fleas constantly biting. So, I wondered at the need to walk the sisters all night to keep them awake…

'No, my friend,' Samuel said, as Francis bristled, ready to defend his decision, 'I am as keen as you are to find the truth behind the tragedies that have befallen your family. I agree that

Chapter Twelve

if Phillipa and Margaret are guilty, they must hang. But, as yet, we cannot say with any certainty that they were involved in casting of spells. If they are, I sincerely hope they confess before we need to resort to torture.'

Samuel heaved a heartfelt sigh. 'But I wondered whether at some stage – possibly after the trial is over – you could use your influence to ensure that in future years, prisoners are confined in a cleaner and more wholesome place. The dungeon in Cobb Hall is fit only for rats, and many prisoners die of disease and sickness whilst awaiting trial. The stench alone is enough to make anyone vomit.'

'Dear Samuel, I fully agree with you. I have never been into the dungeon but over the past few years, I have heard some of my colleagues condemning the place, just as you have done. I can tell you that plans have already been drawn up to build a new gaol in the castle yard, close to the east gate. The old gaol is small and over a hundred years old, and conditions in there are bad enough, so I can readily believe how foul the dungeon in Cobb Hall is. As you know, it is only used to house the very worst criminals – cut-throats, deserters, and of course those accused of witchcraft. But if conditions are as foul as you say, even they deserve to be held in less disease-inducing conditions. Once the old gaol is pulled down and the new one built in its place, the dungeon in Cobb Hall will be cleaned out and used as a store room for the castle.'

Francis held out his hands. 'How soon they will make a start on the new gaol, I don't know. It could well not be for some years yet. Things won't change for Phillipa and Margaret, but perhaps it will ease your mind to know that, eventually, conditions of confinement will be greatly improved for both those awaiting trial and those convicted.'

'It will, Francis. Thank you for telling me.'

*

Margaret had just finished relieving herself when the trapdoor opened. As two of the gaolers came down the ladder, she wondered what they could want at this early hour. It still wasn't fully light outside, although she had lain awake for what seemed like hours, fending off the rats again. She fervently hoped that the gaolers had not come for her.

'Margaret Flower, yer wanted upstairs,' one of them said, his voice close to her ear as he unlocked the manacle. 'Those important gentlemen you saw yesterday are waiting, so get a move on.'

Margaret's heart pounded and she dreaded being questioned again. They'd already branded her a liar and she knew they wouldn't be pleased if she continued to lie. Yet how could she confess to being a witch when she knew she wasn't one? To deny that charge was not a lie.

'Sit down,' Sir William said as she entered the room, and waited until she had complied. 'You have a long day ahead of you. Yesterday you gave us several answers that simply were not true. You know it and we know it. Today, you will think carefully before you reply, and make sure it's the truth. Do you understand?'

His eyes were boring into her and Margaret could not help averting her gaze.

Chapter Twelve

'I am speaking to you, woman, so do me the courtesy of looking at me!'

'I understand what you said to me well enough,' Margaret replied, forcing herself to meet his eyes. 'You said you want me to tell the truth.'

'Then we'll begin. Mr Butler…?'

'Thank you, Sir William. First of all, Margaret, let us remind ourselves of the things you lied about yesterday. If I miss anything out, I'm sure either you or Sir William will be able to remind me. We'll look briefly at the smaller lies first, those that, added together, prove you to be an habitual liar.

Mr Butler glanced down at his papers. 'Ah, yes, as I recall, the first lie was that you still have many friends in Bottesford, when in fact you have none.'

'But it is true that I had plenty of friends until a few years ago. They just deserted me in recent years.'

'Why was that?

'Because of the tales of our mother's whoring at first, when she was only seeing one man! Later on, things got worse when word of the bawdyhouse got round. Their parents would not allow them to be my friend.'

'Remind us of the reason fellow villagers avoided you even more so in recent years, if you would.'

Margaret knew they would know if she was lying and took a breath. 'Bottesford people had come to believe our mother was a witch. They said she put curses on them to cause them hardships, like their crops failing, their animals dying or even their milk turning sour. They also said she cast spells, one of them being to keep all the men coming to the bawdyhouse.

But none of it was true!'

'I see,' Sir William put in, an expression close to a smirk on his face, as he made a note of her reply. 'We'll come back to that later.'

Mr Butler nodded and went on, 'You told us that you and your sister were unable to find employment in Bottesford because there was not enough work to go round. Are you still claiming that to be true?'

'It is partly true, my lord. There is some work to be found in Bottesford, but no one would employ me and Phillipa. At first it was because of their dislike of our mother, but when we opened the bawdyhouse none of the women would even look at us and the men wouldn't employ us because of their wives.'

'Now we come to one of your bigger lies,' Mr Butler said, rummaging through his papers. 'You lied about why you left employment in the laundry at Belvoir Castle, but then we learned of your dismissal due to the theft of food and also for sullying the earl and countess's bed.'

'I lied because I was ashamed of what I'd done, just as I was ashamed to admit that we ran a bawdyhouse.'

Sir William ceased writing his notes and stared at her again. 'Tell us, honestly, how your mother felt about you being dismissed from your work at the castle. I can hardly believe she didn't mind when the only other sources of income at that time were the payments received from your bawdyhouse and from the sale of her herbal remedies and potions.'

Margaret examined her fingers again, but realised she would have to answer truthfully. 'She was angry, my lord, but there was nothing she could do about it. Besides, Phillipa was not dismissed because of me, so there was still her wage coming in every week.'

'Ah, yes. Phillipa did not sink as low as you and steal from her employer or defile her bed.' Sir William's voice was filled with contempt and Margaret shrank further into her shell. 'Your sister was also more honest in her replies than you. She admitted that her place at the castle came to an end a short while later. Why was that?'

Margaret bit her bottom lip, reluctant to say what they wanted to hear, but not seeing any alternative. 'The countess dismissed my sister because of the gossip around the castle about our mother.'

'Which was…?'

'The women were calling our mother a whore and a witch, as I said before. But they were taking their hatred of Ma out on Phillipa, and shouting at her and threatening her in the castle corridors. They would have attacked her a few times if the housekeeper, Mistress Abbott, hadn't stopped them.'

'How did your mother feel about both of you being dismissed from service at Belvoir?'

'She was very angry, Sir William. In fact, I'd never seen her as angry as she was on that day in all my life.'

Mr Butler replaced his quill in its stand and focused on her. 'Tell us exactly what your mother said on that day.'

Margaret stared at him and swallowed hard, knowing a truthful answer to this question would be damning to Joan Flower. But Joan was dead, and it wasn't her or Phillipa who had said those words.

'Well, out with it,' Mr Butler snapped. 'What did your mother say?'

'She... she said she would get revenge on the Manners family if it was the last thing she did.'

'Ah, now we're getting somewhere.' Mr Butler almost purred his satisfaction at her answer. 'Now, tell us exactly how your mother went about getting her revenge.'

'She did nothing, my lord. Ma said those words in anger, but she didn't really mean them. She knew how kind Lady Cecilia had been to have found work for us in the first place. Besides, what could a single woman have done to hurt such a powerful family as the Manners?'

'Damn it, woman!' Sir William slapped his hand on the table. 'That is what *you* are going to tell *us*. We all know what she did, but we want to hear you saying it.'

'I can't remember her doing anything. It was five years ago when me and Phillipa were dismissed from Belvoir Castle. That's a long time.'

'You have already admitted to hearing your mother threatening to wreak her revenge, so if you can remember that much, do you expect us to believe you don't recall whether or not she did anything about it?'

Margaret sat there, staring at the stone floor. 'She did nothing, my lord.'

'Did your mother have any familiars?'

'I never saw any, if she did.'

Sir William let out an exasperated sigh and the two interrogators moved a short way from their table to whisper together. Margaret waited trying to control the sensation of sickness

Chapter Twelve

welling up in her stomach. Absently, she wondered how that could be when she had eaten nothing since the bowl of thin soup the previous morning.

'Look at me, Margaret,' Mr Butler said once both men were re-seated. 'We are going to ask you some very important questions before we draw this session to a close.' Margaret confirmed she understood. 'How we continue our questioning later will depend on your answers now. Do you understand that?'

'I understand.'

'Good. I shall ask some of the questions and Sir William will ask the others. So, my first question is simple: do you admit that in her anger and need for revenge, Joan Flower cast a spell to cause the illness and subsequent death of Henry, Lord Roos, and that you and Phillipa assisted in that spell?'

'No, Mr Butler, that isn't true,' Margaret replied, as calmly as she could. 'As I told you, our mother performed no spells, so how could my sister and I have taken part in them?'

'Did you and your sister take part in three other spells with your mother that were also cast to harm the Manners family?'

'No, my lord, there were no spells cast by any of us.'

Both men noted her responses in their papers, then Sir William asked, 'Do you confess to being a witch and giving yourself to the Devil?'

'I am no witch, and I have never given myself to the Devil! I would never do either of those things.'

Sir William heaved an irritated sigh. 'Very well, it's been a long morning, and Mr Butler and I are in need of refreshment. We will leave you now for a couple of hours or so, during which time you will have a mug of water before being taken back to the dungeon in order to relieve yourself. Then the gaolers will ensure you stand on that stool until we return.

'Be assured, Margaret Flower, we will require more answers when we do.'

*

In her queasy and weakened state, Margaret's time on the stool was agony. Several times she lost her balance on the narrow seat and would have toppled off had not one of the gaolers steadied her. The two hours seemed to go on forever until, eventually, her two inquisitors returned.

'You can get down now,' Mr Butler said, as the cold January air swept in from the castle yard. He pushed the door closed and the two men took their usual seats, placing the papers they had taken with them back on the tabletop.

As Margaret stepped down, her aching legs gave way and she tumbled, cracking her right knee as she landed on the hard, stone floor. On the verge of tears, she rubbed her knee to alleviate the pains shooting down her leg.

'Pick yourself up and sit down,' Sir William's voice rang in her ears. Margaret did as she was told, the smell of strong wine emanating from the two of them adding to her constant nausea. 'So, we'll repeat some of the questions to which the answers you gave this morning seemed a little vague. If you cannot make them more convincing, I'm afraid you will find that today will become never-ending. You see, Margaret, we must be able to make better sense of your answers for our colleagues' sake.

'Mr Butler, I believe you will ask the first question…'

Chapter Thirteen

In which the interrogators target Margaret

Belvoir Castle, Lincolnshire: January 23 1619

Lady Celia Manners had been in a state of constant agitation since her husband left Belvoir for Lincoln in the second week of January. Having no intention of constantly pestering him whilst he was involved in the interrogation and trial of the Flower women, all she could do was wait. The declining health of their only surviving son added to her anxiety, and she clung to the hope that once all three witches were dead, little Francis would recover.

So she was particularly pleased when George Villiers arrived. Having someone to converse with other than sixteen-year-old Katherine, who made no effort to disguise her resentment of her stepmother, the days wouldn't seem quite so long.

'It is my pleasure to be here with you and Lady Katherine,' Sir George replied in response to Cecilia's remark regarding how much Katherine looked forward to his visits. 'If you will permit me, I will stay for a few days. I have no pressing engagements for the next week and the king is not expecting me back in London until after Candlemas. He has graciously permitted me this time away from Court in order to deal with legal affairs involving our hall and lands. If I can brighten your days just a little while the earl is away, I will consider my stay here a success. I cannot deny I am also looking forward to seeing your little son again. The last time I saw him he seemed much improved.'

Celia shuffled a little in her fireside chair in the morning room and heaved a sigh. 'Yes, that is the way this illness seems to be. Sometimes we build up such hopes of Francis recovering, as he does from time to time but, unfortunately, he has taken a turn for the worse this past week and looks as though he's wasting away. Perhaps seeing you again will help to boost his spirits a little. I try to sit with him as often as I can and read to him or tell him stories, but he falls asleep so often. It's as though he hasn't the strength to keep himself awake. Each time the illness overwhelms him, all we can do is pray for his recovery.'

'Francis is asking for you now, Cecilia,' Katherine said, coming into the room and flashing a smile at Sir George without looking at her stepmother. She perched on a small, two-seater settee close to the fireside chairs and straightened her elegant silk skirts. 'It's almost his lunch time and I imagine his nurse would be glad of some assistance.'

As always when her stepdaughter spoke to her, a wave of anger washed over Cecilia. In the last few years, Katherine had started addressing her by her Christian name rather than as Mother, and her tone was decidedly frosty. No doubt the girl missed her father when he was away, but her increased hostility towards her stepmother during those times was inexcusable. It particularly embarrassed Cecilia when Katherine openly flaunted her animosity in front of guests.

'Why don't I pay a visit to little Francis, Lady Cecilia?' George offered. 'You said he's always pleased to see me and

Chapter Thirteen

I'd be happy to help with his lunch and have a chat with him for a while.'

'He asked for Cecilia,' Katherine said, pouting, 'so I think she ought to go.'

'Lady Katherine, I think Lady Cecilia deserves a little break from her duties now and then, don't you? And since I am here to be of assistance at this difficult time for your family, I would gladly sit with your little brother.'

'He's my *half*-brother, Sir George, and I'm glad he likes you because he certainly doesn't like me.'

Cecilia inwardly fumed. 'Perhaps if you were nicer to him, he would do.'

'Lady Cecilia is right, Lady Katherine, so why don't you come with me to the nursery and we will talk to little Francis together?' George gave Cecilia a questioning glance. 'Would that be acceptable to you, Lady Cecilia?'

'I see no reason to object,' she replied. 'But I must insist that you just call me Cecilia and my stepdaughter, Katherine. After all, now that you're a marquess, you are of higher rank than Francis, so I'm sure you can dispense with our titles.'

George flashed a wide smile and rose to his feet, and Cecilia couldn't help thinking how dashing he was. It was easy to see why he was King James's favourite. She also thought he would make a most agreeable husband for Katherine, if not for his Protestant faith. 'If you are both happy to visit Francis, it would give me a little time to see our cook about lunch today, and have a quick word with Mistress Abbott about the housekeeping.'

'Thank you,' Katherine said, standing beside George. 'I'd be happy to accompany Sir George to see little Francis.'

Cobb Hall, Lincoln Castle: January 24 1619

At precisely nine o'clock on the day following Margaret's last interrogation with Sir William and Mr Butler, she was brought to stand before her inquisitors again. Having been permitted no sleep the previous night, her eyes were hot and gritty and she was desperately in need of rest. The fact that she'd had nothing other than sips of water for the past two days added to the extreme weariness and ongoing nausea she felt.

This very room had been her prison, in which she had stood through the long, dark hours of night, trying to fight off her rising fatigue. Three times she had felt her eyelids closing and each time she had been walked around the room for an hour by two gaolers grasping her arms. Oftentimes she thought of Phillipa, and wondered what was happening to her – or were their interrogators leaving her sister alone until they had finished with her?

Now she stood before their table again, but today, two different men entered the room and seated themselves behind the table. In her exhausted state she looked round for the stool, realising she hadn't seen it all night, and feeling the glares of the two men boring into her.

'You will stand for this interrogation,' one of the men snapped at her. He was thickset and dark-headed, and Margaret stared at him as he tweaked his dark beard, hoping she had misheard what he'd just said.

'I only want to know where the stool is, so I can sit down,'

Chapter Thirteen

she said, gasping as he rose to his feet and loomed over her like a giant.

'Are you deaf, Margaret Flower?'

'No, sir.'

'Well hear this. For this interrogation you will stand.'

Margaret hung her head, close to tears before the questions started. But the tall man sat down, and like Sir William and Mr Butler had done, the two of them rustled through their papers as though they were deliberately keeping her waiting.

'Now, Margaret,' the same man went on, 'I am Lord Willoughby, Deputy Lieutenant of Lincolnshire, so I work very closely with Sir Francis Manners, whose family you have grievously harmed with your witchcraft.'

'No, that isn't true! I played no part in any witchcraft.'

Lord Willoughby surged to his feet again, enraged. 'If you speak out of turn like that again, you'll be flogged! Is that clear?'

'Yes, my lord. It is clear.'

'I was about to introduce my colleague when you so rudely interrupted,' he said, sinking to his seat. 'Beside me is Mr Henry Hastings, Sheriff of Leicester. Mr Hastings has had many years' experience in interviewing witches, and you can take my word that he will see straight through your lies.'

Margaret considered Mr Hastings, seeing an ageing, white-headed man, whose stern features and stiff demeanour sent a shiver down her spine. These two men seemed even less likely to treat her kindly than Sir William and Mr Butler, and she knew they would go over the same questions again and again until she was ready to collapse – or had confessed to dealing in witchcraft. But from somewhere deep inside she drew courage, and swore to herself she would never confess to being a witch. After all, it was the truth.

The rest of the day followed the same pattern as the previous one. Margaret was made to stand on the stool for two hours again while the interrogators retreated for food and drink, and the morning's questions were repeated in the afternoon. Mr Hastings, in particular, focused on spells that she was accused of casting while Lord Willoughby constantly reminded her of the various lies she had told and his inability to believe a word she said. By the time the late January daylight was fading, Margaret knew they had drawn no more from her than Sir William and Matthew Butler had done yesterday.

But she was horrified to learn she was to spend another long night deprived of sleep and food and, deep down, she knew that tomorrow would be even more gruelling than it had been today.

*

In the reeking dungeon, Phillipa had also been denied food for two days, though no one had questioned her at all. From where she was chained, she could see the ladder and trapdoor, so she knew that Margaret hadn't returned, other than being brought down to relieve herself two days ago. By now, Phillipa was becoming frantic to know what was happening to her sister.

'That'd be tellin' now, wouldn't it?' The gaoler she had come to know as Harry reacted to her question by shoving her back, down to the straw, and turned to walk away, chuckling to himself.

Chapter Thirteen

'At least tell me if she's still alive,' she pleaded to Harry's back, heaving herself up to her feet again.

He turned round and grinned. 'She's alive all right, but not feelin' at 'er best, shall we say? But I tell you this, she looks better today than she'll look in a couple of days. Them interrogators 'ave got some nasty surprises waiting for 'er if she doesn't cough up what they want to know. Then, Phillipa Flower, it'll be your turn.'

Phillipa's heart pounded as fear threatened to overwhelm her. She could be brave when simply being questioned, no matter how intimidating the inquisitors were, but torture was a different matter. Visions of the pilniewinks flashed into her head and she retched, though there was no food to be spewed from her empty stomach. She thought of her mother's dreams and could see how real they were. Phillipa didn't understand how her mother's dreams could have been so... so prophetic. But the fact that she'd had the dreams at all made sense of her desperate fear of being taken to Lincoln Gaol.

This place was a hell-hole, if ever there was one.

*

Cobb Hall, Lincoln Castle: January 25 1619

The long night was even harder to bear than the previous one for Margaret and she was finding it difficult to keep her eyes open and her legs from collapsing beneath her. She lost count of the number of times she was walked around the floor of Cobb Hall and, on this occasion, she was not even permitted outside to relieve herself at the side of the building. She had no other choice than to pass water where she stood, soaking her skirts in the process.

'This is nothing compared to what you'll get t'morra if you don't tell them interrogators what they want to know,' the gaoler called Harry said as he and another forced her to walk faster round the room. 'They all spew out the truth, as well as their guts, once the tortures get nasty. It's always best to confess before they start with their instruments. The screamin' does our 'eads in, don't it, Jack?'

'Aye, especially once the pilniewinks come out, or the caspie-claws. They'll mebbe let you have a peek at them tomorrow, so you know what you've got to look forward to. Then there's always the iron spider. Now that's summat that makes all the women scream when they're told what it's used for, don't it, Harry?'

Harry nodded. 'As I said, it's always best t' talk before they start with these devices. Yer'll talk in the end, anyway, so yer might as well save yerself some nasty pain.'

*

When morning came and Margaret was thrust before Lord Willoughby and Mr Hastings, the absence of the stool made her fall to her knees and beg to be permitted to sit – only to be yanked up again by the gaolers.

'You look a little weary, Margaret,' Mr Hastings said, his silky voice full of contempt. 'But if you wish this interview to be over quickly, all you have to do is tell the truth.'

Chapter Thirteen

He focused on the gaolers. 'Has this woman had water to drink this morning?'

'No, Mr Hastings. We did as we were instructed.'

'Very well, you may go, but remind whoever is on duty now to be alert for our call. We may wish to use the caspie-claws if this woman refuses to co-operate.'

'Now, Margaret, answer these questions truthfully.' Margaret nodded, wondering what the caspie-claws was as her eyelids threatened to close. 'If you fall asleep where you stand, you will drop to the floor, and we'll be forced to throw that bucket of water over you.' He tilted his head to indicate a wooden pail standing against a far wall. 'I'd try to stay awake if I were you.

'Shall we continue?' Margaret nodded. 'You are charged with being a witch and giving your soul to the Devil. Is that charge true?'

'No, Mr Hastings.'

'Have you had sexual intercourse with one or more familiars?'

'I don't have any familiars.'

'Did you take part in casting spells with your mother in order to cause the illness and death of Henry Manners and the ongoing sickness of young Francis Manners?'

'I did not, Mr Hastings.

'Did you take part in casting a spell to render the Earl and Countess of Rutland unable to have more children?'

'I don't know any spells and wouldn't know how to cast them.'

'That is not what I asked!'

Mr Hastings' raised voice made Margaret gasp and she

covered her face with her hands, knowing they would keep up their onslaught of questions until she admitted she was guilty of something.

'Margaret,' Lord Willoughby said, his voice calm and soothing, 'look at me.' She dragged her hands down her face and stared at him. 'Now, Mr Hastings seems to have said something you feel guilty about so I suggest you share it with us.'

'I am not guilty of anything, so I have nothing to share.'

'But you are guilty of lying, aren't you, Margaret, so how can we believe what you have said today?'

'Because today I have told the truth.'

Mr Hastings shook his head, tutting. 'I'm afraid Lord Willoughby and I aren't convinced you have, so we are forced to start again at the beginning.'

The same questions were thrown at Margaret again and again, and she repeatedly denied everything. At midday the two interrogators left to find refreshments and to rest before continuing, leaving strict orders with the gaolers to ensure the accused had no chance to sit down or sleep. For the first hour she was forced to stand on the stool again, and repeatedly fell off as her eyelids drooped. For the second hour she was walked around the castle yard, wearing only the thin woollen dress she had come here in against the biting January wind.

When the afternoon session started, her teeth were chattering and she felt as though she would pass out at any moment.

Lord Willoughby opened the questioning. 'Tell us what we want to know, Margaret, and you'll be taken back to the dungeon where, at least, you can have something to eat and be able to sleep.'

Chapter Thirteen

'I don't know what else you want me to tell you when I've already told you all I know.'

'Tell us first about the spells in which you participated with your mother and sister.'

'I told you, I didn't take part in any spells.'

'But we know that's a lie.' Lord Willoughby heaved an exasperated sigh. 'All three of you were involved in those spells, and we have witnesses who will testify that your mother told them all about what you did.'

Margaret was too woozy to fully understand what he'd said, but she picked up on one word. 'Witnesses…? What witnesses?'

'That's what I said, and these witnesses will be in Lincoln any day now, and will be questioned about what Joan Flower told them.'

'You mean those three cunning women? They'd admit to anything to take the blame away from themselves.'

'What could we blame them for, Margaret?' Mr Hastings asked, leaning forward against the table, eager to hear her answer.

In her state of exhaustion, Margaret replied, 'They wouldn't want you to know it was them who gave our mother the spells in the first place.'

She watched the two inquisitors share a smirk and suddenly realised what she'd said. 'But Ma didn't want their stupid spells. They're just saying she did so that you wouldn't accuse them of casting the spell themselves.'

'Come now, Margaret,' Lord Willoughby soothed. 'Those women had no motive for wanting to harm any of the earl's family, whereas – as you told us yourself – Joan Flower did.

267

Take Height, Rutterkin

She would do anything to get revenge on the Manners family for dismissing both of her daughters from their service.'

'But I told you, Ma did nothing! She always said things she didn't mean when she was angry.'

'That may well be,' Lord Willoughby agreed, 'but on this occasion your mother *did* act, by casting spells that she was given by the cunning women she associated with.'

'Tell us what part you played in those spells.' Mr Hastings was watching her intently and she knew she would have to admit to something, just so they'd let her sleep.

'I watched as my mother cast a spell to do some hurt to little Henry Manners. I didn't want to be involved with it, but she insisted.'

'Go on,' Lord Willoughby urged. 'Describe how the spell was performed and how Joan Flower intended Henry to be hurt.'

Margaret's eyelids constantly drooped as she spoke. 'My mother used an old glove of little Henry's. She put it into a bowl of boiling water and kept stabbing it with her knife. Then she chanted a rhyme about bringing hurt to the child before burying the glove in the garden beneath the willow tree. But Ma said it wasn't a real spell and she only did it to help her feel as though she'd really taken revenge on the family.'

'You have omitted to explain what your mother meant by "doing some hurt" to the child.' Lord Willoughby's eyebrows rose in anticipation of an answer.

'Ma thought that if the spell worked at all, it would just cause Henry to fall sick for a while then he would get better. She never intended his death, I swear it.'

Chapter Thirteen

The two men whispered together for some minutes, and Mr Hastings said, 'By saying that your mother used an item of clothing to bewitch the child, you are, in fact, confessing that she practised maleficent witchcraft.'

'I don't know what it's called, but she did use a glove.'

'Do you still claim that this was the only spell your mother cast?'

'As far as I know, it was, Mr Hastings.'

'And it was just you watching it?'

'Yes.'

'Where was your sister while this was going on in your cottage?'

'Out, as she often was, with Tom Simpson, most like.'

After more whispering, Lord Willoughby looked at Margaret and shook his head. 'We're agreed that you have told us very little of what you know of this whole sordid affair. You have, at least, confessed to us that Joan Flower cast one spell, and claim that you merely watched because she insisted. So, I'll ask you again, have you ever taken part in witchcraft?'

'No, I only watched – and that was because my mother made me.'

'Was your mother a witch?'

'No, Lord Willoughby. As I told you, she cast the spell believing it wouldn't work.'

'But the spell came from the cunning women who believed it did work.'

'Only for those who were real witches, which my mother was not.'

'And yet, she died after eating consecrated bread, as only a person who had sold their soul to the Devil would do. Have you sold your soul to the Devil, Margaret?'

'No, I have not, and I know my mother hadn't done either.'

'And you deny having a familiar to act as a link between you and Satan?'

'Yes.'

Mr Hastings shook his head. 'You are still not being honest with us. We believe you are as much a witch as your mother; you have made a pact with the Devil and have at least one or more familiars. Gaoler!' he yelled and waited for one to make an appearance. 'Bring in the caspie-claws.'

Margaret felt sick as those words registered. The gaolers had said something about that earlier but they didn't say what it was.

'Where do you want it?' the gaoler asked, carrying in a strange looking metal object.

'Over here, if you would,' Mr Hastings said and the object was placed on the table.

'You can probably guess what this device is used for, can't you Margaret?'

'It looks like something you could put round someone's legs to stop them walking,' Margaret said, wide-eyed as panic and fear took hold.

'You are partly right.' Lord Willoughby nodded, his constant glare boring into her. 'They are certainly put on the legs, which is why they are often referred to as leg-irons. But there is so much more to say about the caspie-claws than that.'

He left her to ponder on his words for a moment before continuing. 'What would you say if I told you that we put them on a glowing fire until the iron gets red-hot?' Margaret

Chapter Thirteen

gasped, anticipating what he would say next. 'Then we screw them onto the accused person's legs and leave them to roast. Needless to say, the smell of roasting flesh turns the stomach and, believe me, those legs would never work again. And naturally, we generally find that the unfortunate person in those leg-irons tells us what we want to know long before he collapses, unconscious, with the pain.'

Margaret couldn't speak. Her breath came in terrified pants as she realised they would do that to her if she didn't tell them what they wanted to know.

'I see that knowledge of the caspie-claws' purpose has had the desired effect on you,' Mr Hastings said, his bushy white eyebrows raised. 'It has that effect on most people. If someone threatened to roast my legs while I was still alive, I'd probably react that way. But we'll give you a little more time to rethink some of your answers before we have a brazier set up to heat this fascinating device.'

Lord Willoughby rose to his feet. 'Evening is upon us and Mr Hastings and I need to return to our lodgings to dine and rest before another long day tomorrow. We must hope that your answers will be a little more enlightening when you face Sir William and Mr Butler again.

'Gaoler,' he called, 'ensure this woman has another sleepless night, with only water to sustain her, then keep her in one of the small cells with whoever's on duty. Sleep is not for her until she's been interviewed tomorrow afternoon. Oh, and leave both the caspie-claws and pilniewinks handy in here. They could well be needed if we're dissatisfied with replies from either of the accused tomorrow.'

Chapter Fourteen

In which interrogations become ruthless

Cobb Hall, Lincoln Castle: January 26 1619

Two gaolers came for Phillipa soon after daybreak the following morning. 'Your turn to talk to the gentlemen again,' Harry said as the other waited at the foot of the ladder. 'They don't seem in too good a mood, either, so yer'd best be tellin' 'em what they want to 'ear or yer'll be fer it.'

As most of the gaolers, Harry showed little kindness to the prisoners and took great pleasure in describing what was likely to happen to them over the days and weeks of their incarceration. With Phillipa, taunts of the inevitable noose were ever present, but not before several of the gaolers had filled her with fear of what the interrogators could do to her.

'Yer might get to meet the caspie-claws today,' Harry went on as he unlocked the manacle. 'Now there's a thing to be scared of. Yer sister met our caspie yesterday and didn't like it one bit. It'll be interestin' t' know what you make of it.'

Phillipa refused to ask what the caspie-claws was and give him the satisfaction of seeing her tremble. 'Where's my sister?' she demanded instead. 'Will she be brought back here soon?'

'Yer might catch a glimpse of 'er up there,' Harry replied, pointing up the ladder. 'Then again, yer might not. Yer'll soon see for yerself.'

*

Chapter Fourteen

The room was empty as Phillipa came through the trapdoor, but she caught sight of the pilniewinks and another, larger, device on the table that she decided must be the one that Harry had talked about. But she hadn't time to dwell on it as the outer door opened and two officious-looking men she'd never seen before came in to stand behind the table.

'Sit down,' the taller, more heavily built of the two ordered, pointing at the stool as he and an elderly, white-headed man took their seats behind the table.

Phillipa obeyed and watched them rustle through their papers and place their quills in their stands.

The older man fixed Phillipa in his steely glare and introduced his colleague as Lord Willoughby, Deputy Lieutenant of Lincolnshire and himself as Mr Hastings, Sheriff of Leicester. 'We won't tolerate lies,' he told her, 'so I suggest you answer our questions truthfully the first time we ask them. And we don't want any backchat from you, which our colleagues, Sir William and Mr Butler, inform us you are prone to do. Understood?'

'Yes.'

'Good. Tell us what you are charged with.'

'Witchcraft. Our accusers believe my sister and I, and our mother who is now dead, put a spell on their son, Henry, Lord Roos, causing him to fall sick and die.'

'And did you?'

'No, Mr Hastings. I don't know how to cast spells, and I would never have wished to harm Henry. He was a pleasant child.'

'Did you cast a spell to the same effect to harm the earl and countess's younger son Francis?'

'I did not, for the same reason. I was also fond of the little boy, who was not much more than a babe when he fell ill.'

'Are you guilty of casting a spell to prevent Sir Francis and Lady Cecilia having more children?'

'No, Mr Hastings. I wouldn't know how to cast spells for any reason.'

Mr Hastings picked up his quill and began noting her responses on his papers, and Lord Willoughby commenced his questioning: 'Phillipa Flower, we have previously ascertained that your mother, Joan Flower, choked on consecrated bread, so proving that she was, indeed, a witch, and had sold her soul to the Devil. So why should we believe that you are not also a witch and have formed the same pact with Satan?'

'Because it's the truth, my lord, and I don't believe my mother was a witch, either. I don't know why she choked, but I do know she was terrified of coming here and would have done anything to avoid it. Maybe she stuffed something else down her throat with the bread to make sure she choked.'

'Your mother was right to be afraid of facing her accusers, Phillipa. Witches are shown no mercy here, especially those whose deeds are too evil for good, law-abiding people to comprehend. We already know that Joan Flower was practising witchcraft in your village, and was feared and hated by fellow villagers. So, why should we believe her to be innocent of casting spells to harm people she believed to have hurt her?'

Phillipa stared back at Lord Willoughby. 'My mother had always been disliked in Bottesford because the Manners family favoured her. Envy was what other villagers felt and envy can make people do and say terrible things. Whenever anything

Chapter Fourteen

bad happened my mother was blamed for it, and soon they started calling my sister and me witches, too. Opening the bawdyhouse made matters worse amongst the women. But when people are as poor as we became, with no work for any of us at the castle or in the village, the bawdyhouse was our only option.'

'Do you know Anne Baker, Joanne Willimott and Ellen Greene?' Henry Hastings tapped the end of his quill on the tabletop, impatient for her answer.

'Yes, they are cunning women. My mother sometimes met with them at Anne Baker's house to learn more about herblore and how to make healing potions and balms.'

'Isn't it true that those women also practise witchcraft and know curses and spells to use for many purposes?'

'If they are witches, Mr Hastings, I haven't heard of it. They are simply healers of the sick.'

'Do you have one or more familiars?'

'No. I am not a witch, so I don't have familiars.'

'Did Joan Flower have a familiar?'

Phillipa averted her eyes and swallowed hard. 'No, she did not, for the same reason that I have not.'

'Your hesitation in answering that question leads me to believe you are lying,' Mr Hastings said, picking up his quill to record her answers. 'But we'll come back to that later.'

Lord Willoughby glared at Phillipa and heaved a sigh. 'Tell us why Thomas Simpson believes you have bewitched him if, as you say, you are not a witch.'

'Tom Simpson is a simpleton who has been besotted with me for years. His mother, Jessie, forbade him to come to our bawdyhouse, but it was his own choice to do so. He told everyone it wasn't, and that I must have bewitched him. It was a stupid lie so that his mother wouldn't be angry with him. Jessie Simpson and Agnes Peate were two of our mother's worst enemies in Bottesford. Agnes Peate hated my mother because her husband came regularly to our bawdyhouse to be with Joan. It was Jessie and Agnes, with a few other hard-faced goodwives, who spread the rumours that my mother was a witch.'

The two men shared a look and Lord Willoughby returned to writing things on his papers.

'What happened to the glove of Henry, Lord Roos?' Mr Hastings asked.

Thrown momentarily off guard by his question, Phillipa stared at the metal device on the table and absently rubbed her neck. 'I don't know anything about a glove,' she said, realising that if they knew about it, they must know about Joan Flower's spell. She wondered if Margaret had confessed to being part of its casting.

'That's a lie and we all know it! Another point we'll come back to later.' Phillipa flinched at the vehemence of his outburst. 'Do you have a willow tree at the bottom of your garden?'

'Yes, Mr Hastings, our mother used its bark to sell to people in need of something to relieve pains like toothache, or cuts and other injuries from accidents. Willow bark has been used for centuries to –'

'Yes, yes, we are aware of the benefits of willow bark. What is it you are avoiding telling us about your willow tree? What secret does it hold?'

'None that I know of.'

Chapter Fourteen

Mr Hastings gestured at Lord Willoughby. 'My colleague and I have made careful note of everything you have lied about today. We were led to believe that you were a little more truthful than your sister, but it seems that is not the case. Stand up, woman!' he ordered. 'Come and stand at the side of the table while we show you something.'

Her heart pounding, Phillipa obeyed.

'What do you think this is used for?' Lord Willoughby asked, tapping the metal device on the table with his finger. 'Your sister's guess was partly correct, so I'm sure you will say something similar. It is called the caspie-claws, if that is of any help.'

'It looks as though it would fit around the lower half of someone's legs... below the knees, I mean. It would stop them walking.'

'Yes, the same answer as your sister gave yesterday. What do you think would happen to the iron if we put the whole device on a brazier for some time?'

Phillipa gasped and her breath caught in her throat. 'No... you surely wouldn't use it on a person when it's red hot!'

'That's exactly what we'd do if someone was stubborn enough to conceal the truth from us for long.' Lord Willoughby nodded as he spoke. 'The liar would be strapped to a chair and the caspie-claws screwed to his or her legs so that the flesh sizzled as it roasted. It causes quite a stench.'

Phillipa retched, but her stomach contained nothing that could be ejected and she swallowed down the bitter bile.

'Naturally, we try gentler means of persuading the accused to be truthful first, including just speaking to you as we are doing today. If that fails, we are forced to deprive you of sleep and food for three days and nights – something your sister will tell you is not very pleasant. Last night would have been her third sleepless night and Sir William and Mr Butler are looking forward to interviewing her later.'

Mr Hastings picked up the pilniewinks. 'I believe you've been introduced to the pilniewinks – or thumbscrew, as it is sometimes called – and you didn't care for it overmuch. After hearing about the caspie-claws, most people see the pilniewinks as the lesser evil, but believe me, the pain caused by the thumbscrew makes men scream. Though, I agree, the caspie-claws should be avoided at all costs…

'So, Phillipa, we have noted your lies, and next time you are questioned, think very carefully before you answer.'

'Gaoler!' Lord Willoughby yelled. 'Tonight, this woman will be enjoying a wakeful and hungry night. She must not doze off and you know what to do if she does. Take her below for now. She can reflect on her lies while she savours the aroma of stinking straw for a few hours. Margaret Flower can be brought back in here to await the arrival of Sir William and Mr Butler.'

*

The White Hart Inn, Lincoln: Evening, January 26 1619

'I suggested this meeting in order to discuss the progress we've made so far,' Francis said, glancing round at his colleagues, once again seated at the table in his inn room. 'From what I've heard we've had a significant admission from Margaret Flower and

Chapter Fourteen

that greater pressure will now be placed on Phillipa. William and Matthew were the last to interrogate Margaret, so perhaps you could fill in the details for us all?'

Sir William tilted his head at Francis and smiled. 'It would be a pleasure, especially as Matthew and I feel that things have started to move in our favour, thanks to the results gained by Lord Willoughby and Henry. As we thought from the outset, Margaret is the weaker of the two sisters, and she has already let a couple of things slip, which we will, of course, pursue. Matthew…?'

'Margaret is becoming increasingly confused when questions are thrown at her rapidly,' Matthew Butler started. 'When she hasn't the time to formulate an answer, she is likely to say something containing a grain of truth that we can pounce on. The first thing she let slip was that the cunning women gave Joan Flower the spell with which to bewitch Henry, Lord Roos. She also admitted that her mother *did* cast the spell and even described how it was done, maintaining that Phillipa was out of the house at the time. But, as yet, Margaret has not confessed to taking an active part in the spell's casting, or to being a witch herself. She claimed that her mother insisted she watched, nothing more.'

'And was that same spell used to bewitch my younger son?' Francis asked, his grief ever present. 'My apologies for interrupting, Matthew, but this is of great importance to me. Perhaps the cunning women know some means of breaking this spell. Failing that, it is said that the deaths of the witches who cast the spell will see it broken. My wife and I live in hope that at least one of those is true.'

Lord Willoughby heaved a sigh. 'We can't answer your question, as yet, Francis, but we all feel your pain. We won't cease trying until we get every answer we want, from the cunning women as well as the sisters. Have you had news regarding when those three are likely to get here?'

'I have, only today. They have now all been located and will be taken back to Belvoir Castle within the next day or so. It seems that Joanne Willimott was hard to find. She has no regular home and spends much of her time wandering around the open fields and woods around Goadby, often sleeping in old shepherds' huts and abandoned barns. But she has been found, at last. Once they've been allowed to rest and eat at Belvoir, they will be brought here by cart. The drivers plan to stay at Ancaster overnight so we can probably expect their arrival in about a week.'

'That is good to hear,' Samuel Fleming remarked. 'We need to know more about the parts they played in all of this.'

'We wondered if you ought to send men back to the Flower women's cottage in Bottesford, Francis,' Lord Willoughby said, gesturing at Henry Hastings. 'According to Margaret, the spell her mother used to bewitch Lord Henry involved an old glove of his that they had found. Joan Flower apparently buried the glove beneath the willow tree at the bottom of their garden. If we could find the glove it would be a significant piece of evidence at the trial.'

Outraged murmurs of 'maleficent magic' filled the room and Francis thrust his fingers through his dark hair. 'Such wickedness is beyond belief. I'll send some men from the castle first thing tomorrow.'

Chapter Fourteen

'One other point of note before we finish, gentlemen, if you'd bear with us a little longer.' Henry Hastings acknowledged the nodding heads. 'Today Lord Willoughby and I questioned Phillipa again and although she didn't say anything outrightly incriminating, her hesitation in answering two of our questions suggested she was lying. For one thing, she denied knowing anything about the glove, or where it was buried. Nor did she admit to knowing anything of interest regarding the willow tree. Despite Margaret's claim that Phillipa was not present during the casting of the spell, we can assume that either Margaret or Joan Flower would have told her about it when she got home. However, we are of the opinion that Phillipa was present at the time and pressure must be put on her to admit to that.

'The second thing is also interesting. When asked if her mother had a familiar, Phillipa's hesitation and strange reaction suggested that Joan Flower *did* have a familiar. So now we also need to find out more about that, which inevitably leads to the question of whether Joan's daughters also had familiars.'

*

Cobb Hall, Lincoln Castle: January 30 1619

For three days neither Margaret nor Phillipa let slip anything further regarding either their own, or their mother's roles in bewitching members of the Earl of Rutland's family. Though threats of the pilniewinks, the caspie-claws and even the rack, had been repeated during every interrogation, as yet, no move had been made to turn those threats into actions. Yet very little food and continued sleep deprivation rendered both sisters in a state of near collapse. Margaret's mind wandered often, re-enacting happy memories of the past. Although Phillipa envied her the means of escape from present circumstances, she knew that in that fragile, childlike and vulnerable state, Margaret could easily say something that would condemn them both to the gallows.

At times Phillipa silently screamed at her pa, John Flower, for dying and leaving his family alone and impoverished. At other times she screamed at her mother for even contemplating casting spells as a means of revenge – and bringing her daughters to this. Then she remembered ridiculing Joan and accusing her of losing her nerve for not casting that very first spell for which Phillipa had stolen the faded, old glove of Lord Henry's. Joan Flower alone had performed the spells, but Phillipa knew that some of the blame for their disastrous outcome must be laid at her own feet.

One innocent child had met his death and another was said to be drawing closer to his as the months ticked by. Joan Flower was dead, forever labelled as 'witch', and there was little hope that she and Margaret would be branded otherwise.

Margaret was up there now, being interrogated again, and this afternoon it would likely be her turn. If Margaret confessed to anything further, Phillipa knew that she would only manage to deny it for so long before – one way or another – they forced her to confess to their version of the truth.

*

Chapter Fourteen

'Open your eyes, Margaret!'

Sir William's voice seemed to reverberate inside Margaret's skull and her eyes shot open. 'Phillipa and me are having so much fun playing Blind Man's Buff with Pa,' she said with a big smile on her filthy, gaunt face. 'It's a new game, brought here from France by some rich folk, Pa says. People everywhere are playing it now, even in the hall at Hucknall where he works. He won't let Ma play with us, though. He's angry with her 'cos she's done something naughty.'

Sir William drew breath to yell at her to come to her senses, but Matthew Butler laid a hand on his arm to stay him. 'She seems to be getting somewhat delirious if you ask me,' he whispered. 'Play along with her nonsense talk for a while. She may well say something of use to us while she's in this state.'

William nodded. 'What could your ma have done that was so naughty, Margaret?'

She pressed her finger to her lips. 'Shh… it's a secret.'

'If you tell me, I promise to keep it to myself.'

Margaret giggled like a five-year-old. 'Pa says she's been casting spells to make people poorly, and he didn't like that idea at all. He told her she should be nice to people.'

William and Matthew shared a glance, and Matthew gestured to William to continue with his questions.

'Well, your pa is right; we should always be nice to people. Your ma must have cast some nasty spells to make him so angry. I hope she didn't cause anything bad to happen.'

'Pa said she made the two little sons of the earl and countess at Belvoir Castle to become very sick… so sick that one of them died. She did it with a spell she got from those three

Take Height, Rutterkin

cunning women. Pa doesn't know that me and Phillipa helped her with the spells and we're not going to tell him. He'd be really angry with us, too, if he knew. And he doesn't know what Rutterkin can do. He thinks Rutterkin is just an ordinary cat.' She lowered her voice conspiratorially. 'But I'll tell you another secret: he isn't! He's Ma's familiar – and he can fly!'

Margaret drifted back into an exhausted sleep and toppled sideways off the stool, waking abruptly to stare at Sir William and Matthew Butler. 'No, I can't be here! No, no, no!' she cried over and over. 'I was at home in Bottesford.' She dragged herself up and sat again on the stool. 'I want to go home! Where's my pa?' she wailed. 'I don't like this place.'

'No, it isn't too pleasant,' Matthew agreed, 'especially when you're so tired. We just have a few more questions for you then can go and have a nice sleep. Now, my first question is this. Have you any familiars, Margaret?'

'No, I have never had any of my own.'

'But your mother had one, didn't she? You told us that earlier. What was his name again…?'

'Rutterkin. He's such a pretty cat, but I don't think he's a familiar. He just sleeps all day on Ma's lap, or on her chair when she's busy. He doesn't like to go outside much, especially when it's cold. Is someone looking after him while I'm here, Mr Butler?'

'Yes, someone has been sent to make sure he's being fed. He wouldn't be able to fly very far if he didn't eat, would he?'

Margaret giggled again, her mind wandering as the fogginess of sleep crept over her. 'He flies so well, or at least that's what Ma says. He carries spells sometimes.'

Chapter Fourteen

'Yes, we'd heard that familiars can do that. Can you remember how many spells Rutterkin has carried, Margaret?'

'Well,' Margaret said, pouting. 'Ma ordered him to take four, but he's a stubborn little cat and would only take two.'

'Do you recall what the two that Rutterkin refused to carry were?'

'Yes, but Pa says that has to be a secret, too.'

With that, Margaret dropped from the stool like a swatted fly, to lie senseless on the stone floor.'

'Gaolers!' Sir William yelled, 'get this woman back to the dungeon and bring up her sister.'

*

'No, Sir William, I don't confess to being a witch or to giving my soul to the Devil.'

Phillipa's weary gaze moved from one man to the other. After several sleepless nights and little food, she was exhausted and so very weak. But she knew she must appear strong and not allow these men to make her confess to things that simply were not true. 'I can think of no way to make you believe that, other than to keep repeating it every time you ask. No matter what our mother did, the only part my sister and I played in the spells she cast was that of onlookers.'

'But you do agree with Margaret that your mother was a witch.'

'I never saw her as a witch. The spell she cast on Lord Henry was done out of frustration – and anger. Our mother was always quick to lose her temper but, to our knowledge, she had never dealt in witchcraft and only visited the cunning women to learn more about herbal cures. She believed the spell they gave her wouldn't work because she wasn't a witch, in the sense that they were thought to be.'

'It sounds as though you believe the cunning women dealt in something other than herbal remedies.' Sir William's green stare seemed to bore into her. 'Do you?'

'Like most people in Bottesford, I had heard the rumours about Anne Baker and what she was supposed to have done,' she admitted. 'They said she had crossed the bounds between white witchcraft and black. But those people were just angry with her because a few of her cures hadn't worked. I don't know about the other two women because they don't live in our village.'

'Do you have any familiars?' Mr Butler raised his eyebrows.

'No. I am not a witch.'

'Does Margaret have any?'

'No.'

'Did your mother have any familiars?'

'No, Mr Butler. She had a little white cat, which she adopted when it refused to leave our doorstep when it was a kitten. But that's all Rutterkin is… a cat.'

'Stop lying, woman!' Sir William's eyes bulged and his face grew red. 'We're stopping being nice right here. Your sister has already confessed that Rutterkin can fly and carried your mother's spells to their destinations. So your lies simply won't work.'

Phillipa tried to focus her bleary eyes on his. 'My sister has always had a fanciful imagination. Rutterkin rarely moves out of Ma's chair, let alone flies!'

Chapter Fourteen

Sir William's move around the table was fast and the sharp slap he delivered across Phillipa's face resounded around the stone walls of the room.

She rubbed her cheek, the sting of the slap bringing tears to her eyes. She wiped them away and stared up at her assailant as he glared down at her, swearing to herself not to give him the satisfaction of seeing her cry. 'Your slaps can't make me admit to things that simply aren't true. Rutterkin wasn't my mother's familiar and he certainly can't fly.'

Sir William's second blow came as a backhanded strike across Phillipa's other cheek, so forceful it knocked her to the floor. 'Get back on the stool,' he ordered. 'I ask you again whether your mother's familiar flies. If you give me the wrong answer this time, your nose may not withstand the next blow.'

'Rutterkin is just an ordinary cat and cannot –'

The fist to her face knocked Phillipa backwards off the stool, and she clutched her nose, warm blood trickling through her fingers. Her brutalised and most likely broken nose was agony and there was no way she could have stopped her tears from flowing down her face to mingle with the blood.

'Get back on the stool,' Mr Butler ordered, and dreading what they would do next, Phillipa dragged herself from the floor.

Sir William retreated behind the table and Phillipa continuously swiped her sleeves across her face to mop up the blood. But the flow was still steady, and to touch her nose brought further tears to her eyes. Mr Butler threw her a piece of rag and she bent to retrieve it from the floor beside her.

For some moments, no one spoke and gradually the flow of blood lessened.

'Now, Phillipa,' Matthew Butler resumed, 'today you have been subjected to the gentlest form of physical persuasion we reserve for those who refuse to cooperate with our questioning. Next time, if you persist in remaining stubborn, you could well suffer a broken arm, or possibly lose your fingernails, or an ear. If your obstinacy continues after that, we'll have no other choice that to demonstrate the use of the pilniewinks or the caspie-claws on you. Do you understand?'

'Yes,' she mumbled through bloodied and swollen lips.

'Good. Now, I'll repeat a few more questions which we expect you to answer truthfully. After all, you don't want to make Margaret look like a despicable liar, do you? Tell us, can your mother's familiar, a cat called Rutterkin, fly?'

She hesitated, but at the sound of Sir William's chair scraping back, she said. 'Yes, Rutterkin can fly.'

'Thank you for being honest at last,' Mr Butler said, as Sir William wrote her answer down. 'Two more questions for today. On the day your mother cast the spell on Lord Henry, did Rutterkin fly away to Belvoir Castle, carrying the spell to the boy?'

'He ran out into the garden, but Ma said he would then fly to the castle and find little Henry.'

'Excellent, Phillipa. See how easy it is to be honest?' Sir William's sneering praise at her submission sickened her and she glowered at him. 'Now,' he continued, 'your sister has admitted that both you and she were willing participants in the spells your mother cast. The previous time we asked her, she was adamant that you were not in the house. Margaret seems much more willing to be honest than she was a while ago.

Chapter Fourteen

Lack of sleep and food have certainly helped her to see reason.'

Phillipa inwardly screamed at the injustice of it all. The real truth was very different to the false honesty that these interrogators were determined to hear. She and Margaret had been no more than witnesses to their mother's spells. But Phillipa knew that by the time they had been subjected to more deprivation and pain, they would have been forced to confess to very much more.

'Margaret wasn't lying when she said we were there, nor was she lying when she said we took part in the spell.'

'And you agree that the spell was carried to Lord Henry by Rutterkin?'

'Yes,' Phillipa sputtered as blood continued to gush from her nose and into her mouth.

'Good. We'll pursue the extent of you and your sister's participation in these abhorrent spells next time we meet.

'Gaolers!' Matthew Butler called and two rapidly appeared. 'Get the two women accused of witchcraft in separate cells on this floor, starting with this one.' He flicked a finger in Phillipa's direction. 'Then bring Margaret up from the dungeon. Keep them in those cells for tonight, with a guard posted with each. Ensure that neither of them has chance to sleep and walk them around this room when necessary – at different times, of course. They may have water but no food. Interrogations will resume tomorrow.'

Chapter Fifteen

In which the Flower sisters are examined and the cunning women are questioned

Cobb Hall: January 31 1619

After another sleepless night, once again worsened by the withdrawal of food, Margaret's mind continued to fail her. Brought before Lord Willoughby and Henry Hastings from the cell in one of Cobb Hall's ground floor recesses, she did not recognise either of them and continuously asked where she was and when could she go home to Ma and Pa.

'The woman's state of delirium can only be beneficial to our questioning,' Lord Willoughby whispered. 'We may even get her to admit to giving herself to the Devil without resorting to persuasion.'

Henry nodded and Lord Willoughby made a start.

'Now, Margaret, you may remember that my name is Lord Willoughby. I must say, you look very tired today and probably need a nice long sleep. Think how cosy it would be back in your own bed in Bottesford.'

'Yes, it would be nice, but I'd need to eat some of Ma's mutton stew first. I'm too hungry to sleep.'

'Your ma's stew sounds extremely appetising. Perhaps she'll make some for you later.'

'You'll have to take me home in your cart because I don't know the way.'

Chapter Fifteen

'We have a few more questions to ask you first, and if you answer them truthfully, Mr Hastings and I might do that. Does that sound like a good idea?'

Margaret's nod was followed by a wide yawn and her eyelids drooped.

'Stay awake, Margaret,' Henry said. 'This is our first question. Are you and Phillipa witches like your Ma?'

Margaret's face creased into a puzzled frown. 'No… although we helped Ma to cast those spells.'

'What did you do to help?'

'Well, we both had a few stabs at Lord Henry's glove when it was in the cauldron of boiling water… and we helped to dig a hole under the willow tree to bury it.'

'What about the glove of little Lord Francis? Did you bury that one, too?'

Margaret's head fell forward as she drifted into an exhausted sleep. Henry came round the table and shook her gently. Wake up, Margaret. What did you do with the glove of little Lord Francis after you had boiled and stabbed it?'

'I remember Ma lifting it out of the water with her little knife and putting it on a cloth to cool.' Margaret blinked a few times as she thought. 'Then she wiped it along Rutterkin's back and threw it in the fire.'

'Why didn't she bury the glove as she did with Lord Henry's?'

Margaret shrugged and pulled a face like a puzzled child. 'She just said there were different ways of doing the spell. This time the glove would burn but the spell would fly up the chimney and across the sky to the castle to find little Francis.'

'Now, Margaret,' Lord Willoughby said as Henry sat down beside him, 'I want you to think hard and tell us if this spell needed any words saying with it.'

'Ma chanted things for some of the spells, but I don't remember everything she said. I know she said something about the Devil in the spell she put on Lord Henry. Pa was so angry about that when I told him – and Ma was angry with me for telling him. She said it was supposed to be our secret and no one else's.'

Lord Willoughby shared a triumphant look with Henry. 'Can you remember some of the words your ma used about the Devil? You're a clever girl, Margaret, so I think you probably can.'

'I remember bits of it. It started, "In the name of the Devil, this glove I destroy...." and then something about burying it in the earth until it rotted. It was a funny chant but she said the words just came into her head. Then she told Rutterkin to "take height and to the castle go", or something like that.' Margaret giggled to herself for a moment. 'She said the same thing to Rutterkin when she put the spell on little Francis, but the spell went up the chimney, so I don't know whether Rutterkin took it after he'd run outside or if it flew to the castle all on its own. Pa was very angry about it all and wouldn't let Ma play Blind Man's Buff with us.'

'Margaret, did you and Phillipa become witches like your ma? I suppose it would have been nice for you all to be the same.' Henry Hastings waited but Margaret's head again fell forward as exhaustion overwhelmed her. 'Margaret!' he snapped, but she was too deeply asleep to hear. Again, he came round the table and shook her by the shoulder until her eyes slowly opened. 'Are you and Phillipa witches like your mother?'

'Maybe we are,' she slurred. 'We did the spells with her in our cottage.'

'Have you and Phillipa made a pact with the Devil?'

'I don't think so, Mr Hastings. Pa wouldn't have let us. He didn't like the Devil one bit. I'm so hungry and want some of Ma's mutton stew now.'

Henry called for the gaolers as Margaret drifted back to sleep. 'Get her in the cell and give her some soup and a crust of bread. Then allow her to sleep for a couple of hours but no more. She'll be having another sleepless night tonight.'

*

Lord Willoughby and Henry Hastings enjoyed a hearty meal with a couple of glasses of fine, red Bordeaux at the White Hart before heading back to Cobb Hall to interrogate Margaret's elder sister. When Phillipa was brought from her cell, Henry shared a look with Lord Willoughby. The woman had evidently angered Sir William and Matthew Butler. Most of her face was swollen and of a deep, blue-black, and her once straight nose was twisted and obviously broken. Her defiant stance had been beaten from her and in her state of defeat, hunger and exhaustion, she dragged herself to the stool.

'Well, Phillipa, it looks as though you have greatly annoyed someone,' Henry started, eliciting a sour look from the once pretty and spirited young woman. I can only imagine you didn't tell Sir William and Mr Butler the truth.'

'I told them the truth but they wouldn't have it. The only words they would accept were those they put into my mouth by violence. So now I have told lies to aid your purpose, and you will send Margaret and me to the gallows.'

'We have a few more points to clarify before we can do that,' Henry replied, 'and I hope you'll be honest in your answers today and avoid further persuasion. First of all, your sister admits that because the three of you took part in the spells cast in your cottage, you and she are probably witches like your mother. Is that true?'

Lord Willoughby shuffled his bulky form on his chair, and Phillipa cringed, evidently thinking he was about to come round the table to beat her.

'I suppose it must be.'

'You have already agreed with your sister that your mother's cat, Rutterkin, carried some of the spells to Belvoir Castle. Margaret has admitted that four spells were cast. Tell us about those four.'

'Besides those on the little boys, I can only think of one other that I took part in, and that was the one on Lady Katherine.'

'Go on,' Lord Willoughby urged. 'Explain what the spell was intended to do. Margaret has given us her version of events, now we wish to hear yours.'

Henry shared another look with Lord Willoughby, confident that Phillipa would believe Margaret had already given her account of that spell.

'The three of us put the same spell on Lady Katherine that we'd put on the two boys,' Phillipa confessed. 'But instead of a glove, we used a lace-trimmed handkerchief that Ma had taken

Chapter Fifteen

from the girl's bedchamber at Belvoir Castle. We all prodded it in the cauldron but when Ma wiped it across Rutterkin's back and told him to fly to the castle with the spell, he refused to move. So Ma just threw the handkerchief on the fire.'

'Are you saying that because Rutterkin refused to carry the spell, it didn't work?'

'It might have worked, a little. We heard that Lady Katherine was sick for a day, then she got better again.'

'Your sister told us the words that Joan Flower chanted whilst the spells on the two little lords were being cast. Tell us what you remember of them.'

Phillipa hesitated, but eventually, she said, 'I only remember Ma chanting words for the spell on Lord Henry. She didn't say them while putting the spell on little Francis or Lady Katherine. It began, "In the name of the Devil, this glove I destroy". Then she said something about burying the glove so it would perish, just like the family who caused harm to her family would do.'

'That family being the Manners family?'

'Yes, Lord Willoughby.'

Then Henry asked, 'Did your mother chant words to Rutterkin during the casting of spells on both little boys and Lady Katherine?'

'Yes.'

'Do you remember what she said?'

'Not properly, but she ordered him to fly to the castle and "do some hurt" in all three spells, although, as I told you, Rutterkin refused to fly with the spell on Lady Katherine. I don't know what Ma meant by "hurt" but I know that Lord

Henry became very sick and died, and Lord Francis is still very ill. Ma didn't know if it was her spell that had caused Henry's death until we did the same spell on Lord Francis – although we didn't bury that glove, Ma threw it in the fire.'

'That you cast a spell at all is devilish witchcraft!' Henry's anger at these confessions was growing as his sympathy for Sir Francis welled. 'Maleficent magic requires a witch to have made a pact with the Devil. Margaret told us that all three of you had done so,' he added, hoping his lie would catch her out.

For a moment, Phillipa seemed unsure how to reply, but then defiance flashed in her eyes. 'I made no pact with the Devil, nor did Margaret. I can't say whether our mother did, or not. She spent a lot of time with those three cunning women, so what she did when she was at Anne Baker's house, I don't know.'

Lord Willoughby asked, 'Have you and your sister any familiars of your own?'

'No. There was just Rutterkin in the cottage, and he made it clear to Margaret and me that he was there only for our mother. He stayed close to her when we were in the house, and often scratched or bit my sister and me if we went near when he was on Ma's lap.'

'So you haven't been sucked by demons in the guise of pretty animals?'

'No!' Phillipa shook her head in wild denial. 'I haven't got any familiars!'

'Can you prove that? Can you truthfully say that you have no teats or marks on your body where your familiars have fed on your blood?'

Chapter Fifteen

'I know I haven't. You'll just have to believe me.'

'That's where you're wrong, woman,' Lord Willoughby said with a sneer. 'We don't have to believe you, and after all your lies and deception what we need is proof that there are no teats on your body before we continue with our questions. A local midwife will be brought in and in a day or two, you and Margaret will be examined. There'll be no sleep for you tonight, either, which will give you time to think about answering truthfully regarding the pact you made with the Devil.'

Lord Willoughby called the gaolers. 'Both women will remain in those cells tonight and not be permitted to sleep. They can have water but no food. Take them outside to relieve themselves and walk them around in here if they show signs of falling asleep.

'One of you get over to Mary Ingram's house. Tell her we should be in need of her services within the next few days and to be ready to come at our call. She can expect the usual rate of pay for a day's work, plus an extra bonus if the results are to our liking.'

*

It was two days later, a Saturday, the second day of February, when the midwife arrived. Carrying a bag with the implements required for the examination of witches, the woman, with two of her assistants, arrived at Cobb Hall at nine o'clock in the morning. The beginning of February was bitterly cold. It had snowed in the night; puddles around the castle yard were glassy and hard, and they entered Cobb Hall accompanied by an icy blast.

They were greeted by Lord Willoughby, who had organised this further test of the accused in his capacity as Deputy Lieutenant of Lincolnshire. 'I won't attempt to tell you how to do your job, Mistress Ingram. You and I have met on several such occasions and I have no doubts whatever about your abilities. But I urge you to be particularly thorough in your examinations of these women. They have been involved in the most heinous, devilish practices and caused immense grief to the Earl and Countess of Rutland. If anyone in this land deserves to hang, it is these two sisters.'

'I understand, and you will have the results you want,' Mary Ingram replied. 'Never yet have I failed to find Devil's marks and teats on women involved in witchcraft. It may take some time with each, but it will be worth your while to be patient.'

'Good. The gaolers will be outside your door should you need assistance, and I will be in here. I know you have never required further aid than that from your own good ladies in the past. I suggest you start with the younger sister, Margaret.'

*

Margaret was sitting on a stool when the three women entered. The gaoler assigned to keep her awake promptly left and Mary Ingram introduced herself and explained to Margaret what she and her assistants were about to do.

In her weary and starving state, and her skin itching and sore from umpteen flea and rat bites, Margaret nodded. But when two of the women yanked her to her feet and started lifting her dress to pull it over her head, she became confused and panic set in. Arms flailing and feet kicking out, she attempted to stop the assault, until the sharp rap of a stick across her back stopped her dead.

'That's better,' Mistress Ingram said as Margaret's dress fell back into place. 'You have no choice as to whether this examination takes place, and if you resist in that way again, the two gaolers outside this door will come in, strip you naked and hold you down while I get on with my task. Or, you could choose to behave sensibly and let us continue our job without a fuss. Either way, this examination will be done.' She gestured to her two assistants. 'At least the three of us are women, and I expect that the presence of two men in here to watch could be even more traumatic for you.'

Margaret remained silent, shaking with fear at what they would do to her. 'Get this filthy dress off her,' the midwife ordered, 'and sit her back on the stool.' Then she rummaged through her bag and took out a pair of scissors.

As Mistress Ingram picked up a handful of the once glossy, fair hair, Margaret let out a loud wail. 'No, No! I beg you not to cut off my hair. Why are you doing this to me?'

'We've found Devil's marks and teats in the strangest of places on the bodies of witches in the past, my girl, and I can tell you, there won't be a single inch of your body we don't search. Now keep quiet while we work. If you cry out again, you'll feel the weight of this stick.

'Pass me the razor, Sarah,' she said, once Margaret's hair had been cut to barely a quarter of an inch all over and the long tresses lay heaped on the floor. One of the women passed her an open razor folded into its handle. Mistress Ingram flicked it open and proceeded to shave Margaret's scalp.

'Good, now that's done, we'll shave the rest of you. On the floor, if you will.'

Margaret gasped. 'You can't need to shave my private parts! Why would you want to look there?'

'As I said, we've found Devil's marks and teats on every part of the body. Where better to hide them than underneath hair, wherever that hair may be? Now, on the floor, legs open wide.'

The rest of the examination was gruelling and extremely humiliating for Margaret. The women scoured her body, in her ears, inside her mouth, under her breasts and arms, and even inside her most private parts, front and back. Mistress Ingram pointed things out to her assistants a number of times for them to make note of but, whatever they said, Margaret couldn't hear.

'Dress yourself before the gaoler comes back in,' Mistress Ingram ordered, rummaging in her bag and pulling out a thin mop cap and handing it to Margaret. 'Wearing that may help to stop you feeling completely exposed and humiliated when your face further interrogations and a trial.'

Margaret could feel no gratitude to this woman who had left her without a shred of dignity, but she said, 'Thank you,' whilst trying desperately to stop herself from wailing like a banshee.

*

In the afternoon of that day, Phillipa was subjected to the same harrowing and debasing ritual that Margaret had suf-

Chapter Fifteen

fered earlier at the hands of a midwife and her assistants. Lord Willoughby had warned Mary Ingram that Phillipa was the more insolent and outspoken of the two sisters and to treat her firmly and harshly if necessary. But Phillipa was subdued, and already resigned to the fate that awaited her. Whatever these women did to her now was nothing compared to facing the hangman's noose. Her life was already over, the interrogators had condemned her as a witch, and she could only hope that hanging would be quick, and not as terrible as it sounded.

Phillipa remained docile and silent throughout the degrading ritual, even when the midwife cut off her thick, dark hair and shaved her body so that not a single hair was left. Then she was poked and prodded all over – 'examined' they called it – as the three women discussed the many flea bites she had gained in that reeking dungeon, and the odd mole she had on her chest. Even the scar on her shoulder, from when she had fallen from a tree as a child and the skin was gashed open, was prodded and noted down. Phillipa willed the time to pass until, finally, it was over and she was permitted to put her dress back on, and a mop cap that Mistress Ingram gave her.

She sat on the stool as they left and the burly, gruff gaoler she had rarely seen appeared.

'On your feet,' he ordered. 'It's back to the dungeon for you tonight. You'll be allowed water and a bowl of soup but nothing more.'

'Will my sister be taken there once the midwife has finished with her? I haven't seen her for so long.'

'She's already there now. Margaret had her turn with the lady this morning. And don't the pair of you look a real treat now?'

Take Height, Rutterkin

The gaoler chuckled as he shoved her to the trapdoor, and only the thought of not being permitted to see Margaret stopped Phillipa from turning round and kicking him in a place that would render him grovelling on the floor.

*

While the examinations of Phillipa and Margaret Flower were taking place in Cobb Hall, Sir Francis agreed to hold the preliminary interview with the cunning women in the old county gaol, one of several buildings in the castle yard. With him would be his brother, Sir George Manners, and Samuel Fleming.

The three women were hauled from the cart and taken straight to face their interrogators inside the old Tudor gaol, a squat, slightly rectangular building of two storeys, both of which were low ceilinged. Immediately through the solid oak door was a central reception area, where the gaolers sat around a small table during periods of quiet inactivity. A corridor at either side of this room each led to two cells, all large enough to comfortably house half a dozen prisoners – although Francis knew that if the need arose, several more would be squeezed in. On the upper floor were four more cells, two of which were retained for the interrogation of prisoners. The other two were currently empty.

The women were escorted upstairs by two of the castle guards and taken into one of the interrogation cells. Beneath a barred window high in the wall opposite the door was a wide table, behind which sat Sir Francis, flanked by Sir George Manners and Reverend Samuel Fleming. A number of stools were stacked along the wall to the right of the interviewers and

Chapter Fifteen

the women were instructed to take one each and sit facing the table. Seemingly satisfied that procedures were in hand, the guards left to stand watch outside the wooden door with an iron grille at eye level.

The three women appeared visibly shaken when they realised that the Earl of Rutland and the Member of Parliament for Lincolnshire would be questioning them. Pleased with that response, Francis hoped their presence would be sufficiently intimidating to the women to ensure their truthfulness.

'Reverend Fleming,' he said, twisting to address his friend, 'since you are already acquainted with one of these women, would you like to lead the questioning?'

'Thank you, Sir Francis, I would.' Samuel focused on the women. 'I am acquainted with all three women, since the two who live elsewhere are regular visitors to Bottesford. Unfortunately, I can't say I've seen any of the three amongst the congregation during Sunday Services at Saint Mary's.'

He held out his hand to each of the women in turn as he addressed them. 'Anne Baker you are a native of Bottesford; Ellen Greene, you hail from the village of Stathern; and Joanne Willimott, I believe the village of Goadby is your home.'

The women each confirmed that to be true and Samuel went on. 'Sir Francis has called this interview in order to ascertain certain facts. We ask that you answer truthfully, or future interrogations will not be so pleasant. Do you all understand?'

Again, the women stated they did and Samuel nodded. 'I am about to put to you what we know of your activities in Bottesford and its surroundings and will pause at times to enable you to confirm or deny what I have said.

Take Height, Rutterkin

'You are each acquainted with Joan Flower and her daughters, Phillipa and Margaret, and were accustomed to meeting with Joan every Saturday, generally at Anne Baker's house, to discuss herblore and the making of herbal remedies. Joan, herself, enjoyed making potions and balms and had begun to sell a goodly number of them before accusations of her involvement in witchcraft circulated in the village and at Belvoir Castle.'

The three women silently nodded so Samuel pushed on. 'You will know that Joan and her daughters have been charged with the heinous crime of bewitching both sons of the Earl and Countess of Rutland, and of putting a spell on Sir Francis and Lady Cecilia to render them unable to conceive more children. I trust you have also been informed of Joan Flower's death on the journey here and that Phillipa and Margaret alone now face those charges?'

The three confirmed that they knew of the charges and of Joan's death.

'It has recently come to our knowledge that Joan Flower obtained the spell with which she bewitched the earl's elder son, Lord Henry, from you three women.' Samuel hushed the murmurs of denial with a raised finger. 'I put it to you that Joan must have cast the same spell on little Lord Francis, and acquired the spell she put on the earl and countess from you. If all this is true, then we can only deduce that you three are also practising witches.'

Francis watched the women's faces blanch and terror fill their eyes at the realisation that they could also be facing charges of witchcraft.

Chapter Fifteen

'Anne Baker, do you have anything to say about the spell you provided for Joan Flower?'

'I do not deal in witchcraft, Rector, and have never given any spells to Joan Flower or anyone else. I am a cunning woman – or a wise woman, as some would say. I make healing remedies for folk who cannot afford physicians' fees.'

'Joanne Willimott, what is your response to the allegations against you?'

Joanne twisted a long strand of grey hair around her finger. 'I've grown herbs and sold healing potions to earn a little to live on since my husband died seven year ago. Like Anne, I am what people often call a cunning or a wise woman.'

'Ellen Greene, what do you know of spells and their uses?'

'I know nothing about spells and wouldn't know how to use one if I was given it.' Ellen tried to smile but failed, her usually rounded face now ashen and drawn. 'I, too, am simply a cunning woman who deals in growing herbs to make healing remedies to sell.'

Francis said nothing but nodded at Samuel to continue.

'As cunning women, all three of you are known to sell charms and sigils as well as herbal remedies. I wonder if you also sell curses?'

'We do not sell, curses, Rector,' Anne Baker answered for the three of them. 'Our charms and sigils are sold only with the intention of causing good things to happen.'

'Wouldn't you say that even charms and sigils are akin to witchcraft? After all, your charms work on a person's mind to make them do something they would not normally do.'

'We don't think of it that way, Rector,' Joanne Willimott

responded. 'Our charms help people to see things more clearly so they can make their minds up.'

Samuel did not pursue that point. 'There have been rumours in Bottesford that all three of you have practised witchcraft for some years. Nothing has yet been proven, although there are those who maintain you each have familiars.'

He paused and held out his hand to single out Anne Baker. 'It is believed you have long practised black magic in Bottesford, and have been accused of doing several evil deeds. Allegations have been made against you regarding the bewitching of William Hough's wife, Elizabeth. Seemingly, you did so because she gave you alms of stale bread. It is also known that you were badly beaten by William Fairbarne because he believed you sent an illness called Plannet to his young son, Thomas, who died as a result. If that isn't enough, you have also been accused of rendering a village man incapable of fathering a child…

'You are said to have brought about these evil deeds by performing maleficent magic, in which you used your victims' hair, or clippings of toe and fingernails to cast the spell. The charges seem to go on, don't they, Anne?'

'None of them are true, Reverend. They are hateful lies, made up to lay the blame on me when, in many cases, people died of illnesses my herbal mixtures could not cure because their families had left it too late to ask for my help. And Andrew Gill's inability to father a child had been ongoing long before he came to me for a cure. Then there are many diseases and illnesses that neither physicians' medicines nor cunning folks' remedies would ever cure.'

Chapter Fifteen

Samuel nodded. 'Thank You, Anne.' He indicated the ageing Joanne Willimott. 'Joanne, in your village of Goadby, accusations of witchcraft have been made against you regarding the killing of John Pratchett's wife and baby. In addition, you sought to divert the blame from yourself by pointing the finger at one Gomaliel Green, a shepherd from Waltham who, according to you, had a white spirit in the form of a mouse. Do you deny any of this, Joanne?'

'I deny killing anyone, Rector. John Pratchett's wife and newborn son were barely alive by the time John came to me for help, so I had not enough time to save them. And I only mentioned the shepherd because he had told me about his familiar. As you say, only witches have familiars, so I wondered if he'd had anything to do with those deaths.'

Finally, Samuel indicated Ellen Green, a younger woman than Anne Baker and Joanne Willimott, being closer to Joan Flower's age. 'It seems you've had no accusations of witchcraft against you, Ellen, but I'm asking you now, do you deal in witchcraft?'

Ellen was silent for some moments. 'There are folk who will say I do. But if you asked them, they'd have no proof to back up their allegations, other than the fact that I have a mole living in my garden, which I have called Moldiwarp. I just enjoy being a cunning woman, making my potions and selling charms and sigils.'

'Very well, time is moving on, so we will leave that point for now. You all realise that you have been brought here to give evidence relating to the trial of the Flower sisters...?' The women affirmed they did. 'We will be requiring testimonies from you, Joanne Willimott and you, Anne Barker, concerning your claims as to what was revealed to you both regarding the spell Joan Flower cast on the Earl of Rutland's elder son.'

Samuel gestured to Sir Francis and said to the two women in question, 'The earl will question you himself on this matter. Sir Francis…?'

'My thanks, Rector. I'll start with you, Anne Baker, since you live in Bottesford and probably knew Joan Flower better than Joanne Willimott did. Tell us, without lies or omissions, who you encountered on your return from a trip to Northampton some years ago and what was said.'

'Yes, my lord. Let me see, it must have been about three years ago. I –'

'Stop there,' Francis ordered. 'This encounter was six years ago, not three.'

'You are right, my lord, six years it was. Time goes by so fast and I lose track of it sometimes. I was getting close to home when I met Jonathan Peate and Edmund Dennis, on their way home from a day's work at Belvoir Castle. They told me that your eldest son, Lord Henry, was dead, and that Joan had admitted to Jonathan, her lover, that she had cast a spell to harm the child, using one of his gloves. She had buried it in her garden and gloated about how it would rot and waste, just like the body of Lord Henry.'

'Nothing further was said?'

'No, my lord.'

'Then let's hear what you know about this whole vile business, Joanne Willimott.'

Joanne sat for a few moments as though in thought, then

Chapter Fifteen

began to ramble. 'There are several local men and women who can wield evil powers and do harm to many good people. They aren't at all like me, who only seeks to do good magic and help people to –'

'That isn't what I asked you!' Sir Francis heaved an irritated sigh, but he was too impatient to find evidence of the Flower women's guilt to listen to the ramblings of a confused old woman. 'Tell us what happened when you met Joan and Margaret Flower not long before the three Flower women were arrested.'

'Yes, lord. I will. I met Joan and Margaret at Blackborrow Hill a week before their arrest and we walked back to Joan's house together. While I was there, I saw Joan's other two familiars – as well as Rutterkin, that is. One was a rat and the other was an owl. Joan told me that although she could not harm the Earl of Rutland himself, she had brought harm to his son, who was now dead. And her familiars had assured her that she would never be condemned for Lord Henry's death.'

'Damnable witchcraft!' Francis yelled. 'King James is right to want you all hanged. What about you, Ellen Greene?'

'I have been a cunning woman for some years, and people call me a witch. I don't deny practising magic, though I did lie about that to Reverend Fleming. I have two spirits at my command: a mole called Moldiwarp and a kitten that doesn't have a name. I confess I made a pact with the Devil, and I have bewitched to death several members of the community. I don't know why I did all that. Sometimes I think I'm losing my mind. But I enjoyed giving that spell to Joan Flower when she came to Anne Baker's house asking for one. I knew my two friends wouldn't have given her one and she sounded desperate to me. So I gave it to her and explained how to cast it.'

Francis groaned. 'The three of you will remain confined in the gaol here until the Flower sisters' trial, during which you may, or may not, be called as witnesses, depending on whether time allows it and if the judges deem your presence necessary. After that, all three of you will most likely be tried for witchcraft. That may be here at Lincoln, or in Leicester. Enquiries need to be made with regards to that. I will, of course, advise that it should be Lincoln, since the details of your crimes are already known to us.'

Francis glanced at George and Samuel. 'Are there any further questions either of you would like to ask at this time?'

Both said they had nothing more, and Francis called the guards. 'These women can now be confined in one of the cells on this floor. They are to be witnesses at the Flower sisters' trial, and as yet, have not been proven guilty of any crime. They will need to be fed during that time and taken outside regularly to relieve themselves. They are not to be maltreated in any way, and I'll be checking regularly that my orders are being carried out. Is that clear?'

'It is, my lord,' the younger of the two men replied.

'Then you can start by bringing them some fresh water, and they will need food this evening. Make sure it's not rotting or mouldy.'

The earl and his two companions left the room. Once in the castle yard, Francis said, 'Tomorrow, the three of us will interview the Flower sisters.'

Chapter Sixteen

In which Phillipa and Margaret Flower are interrogated by Sir Francis, Sir George Manners and Samuel Fleming

Cobb Hall, February 4 1619

Soon after nine in the morning two days later, Sir Francis entered Cobb Hall, accompanied by Sir George and Samuel Fleming. The three men stamped the snow from their boots in the doorway before coming to sit at the table. For a while, they referred to their paperwork, which contained records of all interrogations of Phillipa and Margaret to date, as well as the midwife's findings during her examinations of the sisters.

The three men reiterated priorities to be addressed during today's questioning and clarified which forms of persuasion they would use should the women still prove uncooperative. It was vital to Francis that the sisters confessed to making a pact with the Devil. Having them executed was the only way to break the spell on his young son. Francis was also determined to force the truth from their lying mouths regarding the infertility spell they had placed on him and Cecilia.

'Have the sisters brought up now, if you would,' Francis said to the gaolers Harry and Jack, hovering near the trapdoor. 'We'll question them both together.'

Phillipa was the first to appear and shuffle towards the table. Francis was shocked by the young woman's appearance, and Samuel's appalled gasp did not escape his notice. Desperately thin and filthy, with a thin mop cap on her shaven head, Phillipa's face was swollen and several shades of black, purple and blue. But it was her badly broken nose that drew the eye. It took Francis every shred of resolve to stop himself feeling sorry for her. This woman was a witch who had already taken one of his sons from him and left the fate of his desperately sick, younger son hanging in the balance.

Margaret followed behind, her scrawny frame, grimy skin and dress, and the mop cap to hide her bald head, just the same as her sister's. But Margaret's face had not been punched. Instead, she wore the vacant expression of one to whom all awareness had vanished, her sunken, black-rimmed eyes deep pools of blue.

'Sit down,' Sir George ordered, having been elected to open the questioning. 'I'm sure you both recognise the Earl of Rutland and Reverend Samuel Fleming, although my face might not be as familiar to you as theirs. My name is Sir George Manners, brother of Sir Francis and Member of Parliament for Lincolnshire. I will address my questions to each of you in turn, and request that neither of you answer any that are not directed at you. If I wish to address a question to both of you, I will say so. Is that clear?'

Phillipa and Margaret both nodded and George went on, 'Firstly, we need to reach an agreement regarding which spells you were both involved in casting with your mother, Joan Flower. The last time you were both questioned it was by Lord Willoughby and Mr Hastings, and on that occasion, Phillipa, you confessed to your involvement in casting three spells and

Chapter Sixteen

maintained you knew of no others. Remind us again what those three spells were.'

'They were on the earl's three children: one on each of his two sons and one on Lady Katherine, which didn't work – at least it only worked for a very short time.'

Sir George fixed his attention on Margaret. 'You confessed to helping your mother with the two spells on the earl's sons.'

'Yes, I watched Ma do them and helped to stab the gloves.'

'But you also mentioned something about other spells being cast in your cottage, didn't you, Margaret?'

'I can't remember. I was very tired and couldn't keep awake.'

'You're obviously awake now, so *think* about how many spells the three of you cast!'

Margaret cringed at George's raised voice and Francis thought how like a frightened mouse she looked. 'We did four spells, Sir George'.

'And the three of you partook in the casting of them all?'

'Yes.'

Sir George switched his focus to Phillipa. 'Since Margaret has just told us that you were present when this fourth spell was cast, you can tell us what it was. The last time you were asked you claimed only to remember three.'

Phillipa glanced at Francis and he could see she feared what his reaction would be. 'It was a spell of infertility, placed on the Earl and Countess of Rutland, Sir George.'

'And how was it done?'

'Our mother boiled a small cauldron of water and put it on the table, then made a small cut on her arm with her knife and let a few drops of blood fall into the water. Then she put a

313

pair of Lady Cecilia's gloves she had taken from the castle into the cauldron with some wool from the mattress the countess had given to Margaret when she dismissed her. Next –'

'You mean the mattress from our bed that your sister and some lover had befouled while we were away!' Francis shot an enraged look at Margaret and took a few deep breaths to calm himself. 'Continue.'

'Ma swirled the gloves and wool around in the water with her knife, and chanted some words before lifting them out to cool on a drying cloth. Then she wiped them across Rutterkin's belly while Margaret and I held him still. Ma said Rutterkin didn't need to carry this spell to the castle because it was powerful enough to work without that.'

'What words were said during the performing of this spell?'

'I can't remember exactly, Sir George, but I can tell you some of it. It started, "Barren womb, until the tomb", and something about infertile seed not doing the deed.'

'Do you remember any of it, Margaret?'

'I… I remember only one part, but you won't like it at all. Our pa didn't either when we told him about it. It said that the Manners family would soon be no more. Pa wouldn't let Ma play *any* games with us after that because she'd done too many bad things.'

Francis felt Samuel's hand on his clenched fist as he struggled to control his rage. He nodded as he calmed, and asked Samuel to put his questions to the sisters.

'You both confess to taking part in these abhorrent spells with your mother, yet you both claim not to have made pacts with the Devil. We all know that witches can only cast spells

Chapter Sixteen

because they have given themselves to Satan. What do you say to that, Phillipa?'

'I have never given myself to the Devil, Reverend. But if doing as I was told by our mother means that I made a pact with him without realising, then that must be what happened. I have never seen the Devil or been a part of a coven. People say that witches meet the Devil at their monthly Sabbaths, where they feast and dance, but other than hearing people whispering about those gatherings, I have no idea of what really happens at one.'

'What about you, Margaret? Do you deny making a pact with the Devil?'

'I can't remember doing that, Reverend, but I do remember the spells we did.'

Samuel heaved a sigh, 'Well then, we'll move on. Yesterday you were both examined by a midwife who searched your bodies for signs that you had given yourself to the Devil.' Both women stiffened and Francis wondered if they thought they'd be subjected to that again. 'We had our report from Mistress Ingram before she left the castle,' Samuel continued, 'and I am about to tell you what she found. Do not interrupt before I've finished. Then you will answer further questions on this matter.

'Firstly, the lady found teats on both of you. It seems that you, Phillipa, have a pronounced teat between your breasts that –'

'That isn't a –' she started but George moved quickly and knocked her from the stool with a backhanded strike across the side of her head before she said more.

'Interrupt again and the gaoler will bring me the pilniewinks! Get back on the stool and do as the reverend asked.'

'Thank you, Sir George,' Francis said, and nodded to Samuel to continue.

'You also have a horizontal, jagged stripe behind your right shoulder, Phillipa. It's about three inches long, with the appearance of skin that has been ripped apart but healed again. Mistress Ingram believes it to be typical of marks made by the Devil when a person first makes his or her pact with him. The marks vary in size and shape, but Satan often draws his long claws across the skin in order that his followers can identify each other.

'Those are the two most pronounced marks the midwife found on you, Phillipa, although she found numerous red lumps all over both of you, some raised more than others, which she believes could also be teats. You can have your say about that once I've revealed what the midwife found on your sister.

'Now, Margaret, a teat was found just above your buttocks.' Francis watched the younger woman's brow crease in puzzlement, then she opened her mouth to speak. But the sight of Sir George ready to pounce evidently put a stop to that. 'And as I said, you also have several red lumps across your body and a Devil's mark on your left upper arm. Yours takes the form of a short gash at either side of your arm which, according to Mistress Ingram, was where the Devil grasped you, and his nails sank into your flesh.'

'Thank you, Reverend,' Francis said. 'We'll now hear what you both have to say regarding these marks. Phillipa first.'

'The mark the midwife calls a teat has been there as long as I can remember,' Phillipa started. 'My mother called it a mole,

Chapter Sixteen

probably because it looked like a tiny, brown mole hill. The scar on my shoulder is from when I fell out of our oak tree when I was nine. I landed on Ma's garden rake, which she'd been using earlier. It cut into my shoulder, making it bleed a lot. When it healed up it left the scar. And the red lumps on both of us are bites from the hundreds of fleas that live in the dungeon straw and feed on the blood of prisoners.'

'Margaret?' Francis said without further questioning Phillipa.

'Ma says I have a small wart at the bottom of my back, where the reverend said the midwife found a teat. It has been there for about three or four years and I think it is getting smaller now. I don't know what those marks on my arms are but I have been bitten by the dungeon rats so many times. The red bumps are flea bites, as Phillipa said.'

'Since we have the word of a midwife experienced in seeking out teats and Devil's marks, we can discount your explanations as feeble and unworthy of consideration,' Sir George sneered. 'No one would take the words of witches over those of such a highly respected member of the community.'

Sir George searched through his papers for a moment before focusing on Phillipa and Margaret. 'Now we'll go back to another important issue, which is whether or not either of you had any familiars. Margaret can answer first this time.'

'I don't really know what a familiar is, Sir George, but if you mean animal friends, I have a few. Ma didn't mind sharing Rutterkin with me, but I know he liked her better than he liked me. Pa says I should stay away from him because he bites and scratches me instead of letting me pick him up to cuddle

317

like I do with my other animal friends. Besides Rutterkin, my best friends are Little Robin and Spirit. Little Robin is one of our hens, but she has a red-brown breast, and reminds me of a little robin redbreast. She doesn't really like to be cuddled but she lets me pick her up sometimes. Spirit is a little brown rabbit that comes into our garden to eat our herbs. Ma says she's a cheeky little thing, but she's certainly got spirit. So that's why I call her Spirit.'

The three men shared an exasperated look and Sir George went on, 'Have you any familiars that visit you to suck on your body, Phillipa?'

'No, Sir George.'

'Enough of your lies!' George raged. 'Sir Francis, I suggest we use the caspie-claws on both of these women to make them speak the truth!'

'Perhaps a few more nights of sleep deprivation would be in order before we resort to that,' Samuel whispered as the women wailed. 'The Court of Assize will not be meeting until the beginning of next month, so we have plenty of time to get these confessions. If we are unsuccessful after another period of enforced sleeplessness and food withdrawal, I will not object to whatever harsher method of persuasion you choose.'

Francis nodded his agreement, and George shrugged in resignation. 'As you wish,' he said, 'but in my opinion, they are obviously guilty of all charges levelled and deserve no leniency from us whatsoever. The sooner they confess the better, and we can go home until the trial is held.'

'Let's try Samuel's way first, George,' Francis soothed. 'A few more days here won't make much difference, and we're all

Chapter Sixteen

comfortably housed at suitable inns. I'll explain what we've decided to the others over our meal tonight. I'm certain we'll get the last part of the required confessions very soon.'

*

For three days and nights, Phillipa and Margaret were imprisoned in separate cells in recesses on the ground floor of Cobb Hall. As was the case during previous periods of enforced sleeplessness, they were given water but no food. They were also walked increasingly often if they showed signs of falling asleep.

Phillipa knew she was weakening and by the third night she pleaded to be permitted to sleep. To make matters worse, both she and Margaret were frail and faint from lack of food, their near-fleshless frames finding any kind of movement a torment. Phillipa also realised that Margaret had found the ordeal truly traumatic. Already exhausted from several sleepless nights, her sister's state of delirium worsened. So much so that when the gaolers claimed to have seen her spirits sucking her body in the night, she believed them; she'd just been in her garden playing with them.

On the morning of the seventh day of February, over a month after their arrest, the sisters were dragged from their cells to face three interrogators. Phillipa was horrified to see a brazier glowing brightly to one side of the room with a wooden chair close by to which a number of leather straps had been attached. Between the two, a metal caspie-claws stood on the floor. Margaret's terrified whine told Phillipa that she had seen them, too.

Behind the table was the Earl of Rutland, with Sir George to his right and Lord Willoughby to his left. Phillipa panicked still further at the realisation that Reverend Fleming wasn't here, the only one of the interrogators who could possibly plead for lenience for herself and Margaret. Inwardly she screamed at the injustice of all this and hoped that in an act of great love and compassion God would strike her and Margaret down before the barbaric caspie-claws could be heated.

'I see from your faces that you have noted what we intend for today if you do not speak the truth.' Sir Francis looked from one to the other, and Phillipa could see only loathing in his eyes. 'You have tried our patience with your despicable lies. You are both witches and murderers. My son… my heir… is dead because of your evil deeds, and my only surviving son seems destined to be taken from us soon. I hope you are satisfied with the results of your witchcraft and that the Devil will reward you in the next life. You are both destined to burn in Hell for all eternity for your wickedness.'

Sir Francis stopped abruptly and stared at them for a moment. 'Lord Willoughby has joined us today as a man skilled in applying the caspie-claws to the legs of witches. He will ensure the device glows hot enough to roast your legs right through. Whoever takes second place will have the pleasure of seeing the caspie-claws in action on her sister.

'Needless to say, a full confession of you making a pact with the Devil and using familiars to do his bidding will save us the bother of heating the instrument. It will also spare you from a great deal of pain.'

Sir Francis turned to Lord Willoughby. 'I believe we ar-

Chapter Sixteen

ranged for you to question the women first.'

'My thanks,' Lord Willoughby replied, fixing his searching gaze on Phillipa and Margaret. 'I have read through the interrogation records and note what you have confessed so far. I find it quite preposterous that either of you can deny giving yourself to Satan in view of the spells you admit to casting, and the Devil's marks and teats found on your bodies. Let us see if we can persuade you both to tell us what we want to know without having to resort to a most unpleasant form of persuasion.

'Tell us again about your familiars, Margaret. It seems you shared an interesting secret with one of our gaolers last night.'

Margaret's eyes began to close and she swayed on her stool. Sir George came round the table and shook her awake. 'Answer Lord Willoughby's questions and you can go back to the dungeon to sleep,' he said. 'You'd like that, wouldn't you, Margaret?'

'Yes,' she replied, and listened while Lord Willoughby repeated the question.

'Two spirits come often to suck on me,' she said. 'One is white and the other is black-spotted. The white one sucks under my left breast and the black-spotted one sucks deep within my private parts.'

'Do these spirits promise you anything in return for your sexual favours?'

'They promise to do everything I ask them to.'

'So, you are confessing that by bestowing sexual favours on these creatures… these devils… they enable you to brandish your power and do evil?'

Take Height, Rutterkin

'Yes, Lord Willoughby.'

'Are these the spirits that visited you last night?'

Margaret shook her head. 'Last night one with a big black head like an ape came, but I couldn't understand what he said so he went away again. Then my own familiars came. But I think I was back in my own garden last night, because I've only ever seen them there before. Rutterkin, Little Robin and Spirit don't like to leave our garden.'

Phillipa could see that Lord Willoughby was becoming annoyed with Margaret's ramblings. 'By admitting you have these imps and devils sucking on you, you must realise that the only way that can happen is by you making a pact with the Devil. And we have every reason to believe that you, Margaret, along with your mother and sister, did that with the sole purpose of using your evil power to get your revenge on people you felt had wronged you: people like the Manners family.'

'Lady Cecilia should not have dismissed me from service at the castle. I worked hard in that laundry – and in the hen house. I always loved hens, that's why the Devil sent me Little Robin.'

The three men looked at each other and nodded. Margaret's words were written down and Lord Willoughby turned his attention to Phillipa. 'Tell us about your familiars.'

Phillipa realised she'd have to make a similar confession to Margaret's or the caspie-claws would destroy her legs and she would undoubtedly hang anyway. Their lives would soon be over and all she had done was to watch her mother perform spells she did not believe would work.

'I only have one familiar,' she said, 'a white rat who sucks

Chapter Sixteen

my left breast. He has been visiting me for almost four years now.'

'And what did this creature promise you in return?'

'He promised to make Tom Simpson love me and keep him coming to our bawdyhouse – which he did. But his vengeful and controlling mother turned him against me.'

Lord Willoughby looked squarely at Phillipa. 'As I said to your sister, admitting to having imps and devils sucking your blood can only be possible if you have given yourself to the Devil. So, I ask you, Phillipa, do you confess to making a pact with the Devil?'

'Yes. I made it at the same time as Margaret. Our mother made hers a few weeks earlier.'

Sir George slammed his hand on the table. 'If you had admitted that to start with, you would have saved yourselves several sleepless nights, lack of food, and you, Phillipa Flower, a beaten face!' He shook his head as though expressing his despair at the pointless waste of time and effort, and Phillipa stared at this high-born lord, who had known nothing in his life but luxury, like the rest of the interrogators. Yet they used their titles and influence to force false confessions from poor people, using threats of horrendous torture – and sometimes turning those threats into deeds.

'But, at last we have your full confessions and we can now prepare for your trial,' Sir George said, his expression grim. 'If the judges find you guilty, you will both hang. A fitting end to all witches.'

Chapter Seventeen

In which the Flower sisters are judged

Phillipa and Margaret spent the next two weeks in the dungeon, left alone for the most part. Interrogations had ceased and they were disturbed only by the daily appearances of the weasel-faced chaplain, who used his visits to berate them for their wicked deeds and in making sure they knew they'd spend eternity in Hell. Not one word of prayer was offered. Even the comings and goings of the gaolers, who took pleasure in throwing taunts about the imminent hanging, were preferable to the visits of the sanctimonious chaplain. By talking to the gaolers, Phillipa could, at least, find out what was happening beyond this reeking dungeon.

'It'll be a fun day fer the folk of Lincoln,' Harry said one evening as he dished out the watery soup and hard bread. 'They love a good 'anging, especially when it's witches being hanged. Their bald 'eads make everyone laugh.'

Chained to the wall, three feet away from Phillipa, Margaret drank her soup, pretending not to hear as she dipped the hard bread into the tepid liquid to soften it. 'We've got the trial first,' Phillipa threw back at Harry, 'and who says the judges will find us guilty?'

'They find all of 'em guilty, especially witches. Course, not all prisoners hang. Some 'ave to spend time down 'ere, or in the gaol yonder. But witches…? Nah, they ain't goin' t' let witches live, now, are they? King James 'imself said 'e wants

Chapter Seventeen

all witches to hang. And 'e's told all them interrogators to use torture to get confessions out of 'em. You two were right to confess before the caspie-claws took a likin' to yer. We've 'ad to carry a few witches out to the hangman's cart 'cos their legs and feet had almost burnt right off.'

Phillipa couldn't bear to hear again what that barbaric torture did to a person and said the first thing that came into her head. 'Do you know when the trial will be?'

'I 'eard talk about it bein' sometime in early March, and we've only another full week left in February. So, you 'aven't got long to wait.'

*

At the end of the third week of February, the eighteen Lincolnshire gentlemen who would form the grand jury at the trials to be presented at the next Court of Assize arrived in Lincoln. The group comprised representatives of the three subdivisions of Lincolnshire – Lindsey, Kesteven and Holland – and were all members of the landed gentry. As Lord Lieutenant of Lincolnshire and the biggest landowner amongst them, Sir Francis received them and led the meeting, the purpose of which was to decide which were true cases to answer in court and which were not.

When the case against the Flower sisters came under consideration, Francis told them, 'Since I am the main accuser in this particular case, I can say nothing about it. You must decide for yourselves from the information provided by the interrogators and the women who examined the sisters if you believe it's a true case to answer.'

The men agreed and continued to peruse the findings, taking little time to decide that the case against the Flower sisters was a valid one. All Francis could do now was to bide his time until the coming of the judges who would preside over the trial.

He had only a few days to wait. On the twenty-fourth of February, the two judges appointed by King James from the higher courts around London, entered Lincolnshire with their attendants, to be greeted by trumpeters and welcomed by the sheriff's bailiff. On nearing the city of Lincoln, they were received by Sir William Pelham, the county's high sheriff, along with a number of the Lincolnshire gentry and other local officers. This company of august gentlemen was further swelled by pikemen and liverymen in colourful, ceremonial dress, and the splendid procession made its way to the city to the accompaniment of joyful music, the ringing of bells and a general atmosphere of celebration.

As they passed through the city wall into Lincoln on the last day of February, Sir Francis, his brother Sir George, and Lord Willoughby, were amongst some of the eminent local gentry waiting to welcome them. After a brief discussion on the state of affairs in the county, the company made its way to the imposing medieval cathedral for prayers and a sermon by the sheriff's chaplain. As Francis had expected, on this occasion, the service focused on the evils of witchcraft.

For appearances' sake, Francis took the pomp and ceremony in his stride, whilst inwardly his impatience for the trial to begin simmered. Only the conviction and hanging of these

Chapter Seventeen

witches could bring a sense of normality back into his life: a life that had been turned upside down by the evil doings of the Flower family.

*

Shire Hall, Lincoln Castle: March 4 1619

At seven o'clock on a cold and crisp morning in early March, citizens of the city of Lincoln and nearby villages thronged through the east gate of Lincoln Castle, heading for the old medieval Shire Hall. They surged into the courtroom in jovial holiday mood to enjoy watching witches and other felons wailing and begging for mercy when pronounced guilty and sentenced to hang. Francis never failed to be incensed that the crowds of illiterate, and sometimes drunken, spectators were permitted to watch – and frequently disrupt – the proceedings of what he saw as gravely serious matters. Worse still was the fact that the disorderly public could enter the courtroom at the same time as the judges and jury and other officials required for the trial to operate. Francis had often fought his way through to his seat, jostled along by a moving convoy of people who treated trials as entertainment laid on for them to enjoy. And today's gathering was no different.

Garbed in formal black cloaks and hoods, the two presiding judges took their seats in the middle of a raised bench to one side of the large, rectangular courtroom, flanked by some of the county's high-ranking gentry and officials. Amongst them were Sir Francis and Sir George Manners and Lord Willoughby.

Samuel Fleming had also joined them in order to give evidence during the trial.

It had not escaped Francis's notice that both of these celebrated judges were skilled in dealing with cases of witchcraft, which instantly told him that King James would be taking a keen interest in this case. Sir Edward Bromley, Baron of the Exchequer and a renowned witch hunter, had convicted the Pendle witches at Lancaster seven years ago, while Sir Henry Hobart was Lord Chief Justice of the Common Pleas, a position carrying national responsibility for the civil law.

Opposite to the judges, and presently awaiting the arrival of the Flower sisters, was the prisoners' dock, behind which the jurymen now sat, waiting to be sworn in. A number of minor officials, including the record keeper for the county and several court clerks, were seated around a low oval table in the middle of the room. With them were Sir William Pelham, Sheriff of Lincoln, and his undersheriff, whose responsibility it was to maintain order in the courtroom.

The tiered benches along the walls were soon crammed with the multitude of onlookers, behaving as though a bawdy play were about to start. Several of the sheriff's officers stood sentry in prominent places amongst them, ready to toss outside anyone who persistently yelled out or became involved in disagreements and scuffles.

At the oval table, a crier rose to his feet to demand silence in the courtroom. Once everyone had settled, a clerk read out the names of all taking part in the trial, including the judges, the various officials, and the prisoners. Then a bible was passed along all eighteen members of the jury and, in turn, each man

Chapter Seventeen

repeated the juror's oath:

I swear by Almighty God, I will faithfully try the defendant and give a true verdict according to the evidence...

Francis watched, itching for them to get the formalities over with and the questioning started. In due course, a clerk called for the prisoners to be brought in.

†

Phillipa and Margaret were garbed in the same clothing in which they had been captured over two months ago, and after all those weeks in the rancid, rat and flea infested conditions of the dungeon without a single wash, their skins and dresses were covered in filth, and the stench of those foul conditions clung to them. The flimsy mop caps did little to hide their shaven heads.

The crowds jeered, hooted and ridiculed and the sheriff and undersheriff rose to their feet. Sir William held up his hands and yelled, 'Silence in court!' The noise duly abated, and many heads turned to ensure that none of his officers were coming towards them, aiming to turn them out. Eventually, the clerk of the court ordered the sisters to raise their right hands and plead guilty or not guilty.

Phillipa was determined to put on a brave face and not give these people the satisfaction of seeing her weep or beg for leniency. Beside her, Margaret whimpered and could barely whisper her plea of 'not guilty', the reply they had decided to keep to throughout the trial, no matter what words the judges tried to put into their mouths. But Phillipa knew that her sister was easily intimidated by harsh voices, let alone the threats they carried, and that Margaret's damaged mind could cause her to say the most unexpected things. She also knew that despite her own attempts at an appearance of fortitude, they were here to be judged on confessions already made – and that their fate was already sealed. Her fingers moved to her crooked nose and she glared with loathing at Sir William, sitting below her at the table.

As the prime accuser, Sir Francis was called to give his evidence first. He rose to his feet and Phillipa stared defiantly at him, causing him to shuffle a little. She grinned, knowing her stare had had the desired effect, and the spectators yelled and hissed at her response.

'I accuse Phillipa and Margaret Flower of wilfully casting spells that have already killed one of my sons and left our younger son gravely ill. We have little hope of young Francis surviving for much longer. These witches even attempted to do the same to my daughter, Katherine. Thankfully, their spell did not have the long-lasting effect it had on my sons.'

Sir Francis's words hung on the air of the courtroom and Phillipa knew that the court's sympathies with Sir Francis would increase the gravity of the accusations against her and Margaret.

'In addition to that, they cast a spell to prevent my wife and I from conceiving more children,' Francis went on, looking round the courtroom, evidently playing on the jury's pity. 'They were determined to put an end to the Manners family completely. So far, it pains me to say that the countess and I have been unable to conceive a child for the past six years.'

Chapter Seventeen

Murmurs of sympathy passed around the room, leading to shouts of, 'String up the witches! The wicked creatures deserve to die!'

Again, Sir William was forced to bring an end to the incensed yells.

'Thank you, Sir William,' Sir Edward said, once silence resumed. 'The charges against these sisters are, indeed, grave. Other than their own confessions of guilt, do you have further proof that they cast these spells?'

'I do, Sir Edward. I sent men back to their cottage in Bottesford to seek a glove that once belonged to my elder son, Lord Henry, and was used by Joan Flower and her daughters in the spell they cast upon him. Margaret Flower confessed during interrogation that the glove was buried beneath the willow tree in their Bottesford garden. And that was where my men found it.'

Francis unfolded a piece of cloth to retrieve a small kid glove and held it up for the jury to see. It was black and rotting after six years in the ground, and again the spectators murmured of the wickedness of the witches.

'In addition to this, we have numerous statements from villagers about the curses – in the Devil's name, I might add – laid upon people in Bottesford by Joan Flower.' Francis held up several sheets of paper. 'The results of those curses, along with the victims' names, are written down with these statements for all to see. Joan Flower's curses resulted in everything from the sickness and deaths of people and livestock, to the failure of their crops, foods turning rotten for no reason at all and a sudden storm and lightning striking someone's home. Most villagers agree that Phillipa and Margaret are just as much witches as was their mother. One young man, by the name of Thomas Simpson, truly believes that Phillipa Flower bewitched him in order to keep him going to their bawdyhouse. His statement to that effect is recorded in here with the rest.'

Enraged shouts filled the room and Sir William and his deputy stood to regain order.

'I must also add that we interviewed three of the cunning women known to Joan Flower,' Francis went on. 'Two of the women have given us further evidence regarding the spell Joan cast that killed my elder son. One of them also confessed to having provided Joan Flower with the spell in the first place.' He glanced sidelong at the seated judges. 'The women are in custody here in the castle, my lords, should you request their evidence to be given in person.'

'That won't be necessary,' Sir Edward replied. 'What they said is clearly written in these documents, though we have noted that the names of Phillipa and Margaret Flower do not feature greatly in their recollections.'

'No, my lord, but if we take into account how closely the Flower women worked and schemed together in their cottage, I'd say we can safely assume they were involved. The sisters have already confessed to taking part in the spells with their mother, and their loose morals are obvious. Rector Samuel Fleming lives close to the Flower women's cottage, and I feel it would be of use to this trial to hear what he has to say about the goings-on inside that cottage in recent years.'

'Indeed, it would,' Sir Henry agreed, taking his turn at questioning. 'The characters of the accused must always be

Chapter Seventeen

taken into account. Rector, please share your knowledge of these women with the court.'

Phillipa's hopes for a kind word from the reverend plummeted. As a witness, Reverend Fleming needed to take the oath to speak nothing but the truth, though she knew he would always tell the truth, no matter how he felt. A glance at Margaret told Phillipa that her sister had retreated inside herself rather than accept the events occurring around her, and was staring vacantly ahead, as though in a trance.

'I have known these two young women all their lives,' Samuel started, 'and I christened both in Saint Mary the Virgin's Church in Bottesford. I also knew their father, John Flower, a kind and honourable man who loved the Church. But their mother, Joan, was not a church-goer, a fact that added to people's assumptions regarding her being a devil-worshipper in later years. John worked away from the village for much of the time and Joan only took her daughters to church when John was home.'

Samuel's gaze met Phillipa's, his sadness evident. 'When John Flower died, the family became desperate for coin to live on, and after Margaret was dismissed from service at the castle, she and her mother opened a bawdyhouse. By that time, the family was despised by every woman in the village, some of whom were also servants at Belvoir Castle. Not wishing to work with a woman from a family of such ill repute, they had taken to calling Phillipa unseemly names. They even resorted to physically threatening her along the castle corridors. Naturally, Lady Cecilia was obliged to discharge her from service and I'm sad to say that Phillipa had no other option than to join her mother and sister in the bawdyhouse.

'Things went from bad to worse after that. Raucous laughter and loud singing could be heard from inside their cottage every night of the week, and the coming and goings of men seemed endless.'

'I see,' Sir Henry said, nodding. 'Explain to the court, if you would, Rector, why Margaret was dismissed from service at the castle.'

Samuel glanced at the two women and again, Phillipa knew he would be obliged to answer truthfully. 'Margaret was dismissed for two reasons. The first was for the theft of foods from the castle kitchens on a number of occasions. The second was because she and a male member of staff had thoughtlessly taken the liberty of using the earl and countess's bed for a lustful romp while the earl's family was away from home. They were caught by a chamber maid who had entered the room in order to clean.'

Calls of 'strumpet!' and 'thief!' erupted from the onlookers. Sir William and his deputy rose to their feet and the calls abruptly stopped.

'Thank you, Rector,' Sir Edward said, choosing to overlook the interruption. 'You have given us a good idea of the lewd and untrustworthy nature of the accused. So now we move on.' He fixed his steady gaze on the sisters. 'Tell us, Margaret, why you confessed to casting spells with your mother and yet today you plead not guilty to witchcraft and of making a pact with the Devil.'

In the following silence, Margaret gazed round at the many faces staring at her and shook her head violently. 'Pa says he won't let me play Blind Man's Buff if I make spells with Ma.

Chapter Seventeen

He says it's a wicked thing to do.'

'But you *did* cast spells with her, didn't you?' Sir Edward prompted. 'Tell us what you did.'

Margaret face creased into an inane smile as she thought. 'Yes, I did, didn't I? I stabbed the little gloves of Lord Henry and Lord Francis, and stirred them about in the water. And I helped to dig a really deep hole under the willow tree so we could bury Lord Henry's glove. Oh, and I held Rutterkin still while Ma rubbed Lady Cecilia's glove on his belly. That was part of a spell that would mean the earl and countess couldn't have any more children.'

Shouts and jeers from the spectators were again quietened by Sir William and his deputy.

Sir Edward nodded his thanks at Sir William and continued, 'You also made a pact with the Devil, didn't you, Margaret? It says you did in here.' Sir Edward held up his wad of notes from the interrogators, and Phillipa knew that after Margaret's gleeful confessions whatever she said to deny the charges now would be scorned by the court.

'I did, your lordship, but I mustn't tell Pa that because he thinks I didn't. The Devil sent me plenty of friends to play with, like Little Robin, Spirit, and Rutterkin. He also sent two imps to suck on my body, one white and one black-spotted.'

'Thank you, Margaret,' Sir Edward said, before addressing the eighteen men seated opposite him, behind the prisoners' dock. 'Gentlemen of the jury, having read the findings of the interrogators and the midwife who examined the women's bodies for Devil's marks and teats, you will recall that both of these features were found on the sisters: indisputable proof of their pacts with the Devil.'

'She found no Devil's marks or teats on either of us!' Phillipa called out. 'The scar she found on me was from an accident I had as a child, and the mark she said was a teat was a mole! The other marks were rat and flea bites from the reeking straw of the dungeon!'

The spectators erupted with enraged shouts: 'Stinking liar… filthy devil worshipper… the midwife's never wrong… the dungeon's too good for the likes of you…!'

'Silence in court!' Sir William yelled, though his voice was barely heard above the rumpus. More of his officers streamed into the room and began marching people outside and, at length, the rest calmed down.

'We can well understand your feelings towards these witches,' Sir Henry said, addressing the remaining spectators. 'They have caused so much heartache for the Earl and Countess of Rutland, who are known far and wide for their kindness and generosity of spirit towards the people who dwell on their estates. That they have become the targets of wicked and vengeful women is truly deplorable. The harm done to Sir Francis and Lady Cecilia by their vile spells cannot be undone, and will have long-lasting effects. Which is, of course, exactly what these witches intended.'

'Sir Henry,' Phillipa said, quietly now after her outburst. 'The vengeance you speak of was our mother's, not ours. All we did was watch while she cast those spells, because she told us to.'

Sir Henry stared coldly back at her. 'It is easy to deny your

Chapter Seventeen

confessions when you face the gallows. It's too late to withdraw those confessions now.'

'But they were made under the threat of roasting our legs in the caspie-claws if we didn't! What person would not confess when the alternative is such a merciless torture?'

'You heard what Sir Henry said, woman!' Sir Edward's face reddened as his anger rose and his patience ebbed. 'The time to deny your guilt has passed. We have heard the evidence against you from a number of sources and the jurors must now decide on your innocence or guilt.'

Phillipa held her tongue, along with the rest of the court, as Sir Edward addressed the jury. 'In reaching your verdict I charge each of you to consider what your own conscience and the evidence you have heard in this court tell you. I also urge that the eighteen of you come to a unanimous verdict. The prisoners are either wholly guilty or wholly not guilty. Who is acting spokesman for you?'

A tall, thin man stood. 'I am, your lordship. My name is Richard Burroughs.'

'Then, Mr Burroughs, do you, the jurors, need time to reach your verdict?'

'Only as long as it takes for each man to pass along his paper with his verdict written on it and for me to count them, my lord. We do not need to leave the room unless our verdict is not unanimous.'

'Very well.' Sir Edward swept the court with his commanding gaze. 'We will have silence while the juror's verdicts are collected. Anyone who disobeys that order will be taken directly to the gaol across the castle yard.'

At length, Mr Burroughs stood and Sir Edward asked, 'Do you find the accused guilty or not guilty?'

'Guilty, my lord. Unanimously.'

The spectators erupted with cheers and whistles until Sir William stood and his men closed in along their rows.

But Phillipa could not hold back her fury at the injustice of it all. Their own side of the charges had been given no consideration whatsoever. No one had spoken in their defence, and they were both assumed guilty before the trial even started. Inside she was screaming that she and Margaret had only confessed under the threat of cruel torture, and still being hanged after it.

'Since you believe us guilty of Devil worship, I'll play along with that,' she yelled, thrusting out her arm and circling to take in the court:

> *May the Devil strike you all dead*
> *And you dwell in Hell for eternity*
> *Stoking Satan's fires*
> *While your roasting flesh falls from your bones*
> *Charred meat for the devilish hounds.*

Sir William leapt from his seat and into the dock, striking a blow across Phillipa's head that rendered her dazed and sprawled across the floor. The spectators were on their feet, cheering on the action, their arms waving. Sir William held up his hands for quiet and eventually, silence resumed.

Sir Edward was incensed. 'The woman has pronounced her own death sentence, and in doing so, also that of her sister!'

Phillipa dragged herself to her feet and stood beside Mar-

Chapter Seventeen

garet while the square of black fabric, known as the black cap, was placed on Sir Edward's head before he delivered the death sentence. 'Phillipa and Margaret Flower, on this, the fourth day of March in the year sixteen hundred and nineteen, you have been found guilty in accordance with the witchcraft statute of sixteen hundred and four. You have consulted with, and acted in accordance with the Devil's will, and it is you who will spend eternity in Hell. From this place, you will return to the dungeon from which you came, and on the eleventh day of March you will be taken to the place of execution to hang by the neck until you are dead.'

*

The day after the trial, the gaoler named Harry came down to the dungeon to speak to Phillipa and Margaret. Phillipa had spotted him among the spectators at the trial and realised it must have been his day off. And now he'd probably come to gloat and ridicule, as he usually did. In her vacuous state, Margaret continued singing little children's rhymes and didn't even know that Harry was there...

> *To market to market to buy a fat pig*
> *Home again, home again, jiggety-jig...*

''Ow yer bearing up?' Harry asked Phillipa, squatting down beside her.

She glowered at him and he grinned, but facing death in less than a week, she was in no mood to be nice. 'Go away and take your mockery with you. How would you feel if you were going to be strung up to dangle in front of crowds of jeering people, all happy to watch you choke to death?'

'I'd not like it one bit,' he said, without the grin. 'My wife didn't like it, either.'

Phillipa stared at him, thinking she'd misheard. 'Do you mean your wife wouldn't like the idea of you being strung up, or the idea of being strung up herself?'

'I don't mean either. She *was* strung up and left danglin' till she was dead. At least they let me take 'er body for a decent burial once I got back 'ome. She was a cunning woman… grew lots of 'erbs and made 'ealing potions. She was kind and caring but they still called 'er "witch". They took 'er while I was away for a few days sellin' the leather goods I made in Manchester.'

'Manchester? That's a long way from here. And if you work in leather, how come you're a gaoler now?'

Harry shrugged. 'It was the only job open to me when I arrived in Lincoln. I'm thinkin' of moving somewhere else to look… Manchester, p'raps.'

'I wish you well in that,' Phillipa said, unable to think of Harry's future when there was no future for her and Margaret.

'Do you know, Phillipa Flower, I've never known a woman as spirited as you, or as brave. I know from past experience there's no justice to be 'ad when someone's declared a witch. My wife – Judith 'er name was – was no more a witch than you or yer sister. All she did was make 'erbal cures to 'elp people, but because other members of 'er family in Pendle 'ad been charged with witchcraft the year before, she didn't stand a chance. But it was six years ago and in the past. I try not to think about it. But your rough treatment 'ere has really nettled.'

Chapter Seventeen

Phillipa scowled. 'I wouldn't have thought so, considering the way you've taunted and ridiculed us. I am no witch and neither is Margaret.'

'I believe you. I watched 'em interrogate you often enough and admire yer guts for 'olding out as long as yer did, especially when you were kept awake and starved for days on end. Reckon they'd 'ave used the caspie-claws and the pilniewinks, too, if yer 'adn't confessed when yer did. And I 'ave to be nasty to prisoners or the rest of the gaolers would think I was soft and not fit to do the job.

'You could 'ave a good life ahead of yer, if we could just get you out of 'ere,' he added, totally surprising her.

She stared at him, wondering if he really meant that. 'If only,' she said. 'I doubt if anyone has ever escaped from this dungeon.'

'There's a first time for everythin', Phillipa Flower. Anyways, I'll leave you to think about whether you'd be willin' to try after yer've seen the reverend. 'e's up there waiting to talk to the two of you. We'll 'ave another little chat about what I said when I've come up with a good plan.'

Harry climbed up the ladder and through the trapdoor, to reappear moments later, leading Samuel Fleming down with him. 'I'll leave you to talk in private,' he said, turning to leave. Then he turned back and said, 'Oh, and Reverend, if yer've time. I'd like a quick word with you when you're done down 'ere.'

†

'I am here to pray with you both, as I said I would if you were found guilty,' Samuel said as he reached Phillipa and Margaret.

Take Height, Rutterkin

'Shall we kneel…?'

Phillipa yelled at Margaret to stop her mindless singing and get to her feet. 'Reverend, this straw isn't fit for you to kneel on. Your cassock will be covered in filth if you do, and fleas will likely jump on you.'

The look of concern on Phillipa's grimy face tore at Samuel's heart. 'My child, that is the least of my concerns today. Please, both of you, kneel with me.'

'I don't want to pray,' Margaret said, her face reflecting a childish pique. 'Ma will be cross if she finds out. She doesn't believe in God. Is she up the ladder, waiting to take us home?'

'No, Margaret, your ma hasn't arrived yet. Perhaps she'll come another day. So, shall we say The Lord's Prayer together..?

The three of them knelt and Samuel, started…

> *Our Father, who art in heaven*
> *hallowed be thy name…*

Phillipa's voice was choked with emotion as they chanted along with Samuel and when they had finished, she said, 'We haven't said that prayer since before Pa died, Reverend. As Margaret just said, Ma wouldn't allow us to pray. It felt good to be saying it again.'

'It is a wonderful prayer, Phillipa, especially so for you two in these last days. The lines…

> *Forgive us our trespasses,*
> *as we forgive those who trespass against us…*

are particularly applicable. If you say this prayer often in the

Chapter Seventeen

coming days, knowing that God does forgive us our sins, it will be of comfort to you.'

Samuel's heart was heavy, his thoughts filled with the terrible ordeal these two young women faced. Having already been subjected to weeks of filth and squalor, gruelling interrogations, sleep and food deprivation and threats of unbearable torture, they now faced the end of their lives. But having heard the sisters pray, Samuel now knew one thing for certain: Phillipa and Margaret Flower were not witches, even *if* their mother had been one. If witchcraft was responsible for the sorrows that had befallen Sir Francis's family, it must have been inflicted by their mother. No witch who had sold her soul to the Devil could ever pray to God. The words would simply come out as a jumbled, nonsensical ramble.

The saddest thing about having this revelation now was that there was absolutely nothing Samuel could do about it.

Chapter Eighteen

In which the Flower sisters face the gallows

Lincoln Castle: March 10 1619

'Well now, Phillipa Flower, the day yer've been dreadin's almost 'ere,' Harry said, squatting down on the straw beside her soon after daybreak. 'Yer 'anging's all set for one o' clock tomorrow, no sooner, no later, so we need t' make sure yer get to the gallows on time, especially as me and Jack've volunteered to drive the cart. The 'angman won't be 'appy if we're late.'

Phillipa glared at him, wondering how he could profess to be sympathetic to their plight on one day and so callous on another. 'I don't want to know all this, and I'm glad Margaret's still asleep and not listening to your stupid taunts. If you're trying to make me feel worse than I already do, let me tell you that nothing you say could do that.'

'Go away and gloat somewhere else!' she shot at him when he didn't budge. But her bravado was superficial and tears rolled down her cheeks. She stared at the brightening sky through the arrow slit of the recess, wishing with all her being she could be free to go home and enjoy the new day. But the thought was soon dashed; she now had no home to go to. The Flower family would always be witches to Bottesford folk.

'How can you be so… so *cruel* as to talk to me like this? Do you think I have no feelings at all? The thought of being strung up on the gallows terrifies me, though I try to be brave.'

Chapter Eighteen

'I wouldn't believe you if you said you weren't terrified, but I did warn yer. Most people who come before them 'igh court judges are found guilty, whether they are or not. Especially those accused of witchcraft. The judges make sure they stay on the right side of King James. They say the man's obsessed with 'unting down and 'anging witches. 'e'd be better takin' more care of the poor folk in 'is lands than chasin' witches if you ask me. Few of us 'ave anything good to say about 'im.

'Have you 'ad a think about escapin'?'

Phillipa nodded wearily and rubbed her aching brow. 'Yes, and I can't see how it could be possible. You wouldn't have a chance of getting us out of Cobb Hall, let alone the castle. We can't simply climb up that ladder and head for the gates. For one thing, Margaret's lost her mind. She has no idea what's going on from one minute to the next, and would probably start singing and telling everyone in the castle we were leaving. I doubt she'd ever be the same again, even if she were to live. She'd need to be constantly looked after. Our lives were doomed as soon as our mother cast a few meaningless spells and started hurling curses at the miserable village goodwives.'

'I meant just you,' Harry said, after listening to her rambled reasoning. 'I can't do anythin' for yer sister. And as you just said, Margaret wouldn't 'ave a life worth livin', even if she did get out of 'ere. But you, Phillipa Flower, are a different matter. Though you might not agree to doin' what I suggest. It's taken a bit of plannin' and we're lucky that events 'ere in the dungeon 'ave played out well fer us.'

'You'd better tell me what this plan is, then.'

'Tomorrow mornin' we need you to die – at least, you need

to *pretend* to be dead. As soon as Margaret wakes, tell 'er yer feel sick as a dog and have pains in your guts. Play it up for a bit, then drop to the straw, facing away from yer sister or she might see yer breathin' or yer eyelids flickerin'. I'll come down t' see what's goin' on as soon as she starts shoutin' and wailin'. If she doesn't make a fuss, I'll come down 'alf an hour later and take it from there.'

Phillipa couldn't begin to guess where Harry was going with all this but she nodded and let him continue.

'As yer know, prisoners die in 'ere all the time, usually from gaol fever. A man died yesterday afternoon and a woman about yer age died in the night, so no one's goin' t' question another death down 'ere tomorrow. Me and Jack will bury the man this afternoon, and the woman's due for burial tomorrow mornin'. So we just need to swap 'er body for yours. She's about your height and just as skinny. We'll shave 'er head, put your dress and mop cap on 'er, and rub more dirt and grease on 'er face and legs. No one will be able to tell it ain't you.'

Phillipa shook her head before the glimmer of hope sparked by Harry's words took hold. 'I'm not brave enough to try to escape; the mere thought of being found out terrifies me. Besides, I don't know whether I can trust you. You've never tried to help either of us since we've been in this filthy place, though you haven't been cruel to us like some of the gaolers. But why would you risk your own life to save me?'

'Because I know yer innocent, and I don't want t' see yer 'ang. And as fer not bein' brave enough, I've never met a woman as brave as you in me life. No one's ever stood up to them interrogators before.' Harry smirked.' You really got Sir

Chapter Eighteen

William's goat. I was glad yer eventually confessed, or you'd be sittin' 'ere with charred, useless legs and still facin' the gallows…

'Ain't the thought of havin' a life ahead of yer worth the risk of tryin' to escape?'

Phillipa squeezed her eyes shut as teardrops welled. 'How can I leave Margaret to face the gallows alone?'

'She'd 'ang whether you were with 'er or not, and there's no way of gettin' 'er out. Besides, if we follow my plan, she might not realise you aren't there. So will yer at least try t' save yerself?'

Phillipa covered her face with her hands as the enormity of what she was considering overwhelmed her. If she managed to get away, would she ever forgive herself for abandoning Margaret? Then she thought again about what Harry had just said about Margaret hanging anyway, and whispered, 'Yes, I will… at least I think I will,'

'There's no time to be undecided now. It's either yes or no. If it's yes, I can let Jack know we're goin' ahead with my plan and can make the final preparations. I need a definite answer, now. Will yer go along with my plan to escape, or not?'

Phillipa momentarily closed her eyes as indecision raged. Then she simply said, 'Yes.'

*

Lincoln Castle: March 11 1619

Phillipa spent her last night in the dungeon tormented with guilt at having agreed to saving herself and leaving Margaret to her fate. On top of which, the closer it got to morning, thoughts of what they could do to her – as well as to Harry and Jack – if they were captured, caused her to break out in a cold sweat.

Harry came down to the dungeon soon after dawn. Margaret was still sleeping and he squatted down beside Phillipa.

'From the look on yer face, I'd say yer've been thinkin' 'bout changin' yer mind,' he whispered. 'I 'ope you 'aven't, 'cos everythin' else is goin' t' plan.'

'I haven't changed my mind,' she whispered back, 'although if you'd asked me a couple of hours ago, that wouldn't have been my answer. The thought of being captured and brought back here to be tortured before I hang petrifies me.'

'I understand that, but Jack and me will do our best to make sure yer not caught. And there's no reason yer should be if we stick to my plan.'

Phillipa nodded and Harry said, 'Remember what I told yer yesterday about pretendin' to be sick and droppin' to the straw?'

'Yes'.

'You need to do that soon after Margaret wakes. She must believe yer dead, so put on a good show for 'er. I'll come down when she starts yellin' and carry yer body up to our gaolers' room. You can take off yer dress for the dead woman in there. I've got another for yer to put on, as well as a thicker and bigger mop cap. Jack's shavin' the woman's 'ead up there now.'

Margaret suddenly shuffled and Harry stopped whispering. But her steady breathing resumed, telling them that Margaret was still asleep.

'Jack and me will bring the woman's body down 'ere and lay it in a place where it can be collected later for them to 'ang,'

Chapter Eighteen

Harry continued. 'We'll put you in the cart, wrapped ready for burial in a corner of the castle grounds where all 'anged felons are buried, seein' as most families don't want the bother.'

Phillipa frowned, not understanding. 'Did you say they'll hang the corpse?'

Harry nodded. 'The crowds wouldn't be 'appy to see only one witch danglin' when they were expectin' two, and we don't want to cause any riots. They'd rather see the corpse danglin' than be told the witch died in the gaol. But it won't be you they're 'anging, will it?

'I 'aven't time to tell yer more now, but I need t' know before I go that yer'll fake yer death as I said, and won't move a muscle when Jack 'elps me t' carry yer up the ladder. You must trust me, Phillipa Flower, or my plan won't work and me and Jack'll be strung up as well as you.'

Soon after Harry's retreat, Margaret roused and immediately started singing another childish rhyme. She turned and smiled at Phillipa. 'I think we'd better get out of bed before Ma comes and shouts at us for being lazy,' she said, slowly standing up. 'There'll be the eggs to collect and the cottage to sweep and tidy before we go to the market. Is Pa coming home this weekend, Phillipa? I hope he is.'

'I hope so too. It's fun when Pa comes home, and we always bake nice things. Pa loves his meat coffins, and we enjoy baking them. But I don't think I'll be able to eat one today. I feel so ill…'

Her heart pounding, Phillipa pushed herself to her feet, then grasped her belly and groaned, as though in great pain. She doubled over, pretending to retch for some moments. 'I feel really bad, Margaret,' she said, swiping her sleeve across her mouth before clutching her belly as though she could wrench out the griping pains. 'I've had sickening pains in my guts all night and I ache all over. I think I might have gaol fever and be dying...'

Phillipa dropped to the straw, as instructed, facing away from her sister, who was manacled and chained to the wall, two feet out of reach of her in the alcove.

Margaret fell to her knees, laughing. 'No one dies just like that, Phillipa, so get up and stop being silly. We need to go to the market with Ma. Get out of bed and get dressed before she goes without us.'

Margaret reached out to Phillipa's motionless body as far as the chains would allow. 'Get up!' she shouted. 'We need to go downstairs!' When Phillipa still didn't stir, Margaret said, 'If you don't get up now, I'll shout for Ma...

'Ma! Ma!' she yelled at the top of her voice. 'I think Phillipa's dead!' Evidently struck by her own words, Margaret started screaming, 'She's dead!' she shrieked as two gaolers hurried across the straw from the ladder, then continued to squeal like a wounded pig.

It took all of Phillipa's strength not to turn to see what was going on. But then she heard Harry's voice trying to calm Margaret down. She opened her eyes for long enough to see that he'd moved to the middle of the dungeon where his voice could be heard by all prisoners.

'Another of your cellmates has just died of gaol fever, and she was due for 'anging this afternoon,' he yelled. 'We'll take 'er upstairs to wrap ready for burial with the woman who died

Chapter Eighteen

yesterday. Yer'll just' ave t' cover yer ears till 'er sister stops squealing.'

Harry unlocked the manacle around Phillipa's wrist and hoisted her inert body over his shoulder, as only someone used to doing this work could do, and followed Jack slowly up the ladder. The two men manoeuvred her through the trapdoor and across Cobb Hall to one of the gaolers' rooms where Harry lowered her to the floor. He put a finger to his lips, indicating she should keep quiet. She glanced at the body of the young woman on a table, garbed only in her shift, with her head shaven and her face, arms and legs covered in filth and grime. Phillipa's only thought was that, at least, her suffering was over.

'There's a dress and cap for yer over there,' Harry whispered, tilting his head towards one of four wooden chairs in the room. 'They should both fit yer well. We'll stay outside while yer change clothes, so knock on the door when yer've done. Then we'll get yer dress and cap on the woman and wrap 'er in a shroud before we take 'er back to the dungeon, just in case any of the officials come in 'ere when we're supposed to be burying 'er.'

'You won't put her near to Margaret, will you?' Phillipa whispered back, guilt again engulfing her at the thought of Margaret, left behind to hang. 'If no one reminds her I'm dead, she'll soon forget she watched me die.'

Harry shook his head. 'We'll find an empty alcove. Now, we'll leave you to get yerself changed.'

Trembling with fear at the thought of one of the officials suddenly bursting through the door, Phillipa changed her clothes and tentatively knocked on the door.

'I told you the dress'd fit yer well, and no one will know yer've no 'air with that cap on,' Harry said. 'Right, now we need to wrap yer in sackcloth for burial. Then we'll get you in the cart so I can drive it over to the graveyard – if we can call it that – before we 'ead to the gallows later on.'

The sackcloth smelt of rotting vegetables, but the two men had, at least, left gaps around her face so she could breathe. The cart rolled across the castle yard and she was thankful to be lying on a pile of old blankets. But her stomach lurched and she froze with fear when they came to a halt and someone standing very close to them spoke to Harry.

'Another death in the dungeon?'

''Fraid so, Gerard. Gaol fever takes most of 'em, especially those who spend months down there. The dungeon's a stinkin' 'ole, if I'm honest.'

'I thought I'd seen you and Jack heading to the graveyard earlier. The grave's all ready, I take it?'

'Aye. It's best to do that beforehand, so it only takes one of us to finish the job later. Fillin' in's always easier than diggin' out.'

'I'll let you get on with it, then. No doubt I'll see you at the hanging later.'

The cart rumbled on and Harry hummed to let Phillipa know she could relax a little again. When they next halted, she guessed they'd reached their destination.

'I've turned the cart so the 'orse is facin' the castle yard,' Harry told her. 'Not that this patch of earth they call a graveyard is overlooked, but we still need to be on our guard. We'll get the sackcloth off yer so I can wrap it round a rolled-up

Chapter Eighteen

blanket. It needs to look enough like a body so if anyone arrives when I've just started shovellin', they won't start askin' awkward questions. At least that castle guard only took a quick look in the cart.

'Anyways, once I get to work, yer'll need t' get yerself under the blankets. Once we 'ead off t' the gallows, I'll put a couple of coats and tunics on top of the pile so it looks like a pile of old clothes. Later on, yer sister and the woman's corpse will be in the back with yer, so Margaret mustn't see yer. Jack'll be drivin', so I'll sit between Margaret and the blankets. Did you hear all that?'

'Yes. Is it far to the gallows?'

'Not much more than a ten-minute walk. The gallows is a great eyesore outside the north-west corner of the castle walls, where there's plenty o' space for the big crowds that gather at 'angings. It'll take about the same time with the cart, especially if folk get in our way once we're through the castle gate. We 'ead towards the cathedral, then turn left onto Bailgate, then left again onto Westgate as far as the corner in the castle walls.

'Oh, I almost forgot, it will be Reverend Fleming, not the miserable prison chaplain, who comes to say the final prayers with yer. He mentioned it t' me when I spoke to 'im a few days ago. The reverend asked to do that, because yer from his parish and 'e knows yer both. 'e's goin' straight back to Bottesford after that. 'e seems like a nice man, for a priest.'

'He is, and I wish Ma had taken Margaret and me to more of his services when we were growing up.' Phillipa squeezed her eyes tight shut in an effort to stop the gathering tears from rolling down her cheeks.

Take Height, Rutterkin

*

At twenty minutes past twelve, the cart pulled up outside Cobb Hall. Beneath the blankets, facing the side of the cart so the gap left to enable her to breathe couldn't be seen, Phillipa lay, fraught with unease as Harry and Jack made their way inside to bring Margaret, and what was supposedly Phillipa's corpse, up from the dungeon. But when the outer door opened, she couldn't fail to hear Sir William's piercing tones.

Cold fear gripped her. Had their plan been discovered and did the officials know that the woman's corpse wasn't that of Phillipa Flower? She hardly dared breathe as she waited, dreading the blankets to be snatched from her and Sir William to punch her again. Then she felt motion in the cart and could hear Harry humming softly to let her know it was him.

'Lay her over that side, Jack. I'll get the shroud off 'er and prop 'er up so she can be seen by the crowds while you get back and fetch Margaret Flower up.'

'Right, let's get you sitting up, so folk can see yer 'ere,' Harry said, evidently talking to the corpse.

The door opened again and Phillipa heard Margaret's cheerful voice as she spoke, presumably to Jack. 'I hope you're taking me back to Bottesford. I've been out with my friends for so long today and Ma will be wondering where I am. It's such a lovely day for a ride and I love the sun on my face.'

Phillipa almost choked on her grief, coupled with self-hatred at leaving the sister she loved to a fate she did not deserve.

'Let's get you on the cart,' Harry said, with a bump that told Phillipa that Margaret was now very close. 'Sit down by this side.'

Chapter Eighteen

'Shhh, Phillipa's nodded off,' Margaret chided, evidently referring to the corpse as she sat. 'And she won't want waking up.'

'No, she won't, so we all need to be quiet for a while,' Harry replied as Phillipa felt him squatting down between the pile of blankets and Margaret.

The cart started to move and Phillipa heard the first calls and heckles from people around the castle yard: 'Good riddance to the witches! The Devil will take his own! I hope you both burn in Hell!'

'Who are they all so angry with?' Margaret's child-like voice was almost lost amidst the number of yells. 'I can't see any witches around here.'

The cart moved on, the rattling and bumping of the wheels telling Phillipa they were now on the cobbled city streets. The fired-up crowds shrieked abuse at the witches, jeering at their bald heads beneath the mop caps and their filthy faces.

'Don't do that, Margaret,' she heard Harry say. 'If you pull faces at 'em, they'll shout and jeer all the more.'

'Well then, they should move out of our way so we can get through. I still can't see the witches they're calling names, but if we don't get a move on we'll never get back to Bottesford.'

After the second left turn, Phillipa guessed they were on the final stretch to the gallows. Her heartache at the thought of what Margaret was about to suffer now overriding the dread she felt of being caught.

'Right, Margaret, when we stop, Reverend Fleming will be joining us on the cart,' Harry said. 'He's asked to say prayers with you and Phillipa because he won't be seeing you again after today.'

Take Height, Rutterkin

'Why? He isn't leaving Bottesford, is he?'

Phillipa could sense Harry searching for a plausible answer. 'No… but I think your ma told him that *you* are. You'll have to ask her more about that when you see her.'

'Oh, I hope we aren't leaving for good. I like Bottesford and don't want to live anywhere else.'

'Well, we seem to have arrived and…' Harry's voice was drowned by the sudden roar that erupted from the jubilant hordes as the cart rolled into their view. But the yelling and whistling was brief and they quietened to an expectant hush. Then Phillipa felt someone climbing onto the cart and Samuel Fleming's familiar voice addressing her and Margaret.

'Phillipa and Margaret Flower, we will say The Lord's Prayer together, as we did a short while ago. It is our final chance to help you repent of your sins so that God will welcome you into Heaven. There is little space on the cart so there's no need to kneel. God will hear your prayer, just the same.'

'I think Phillipa's still asleep, Reverend. Should we wake her?'

'Your sister isn't asleep, Margaret, she's just feeling unwell today. I'm sure she'll feel a lot better once you all get home. She will hear our prayer and say it inside her head.'

Phillipa realised that the reverend's words were meant for her rather than the corpse and wondered how he knew she wasn't dead.

The crowd remained quiet as Samuel recited the words of The Lord's Prayer and Margaret and Harry said them aloud with him.

'Now, Margaret, Harry will bind your wrists and loop the

Chapter Eighteen

remaining lengths of rope through that ring you're leaning against. He will hold the loose ends in order to keep you steady as you push through these unruly crowds. He will also bind Phillipa, of course.'

'That's all right, as long as he unfastens the bindings later. I don't like being tied up.'

'I'll take my leave now, Margaret, and I feel sure that one day, we will meet again in the presence of God.'

Phillipa felt movement on the cart and knew that the reverend had gone and that Harry would now be binding the wrists and putting nooses around the necks of Margaret and the dead woman. Harry yelled to someone to catch the long ropes of the nooses as he threw them up to the gallows bar, and soon the cart began a slow, steady move.

Within moments, Phillipa heard Margaret's screams. Then came the terrible sound of her and the corpse being wrenched from the cart to dangle from the gallows bar. Margaret's screams become no more than a strangulated gurgle as she writhed with the agony of being slowly choked to death. The strangling twist, they called it.

The crowd cheered and whistled, and Phillipa sobbed. Her sister did not deserve this horrendous end. If only there had been some way of saving her, too.

'It's more than our lives are worth to lash the horse and gallop away fast.' Harry must now have sat beside her, because Phillipa heard his voice clearly. 'They'd have the guards after us if we did. A slow strangulation's what the crowds love to see, not a sudden death from a broken neck. Be patient with the slowness, Phillipa, but no one's giving us a second glance at this speed. All eyes are on the show they came to watch, including the eyes of all those fancy lords. We'll soon be out of the city, well away from them all and on our way to start a new life.'

Beneath the blankets, Phillipa's heartbreaking grief dispelled all thoughts of her own freedom. She knew that thoughts of Margaret squirming at the end of a rope would stay with her for ever, and that she would never find solace enough to live a normal life, no matter how far away Harry took her.

'We've just left the city and are now on the road to Newark,' Harry said after what seemed to Phillipa like hours. 'So this is where we say goodbye to Jack and the cart. No one back in Lincoln knows yer missin' and Jack'll tell the sheriff, I decided to move on, and got off the cart in the middle of Lincoln. So 'e needs to get back quick, if that story's t' be believed. The cart'll be needed later today to take the bodies back t' the castle for burial. Jack's volunteered to do that so no one notices you aren't one of the corpses. The graves will've already been dug ready for 'im by the time 'e gets back.'

Phillipa emerged a little from beneath the blankets. 'But where will we go from here and how will we live? We have no money and I haven't even got a coat to put on.'

'A good coat 'as been sittin' on top of yer along with mine since we started out for the gallows. It was my wife's, same as the dress and cap you're wearin'. There's also a bag with other things of 'ers in it under the clothes, and you can 'ave whatever you want from it. They're no good to 'er now, are they? And I've been saving most of my wages for the past few years 'cos I always knew I'd be movin' on. A gaoler's life isn't fer me. As to where we'll go, I've a few ideas about that, but the first part

Chapter Eighteen

of our journey anywhere is already sorted. An acquaintance 'as kindly offered to 'elp with that.'

They said their thanks and goodbyes to Jack, donning their coats as Phillipa wondered who this acquaintance could be. Harry handed Jack a half crown and half a dozen shillings for the risks he'd taken on their behalf, and packed the rest of the clothes into the leather bag. As the cart turned and trundled back to Lincoln, they began a slow walk along Newark Road.

'Before we meet this person, Phillipa, we need to stop at the first stream or pond we see so yer can 'ave a wash. After all yer weepin', yer've got cartwheel tracks down yer filthy cheeks.'

*

Samuel Fleming waited inside his coach on Newark Road, unable to keep anxiety at bay. Joseph had hopped down from his driver's seat and was somewhere in the middle of a nearby copse, relieving himself before the journey resumed. He was a good lad, and Samuel had paid him well for his services as coachman, Young as he was, Joseph had made two journeys to Lincoln without a fuss. The question now was, could Joseph keep indefinitely quiet about today's escapade to pick up Phillipa and Harry? Even an extra bonus wouldn't prevent an odd slip of the tongue.

A tap on the coach window told Samuel the two new passengers were here. He opened the door quickly, ushering them inside and urging them to crouch down and keep silent as the young coachman returned.

Take Height, Rutterkin

'Ready for off, then, Reverend?' Joseph asked cheerily as he climbed up to the driver's seat. 'Newark next stop, I reckon.'

'Yes, thank you, Joseph,' Samuel replied. 'Anywhere in the town will do, so there's no need to veer off the main route home.'

Once they were moving again, Samuel said, quietly, 'When we stop in Newark, I'll send Joseph to have a look round for a few suitable inns, should I wish to stay in the town anytime in future. That will give you time to leave the coach and disappear from sight before he returns. If he doesn't know you were here, we won't have the worry of him letting slip that he'd seen you at a later date.'

Samuel could not help but notice the harrowed look in Phillipa's eyes and his heart went out to her. 'I don't know what your plans are from here on, and it's best we keep it that way. I can only wish you both God speed, and hope that the dreadful memories of today fade, with time. You, Phillipa, have lost everything in your life and have been treated most cruelly for the past two months. I shall pray that good health is yours again before too long. And Harry, Jack told me of your wife's fate, and I cannot express my condolences enough. These are difficult times, but I hear that King James has had a change of mind regarding witch hunting this past year. He is now not so certain that all those accused of witchcraft really are witches, and is urging caution in the arrest and trial of anyone denounced by fellow citizens of the crime. Not before time, I might add.

'You have a fine young man in Harry, Phillipa. When he approached me last week with his escape plan, you and Mar-

Chapter Eighteen

garet had just prayed with me, and I knew then that neither of you were witches. At the time, all I could do was wish him success with his plan and pray you wouldn't be caught. But after giving the matter some thought, I realised how I could help. Helping you to flee quickly from Lincoln was the least I could do.

Samuel heaved a sigh, his own heartache over so many aspects of this whole, sordid affair a heavy burden to bear. 'Harry's plan gave us a way of saving you, Phillipa, though I know that both you and I will carry our sorrow that Margaret couldn't be saved for a very long time. As for your mother, I don't suppose we'll never truly know if, in her state of desperation and destitution, she had given herself to the Devil.'

Samuel reached into the pocket of his cassock and pulled out a leather purse. Opening it, he tipped the contents onto his palm, giving three of the gold crowns to Phillipa and three to Harry. 'This isn't much for the life ahead of you, but it may help you to travel to wherever you decide to stay and ensure you don't starve while you do so. Half of it is more than enough to buy a horse and cart. And this,' he added, reaching behind for a large sackcloth bag, 'contains enough food to last at least a couple of days. I'm sure you can buy ale cheaply enough from any inn or tavern. You probably ought to stay at an inexpensive inn in Newark for at least tonight. I fear that you, Phillipa, are in no state to walk very far.'

Overcome by his kindness, Phillipa's tears flowed. 'We can never repay your thoughtfulness, or your generosity, Reverend. I'm sorry I never had chance to know you better when I lived in Bottesford.'

Take Height, Rutterkin

'There's no need for talk of repaying me, Phillipa. I am partly motivated by my own guilt… and my own weakness. I allowed people to convince me that the Flower women were responsible for the damage done to the Manners' family. Now I realise how wrong that was regarding you and Margaret, although your mother's part in it all remains unknown. I doubt we'll ever know the cause of such a terrible illness that befell the earl's two sons, but I do know that you and your family were always law-abiding citizens, even though your mother didn't come to church. I knew she was a follower of the old gods, but whether she had become a devil worshipper we can only guess.

'I think destitution and despair led to Joan Flower's downfall which, in turn, brought her daughters down. Margaret would never have stolen from the castle kitchens had she not been worried that you and your mother might starve and there would have been no need to open a bawdyhouse. But we cannot turn back the clock, and once we stop in Newark, you must be gone before Joseph returns.

'I'm sure you and Harry will be good company for each other until you find somewhere to settle. Whether or not that will be together, only time will tell.'

There was little more to be said and the rest of the journey to Newark was made in companionable silence.

Chapter Nineteen

In which returning to normality does not come readily to the Vale of Belvoir and a family enjoys a new life

Belvoir Castle: early March 1620

On the fifth day of March, little Lord Francis, younger son of the Earl and Countess of Rutland, passed away, after being bed-ridden for most of the nine years of his life. Since the family was spending time at their London home of Bedford House when the death occurred, the funeral took place at Westminster Abbey the following day. Now back home at Belvoir, the earl called upon Samuel Fleming to lead a small, family service for the boy in the castle's little chapel. At the end, Celia remained in the chapel to pray and Francis sat alone with Samuel in the morning room to drink their cocoa. There the grief-stricken earl confided in his old friend.

'After all we went through to ensure those witches hanged, the evil spell they inflicted on my son was never broken. Perhaps King James is right in believing that only burning a witch puts an end to any spells she has cast.'

'I doubt if the practice of burning witches will ever return to England, Francis, and I pray it never does. It is a most barbarous way of putting anyone to death.'

'I agree, although since the spell on young Francis continued after the Flower women were dead, I cannot help but wonder. Francis grew weaker and weaker until in the end, he just seemed to fade away. I swear, he had so little flesh on his bones we could count his ribs. We would never have risked travelling all the way to London with him had we not been determined to seek physicians who knew of this strange sickness and had remedies with which to combat it.'

Samuel nodded, sipping his cocoa and hoping his guilt at having assisted Phillipa to escape didn't show on his face. 'The only comfort I can offer at this time is that your son is now at peace in Heaven. His suffering is over. Even the death of a witch – by any means of execution – cannot change what is ordained by God. I was never convinced that executing witches put an end to the spells they had cast, and have been informed that only spells of reversal can do that. Unfortunately, not even the cunning women knew of any such spells that could break the one on Lord Francis, or the infertility spell placed on you and Lady Cecilia. They say that witches store numerous bottles that contain ingredients for the breaking of spells, but I would not recommend anyone ignorant of their contents to open them.'

'No, it wouldn't be very prudent although, as you know, Cecilia and I are now desperate for an heir. The many weeks she spent at Tunbridge Wells last summer were all in vain. Despite the town's claims that the fresh air and sparkling waters offer cures for many illnesses, it seems that infertility isn't one of them. Nothing has improved.'

'Francis, my friend, as with most things, whether or not Cecilia conceives is in the hands of God, not the waters of a spa town. I've no doubt that bathing and taking in the summer air would bring a feeling of wellbeing to most people, and perhaps

Chapter Nineteen

help them to fend off minor ailments such as summer head colds, and coughs. It may also help to reduce the crippling pains in the bones that plague the elderly. But I find it hard to believe that fresh air and clear waters can heal more deeply rooted conditions, including infertility.'

Francis sighed, picking up his cocoa from the small, elegant walnut table between his chair and Samuel's, and taking a sip before putting the cup down again. 'I think the same, Samuel, but Cecilia clung to the hope that it could. She has now accepted the fact that we will have no more children, and I'm finding it hard to cope with her pain as well as my own. Cecilia will not discuss the issue, so it hovers over us like a menacing black cloud whenever we're together, which isn't often nowadays.'

'I feel your grief keenly, Francis, though further words of comfort fail me. But I do wonder, if Lady Katherine marries well, could not a son of hers eventually inherit?'

'He could, if I wrote it into my will, though I know Cecilia wouldn't like the idea, considering that Katherine is not her true daughter. We are also presently involved in discussions relating to a possible marriage between Katherine and George Villiers. Unfortunately, Cecilia has taken a recent dislike to him, which makes everything so difficult.'

Samuel raised his eyebrows in anticipation of further explanation, but it seemed that Francis was not yet ready to supply one.

'You know that George is now a marquess, don't you?' Francis said, instead. Samuel nodded. 'It probably won't be long before the king honours him with a dukedom, and

Katherine is delighted with the idea of marrying such a high-ranking lord.'

'I believe you mentioned that your daughter has been besotted with Sir George since she was young, so would it not also be a marriage of love?'

'On Katherine's part, yes, but over the years, I have learned that George thinks only of himself, and after he and Katherine were wed, he would doubtless continue to spend much of his time at Court. His relationship with the king is common knowledge. James has bestowed numerous titles and estates on his lover over the years, and I'm afraid George has made many enemies because of it. I know I don't have to tell you, Samuel, that envy creeps into all walks of life.'

'It does indeed,' Samuel replied as images of Joan Flower and the unkind Bottesford goodwives flashed in his head. 'You said Lady Cecilia does not approve of the match, either?'

'That is based purely on the fact that he's a Protestant and, as you know and have kindly kept quiet about, we are Catholics. Cecilia knows that once Katherine marries George, he and his shrewish mother will insist she converts to Protestantism.'

'I see. What about you? How do you feel about your daughter marrying Sir George?'

'At first, I thought it a splendid idea, but every time we attempt further negotiations, George demands an even greater dowry. I find it deplorable that a man of his immense wealth and power, with lands and properties all over the country, could demand so much for a dowry.'

'I understand, and commiserate with you, Francis. I can only imagine that Sir George needs more and more money to

Chapter Nineteen

pay for his lavish lifestyle. As you say, he now has the maintenance and running of many estates to pay for, including huge numbers of indoor and outdoor staff at each. And when he's at Court he'll need to keep up the display of his wealth by wearing the most exquisite attire and arriving in the most handsome coach. And when he weds, he'll have the additional expenses of a wife and children to consider.'

'You're right, and I know I shouldn't grumble. It's just that I would not have expected George to be so mean-spirited to his friends. He's stayed at Belvoir on many occasions for several weeks at a time, all at my expense, of course – which I didn't give a thought to until these marriage talks began. Now I've seen a side to George that I rather wish I hadn't.

'But I shouldn't be burdening you with our problems, Samuel. It's just that you have such a patient listening ear.'

Samuel tugged his ear with great exaggeration and both men laughed.

'I hate to break our chat, Francis, but before I leave, could you enlighten me regarding the final resting place of Lord Francis? Earlier, you mentioned your hopes of bringing his tomb up to Bottesford, and I can only agree that having Francis lying beside his brother in Saint Mary's is a splendid idea. Is that still your intention?'

'It is, and I'll give you a definite date for that as soon as I can. At the moment my priority is to keep the peace between Cecilia and Sir George.'

Francis rubbed his brow and Samuel could see that he, too, was desperately in need of sleep. 'At present, Cecilia is too distraught at our son's death to cope with anything else.'

'My heart aches for you both, Francis. You have had so much to bear and I will pray that one day soon you find the peace you so crave.'

*

Bottesford Village, Leicestershire: last week of March 1620

Samuel Fleming's heart was, indeed, heavy. On many nights, sleep eluded him as he tossed and turned, wrestling with his troubled thoughts… and his conscience. It was over a year since the interrogation and trial of the Flower sisters and the awful hanging of Margaret, and Samuel still found it hard to put all of it behind him. So many questions continued to haunt him. Were his motives for assisting in Phillipa's escape truly justified, or were his actions a betrayal of his long and cherished friendship with Sir Francis?

Like leeches to the skin, thoughts of those events still clung to his mind, giving him little respite, night or day.

The long, bitter days of winter had been particularly hard to bear, but now, spring hovered on the doorstep. Samuel longed for the sun to cast its warmth on the hard, frosty earth. His old bones creaked and, even indoors, his head felt permanently cold lest he sat in front of a roaring fire with his nightcap on. Already two years past his allocated three score years and ten, with only a sprinkling of white hair left on his scalp, Samuel knew his time left on God's Earth was limited. He was ready to meet his Maker. Maybe then he'd find answers to some of the things that constantly plagued him.

Chapter Nineteen

'If you continue to speak about wishing to die, Samuel, you will make me very cross,' Esther chided as she removed the barely touched breakfast from in front of him. 'Leaving most of the food on your platter isn't likely to build up your strength, is it? You would also sleep better and not feel constantly cold if you had warm, hearty meals in your belly. Why, you could outlive me if you ate all the nourishing foods that Alice and I cook for you.'

Samuel always smiled at Esther's kindly face, but he knew that wasn't true. Nor did he want it to be. Too often his thoughts returned to the Flower family before John Flower's death had plunged the women into poverty – a soul-destroying state that Samuel was certain had led to their inevitable and heartbreaking end. He often wondered where Phillipa was now, and if she was still with the kind gaoler who rescued her. As for poor Margaret, knowing she had lost her mind didn't ease Samuel's pain when he recalled her panicked writhing as she choked at the end of a rope.

At first, Samuel had truly believed all three of the Flower women to be guilty. Everything pointed to it, from the little white cat that was believed to be Joan's familiar, the buried glove and Joan's strange death at Ancaster, to her daughters' confessions. On top of which were the statements of those cunning women. It wasn't difficult to understand why both the interrogators and judges believed that Phillipa and Margaret must have been complicit in their mother's spells.

But, if the Flower women were innocent of causing the sickness and deaths of the earl's sons by witchcraft, what *had* caused an illness for which physicians had no cure? And if witchcraft really was the cause, who else could have cast those spells, other than the Flower women?

Samuel felt he was going round in circles and his head ached as a consequence. If only he could put the past behind him and move on.

The Flower family's little cottage by the Devon had become a place to be feared over the past year. Village folk avoided it at all costs, some professing to have heard loud singing and ribald jests coming from inside when the nights were dark and the winds were still. Others claimed to have seen the ghost of Joan moving around inside her cottage through the open shutters. Still others were adamant that Rutterkin could often be seen perched on a tombstone in the cemetery. Samuel smiled at that. Alice's husband, Gilbert Nicholls, spent hours every day around the rectory gardens and cemetery. Funny how he had never spotted a little white cat.

But, despite Samuel's sermons urging the villagers to put aside their fearful thoughts and imagined sightings, most folk truly believed that Joan Flower had returned to take her gruesome revenge on those who had brought about the arrest and deaths of her and her daughters.

*

Pendle, Lancashire: early August 1628

The day was hot and the windows and single door of the cottage in the small village of Barley had been opened wide to allow the light breeze in, and the stifling heat from the oven, out. A

Chapter Nineteen

heavily pregnant, dark-headed woman swept her sleeve across her sweaty brow as she rolled out the pastry to make her husband's favourite meat coffins for the evening meal. She smiled as she thought how much the life of a farmer suited him. Harry Beddows loved the outdoors and claimed the physical exertion kept him fit. She felt lucky to have married such a loving and hard-working man. His love for her and their children shone through everything he did. He might not earn as much coin as he would have liked but, with what she made from the sale of her herbal remedies, they managed very well.

Through one of the windows, she could see their two young daughters playing in the stream that flowed across the end of their garden, squealing as they splashed each other with the cooling water. A short distance beyond, the green-swathed slopes of Pendle Hill rose up to greet the cobalt blue sky.

Phillipa felt blessed to have such a life… to have any life at all. Nine years earlier she had resigned herself to facing an ignoble death. It had taken her a year to fully stop grieving, partly for her mother, but mostly for Margaret. Even now, when her thoughts returned to events of those times, feelings of guilt welled as she tried to justify to herself the necessity of leaving her sister alone to face the gallows.

Rarely a day went by when she didn't thank God for sending Harry to her. Harry's love for his second wife and their daughters could not be doubted. Naming the girls after the mother and sister that Phillipa had lost just seemed so right, and Harry had readily agreed. Six-year-old Joan and five-year-old Margaret were happy children. There was no one in Barley to envy or dislike Phillipa, or make her life a misery as the goodwives of Bottesford had done to her mother. Joan and Margaret had plenty of friends and were happy to attend church every Sunday with their parents, the same church in which she and Harry had married, soon after their arrival at Barley.

Phillipa patted her rounded belly, wondering if their third babe would be a boy. In another three weeks they would know, and Phillipa didn't doubt that Harry would love the child whether it be boy or girl.

The August twilight was long, and once the meal was savoured, the family sat outdoors, enjoying the lingering warmth of the evening. 'I need to be up before dawn tomorrow,' Harry told them. 'We've 'alf a dozen steers to get to the market over in Colne. Should bring a good price, too, so I'm expectin' a nice bonus from old Bryan. No one could say 'e's not generous to 'is workers. Most of these yeomen farmers can be tight with their coin, but not 'im.'

'You're such a good worker, Harry, no one can deny that. It's you who keeps Bryan's farm going, and he knows it. You deserve every bonus you get.'

'P'raps you're right, but I enjoy my work and that makes a difference. Not like the last work I did before we moved back 'ere.'

'What was your last job, Pa? I thought you'd always been a farm worker.'

Phillipa shot him a look, willing him not to tell the girls about Lincoln gaol. Having to explain about almost being hanged would be too much for them to understand.

'Well now, Joan, I worked in a tavern in the big city of

Chapter Nineteen

Lincoln. Can't say I enjoyed the work, but I earned enough to enable me to save up for your ma and me to move back 'ere.

'Anyways, it's time to get to our beds. As I said, I've an early start tomorrow. It's almost nine miles from 'ere to Colne, then we've got the steers to sell before we 'ead back, so don't expect me 'ome till late tomorrow… Just look at Margaret; seems she couldn't keep 'er eyes open.'

Harry gently lifted the sleeping child and carried her up to her bed, followed by Joan. Phillipa took their mugs back into the house and locked the door and window shutters before heading up to bed, hoping the unborn babe realised it was time to sleep and not the time to start kicking and keeping its mother awake.

'I 'ope you don't 'ave another of yer dreams tonight,' Harry whispered as they snuggled down beneath the blankets. 'We all need our sleep and yer yellin's enough t' wake the 'ole village.'

'I can't control when the dreams come, and I don't remember what most of them were about the next day, but one of them has become as clear as water recently. There's a man in it who I vaguely recognise, though as yet, I can't put a name to the face.'

'Go on, then, tell me what 'appens in this dream.'

'Nothing of importance has happened yet, but I have the feeling that when it does, it won't be pleasant. There are angry people in it, all plotting ways they could get rid of this man I half recognise. It seems he's made some disastrous mistakes as a military leader, but King Charles refuses to hear anything bad said about him.'

'Let's 'ope this unpleasant thing doesn't 'appen tonight,

then. Didn't yer tell me your ma used to 'ave dreams like yours?'

'She did, and they always upset her. She dreamt about Lincoln gaol, although, as you know, she died before we got there. She knew all about the filth of the dungeon, and the rats. She also knew about some of the tortures. The dreams really frightened her, and her death wasn't something I understood at the time. Looking back, the only possible answer is that my mother *was* a witch and she really did choke on consecrated bread.'

'I don't suppose we'll ever know, but it's all in the past. Right now, it's time to sleep.' Harry's enormous yawn proved his point.

It wasn't until two weeks later that the dream returned. This time, the man Phillipa half-recognised was poring over some maps opened out on a large table in some kind of inn or tavern, surrounded by a number of fellow officers. They seemed to be organising a military expedition overseas.

Phillipa was suddenly aware that one of the men had a dagger gripped in his hand. She yelled a warning, but to no avail. The knifeman pounced, stabbing deep into his prey's back and dropping him to the floor before walking calmly from the room with the rest of the men.

Though the victim meant nothing to Phillipa, she realised she was weeping. No death was pleasant to watch and this was no ordinary demise. It was a planned assassination. She wondered if it had already occurred, or if she was 'seeing' something about to happen. Her mother's dreams had always been predictive, but that didn't mean Phillipa's were the same.

A week later, talk of the assassination in Portsmouth of

Chapter Nineteen

King Charles's constant companion and adviser, Sir George Villiers, Duke of Buckingham, was on everyone's lips. The name suddenly matched the face in Phillipa's dream. She'd caught glimpses of Sir George years ago, while she was working at Belvoir Castle. Taking little interest in political affairs, all she could do was wonder why she should have dreamt about the man's death. There was nothing she could have done to prevent it. Did she, like her mother, have 'the sight'? In which case, was she, like Joan Flower, also a witch? She brushed the thought aside, for now.

At the beginning of September, Phillipa gave birth to a healthy son whom they named Samuel, after a dear old friend. He was a healthy babe who fed well and slept soundly as a consequence. Joan and Margaret were delighted to have a little brother, and Harry was a proud father for the third time.

'He looks like you,' Phillipa said, laying the sleeping child in his crib. 'At least, I think he'll look like you when he's grown. He has your blue-grey eyes and strong jaw. He's also got a sprinkling of fair hair like yours and Margaret's, although I suppose it could darken later on and become like mine and Joan's.'

Harry grinned. 'I'd love 'im whatever he looked like; you know that. As long as 'e grows straight and sturdy and is 'onest and 'ard workin', 'e'll do for me.'

Throughout the month, as the leaves on the trees turned to amber and gold, the cottage was a busy place. While Harry was at work, busy threshing the harvested wheat, the two girls helped their mother with jobs she hadn't time for. Phillipa valued their efforts and was touched by their concern, and a happy atmosphere prevailed. On the last day of the month,

Take Height, Rutterkin

while the babe slept and Phillipa and her daughters were preparing a mutton stew for the evening meal, a small white cat padded in through the open door and stared up at Joan.

'Hello again, Rutterkin,' Joan said, smiling. 'You took your time getting here.'

Phillipa's reaction was swift. 'Don't even think about settling here, you little demon! You've done enough damage to my family.'

The cat arched its back and hissed as she held out the crucifix on a chain around her neck and chanted:

> *Take height, Rutterkin*
> *and go*
> *Fly back to he who sent you*
> *and tell him,*
> *I said 'No!'*

The cat slowly retreated and disappeared outside. Bemused, Margaret stared at her mother and sister as though they'd lost their minds. 'Who sent the cat to us, Ma?'

'No one you know, Margaret, and there's no need for you to worry about Rutterkin.' Phillipa sighed, absently rubbing her crooked nose. 'I've met that pretty cat before and I can tell you, he's an evil little monster, and he causes pain to any family who takes him in. And Joan, if he returns, he is *not* permitted to enter this house. Send him on his way by using your crucifix as I have just done. Is that clear?'

Joan's face was sullen, but she nodded.

'So now you need to get your crucifix out of the storage

Chapter Nineteen

chest you hid it in and hang it round your neck. Will you do that for me?'

Clearly mortified that her mother knew of her covert actions, Joan hung her head and mumbled a reluctant, 'Yes.'

'Good, then let's hear no more about the cat and get on with preparing this stew.'

*

In a grassy glade in the nearby woods, Joan picked up a leafy twig and played with the little white cat. Rutterkin chased the twig as Joan trailed it through the grass littered with an abundance of toadstools, and leapt into the air as she gleefully waved the twig about. After a while, Joan plonked herself down against a tree trunk to rest, and stretched out her legs. The cat did not hesitate to take his usual place on her lap.

'Don't worry, Rutterkin,' Joan murmured to the purring cat, as her thoughts lost themselves in his yellow gaze. 'I don't wear that stupid crucifix when I come to play with you. I hide it under my bed. We'll always be together, in this life and our lives still to come.'

Thank you for reading Take Height, Rutterkin. If you enjoyed the book, a short review on Amazon, Goodreads, a blog, or any site you feel is suitable – Twitter or Instagram for example – would be greatly appreciated. Reviews help self-published authors immensely and are always gratefully received. A sentence or two is all that is needed.

Acknowledgements

My sincere thanks to all those who have helped with the creation and publication of this book:

Cover image created by Louise Bunting (author's daughter)

Central woman, Belvoir Castle and the Cat: images purchased from Shutterstock

Fair-haired girl: Photo by cottonbro from Pexels

Dark-haired girl: Photo by Jaspereology from Pexels

Internal images:
Map of central Bottesford, two sketches of Cobb Hall and the plan of Lincoln Castle (the latter based on an image in the Lincoln Castle Guide Book): Louise Bunting.

*

Editing by Doug Watts: doug@jbwb.co.uk

eBook conversion and formatting by Alan Cooper:
https://www.yourebookpartners.com
email: alanfcooper@me.com

A little more about *Take Height, Rutterkin*

As the craze for witch hunts continued to rage across Europe during the 15-18th centuries, many people lived in fear of being denounced by their neighbours of practising witchcraft. In England, King James 1 was an avid pursuer of witches, urging his subjects to be vigilant in notifying the authorities of anyone they believed to be guilty of practising the dark arts. Most of those accused lived on the outer edges of communities, sometimes for no other reason than they were different, ugly or deformed in some way, were poor, or simply old. Most of them were old and widowed women, particularly those who lived alone, attempting to earn a living without the control of a husband, father of brother. If she grew herbs from which to make potions and balms to sell to neighbours, or kept an animal that could be seen as her familiar, she was especially likely to be denounced as a witch. A few were men, accused of being sorcerers.

Take Height, Rutterkin is based on the true story of a family of three women – Joan Flower and her two daughters, Phillipa and Margaret – who were unfortunate enough to become such targets. They lived in the Leicestershire village of Bottesford, a little over three miles from Belvoir Castle. I have woven my story around key events known to have occurred in the area at that time, including the Flower family's sudden lack of status and financial security sometime after 1611. This is thought to be due to the death of a male member of the family, most likely Joan's husband, who would have been the main breadwinner.

Events really turned sour for the women following their dismissal from employment at Belvoir Castle – and Joan's (alleged) subsequent revenge on the Manners family. The strange illness that struck the earl and countess's two young sons is documented. It is also true that Sir Francis and Lady Cecilia were not successful in conceiving more children after the deaths of their two heirs. On Sir Francis's death, Belvoir Castle, and all his other estates, passed to his younger brother, George.

In those days of fear and superstition, when most people believed in the existence of witches and dark forces, it is easy to understand how the death of little Henry Manners in September 1613, from an illness that no physician knew how to treat or cure, could be attributed to witchcraft. However, it was some years later, in 1619, that Joan and her daughters were arrested on the charge of causing Henry's death and the ongoing illness of his younger brother, Francis, who died a year after the trial and execution of Phillipa and Margaret.

The women's revenge on the Manners family following their dismissal from service at the castle is the key factor in my story that eventually leads to their downfall. There is no doubt that the women were arrested and tried for causing death by witchcraft, but whether or not Joan actually did cast spells on that important and affluent family, and throw curses at anyone who annoyed her, remains unknown. However, that she *did* forms part of the fiction I have created. It is true to say that Joan was a very unpopular figure in Bottesford, known for being of a wild, unkempt appearance, of a 'hostile' nature, impious, and for using foul language. According to Tracy Borman*, Joan was described as 'a woman full of wrath'. So it isn't too difficult to imagine her throwing curses and casting spells when her temper was up.

My book tells the story as it could have played out before and after the Manners family turned their backs on all three of the Flower women in 1613. Making ends meet with no regular income after the death of Joan's husband (possibly a John Flower, although that is also uncertain) had been hard enough, but now they had all been dismissed by Lady Cecilia, no one in the village would employ them. The Flower women soon became poverty-stricken, a desperate state which led them to do things they would not ordinarily have done. To account for the excessive drinking and raucous singing heard in Joan Flower's cottage of an evening, Ms Borman* states, 'It was whispered that their home had become little better than a bawdyhouse'. I have chosen to attribute the women with doing just that. Opening a bawdyhouse became the only means left to them of earning enough to live on. It resulted in the Flower women becoming truly reviled by the village goodwives.

The three women were arrested in 1619, charged with causing death by witchcraft, as indicated in Paragraph 4, above. Following Joan's strange death at Ancaster, Phillipa and Margaret were interrogated and tried in Lincoln Castle. Their confessions regarding assisting their mother in casting spells, and that Joan's did have a familiar called Rutterkin, are likely to have been made after suffering starvation, sleep deprivation and other tortures during interrogation.

The ending of my book, including Samuel Fleming's role in it, is my own creation. According to most sources, Phillipa and Margaret were both hanged outside Lincoln Castle and buried in unmarked graves in the castle grounds. As a point of interest, the location of the gallows in the early 17th century was where I described it, so the women would have been taken there by cart. A century later, the gallows (erected whenever the need arose) was on the top of Cobb Hall. One interesting snippet presented in an online site (Wikipedia) happened to say that Phillipa managed to escape. She went on to live a happy life in Kent and gave birth to three children. Naturally, I jumped at the chance to write my own version of that.

Samuel Fleming was, indeed, present at the Flower sister's trial but there is little more about him after that, other than the fact that he died on either the 12th or 13th of September, 1620, at the age of 72. His bridge still stands across the little River Devon in Bottesford and is still known as Fleming's Bridge. Samuel also had a brother called Abraham, who died suddenly in Bottesford, and a sister named Esther, or possibly Hester, who married a Thomas Davenport.

Other than referral to the various online sites about the Witches of Belvoir, including the Bottesford Community Website,

I have used ***Tracy Borman's excellent book, *WITCHES: James 1 and the English Witch Hunts*** for additional information. I also read a wonderful fiction titled **The Witch and the Priest, written in 1956 by Hilda Lewis**. As the title suggests, the story in that book is quite unlike the one I have written, but as far as I know, it is the only other work of fiction about the Witches of Belvoir. I found it a very entertaining read.

*

Bottesford is a delightful village, although it has grown considerably since my husband and I – along with the first five of our six children – lived there from 1976-1982. There are many more amenities in the village nowadays, but the old things never change. The commanding church, the Buttercross in the old Market Place, Fleming's Bridge, the fish and chip shop and the lovely fords in the Devon where the children – and their mothers –paddled in the summer, are just as I remember them.

About Millie Thom and Her Books

Millie Thom is the author of the four books in the Sons of Kings Series:

Book 1: Shadow of the Raven
Book 2: Pit of Vipers
Book 3: Wyvern of Wessex
Book 4: King of the Anglo Saxons

The books are historical fiction, set during the second half of the ninth century in the Anglo-Saxon and Danish lands during the lifetime of King Alfred. The storylines are ongoing throughout the four books so, ideally, the series should be read in order.

Millie has also published A Dash of Flash, an eclectic mix of 85 flash fiction pieces and short stories, and intends to complete A Second Dash of Flash in the near future.

Take Height, Rutterkin is Millie's sixth book and, although it is still historical fiction, it is set in England in the early 17th century, a completely different time period to her Sons of Kings series. This book is a 'one off' and not part of a series.

As a former history and geography teacher with a degree in geology and an enduring love of the past – including the evolution of the Earth and all who have lived on it – reading and writing historical novels are natural extensions of Millie's interests.

Millie and her husband have six grown up children and live in a small village in Nottinghamshire, midway between the old city of Lincoln and the equally old town of Newark-on-Trent. When not reading or writing, Millie loves swimming, travelling, collecting fossils and taking long walks in the countryside.

Links to Millie Thom and her Books

Amazon UK: http://amzn.to/2MfSLAy

Amazon US: http://amzn.to/2udCDJH

Amazon Au: https://amzn.to/2Kg7WME

Millie can also be found on:

Twitter: https://twitter.com/MillieThom

WordPress: https://milliethom.com/

Instagram: //www.instagram.com/millie.thom/?hl=en

Goodreads: https://www.goodreads.com/author/show/8383271.Millie_Thom

Printed in Great Britain
by Amazon